AZTEC FIRE

Forge Books by Gary Jennings

Aztec

Aztec Autumn

Aztec Blood

Aztec Rage

Aztec Fire

Spangle

Journeyer

Apocalypse 2012

Visit Gary Jennings at www.garyjennings.net.

• GARY JENNINGS' •

AZTEC

FIRE

ROBERT GLEASON
AND
JUNIUS PODRUG

FORGE®

A TOM DOHERTY ASSOCIATES BOOK
NEW YORK

This is a work of fiction. All of the characters, organizations, and events portrayed in this book are either products of the author's imagination or are used fictitiously.

AZTEC FIRE

Copyright © 2008 by Eugene Winick, Executor, Estate of Gary Jennings

All rights reserved.

A Forge Book
Published by Tom Doherty Associates, LLC
175 Fifth Avenue
New York, NY 10010

www.tor-forge.com

Forge® is a registered trademark of Tom Doherty Associates, LLC.

ISBN-13: 978-0-7653-5625-3
ISBN-10: 0-7653-5625-2

First Edition: August 2008
First International Mass Market Edition: April 2009
First U.S. Mass Market Edition: July 2009

Printed in the United States of America

0 9 8 7 6 5 4 3 2 1

For Joyce Servis

ACKNOWLEDGMENTS

Many people helped bring this book to fruition. We particularly wish to thank Tom Doherty, Linda Quinton, Christine Jaeger, Sessalee Hensley, Eric Raab, Melissa Frain, Elizabeth Winick, Hildegard Krische, Maribel Baltazar-Gutierrez, Jane Liddle, and Nancy Wiesenfeld.

Even jade will shatter,
Even gold will crush,
Even quetzal plumes will tear.
One does not live forever on this earth:
Only for an instant do we endure.

>   —Death Song by Nezahualcóyotl,
>   philosopher-king of Texcoco

There is nothing like death in war,
nothing like flowery death
so precious to the Giver of Life:
Far off I see it: my heart yearns for it.

>   —Aztec War Song
>   (Sahagún, *Historia general de
>   las cosas de Nueva España*)

PART I

TWILIGHT OF THE GODS

ONE

BEFORE MY AZTEC uncles were hanged, they took me to the mystery city of Tula to teach me the Way of my people. They expected to die there and even brought along a yellow dog—which, according to our beliefs, would guide them through the Nine Hells after death.

I was sixteen years old.

I will tell you more of the Nine Hells, the Mystery City, and Yellow Dog in a moment, but first let me introduce myself. My name is Mazatl—which means "Deer" in the Aztec tongue, Nahuatl—and Mazatl is the name I have always answered to in our village. By law, however, I must have a Spanish name, and in their language I am called Juan Rios.

The Spanish call all indios "Aztecs," which many of my people resent. In the Spaniards' minds, slaves are beneath contempt, and we indios are indeed enslaved. Few Spaniards acknowledge that we have had a culture rich in art, architecture, medicine, and astronomy and that our culture thrived long before they arrived and destroyed our towering monuments to the majesty of the past. Nor has it occurred to these people whose roots are in Europe that people of the Americas did not need to be "discovered."

In truth, however, I am heir to an even older and mightier people than the Mexica, the first people whom the Spanish condescingly call Aztec: I am of the *Toltec,* a civilization that scholars call the first true "Aztec" because those civilizations that followed—the Mexica-Aztecs, Mayan, Zapotec, and all the others—shamelessly aped Toltec civilization in their art and architecture, most notably in the construction of their own cities and in the rendering of their finest artworks.

Like the Mexica-Aztecs and other empires in central Mexico, the Toltec speak Nahuatl—the melodious tongue of the gods.

My people were a mighty empire when the Mexica-Aztec, the People of the Reed, wandered naked and defenseless, the prey of snakes and crocodiles, jaguars and wolves, living on grubs and weeds and worms. These uncouth savages feared our fury and lusted after our prodigious riches—all the while trembling before our soaring pyramids and illimitable empire. Most of all they stared in awestruck wonder at our Scintillating City of Turquoise Gold, our Invincible Citadel and Sacred Shrine—Tula. To the Aztec, Tula was a city of golden turquoise-laden palaces, where meat, maize, beans, avocados, and honeyed sweets were plentiful as earth and air, where mescal, corn beer, and fermented chocolate flowed like water.

Perhaps most of all, the Aztec envied our science and our skill with numbers. To them our learning must have indeed seemed inscrutable as the sun and stars. Rather than working fields, the people of Tula probed the heavens and through their celestial science and godlike wisdom divined the future.

My Toltec ancestors raised wondrous plants—which cured all the ills that human flesh is heir to. Erecting vertiginous temples and magnificent monuments, we even placated the implacable gods.

Aztec emperors would later claim lineal descent from Tula's royalty, while its high nobility truckled after Toltec wives.

Now all that remained of Tula's golden grandeur was shards and slivers, wrack and ruin—the centuries-ravaged wreckage of a five-tiered step-pyramid dedicated to Quetzalcoatl; cracked, crumbling foundations of other toppled temples; ruins of two ball courts, and the scattered, shattered remains of a Sun King's grandiose palace.

The terraces of the step-pyramid's sloping sides were still embellished with painted and sculpted friezes of marching jaguars and ferocious dogs, of birds of prey devouring human hearts, and of human faces, trapped and staring wild-eyed inside the gaping jaws of serpents.

No, nothing before or since had equaled the Toltec—including the Mexica. Ignorant of art and architecture, the Mexica ransacked the culture of my people. When building their own great city, Tenochtitlán, they pillaged Tula's religion, culture, art—even the concept of themselves as warrior-priests of the sun god. Thus most "Aztec" myths, legends, their pantheon of gods, pictographs, temples, and palaces were imitations of our own culture, our infinite creativity.

Even now the grandeur of our lost Toltec world could be felt—despite the barbarism of the Spanish. Indio ruins throughout the colony were shaped to resemble Toltec edifices, including those of the magnificent Chichén Itzá monuments in the land of the Maya to the far south.

Ayyo . . . Tula had been a great empire a thousand years before I was born—though now it was only an abandoned ruin. The city, however, was not abandoned by the gods of my people—I sensed their presence the moment I reached the pyramid's summit and walked among the forest of giant stone warriors now known as the Atlanteans, a name drawn from the legend of the lost continent of Atlantis rather than the history of my people because no one knows the true name of these mighty warriors.

These fierce stone warriors, standing nearly three times the height of a man, evoked visions of great wars and conquest by a people far superior to those that walk the land today.

I have lived my entire life in a village in the mountains

to the east of Tula. The village is small, fewer than a hundred huts and not really big enough to support a church, though we had our own small chapel. It was said that our village was so small and poor that only priests being punished for transgressions against God and the Church were sent there.

No Spaniards lived in the village except for the priest, and as would be expected for a man sent to purgatory on earth, he was neither a very good Spaniard nor a very devout priest.

Mexico City was two long days' walk to the south. I had never been to the great city, though I had heard many tales of its savage wrath and majestic wonder.

The people of my village subsisted on the maize and beans and peppers we grew. We also mined a sulfur pit in a nearby mountainside.

My people did not grow rich off the sulfur. Unlike gold or silver, it is not precious. There would be a time when we used the sulfur as an ingredient in black powder, but we never profited from the sale of the black powder.

In the end, however, that damnable gunpowder doomed my uncles—and had forced our journey to Tula to fight our last battle.

TWO

WE WERE AN unprepossessing army to say the least—an indio in a frazzled straw hat, homespun cotton clothes, and rope sandals; determined to hurl a spear at a hated foe in his last battle; a priest in frayed and faded clerical garb who said a prayer each time he reloaded his flintlock pistol.

And me—the least dangerous of all.

For the first fifteen years of my life, I had not traveled from the village of my birth any farther than a one-hour walk. But that had been the year before. After my people rose up against the Spanish last year in a War of Independence, my life was turned upside down, and I left my village many times.

Although I had been taught many legends about the ancient city, this was my first visit to Tula. Unfortunately, today we had not journeyed to that golden city to study history but so my uncles could look death in its obsidian eye—and die with honor.

I call both of them my uncles, though neither man acknowledged that tie. Moreover, they themselves are diametrically different and sharply at odds with each other—divided by culture and blood: one is Toltec, the other Spanish.

To understand the colony and its people, one must first be familiar with the Spanish concept of blood purity. To the Spaniard, honor was not determined by knowledge, artistic ability, or even personal achievement, but by the blood in their veins. Not even great wealth made a mixed-blood silver-mine owner sit taller in the saddle than a lowly Spanish muleteer whose blood was unadulterated. With unsullied Spanish blood, one was *presumed* to possess all the noblest virtues of manhood—moral strength in life, bravery in battle, and domination over weaker men and women.

Both of my uncles had pureza de sangre, purity of blood—though one was Toltec, the other Spanish. While our Spanish masters claimed to respect pure indio blood, they only esteemed Spanish blood. And even the blood of Spaniards had an unwritten hierarchy: Spaniards born in Spain who came to the colony to administer it—and rape its wealth and women—were called gachupines, wearers of spurs . . . spurs that roweled and bloodied the backs of the indigenous peoples. Spaniards born in the colony were called criollos.

European-born Spaniards believed that being born in the colony made one's blood less potent, and they reserved the great offices of government and the Church for themselves. Thus the colony's social order demanded that the gachupines dictated to the criollos; the criollos chafed under the contempt of the gachupines while they oppressed the mixed bloods called mestizos and mulatoes and the full-blooded indios.

This business of blood was unfathomable to a boy of my tender years, but one thing was clear: The Spanish were my masters. To show disrespect was to invite the shackle and the whip. To contest their superiority by word or deed was to entice death.

My Toltec uncle was called Yaotl, which means "war" in the language of our people. His name, given at birth, suited him well because he was a true warrior, the strongest and bravest man in our village. Short for a Toltec—and certainly shorter than most Spaniards—he was nonetheless solid and massively muscular with a powerful chest and limbs.

Yaotl practiced the Old Ways, the traditions of warriors who served long-dead indio kings and gods. From him I learned to hunt and fish, to survive on what the land itself provided, whether in arid wastes or in sweltering snake-infested jungles. I could hunt my prey on the run with my obsidian dagger and rock-sling, and I could divine water in places where even lizards shriveled up and died.

My other uncle, Fray Diego, was Spanish. He came to our village before I was born. My people had not seen a priest for years before his arrival. The cynics among us believed the Church had waited until a priest fell so grotesquely from grace they could justify banishment to our embarrassingly barren parish.

Others suspected Fray Diego had provoked his superiors in an internecine power struggle, infuriating them beyond all reason. Fearing retribution, he chose a remote village as distant from their vindictive reach as he could find. The good fray came here to go to ground and officially disappear—rather than to administer the sacraments. Whatever his motives, the fray found more personal absolution in the sacred grape than in holy prayer. The fray himself once suggested that his sojourn in our village was a punishment and a penance for his plethora of sins.

My Spanish uncle was nothing like Yaotl in body or mind. His body was plump, more resembling the bottom half of an hour glass, a consequence of his gluttonous love of tortillas, frioles, and holy wine. But food was not his only gluttonous transgression. Devilishly curious, he devoured knowledge of every sort. Reading voraciously and questioning everything, his skeptical curiosity had not endeared him to the Holy Mother Church.

Fray Diego taught me many things. Because of him I grew up speaking Spanish as well as Nahuatl. He educated me to read the books of our Spanish masters, to write their language; and he introduced me to books and plays in that tongue. His true love were the works of the Siglo de Oro, the Golden Age of Spanish literature two hundred years ago, but he introduced me to the works of many writers and poets, including the plays of Vega, Molina, Calderón, and Moratin, the poetry of Sor Juana, and the novels of Cervantes.

No ordinary priest, he was also not an ordinary man. Omnivorously curious, he admitted to me that his indefatigable investigations of his own Holy Trinity—Women, Wine, and Cards—had predestined his downfall.

His impious passions and amorous adventures were widely reported throughout our village. Some villagers implied on one of his wayward wanderings that he had bedded my mother and conceived a bastardo son, namely me.

Those same wagging tongues in the next breath, however, imputed my paternity to Yaotl as well.

My mother rejected all such tales, maintaining that the ancient Toltec god, Quetzalcoatl—deviously disguised as a royal prince—had entered her bed and, yes, herself as well . . . but had spawned her doting son not with mortal seed but through more immaculate means. The truly vicious argued instead that she was little better than a village puta, who had bedded down both the priest and the warrior in the selfsame night and did not know who my father was.

As for me, I was comfortable having two uncles and no father. Tall and slender like a reed, I looked like neither man, so I accepted that my origins were immaculately conceived and divinely inspired.

When we arrived at Tula, my heart was leaden with dread, and my mind churned with churlish thoughts. My uncles had forbidden me to accompany them to this last battle and had carefully watched the trail behind them after they left the village, intending—if they caught me tracking them—to thrash me within an inch of my life and send me limping back home.

Ayyo. I had left the village before them and stood defiant on the outskirts of Tula when they arrived. Amazed at my audacity, they decided I could accompany them to the ruins of the city, where they would instruct me on the greatness of our people. I promised to return to the village before the Spanish arrived and the battle began—a promise I was determined not to honor.

That promise would be the only lie I would ever tell them.

I was sworn not to run from the enemy of our people, and I had hidden weapons before my uncles arrived.

I was committed to fighting my first and last battle shoulder to shoulder with my uncles.

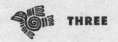

THREE

YAOTL MADE SWEEPING gestures with his arms.

"Long, long ago, this was one of Tula's ball courts." He held up a rough, crudely made rubber ball. "A ball like this was used in the game."

He bounced the ball. It struck the stone floor with a heavy thud and came back up. He hit it with his hip, sending it to me. I caught it but it was heavy and knocked me back, almost off my feet.

"The game is called tlaxtli by our people," he said. "It's a game of life, death, and of war."

"A game of war?"

"Tlaxtli was played as if it were a battlefield. Professional teams traveled from town to town, playing the game. They formed leagues and had great championships every year at El Tajin, the city of thunder north of Veracruz on the coast of the Eastern Sea. The city had twenty ball courts. All the teams went there to play the final champion match. They wore uniforms that represented animals: jaguar, eagle, snake, frog, fish, deer, every kind of animal.

"Like warriors going into battle, their uniforms were padded to protect them against the violence of the matches." Yaotl pointed at his shins and knees. "Wood and leather pads protected the legs. Around the waist, a wide wooden waist yoke absorbed the hardest hits. Helmets protected their heads."

"A hard, savage, brutal contest," Fray Diego said. "You shouldn't glamorize it for the boy. A heathen game, pagans played it, often to the death. One of the many barbaric indio practices we Spanish thankfully abolished."

Diego helped himself to his wineskin.

Yaotl shook his head. "No more savage or brutal than the games called jousts that your European knights played."

"The barbarity of medival knights does not justify heathen folly."

My uncles didn't see eye to eye on many things, but they both agreed on the most important issue—all the people in the colony should be treated equally.

Diego wandered off with his wine-boda while Yaotl enthused over the game of tlaxtli.

"The team that became the champion for the year was rewarded with treasure and women. But . . . ayyo . . . the captain of the losing team—like a warrior who fell in battle—was sacrificed."

"How?"

"A priest cracked open his chest and ripped out his heart."

"A priest like Fray Diego?"

"No, a real priest," Yaotl said, his face contorting in derision, "nothing like that besotted padre-puta. Neighboring empires fought Flower Wars only over land or treasure, so their warriors could be captured and sacrificed."

"So their chests could be cracked like eggs and their beating hearts torn out?" I asked.

"Divine sacrifice requites the gods for sun and rain and maize. Blood empowered them to push the sun and moon across the sky, to force the rain to fall and the maize to bloom. The blood covenant is a sacred gift to the gods, and for the giver, their sacrificial gift is an honor beyond measure."

"I like my heart where it is."

He slammed the ball into my stomach. I pushed the ball back, using my hands.

"The gods received the blood from the losing captain's

body," he said, "but the winning captain was given the heart to eat."

"Our gods have not had their blood feast for centuries. They must be down to parchment and bones. So why then do the sun, moon, maize, and rain continue to prosper?"

"Stop blaspheming the Immortals and focus on the game." Yaotl fixed me with a hard stare. "Remember, no hands. Hit the ball only with your shoulders, hips, buttocks, and knees. You can kick it, but that movement is rarely used. The ball is so heavy it can break your foot."

"What happened to the loser besides his heart being eaten?"

"His head was flayed and dried, then wrapped in rubber and used as a ball. The rubber comes from trees that weep it on the other side of the mountains, where it's hot and wet most of the year. They called it a skull ball and played the next championship tournament with it."

The fray stared at something in the distance.

"Are they coming?" Yaotl asked.

"I see a cloud of dust, but no horsemen yet."

"Holy Mother of Mercy," I said, crossing myself. I didn't know why I did that, but Fray Diego did it sometimes.

The "they" Yaotl referred to were the Spanish. Under Father Miguel Hidalgo—a valiant priest who had declared all people equal—the indios had revolted en masse and lost. They'd died for a cause: for the dream that indios and mixed-blood peons were equal to the Spanish gachupines. . . .

Raising an army, Fray Hidalgo fought battles, freed the indios from their dreaded tribute, and even shattered the africano's shackles. But in the end, a Chihuahua firing squad blew his tortured body into bloody oblivion. Now the Spanish visited their vengeance on all who followed the fray's sacred dream.

Fray Diego claimed that like Hidalgo, he suffered the curse of Odysseus—incurable curiosity—and that curiosity was now about to claim his life. The Odyssean curse had driven him to master gunpowder manufacturing. He knew that one of gunpowder's key ingredients was sulfur, which the village had in abundant quantity. Saltpeter and charcoal were the other two ingredients. They could both be refined out of raw materials readily available to the village. Trees could be burned for charcoal, and the mountain's bat caves combined with the village latrines would supply inexhaustible quantities of saltpeter.

Fray Diego had turned the village's tiny church into a black powder factory that was soon fabricating gunpowder for Father Hidalgo's army of peons. He also organized a small gun factory, rebuilding old muskets and pistols. Yaotl had smuggled the gunpowder and arms to Hidalgo's rebel army under wagonloads of manure.

I was as guilty as Fray Diego and Yaotl. I helped Fray Diego make gunpowder, assisted in rehabilitating guns, and had hazed the mules hauling both black powder and weapons to the rebels.

I admired my uncles for their courage. I had no faith, however, in the Spaniards' view of Christian charity . . . especially as it impacted on our small village.

The meek may be divinely blessed, but we had not been meek.

Although our village was small, its contribution to the insurrection had been vast.

Now, however, the Spanish viceroy was onto us. The king's administrator of New Spain knew my uncles by name. My uncles had come down the mountain in the hope that if they faced the Spanish guns—sacrificed themselves in their own version of the Aztec blood covenant—the village would be spared retribution.

My family had already paid greatly for the transgression. Caught smuggling the fray's guns and powder to rebels, my mother and only sister had been killed.

Like the ball game of tlaxtli, in the war against the Spanish the loser had his heart ripped out.

FOUR

YAOTL FEIGNED INDIFFERENCE to the distant roiling dust. I was less sanguine. The Spanish were coming. The battle would soon be joined, after which we would join our ancestors—and commence our journey through the Nine Hells.

"You must leave soon, return to the village and tell them to stay away from their homes until they are certain the Spanish will not punish them."

"They already know that, you told them before we left."

"Then tell them again." He gestured around him, a sweep with his arms. "Look around you, boy, what do you see?"

"Old ruins—"

"No, you see greatness. A rich and mighty empire built these great stone monuments. Men who stood as tall as gods."

He pointed at the Atlantean Warriors. The giant stone warriors each carried an atlatl, a throwing stick used to hurtle a spear much farther than a man could normally throw it. Spread across the chest of each giant was a butterfly—not a delicate-looking insect, but one of power.

"The collector of hearts," Yaotl said, pointing to a particularly imposing stone deity. "He's a god named Chacmool. The priest placed the hearts in the dish he's holding."

Chacmool was a reclining figure holding a dish on his belly. A sacrificial dagger was strapped to his upper arm.

"People besides ballplayers were sacrificed?"

"By the thousands. To satisfy the blood covenant,"

Diego said, rejoining us. "Another barbaric custom of your indio ancestors that Yaotl makes light of."

"Blood for food," I said.

"Exactly so," Fray Diego concurred.

"Leave us alone and drink your vino," Yaotl said. He nodded at the dust cloud in the distance. It had grown larger. "There are some things the boy should know about his ancestors and soon he will have to go."

Yaotl told me that Tula was also called Tollen. "A large city, perhaps as many as fifty thousand, not counting slaves. With many fine buildings, palaces, and houses for people to live in. All the peoples of the One World admired and envied the people of Tula. When the empire grew weak, the Aztec and other tribes preyed on it. They vandalized the palaces and temples, carrying off the stones to build their own edifices with the same designs they saw here. Then the Spanish took more, using the stones to build the temples they call churches."

"But it was once the greatest city on earth?"

"During the reign of its glorious god-king, Quetzalcoatl."

"The Feathered Serpent," I said.

Quetzal was a bird with bright feathers and coatl was the Nahuatl word for "snake."

"Quetzalcoatl of Tula was the greatest king in the history of the One World," Yaotl said. "He bore the title of god-king because he was born of a virgin mother. Although his father was the king, he did not impregnate Quetzalcoatl's mother. She conceived Quetzalcoatl when she swallowed a piece of jade.

"When Quetzalcoatl was still a boy, his father was murdered and he fled the city. He hid in the wilderness where birds and animals taught him to survive, endure, fight, and prevail—but to also revere justice. Returning as a young man, he raised an army. He conquered the city and became its rightful king. Wise, brilliant, and brave, he forgave his enemies and created a peaceable kingdom in Tula, using knowledge gained from the beasts of the wilderness. Unlike the priest and warrior classes established in power, he did not believe in human or animal sacrifice or cannibalism. Because the people believed so strongly that a failure to sacrifice would offend the gods, he permitted it, but insisted that only flowers and butterflies be sacrificed."

Yaotl told me that this mighty red bearded king of my people was tall, powerfully built, and a master builder who created not just a fabled city but re-created his people as well, introducing them to the arts of sculpting, pottery-making, and jewelry design. Their artistry—as well as their science, mathematics, and military might—would become the pride and envy of the One World.

"No king or nobleman in the One World would eat off plates made anywhere but Tula."

A time of wonder and plentitude. Besides massive ears of maize, bumper crops of beans, avocado, tomatoes, and chocolate abounded. Cotton grew not just alabaster-white but in iridescent rainbow shades, while brightly colored quetzal birds warbled poetry and harmonized melodious songs.

"These are not tales to amuse children, but sacred truth," Yaotl said. "Ask the priest, he'll tell you."

"Yes, it's true," the Fray said. "Fray Bernardino de Sahagún, the priest who recorded the history of the One World, wrote that under Quetzalcoatl's rule, beans were superabundant, gourds gargantuan—too vast to envelop in your arms—ears of maize the size of your thighs. He confirmed cotton of all colors was harvested—red, yellow, brown, white, green, blue, and orange . . . colossal cocoa trees growing grandiose and garish-hued . . .

Incomprehensibly rich, Quetzalcoatl's subjects dwelt in a land of plenty, in a prosperous and serene kingdom, lacking *nothing*. That is what he wrote."

"You see," Yaotl said, "even the Spanish dogs stood in awe of the glory and the dream that was Tula—before, of course, they grew wealthy and fat from raiding our homes, raping our women, and ransacking our land."

Yaotl told me that Quetzalcoatl had spurned the priests and warriors who longed for the old days of conquest and sacrifice. "Despite the bounty Quetzalcoatl dispensed on his people, the priests and warrior class still subscribed to the blood covenant, fearing that without the blood tithe, the people would starve, and their world destroyed."

Quetzalcoatl could create miracles, but he had a fatal flaw that could be exploited by his enemies—his love for his own sister.

"Forbidden lust," Fray Diego said, "for which he'll burn in hellfire everlasting."

"They got him drunk," Yaotl said, "but more than that, they stole his mind with forbidden mushrooms which they mixed in his pulque. Deprived of his senses, the evil priests maneuvered him into his sister's bedchamber. Awaking the next morning in shame and disgrace, he countered charges of incest by declaring himself a mortal god—beyond the laws of humankind. Mortals could err, a mortal god could not.

"He left Tula and journeyed to the Eastern Sea which Veracruz overlooks today. He set sail on a raft made of intertwined snakes to seek out the abode of the gods. Before he left, he told his followers that he would return in a One Reed year."

"I know the rest," I said. Every schoolboy knew the story of Montezuma and Quetzalcoatl. "The Spaniard Cortés had a red beard and hair, and he landed at Veracruz in a One Reed year. The Mexica emperor, Montezuma, thought Quetzalcoatl the god had returned. Cortés's land-fall frightened the emperor into indecision. Had fear of Quetzalcoatl not so paralyzed Montezuma, his army would have easily defeated the small Spanish force."

Yaotl nodded. "True, true, but he waited too long. Cortés bedded the woman Marina, who had quickly mastered both Cortés's language and loins. She forged for Cortés the tribal alliances with which he annihilated their hated foe, Mexicas. Those tribes provided thousands of warriors that fought alongside the Spanish. And of course one day the Spanish dogs turned on those allies and conquered them."

"Uncle, what you are telling me is that the people of the One World were conquered by the Spanish because of the legend of the last great king of Tula."

"A Spanish force of less than six hundred," Fray Diego interjected.

"Revenge." Yaotl's lips smacked with satisfaction. "The ghost of Quetzalcoatl took revenge on the Mexica and other tribes that attacked Tula after Quetzalcoatl left the city. You see, boy, without the mighty king, Tula could not survive because it had incurred the worst possible sin—envy.

"All the other tribes—especially the bare-ass, bare-footed Mexica-Aztecs—looked upon the golden city as a prize to possess." Yaotl shook his finger. "But before the barbarians could destroy the city, after Quetzalcoatl left, its own leaders plundered the city's wealth and dissipated its might. Bringing back human sacrifice, they added a new type of immolation—the arrow sacrifice, no doubt learned from the barbarian tribes to the north. The victim was tied to a rack, white paint applied over his heart, then he was used for target practice while his blood dripped on the ground to fertilize the earth. The victim took much longer to die than having his heart ripped out.

"They built racks on which to mount the decapitated heads of enemies and defeated ball game players. The new priest-kings despoiled the empire through war, greed, and stupidity. One war was even fought over the size of a woman's buttocks."

"What?"

"Sí, it is the truth. King Huemac ordered a subservient tribe to provide him with a woman whose buttocks were four hands wide. When they brought him a woman, he rejected her and insulted the tribe. They called him 'Big Hands' and her rump wasn't big enough for a span of his hands."

"What happened to Big Hands?"

Yaotl shrugged. "Tula was defeated, and he was killed in the war that followed. But things got even worse. Tula called the people of the dry northern desert 'dog people' because they wore animal skins, ate raw meat, and used bows and arrows. The Mexica-Aztecs were the most savage of these barbaric wanderers, and they resented the Toltecs' scorn. As the Mexica-Aztecs grew in power, they eyed the great city with ire and envy. At last, allied with other tribes, they attacked and ravaged the golden city.

"But the Mexica-Aztecs never forgot the greatness and grandeur of Tula. They envied everything Toltec. Their royalty married princesses of the Tula royal blood to improve their 'barbarian' bloodlines. They pillaged Tula's arts and crafts, its mathematics and science, and passed them off on the unsuspecting Spanish as their own."

"Tell him about the treasure," Fray Diego said.

"What treasure?" I asked.

"Quetzalcoatl's," Yaotl said. "Before the god-king left Tula, he is said to have hidden a vast treasure—perhaps under our feet right now, in a secret room beneath the pyramid. Or perhaps in a cave in the mountain. Many men and kings have hunted for his treasure, and their hunt has invariably visited evil luck on the hunters."

Presaging Death, our yellow dog barked at the distant dust devils.

FIVE

THE HOUNDS of hell."

Fray Diego pointed to the west. The dust cloud billowed above a troop of cavalry. The soldier riding point carried the crimson and gold standard of a Royal Militia company.

"Fifty or more," the fray said. Drained of blood, his face was deathly white. His lips quivered, and his jaw trembled in and out.

"Riderless horses will trail them home," Yaotl said, curiously without fear, an odd satisfaction in his voice.

This day came to all warriors—the final day—and he seemed ready for it. He was a great warrior, but I waged war as well. I had mixed gunpowder, rebuilt muskets, and pistols.

In contrast, Yaotl wielded a spear and knife with black, razor-sharp, volcanic obsidian to do the cut-and-thrust work—the weapons of his ancestors.

Still his spear would not carry a tenth as far as the Spanish musket balls I had supplied our troops. A musket ball could blow a hole out the back of a man and pass through three more standing back to back.

Moreover, fighting fifty soldiers and sustaining innumerable wounds conferred greater honor-in-death—at least in Yaotl's mind—than succumbing to a single musket ball.

Indifferent to honor, I was afraid. My knees buckling, my throat burned with the urge to cry. But I could not dishonor my uncles and the memory of my mother and sister and flee. Too many nights Yaotl had instructed me over a campfire on the Way of the Warrior: Never show your back to an enemy. Stand and fight. Die with honor—all wounds in the front, none in the back.

Yaotl killed the yellow dog with his spear. "Put it at my feet after I die," he told the Fray. "He will be our guide through the Nine Hells of Mictlan."

Fray Diego said nothing. Faithful to his own creed, he would not mock Yaotl's.

Yaotl, meanwhile, was still descanting on the Nine Hells of Mictlan. Mictlantecuhtli, Yaotl explained, was the skull-faced king, who ruled the Mictlan Underworld. Those damned to that sepulchral underworld faced nine challenges, one at each hell-level—the challenges of crossing a raging river, avoiding continuously colliding mountains, traversing a ridge of razor-sharp obsidian glass, enduring an icy wind that cut like blades, ducking violently swinging banners, surviving volleys of arrows, negotiating a valley of vile bloodsucking beasts, and scaling slimy rocks. If the challengers prevailed, their souls were scattered as dust, conferring on them the gift of oblivion. However, the Lord of the underworld had one last trick, many said. At the final level Mictlantecuhtli had erected a mystery obstacle that few could triumph over.

Those who failed were doomed to repeat the struggle.

I did not understand why Yaotl feared he would face the Nine Hells.

"You told me," I said to Yaotl, "that when a warrior fell in battle, or was sacrificed, he did not suffer the Nine Hells."

"True. If I fall in battle, I will ascend to the House of the Sun, a paradise across the Eastern Sea. There I will feast on fine food, bed beautiful women, and wage mock battles with my companions. My sole warrior duty will be to rise with the Sun God each morning and serve in his honor guard each day, as he crosses the sky." He shook his head.

"But that was the fate of a fallen warrior when the gods of my people were strong. The Christian God is more powerful. If my gods lack the strength to raise me up to the House of the Sun, Mictlantecuhtli will pull me down into the Underworld."

He gave the fray a small piece of jade. "This goes in my mouth. I will need it to pay toll at the raging river at the first Hell."

Fray Diego pocketed the jade and worked his rosary as he muttered Hail Marys. He saw me staring and smiled. "My son, sheep who are lost seek their shepherd at the first sign of wolves."

"Go, boy, run, race back to the village," Yaotl said.

I hesitated and Yaotl gave me a stinging blow to my head. "*Run!*"

SIX

I RAN, BUT not far. I was not a boy but a man. Reaching bushes, I glanced back and saw that my uncles were no longer watching me but studying the oncoming horse horde. I slipped behind the bushes out of sight. This was the spot where I had cached my weapons: a pistol and a knife.

I'd assembled the pistol myself in the days when we were rebuilding damaged guns in the village chapel for Father Hidalgo. But like all pistols, it fired only one shot and like most pistols, that shot often missed its mark or failed to fire at all. Still, I had the knife for when the pistol failed.

Yaotl schemed to die from countless wounds, and the fray hoped to die quickly soon after slaughtering his fellow men. My dream of death was far more humble: I would kill one Spaniard before a musket ball blew away my brains.

I crouched in the bushes, watching and waiting for my chance.

My uncles prepared to face their foe. Yaotl stood tall—the heir to the tradition of mighty Toltec warriors.

Fray Diego, meanwhile, readied his weapons. Ayyo . . . the good fray did not disappoint me. I almost howled with laughter as I watched him unlimber his arsenal. A man of erudition and imagination, he assembled an assortment of small bombs—clay pots packed with black powder sporting short fuses. Ignite the fuse, hurl the bomb, and duck the debris and blood.

I did not ask Fray Diego if he expected a grateful

greeting when he faced his God at the pearly gates in the afterlife.

The horse-borne force suddenly fanned out, advancing in two long lines.

They aren't fools, I thought.

Had they advanced in a solid column, Yaotl's spear might have found flesh, and the fray's bombs would have hit home. With the horsemen spread out, Yaotl's spear was useless, and the fray's bombs impotent.

My heart sank as musket shots rang out. They had no intention of charging us and fighting it out. They would hang back and shoot.

As if to confirm my fears, Yaotl screamed and sank, knocked off his feet by a musket ball. One bullet winged his arm, another his shoulder.

The Spanish dogs were shooting him to pieces, but nonetheless bent on taking him alive. His journey through hell would begin not in the Nine Hells of Mictlan but in this life.

The fray also understood. His countrymen were not fools . . . at least not the commander of this small company of militia cavalry. As the bullets smacked around him, the fray held up his hands to the heavens, as if imploring them for guidance, faith, and transcendent truth even at the hour of his almost certain death.

Had I felt the urge to pray, I might have asked for something more substantive—perhaps a battery of heavy artillery.

At that point, however, the horse soldiers rode up and dismounted. They kicked and cuffed and punched my uncles before dragging them up to the commander. A young officer who sat tall in the saddle, the commander stared down at the two prisoners, his face a mask of conceited contempt.

Spanish officers in the colonies were often self-styled,

self-equipped, and dressed as much to attract the ladies as to wage bloody war, while the common soldiers were uniformed in simple dark green long shirts and loose pants. The officer in charge was dressed as a god. Like the quetzal bird, he had a green coat and red vest. The epaulets on his shoulder were golden. He dressed to suit his vanity.

Obviously, he didn't fear the wrath of rebels—or Toltec warriors. He stood out like a rooster in a barnyard of hens. Dressed as if he were going to a parade rather than a battle, his mighty magnificence brought home the vast superiority of the Spaniards.

Yaotl stared back at the commander in stony silence and brazen defiance.

"Señor," the fray said politely, "before Christ, we are your humble prisoners. You may do with us as you will— take our lives if you see fit. Please, however, spare our village."

The commander spat in the fray's face.

A tall sergeant, with a black sweeping mustache and diagonal dueling scars traversing his cheeks, dismounted. Unlimbering his member, he urinated on Yaotl.

Pointing to a tree with long, low overarching bows, the magnificently uniformed commander shouted in his best parade-ground voice: "You have ropes. You have a tree. Hang them."

His men took two coiled ropes from the cross-bucks of their lone pack animal and tossed them over the overhanging bows.

I raced from the bushes straight at the nearest cavalryman. He sat on his horse with his back to me. Too young and stupid to consider shooting a man in the back, I let out a war whoop that sent the startled soldier wheeling his horse to face me.

When he turned, I fired the pistol.

The shot went wild but the spooked horse bolted,

throwing the rider off. Leaping onto the prone man, I raised my knife high, preparing to plunge it into his heart. I planned to execute him in the manner of my ancestors, who dispatched their adversaries by ripping out their hearts.

Before I dealt the blow, however, my head exploded.

SEVEN

WHEN I AWOKE, my uncles were twisting in the wind, their heads cocked at hard right angles. Against my will, tears came. I whispered a prayer to Quetzalcoatl for Yaotl and the fray's eternal redeemer, Christ Jesus. I prayed for Yaotl's warrior's heart and for Fray Diego's saintly soul. I wished Yaotl good speed in the Nine Hells and the fray vaya con dios in Christ's heavenly kingdom.

I was trussed up tight, lashed to a tree. I listened as an officer argued with the commander over my life . . . and death.

The commander cracked his riding crop against his boot top; he radiated the instinctive disdain, casual cruelty, and innate arrogance of a Spanish aristocrat. He glared at his men with withering condescension. Perhaps thirty years old, he was a ramrod-straight spit-and-polish martinet with the soul of a counting house and the compassion of a striking cobra.

"It doesn't matter if he's a boy," the lieutenant said testily. "He almost killed one of our men. He's a rebel and should hang."

The captain's glance shot right through me—a gaze blank and pitiless as the sun. I read many things in his features . . . vanity, violence, viciousness, vindictiveness, the cynical sneer of cold cruel command. A supercilious aristocrat, he viewed soldiers as inferiors worthy only of relentless repression and indios as farm animals whose sole purpose in his blighted universe was as a beast of burden born to serve and suffer under the whips and rowels of brutal Spaniards such as himself or—in the case of our women—under their garranchas. We were dray animals and putas, for him and his kind to rape and flog, plunder and exploit, imprison and kill.

All he respected was strength and confrontation. Cringing weakness was worse than open contempt.

I met his glance with derision. "Let me go, Spanish pig, and I'll cut your little garrancha off and feed it to a dog."

He laughed.

And slashed my face with his riding whip.

I choked back my pain, denying him the satisfaction of hearing me whimper. Blood flowed down my cheek and down my chest. Still I did not blink.

"Let me loose—I'll fight you man to man, you castrated male whore."

Slipping a boot out of the stirrup, he sneered—and kicked me in the stomach.

"He has rebel blood," the lieutenant said, "hang him now or we'll face him in battle again."

"Why waste his financial worth on the end of a rope? He's young and strong. We can sell him to the mines. He'll bring a good price. Once he's in the tunnels, he'll never see the light of day again. He'll be an old man in a year, dead in two, and will have served our country well."

Bastardo. Being sold to the silver mines was a slow, agonizing, soul-destroying sentence—death by inches in an endless labyrinth of hot, sweaty, dust-ridden hell-pits. The slightest infraction of rules or hint of insubordination and they strung you up at a flogging post.

"We'll see who's the puta, Aztec. Down in the mines, a young rabbit like you will bring out the macho wolves. The mines are full of them. We'll see who's the real man when they finish hammering your bruised and bleeding ass."

PART II
AND INTO THE FIRE

HOW MANY DAYS I trudged, slogged, limped, crawled, and was half dragged over rough roads and broken country, up hills and through river fords to the transit holding pen of San Jacinto I could not say. Ten days I would guess. Those days passed in a blinding blur of hunger and hopelessness, dust and dehydration, sunstroke heat and bleeding road-blistered feet.

When I didn't keep up, there was also the downward slash of their plaited rawhide wrist-quirts.

Nor was the San Jacinto holding pen much of an improvement. More a waist-deep dirt pit than an actual jail, it was surrounded by a wall of sun-baked mud-brick. Like myself, the sixty-odd prisoners were all as stunned by hunger and thirst, agony and fatigue, filth and heat. Diarrhea was rampant, and the two buckets could not contain the diseased excretions. Most of us lacked the energy to do more than sleep, scramble after the slop they threw at us twice a day, and drag ourselves to the buckets.

Dogs and donkeys ate, drank, and slept better than we did.

They suffered less, too.

We waited in the walled pit of San Jacinto for transport to the silver mines—Guanajuato, Zacatecas, Pachuco. We did not know which one, nor did it matter much. They were all death traps. Prisoners went there to toil, suffer, and die.

I would suffer in agony and ignominy.

I would die in shame and in shackles.

NINE

AT THE END of my first week, I stood in a foul pit with other prisoners and watched a gunsmith struggling to shoulder and unload large kegs of gunpowder for the militia. Small of stature—almost dwarfishly diminutive— he had thin arms and a sunken chest. His eyes were haggard—almost haunted in appearance—his cheeks hollow and drawn. Swaying and staggering under the heavy barrels, his lungs wheezed—so much so I wondered if he was down with a contagion.

Working before an open forge had befouled his face and hands, his tan shirt and trousers, with grimy sweat. He was clearly a man understaffed, overwhelmed, and overworked. He needed a helping hand.

Furthermore, I knew his trade. I had once handled the same explosive for *another* army, albeit an army of liberation.

"Shame about your apprentice, Felix," a tall, sturdily built soldier said to him. "I hear the miserable wretch up and died on you this morning."

"Yes, and after all the work I put into him. He was just starting to learn the gunsmithing trade. Lord knows where I'll find another. Not in this benighted town."

"You could have used his strong back today."

"Mine creaks like a cracked axle."

Ayyo. The poor Spaniard. He had to do a day's work. I called to the man. "Señor Felix, I must talk to you."

He looked up but turned away, ignoring me.

"Señor, I *must* talk to you."

He gave me a look, then strode over to me. "Shut up, boy, or you'll *talk* to the business end of my horsewhip."

No one was close enough to overhear, so I whispered, "I know gunpowder and gunsmithing. I'm also muy hombre—strong as a macho mule. I can unload for you."

"Shut up, boy."

I watched him open a barrel and pour gunpowder into a musketeer's flask.

"Your black powder's too fine," I said, "so fine it should only be used in a pistol's flashpan. Musket powder must be coarser, or the heat and speed of the discharge will split the barrel. The quartermaster will have your cojones for sweetbreads."

The man stared angrily at me, his eyes narrowing.

Well, at least I had his attention.

He finally looked around, confirming that no officers had overheard me. No one was within earshot, and I'd kept my voice low.

He strode over to me. "Make trouble for me, boy, and I'll have *your* cojones. *Now*." He glanced around again, nervous. When he looked back at me, he asked: "What do you know about gunpowder and gun smithing?"

"I made black powder and rebuilt weapons for the army of Generalissimo Hidalgo. That's why they're sending me to the mines."

"So you're a bastardo bandido as well as an idiot Aztec indio."

"I thought the revolución would improve my character."

"The mines will improve your character."

"By killing me?"

"Exactly so."

"Wouldn't it be better if I improved your financial character, señor, and protected your aching back from protracted labor? You'll work less. Your only burden will be the barrels of dinero I will shoulder through life for you. I tell you I know gunpowder like buzzards know carrion. I can rebuild—no, I can make—muskets and pistolas." I lifted my chin with pride and whispered: "I have built a pistola all by myself and shot a militia officer with it. To death. I even mixed the gunpowder and molded the lead ball which I emptied into his gachupine skull."

"They hang men for less. Why not you?"

"I'm young and strong. I'm worth more to them alive, so they sell me to the mines. But they'll sell me to you instead—if the dinero is right."

"You say you can make black powder?"

"And guns."

"The truth is not in you."

"If I lie, our Holy Mother ran a brothel."

Felix shut his eyes and crossed himself.

"You are the devil," he said, his eyes still shut.

"Your devil indeed—but a devil skilled in your trade, and you need me. As you said, you can find no one else. You *will* find no one else."

"If you know so much, tell me what goes into gunpowder?"

"Seventy-five parts saltpeter, fifteen parts charcoal, ten parts sulfur. But the mixture must be caressed because batches vary. Mix it too energetically it will energize you into Holy Hell."

"You have a strong back?"

"Like a prize stallion."

"Cross me, you'll wish you had died in the mines."

"I will make for you the highest quality of powder and the most magnifico weaponry in all of New Spain. You'll make three times as much dinero as you bring in now and forge the finest firearms in the land."

"I'll ask that slave driver of an overseer how much he

wants for an ignorant indio Aztec with vulture vomit for brains."

"I'm a bargain, you'll see." I puffed up my chest. "I'm worth my weight in Aztec gold."

Shaking his head, he turned and walked toward the overseer.

He was cursing the father I never knew and my mother in the foulest possible terms.

PART III
GOLD AND GUNS

TEN

Lago de Chapala, Intende de Guadalajara, 1818

A MAGNIFICENT PISTOLA," Manuel, my best assistant, said.

Sí, another masterwork, by a master craftsman . . . namely me. A flintlock pistol, the walnut handle inlaid with ivory, embellished with elegant whorls of eighteen-karat gold, elaborately embossed staghorn stock and glittering with brass fittings burnished to a mirror-gloss.

From the light filtering in through the shop window, I examined the gold plate containing the name of the gunsmith who had crafted this exquisite weapon: *Felix Baroja of Eibar.*

No, my name was not Felix Baroja nor was I of Eibar, a town in Old Spain's Basque country. I was Juan Rios, and to my Spanish masters I was an ignorant Aztec peon, which many Spaniards thought lower than the beasts. My name may have been Spanish, but my Spanish masters were quick to let me know I was in no way Spanish and hence without any rights at all. I no longer answered to Mazatl because that name was unknown and unpronounceable to my Spanish masters. I lost that name when I lost my uncles to a taut noose and a gallows tree seven long years ago, and I was spared a mine slave's ignominious death.

I stared into a small handheld mirror that I used to peer down the pistol and musket barrels that I forged and fabricated. In my seven years as a bond slave, I'd grown to manhood. My hair was dark and thick, and since my beard was surprisingly coarse for an indio, I had to shave. My eyes, Felix continually warned me, were bold and wary as a hawk's, not submissive enough for "an Aztec indio bastardo," as he liked to refer to me.

Once when he branded me "a bastardo"—due to my problematic paternity—I shot back: "In my case, señor, an accident of birth. You, however, are a self-made one."

He laughed derisively and only continued his endless assaults on the mystery of my true antecedents.

The forge was in a dark, carefully concealed room situated between my work room and Felix's office. I dreaded working the forge. Forge-building was not only dirty and sweltering, sometimes I had to work there in secrecy.

The doors were locked and the windows shuttered. No one else had a key but Felix.

And that enclosed forge shed—where I heated steel over blazing coals, then melted, shaped, and hammered it, often on anvils—was insufferably hot and filthy.

The second shop, in which I otherwise toiled, was in a small building, sequestered behind Felix's office and showroom. The window was draped off most of the time. Only when I unavoidably required light to probe and inspect my handiwork did I push the curtain aside—and only then when I was sure no one lurked outside.

That shed was a typical gunsmithery—shelves crammed with flintlocks, wheellocks, matchlocks, barrels, hammers, handles, trigger housings, damaged pistols of every sort. Tools hung from pegs on the walls—hammers, tongs, awls, files, chisels, hand drills, and pliers. Work benches were equipped with anvils and vises beside smoking braziers.

For reasons of personal pride and mutual self-protection, my bond master insisted on concealing my gun- and powder-making from the public, and I acquiesced. You might think I owed him no less. As owner of the gun shop and gunpowder plant where I lived and worked, Felix Baroja was the man who had redeemed me from certain death in the silver mines. Nonetheless, I served him under conditions that negated any gratitude I might have conceivably felt. The laws—which allowed him to purchase me and if he had so chosen, flog, castrate even, or kill me like a dog—were the ubiquitous laws of the land and the bane of New Spain. In the nearly three hundred years since the Conquest, those laws had allowed Spanish conquistadors and slave drivers to shackle and imprison, exploit and murder my people—annihilating ninety percent of them with their guns and whips, prison mines and forced-labor haciendas. For those three hundred years, the gachupine "spur-wearers" and their criollo brothers had roweled our bloody backs and flanks with their razor-sharp spurs to enrich themselves.

Felix was pure Basque, a gachupine breed from northern Spain that is renown in both hemispheres for its legendary gun-makers. But the exquisite pistol in my hand was crafted not by him but by his bond slave, Juan Rios, in a compound near the shores of Lake Chapala in the Guadalajara region of the New Spain colony.

He reaped the fruits of my sweaty, sweltering, stifling labor and accepted the accolades due me.

The compound was situated by a creek a few miles east of the town of Chapala. Nearly fifty miles long and ten miles wide, Lake Chapala was the largest lake in the New Spain colony, and our creek was one of its tributaries. Thirty miles from Guadalajara, six thousand feet above the ocean shore's elevation, our lake was comfortably ensconced—a fortuitous altitude, which kept the climate temperate year round.

The pistol falsely bore the legend of the Basque gun-maker and his Iberian Peninsula home city for many reasons. My lord and master would not acknowledge to anyone—not even *to me*—that I had designed, forged, and fabricated the weapons, which had made him rich. That his hard-used, long-suffering bond slave was as talented as any gunsmith alive and far more industrious than himself was a fact his gachupine pride would never accept.

An indio slave, whom he routinely ridiculed as his "Aztec cannibal," underwrote both his fame and fortune.

Compounding his vanity was his fear. As I have said, in allowing an indio to master the craft of gun-making, he had breached one of the Crown's most inviolable laws— one that underpinned its entire tyranny. The Crown had not forgotten Father Hidalgo's bloody and costly uprising, and Felix's and my transgression had threatened that tyranny in the most devastating way imaginable. Were the gachupines to learn that Felix was allowing an indio to practice and perfect the craft of pistol and musket manufacturing, the full weight of royal retribution would crash down on the vain, greedy Basque like a volcanic eruption.

Despite the risk, he never once suggested curbing my lucrative labors. While I reaped little for my industry and peril—common food and shelter—he profited extravagantly. His life had grown relatively affluent, his workday exertions reduced to bragging to his friends, bedding down his mistresses, and besotting himself with brandy and vino.

When I first approached Felix, I was hardly more than a boy—a prisoner sentenced to suicidal slavery for backing Hidalgo's Independence Movement. Like many others who'd backed Father Hidalgo, I was deemed an irredeemable enemy of the Crown.

Nor, in truth, had the fury that had fired the country's impassioned rebellion ebbed. With each succeeding year since Hidalgo's death, the padre's dream of freedom had spread and swelled in my heart, in everyone's hearts. Since 1810, when Father Hidalgo first proclaimed the Cry of Dolores on the church steps, his revolutionary vision had never dimmed but had secretly grown.

But that vision had not freed the Good Father's people nor tamed the Spaniards' tyranny.

Seven years ago—at the Battle of Calderon Bridge, not far from Guadalajara—a royal cannoneer's lucky shot had detonated an overloaded powder wagon, its flaming debris igniting furious firestorms throughout his camp. The conflagration razed his army and incinerated their supplies, weapons, ammunition, materiel. Afterward Spanish troops captured and imprisoned Hidalgo, eventually executing him by firing squad.

Another son of the Church, Father Morelos, picked up Hidalgo's struggle. Fighting to the bitter end, he was at last captured and executed in 1815. Since then, scattered bands—some no more than bandido gangs—harassed the Spanish swine in many places throughout the colony. General Guerrero's guerrilla army conducted operations in the China Road region, cutting a bloody swath from Acapulco to the Valley of Mexico. The most stubborn resistance, however, was waged on a small island near the coast of the lake—not far from our small factory—where a band of rebels had held off the Spanish for years.

Nonetheless, all the years of war, rebellion, and rampant banditry had achieved little. The oppression of peons continued unabated. If anything, the criollos exacerbated their depredations, trusting only in violence and terror and the utter suppression of their starved and brutalized subjects.

ELEVEN

I WAS EXAMINING the rifling in the pistol's bore—using my mirror to reflect candlelight down the barrel—when Felix entered. Spiral grooves, meticulously cut into the inside of a barrel's interior, spun the rotating ball as it sped through the barrel. This rifling—as it was called—greatly increased the weapon's accuracy. Despite the benefits of these spiraling grooves, few weapons were rifled because it was expensive and the weapons required continuous upkeep. Black powder and residue from the spinning lead balls filled the grooves, requiring that the barrels be re-bored periodically.

Felix was garishly garbed with a black broad-brimmed, low-crowned caballero's hat and a matching silk jacket, under which he sported a ruffled shirt of imported alabaster linen and a red brocade vest. His tight black breeches were stuffed into knee-high ebony riding boots, which he'd ordered me earlier in the day to burnish to a mirror-gloss and heel with four-inch sterling silver spurs. A plaited wrist-quirt of inky ox-hide rested horizontally in his hands.

"The marques will be here soon," Felix said without preamble, not even bothering to inspect my craftsmanship. "Pray—for your sake—that the pistol more than meets the marques's expectations . . . and mine. Make sure it is in its case and in my hand before the marques's carriage arrives."

"Sí, Patrón."

He swung the wrist-quirt against his boot top, casually cracking the triple three-inch poppers against it. Felix had used that quirt on me more than once when my efforts or attitude did not suit his insufferable vanity or supercilious fancy. And I had resisted the urge to kill him.

He wanted the pistol in his hand so he could present it to the marques as *his* handiwork, not letting the marques know that an indio's skill and sweat had produced a weapon of such singular sturdiness, incomparable precision, and, yes, surpassing beauty. Basking in the grandee's praise, my patrón would then pocket the gold that was the reward for excellence.

As I spoke, my foot nudged saddlebags I'd concealed earlier under the table, pushing them farther out of sight. If Felix knew the contents of the bags—and what I was doing with them—he would have handed me over to the constable, who would have flogged me to the point of death and then dragged me to the viceroy's gallows. Not even the piles of dinero and fame my craftsmanship had lavished on him would have saved me.

"Did you finish repairing his hunting muskets?"

"Sí, Patrón. He will find that all three shoot better than the day he bought them."

"He wants those delivered to his house this afternoon. He won't be taking them into the city with the pistol."

The "city" was Guadalajara.

Felix set an old wheel-lock musket on the table. "This belongs to Ruiz, the grain merchant. Repair it for him, but don't make it like new. It's a piece of junk. He's a bastardo and too cheap to pay what I so indisputably deserve."

Without a muchas gracias, he left the shop.

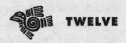

TWELVE

IN THOSE SEVEN years in Felix's gun shop, I had worked diligently at gunsmithing and studied the history of such weaponry and munitions.

The size and shape of muskets and pistols had not changed significantly since these weapons had first become commonplace among Europeans three hundred years ago.

Gunpowder was still poured and compressed into muskets, pistols, and cannons, and a lead ball was still rammed through the barrel and into the breech. Gunpowder was also put in a flashpan on the weapon's top. When the trigger was pulled, the powder in the flashpan ignited the main powder charge in the breech, blowing the ball out the barrel at a speed sufficient to kill a man.

Early on, the shooter had to hold the weapon with one hand and light the powder in the flashpan with the other. A device was needed so both hands could be used to hold and aim the weapon.

The first effective one was the "matchlock." The "match" was a piece of cord attached to an arm and lighted. When the trigger was pulled, the arm holding the match dropped down, igniting the gunpowder in the flashpan.

Ayyo! Having a frighteningly flammable cord near gunpowder was hazardous. Accidents were inevitable, and the consequences could be catastrophic. Moreover, matchlocks in wet weather were notoriously unreliable. At night the glow made it easy to spot the shooter.

Since the weapon was relatively inexpensive to make,

the matchlock remained the preferred musket throughout Europe for centuries.

Gun owners still occasionally sent me one for repair.

The next improvement was a spinning wheel that replaced the burning cord. A metal jaw gripped the flint, and when a shooter squeezed the trigger, a steel wheel with edges rotated against the flint, firing sparks into the flashpan, igniting the powder.

I've been told that Leonardo da Vinci invented the wheel lock, though to hear Felix brag about it, you would think he himself invented it and everything else under the sun.

Wheel locks have been around for three hundred years, back to about the time Cortés was conquering the One World. Due to the high cost of weapons, people passed them down for generations.

The preferred weapon in my own time was the flintlock. Like the wheel lock, a spark from flint was used to ignite the powder, but the flintlock was much less complicated: the flint was held in a small vise called a cock that fell and sparked when it struck a glancing blow to a piece of steel after the trigger was pulled.

Of course, all muskets had one purpose: to kill.

THIRTEEN

AFTER FELIX LEFT, I went to work on the grain merchant's wheel lock. I saw immediately that the spring beneath the jaws that held the flint was missing. Since we had few spare parts for weapons repairs and no extra springs, a new spring would have to be fabricated. Such missing or irreparably damaged parts had to be handcrafted in the shop foundry. The process was not simple, but I had already fabricated entire weapons with our limited equipment.

Consequently, the flintlock had become the weapon of choice for infantry since the seventeenth century. Most of the pistols and muskets I worked were flintlocks.

Thanks to my expansion of Felix's business, the compound—in which I performed my duties as a gunsmith and maker of gunpowder—had grown substantially. It now consisted of several buildings. The buildings stood two hundred paces apart, and each shed was long and narrow. The powder shed's brown mud-brick walls were of double thickness. In the event that one of us accidentally discharged a weapon in the compound, we didn't want it entering the powder shed and causing an explosion.

Beside the two buildings, we had constructed storage areas, a stable and corral for mules, and a bunkhouse for the workers. Felix and his family lived on a hillock far from the destructive range of an explosion in the gunpowder shed.

He also stabled his horses at the main house.

He clearly worried more about his livestock than his workers.

As a matter of law, Felix was not supposed to manufacture guns. The Crown required that all weapons must be imported from Spain and that only repairs be locally done. But as with most Spanish laws, legal exceptions were available for a price. Our favorite method is to call the work a "repair": We start with a part from one weapon, such as a butt-plate . . . and build the new weapon from that point on. That way Felix could claim that he is merely "repairing" the weapon.

The firearms Felix had previously crafted were not nearly as fine as the pistol I had made for the marques in our gun shop. Similar to a blacksmith's shop, the gun shop housed some special tools that were indispensable to gunmaking and to manufacturing the parts needed for weapon repairs: anvils, bellows, hammers, boring and grooving tools and other instruments, as well as a forge, which was a furnace or fire pit where metals could be melted or heated so they could be shaped, hardened, and infused with tenacity.

Muskets and pistols were made with the Damascus barrel technique. The barrel was made by heating thin rods of steel so that they were pliable, then twisting them around a center bar. Wrapping the rods around the center bar created a continuous open seam that had to be filled. Heating and pounding the metal, in what was called a "wielding" process, closed the seam. Inadequately closing the seam caused most defective barrels. Another common defect was making the barrel too hard and brittle. As with a sword, the iron had to give a little or it might crack, snap, or break.

After the barrel was shaped, the center bar was pulled out and a boring tool smoothed the barrel's interior.

The barrel had to be "proofed" to test its reliability. We proofed a weapon by firing two balls at once with twice the powder used for a single ball. If the barrel survived this double load, we'd "pickle" it with an acid bath to remove an iron layer that would easily rust. The pickling made the barrels black and brought out the characteristic Damascus twisted wire pattern on the barrel.

Felix confided in me once after too much wine that while his Damascus barrels were inferior to most of those he'd made in Spain, they were better than the cheap, often defective muskets he had occasionally made for use in the slave trade. In that trade, guns were the profession's legal tender—one gun bought one slave from a native chief or a professional trader. As often as not, the guns were so cheaply fabricated that they blew apart on firing, killing the customers who purchased them.

Through Felix's books and from our occasional discussions, I learned that cleaning the rust off old horseshoe nail stubs and melting them down produced superior gunmetal. That steel could then be forged into long rods used in the Damascus process.

Horseshoe nails were superior to wrought iron because horses were so valuable—in both war and peace—that their horseshoe nail stubs were made from superior steel. I learned that melting pieces of steel carriage springs in with the nail stubs produced an even higher quality gunmetal for the manufacturing of firearms' barrels. The spring steel increased the barrel's resilience and tenacity.

Using that process, the flintlock pistol I made for the marques was a finer weapon than most and not just because of the rifled barrel.

At one point during the colony's crisis in weapons shipments, Felix even let me forge a cannon. The best cannons are cast, usually out of bronze, while lesser expensive ones are made of iron. But a cannon barrel is nothing more than a tube bigger than a musket or pistol barrel, and I modeled my cannon on the Damascus barrel, using the twisted-wire technique.

I'd read that the Chinese had actually loaded and fired gunpowder in bamboo tubes and that after reinforcing bamboo with steel tubes, Arabs had fired metal arrows from the tubes.

Closer to home for me, I had worked with my uncles who had reinforced hardwood to create cannons for Father Hidalgo. Not the best weapons in a battle, but if carefully loaded, they could send a broadside of nails into advancing troops.

I admit, my Damascus cannon was far from a perfect weapon. The problem was that the seams left from the twisting were so large, they had to be partly filled with lead, a soft metal, and that created a weak seal. But with light powder charges, the cannon was useful.

Working for Felix had also honed my skill at making gunpowder. Ayyo! Great care had to be taken when working with gunpowder because few tasks were as dangerous.

Each step involved care—the making, storing, handling, and transporting of the powder. We removed from the shop all metal that could collide, spark, and ignite the explosive. Finished powder was stored only in copper and transported in copper casks, each weighing about twenty-five pounds and covered with leather pouches that were sealed at the top.

The formula for making gunpowder was well known—but making gunpowder is in the end alchemy and the alchemist's art is perfected only by getting the combination exactly right, by tweaking the formula here and there to suit the actual strength of the ingredient. Saltpeter was especially tricky, its purity varying from deposit to deposit. The quality of charcoal differed widely, depending on the type of wood burned and even the age of the tree it came from. Willow or hazel charcoal was preferable for cannon powder, dogwood charcoal for small arms.

I also preferred using urine instead of water in mixing the ingredients, having found that a beer drinker's urine was better than water, and a wine drinker's best of all.

I began by working with the ingredients separately, grinding each by hand into a fine powder. Dissolving the saltpeter in urine in one drum while the charcoal and sulfur were dissolving together in another, I then mixed the compounds together in a wet mixture.

When they were completely blended, the mixture was formed into cakes, the liquid pressed out, and the cakes allowed to dry.

Rather than a fine powder, gunpowder works best when it is "corned" into small granules. Corning is accomplished by grinding and tumbling the mixture, then passing the granules through different-sized wire screens. The resultant grains can range from the size of a grain of corn to a powder.

The requisite size of the grains depended on the powder's purpose. Cannons required a coarser, relatively large grain, muskets a medium grain, and pistols a finer grain.

I determined the powder's potency by firing a musket ball into clay to see how far the powder drove it in. Afterward, I adjusted the mixture accordingly.

Some gunpowder we worked with was reprocessed powder. When the powder on merchant vessels and warships became damp, it had to be revitalized. Felix bought the defective powder and reprocessed it for use in the silver mines. We added urine and saltpeter to the flawed powder, then remixed and screened it, sometimes blending in the other ingredients when it failed our tests.

Another customer, however, was desperate for our merchandise—even more desirous of it than the rich marques and our filthy-rich mine owners. A customer who could not pay and whom Felix and the viceroy's secret police must never know I was supplying.

For the sake of my safety and theirs, I had hidden the saddlebags beneath the table—then kicked them in even farther.

FOURTEEN

WHEN I HEARD a shout that the marques had arrived,
I handed the gun in its case to Felix.

I expected no credit for my work, and Felix never surprised me with any. He kept the torrents of praise—which
our customers lavished on him as his just due—utterly to
himself as a miser might hide and hoard his gold. Even
when our grateful customers lauded his alleged labors to
my face, he never acknowledged my contribution after
they left.

I sometimes wondered if he had deceived himself
into actually believing he had forged and fabricated the
weapons.

Even in the ways by which the Spanish gachupines
evaluated manhood, I was more hombre than Felix. I was
a better gun-maker than he, more skilled with a knife, a
gun, or bare fists. I'd proven it in combat where I had
killed better men than he.

From the way Felix's woman stared at me when he was
away, I believed my garrancha would probe more deeply
and more ecstatically than his, too.

Not that my life was as bad as most peons in the colony.
Even though I was an indio or a mestizo—depending on
which of my uncles had indeed spawned me—I performed work that gave me great satisfaction. Since I lined
Felix's pockets with dinero and drenched his ego in unde-
served praise, he could not abuse or mistreat me too egre-
giously.

He gave me enough to eat, a roof over my head, and
kept me clothed.

True, my accommodations were not lavish. I lived above the stable . . . not where Felix housed his fine horses, but the stable in the compound for the mules that pulled our wagons or carried our products to market.

Living with the stench of manure is just the peon's lot in life . . . at least, according to the gachupines. But I was not born and raised a "tame" peon. I was taught the Way of the Warrior. A warrior doesn't walk in the droppings of another man . . . or the man's animals. A warrior rewards with respect those who have honored themselves in battle, not the thieves and liars who sell them defective guns made of weak wrought iron.

I wanted respect. I wanted to walk down a sidewalk and not have to step into the gutter because a Spaniard was coming. I tired of bowing and scraping to Spanish nobles and hacendados whose contribution to their titles, their fortunes, and their honors was simply the condition of their birth.

Father Hidalgo, Father Morelos, and the other heroes and heroines of the revolution knew that the only way to win our freedom was to kill Spaniards until they understood we were equal enough to drive them from our soil, that all people were created equally.

Because they could kill equally.

Which is why there were two hundred lead balls in one saddlebag and a copper canister of black powder in the other.

If every shot hit home, the bags contained enough to kill two hundred Spaniards.

Ayyo . . . the lieutenant who argued with the commanding officer at Tula that I was infected with rebel blood was correct. They should have hanged me, and perhaps one day I would dance the hangman's jig—after a Spanish torturer stripped my flesh with whips, knives, and hot pincers.

While Felix busied himself impressing the marques with *his* exquisite craftsmanship, I slipped the saddle-bags out from under the shop table and into a secret hiding place in the mule stable.

Why had I stayed and walked in Felix's shadow? The good servant, the loyal indio, humble peon? Because I learned something the day that my uncles fought the Spanish—and lost. The Spanish beat them with superior weapons, muskets that permitted them to stay out of range of my uncle's efforts.

To beat the enemy we needed better weapons.

FIFTEEN

WHILE FELIX WAS off to town to purchase supplies—
and see his current mistress—I prepared to make my delivery. After cleaning up, I loaded the sheathed muskets
onto my favorite mule, Rodrigo, and set off for the hacienda of the marques. The two saddlebags were hidden
beneath a rolled-up canvas tarpaulin.

Along the way, I veered off the road to a hillside where
I came alone to practice my shooting skills. I used two
pistols that I had made. Indios were not permitted to possess arms, so I concealed them inside my loose-fitting
peon garb, one in a holster tucked under my arm, the other
in an ankle holster under my trousers. Both were rifled
flintlocks, their gunmetal forged with melted horseshoe
nails and wagon springs. I had made my pistolas with loving care, making them deadly accurate and remarkably
reliable.

Any Spaniard would have scoffed at them. I had super-
imposed rust and scratches on them, eschewed any and all
embellishment, making them appear as crude as I knew
how.

Targeting small hillside rocks, I loaded, aimed, and
fired my weapons. We test-fired all guns we made or repaired at the compound, and once in a moment of foolish
bravado, I had showed off my shooting skills to Felix. He
had been stunned.

And angry.

I was not only a better marksman than he was, he main-
tained I was better than the Count de Moreno, who was arguably the best marksman and duelist in the colony.

"He showed his skills at a party I attended," Felix said. "I thought he was unrivaled but you are better."

He then forbade me from practicing or even test-firing a pistol—except into our barrel of clay.

"You are to tell no one or demonstrate for anyone your marksmanship," he said.

The wearers of sharp spurs would not be happy to know that the best shot in the colony was a peon.

Or that he had the deadliest brace of pistols in all of New Spain.

From Felix's books, I learned much about the history and manufacturing of firearms. The basic problem with pistols and muskets had been the same for centuries. They are cumbersome and time-consuming to load.

Loading them had always been a laborious process, which involved pouring powder down a barrel from a horn or flask. A ball and wadding was then rammed down the barrel with a rod. Priming powder was put into the flashpan. The weapon was then cocked and fired.

Dampness, however, often destroyed the powder's effectiveness, and residue frequently fouled the barrel.

The typical soldier required up to a minute to load and fire their muskets.

That was fine for armies firing volleys at each other, but in individual combat with an advancing foe, your enemy would run you through with a sword before you were able to fire and reload.

If a shooter, however, loaded his weapon at its breech end—the end of the barrel closest to the flint firing mechanism—the shooter could reload it much faster than a muzzle-loading weapon.

Over the centuries breech-loading weapons had been designed, even fabricated, but they had proven too difficult and expensive to manufacture and too unreliable for military use. Most breech-loading firearms were toys for kings. The English king Henry VIII and a Louis of France both had owned breech-loaders.

I had studied and experimented with the various types of breech-loaders that I'd read about in Felix's books. The one created for the English king three centuries ago especially intrigued me. Rather than opening the breech and pouring powder and a ball inside, an iron tube called a cartridge was inserted under the hammer. The tube containing the powder charge and ball was held in place by a wad at the front.

I soon discovered why the cartridge never came into general use—making them by hand was a long, laborious process that required expert workmanship.

I found a more practical design on a powder delivery trip to the Guanajuato silver mines with Felix. I had observed one officer from an army of the United States—the colony's neighbor to the northeast—on a map-making expedition. He carried what he called a breech-loading flintlock musket.

Felix and I had camped near the norteamericano's group, and I saw the weapon when the man purchased powder from me while Felix was away collecting payment from a mine owner.

That an indio was so curious about his breech-loader—and so obviously knowledgeable about firearms construction—surprised the officer. I piqued his interest enough that he answered my question. He explained that an inventor named Hall had designed the unusual weapon. The chamber at the front of the barrel elevated to receive the charge and was then snapped back down.

I couldn't duplicate the weapon because I couldn't see its exact mechanism, but it inspired me to design a breech-loaded pistol. I created a hinged chamber that lifted up during loading but was tightly sealed and after firing was pushed back down. To covertly create the correct tolerances for the metals took me many months.

For ammunition, the hand-carved ebony butt was hollowed and contained a supply of small paper packets that each held a charge of ball and powder. I also carried extra packets in a deerskin pouch.

To load a pistol, I ripped open a packet with my teeth and poured it into the open breech chamber, ball first. Because the barrels were rifled and would easily foul, the balls were slightly smaller than the barrel and were greased and wrapped in a piece of cotton cloth. Consequently, the smaller greased round left minimal residue in the barrel while the expelled cloth cleaned the barrel as it passed through.

The time for loading the weapon was greatly reduced, but I still had to manually open the flashpan, shake in priming powder, and close it. If a mechanism could have loaded the powder into the primer pan without disrupting the shooter, the loading would have been accelerated.

Over the centuries gunsmiths had struggled with the concept of a self-priming firearm. A Scot minister named Forsythe might have come closest to perfecting the self-priming firearm. I followed his model. I made a small metal box slide over the flashpan and deposit priming powder when the hammer was cocked.

Naturally, I had mixed the finest batch of pistol powder for my handguns—the powder Felix kept for his wealthiest and most important buyers.

Nothing was too good for a thief, eh?

Able to fire a pistol six times a minute, two or three times faster than most skilled shooters, I could now boast—to myself—that I was not only the best shot in the colony, I was also the fastest.

Leaving my practice area, I returned to the road and

urged Rodrigo to hurry to the marques's hacienda. I had an important rendezvous later—one that could only be accomplished under cover of darkness—and I needed to return to the compound before arousing Felix's suspicions.

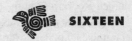

SIXTEEN

I DID NOT come to the revolution on my own.

I was never a scholar, and in my formative years I required tenacious teachers. To educate me, my uncle, Fray Diego, often had to knock knowledge into my head. But I always enjoyed history in which heroes and villains battled it out, and I remembered well his lecture on the region I now lived in.

During those school days in the one-room mud hut that served as our village school, the good fray told me Guadalajara's history differed from other regions in the Valley of Mexico, which was why Guadalajara so quickly answered the Grito of Dolores. The city is about 320 miles from the capital.

"The indios in the Valley of Mexico," the fray had explained, "had numbered in the millions. They had large cities like Tenochtitlán and a high culture in terms of science and the arts. New Galicia, which the Spanish originally called the Guadalajara region, had a much smaller population and no large cities. However, like the Mexica and Toltecs, the indigenous people spoke Nahuatl."

Because of the smaller population, rancheros and small farms developed rather than the sprawling haciendas that characterized other regions. Owning land instilled in them the belief that the gachupines should respect their rights.

The Spanish spur-wearers felt differently.

In 1529, eight years after Cortés's conquest of the Aztecs and the Valley of Mexico, Nuño de Guzmán, a

Spaniard who was jealous of Cortés's fame and treasure, set out with a force of over ten thousand from Mexico City to explore the region and bring it under Spanish control.

Guzmán was a brutal, murderous tyrant who used torture and death to subdue the region. Called Señor de la Borca y Cuchillo because he conquered and ruled by the noose and knife, Guzmán plundered the land, assuming a noble title, Marqués de Tonala, to ape Cortés. He looted villages relentlessly, enslaving the indios in the *encomienda* system, by which the Crown granted a Spanish soldier or colonist a tract of land or a village together with its Indian inhabitants.

Guzmán was arrested and sent back to Spain, but his savage tactics and those of his successors ultimately provoked the great uprising of indios in the region. Called the Mixtón War, it erupted in 1541 and was led by Tenamaxtli.

The indios rose to drive the invaders from the land, taking many towns and besieging Guadalajara. Spanish forces—backed by large numbers of Tlaxcaltec and Mexica warriors—suppressed the revolt.

Not only did Guadalajara answer Fray Hidalgo's Cry of Dolores for independence sooner than most areas, it remained loyal right up to the final battle at Calderon Bridge. From Guadalajara the legendary priest and warrior for freedom led the march with a grand army—only to lose the dream and the war when a lucky cannon shot hit a rebel wagon carrying gunpowder. But the brave people in the Lake Chapala region continued the fight long after the heroes of 1810 were captured and executed.

Late in 1812, people in Mezcala—a small island town on the lake, about twelve miles east of the town of

Chapala—received word that a Spanish force was marching on the town to punish it for aiding a rebel leader.

The town raised a force of about seventy volunteers armed mostly with primitive stone weapons and clubs. They met the Spanish force of nearly twice its size yet inflicted a severe defeat on the trained soldiers.

Within days they battled another Spanish force, defeating it again with primitive weapons. They had captured some flintlock muskets but—not knowing how to load and fire them—found them useless as anything except clubs.

Spanish troops continued to attack Lake Chapala's rebels, and the rebels persisted in defeating them. When the rebels consolidated their forces on the small island of Mezcala, the battles turned into naval warfare, with large Spanish contingents attacking the rebels in small boats.

After the frustrated Spanish ravaged a village in revenge for the island's defiance, the defenders attacked and captured the brutal officer, executing him and a number of his men.

I had made contact with the defenders after working for the gunsmith for a few months. Sneaking powder and ball to them, I began to secretly repair their weapons. Since my compañeros could have informed on me or divulged my name under torture, I was known to the rebels only as the Alchemist.

And I never permitted them to see my face.

After nearly five years of fighting, about a year ago, following an epidemic that had taken a severe toll on the defenders, a peace was finally negotiated whereby the defenders were granted a pardon.

But not all the defenders had given up. And to those bitter-enders, I was still a supplier of weapons, though I arranged for larger amounts of powder and shot to be directed south to Guerrero and his brave army of resistance in the China Road region.

Playing a dangerous game, I knew that it was just a matter of time before I would need my pistols for more than target practice.

SEVENTEEN

I WAS ALLOWED inside the marques's house only because the majordomo was too lazy to carry my muskets into the house. Perhaps the main house of the hacienda was not a palace to the marques. After all, he had actual palaces in Guadalajara and Mexico City. Still, from my poor peon's viewpoint it was a dwelling for a king—no, a god.

And the marques had not donated a drop of sweat— much less shed his blood in conquest—to acquire it. Ayyo, I didn't understand why people like him who had so much had done so little and why people like me worked so hard for almost nothing.

Sí, I resented the gachupines and their criollo brothers, not so much for what they had, but for the way they exploited the powerless. Some of them were brutal bastardos who despoiled the dispossessed, riding roughshod over them, pillaging their land, their labor, their women. Many committed a far less violent but nonetheless devastating sin: They treated us as stupid children who belonged to them as a pretext for our exploitation and enslavement.

Their big haciendas were run as feudal domains—not just places of work but small communities, often with their own chapels.

People were born, married, died, and buried on them.

Debt peonage kept many laborers enslaved to haciendas. Due to almost nonexistent wages and inflated charges for living expenses, the bond laborers could never discharge their debt to the hacienda owner. They were effectively tied to the hacienda as inextricably as a shackled slave.

Midsize haciendas had about two hundred workers and another five or six hundred family members living on them. Larger haciendas had thousands of workers.

Our Spanish masters did not frown on the flogging of workers unless perhaps it incapacitated workers, therefore costing them money.

In the end, the hacienda was an attempt to dominate every aspect of our lives—to transform us into the stupid irresponsible children that our masters continually asserted we were.

Some of us however had different ideas.

Some of us rebelled.

EIGHTEEN

BACK ON MY amigo, Rodrigo, I left the hacienda and followed the main road until I reached a trail that would lead me down to the lake.

I traveled the shore, sticking close to the dense conifers and scrub brush, keeping a close eye on both my front and back trails. I had to make sure the royal patrols weren't tracking the rebels' number-one gunrunner.

I spotted a faint stirring in the dim distance. Fading quickly into the thick trees and brush to my right, I made out the movement of a royal militia patrol I estimated to be ten-man strong. The patrol did not stop or point. They gave no sign of having seen me.

I did not know the exact rendezvous point with the rebels—only the general lakeshore area where they were to intercept me. Even though I was supplying the rebels—and admittedly risking my skin to do so—my risk paled alongside theirs. The viceroy's troops hunted the rebels continually while I was not even under the remotest suspicion.

The rebels could not afford to give anyone too much information as to their comings and goings. Were I to be caught with the contraband and knowing the rebels' itinerary, the royal militia might well suborn or torture the information out of me.

Once the militia patrol was gone, and I was sure I was alone, I would move back into the brush and tree line and light a candle. A boatload of rebels could spot it, but the vegetation would conceal the glow from most passersby.

The viceroy's men knew the rebels were supplied

from this side of the lake. They had consequently increased the lake patrols, but they could not pin down the correct location.

Not yet.

I would have rather dropped the contraband along the shoreline—perhaps behind a stand of trees—and ridden off. I couldn't however—not in good conscience. I had to make sure the ammunition got into the right hands.

For reasons of self-protection.

If the local fishermen or other boaters saw the light and spotted my stash, they might turn powder and balls over to the viceroy for a reward. There weren't that many high-quality gun and powder-smiths in this remote region. They would recognize the powder and balls as premium ammunition and trace them back to Felix and his hard-used assistant in short order.

My role in the brief Battle of Tula would quickly come out and my gachupine masters would stretch me out on the viceroy's gallows or the Grand Inquisitor's rack.

I also needed to meet with the rebels. They sometimes had an important dispatch for me—information on the viceroy's patrols or a weapon to repair.

NINETEEN

WHEN THE PATROL turned off and returned to the main road, I continued up the shoreline. The lake jutted in at one point to less than a hundred paces from the tree line. I led Rodrigo in among the trees there. Wrapping his reins around a tree limb, I cross-hobbled his rear hocks and removed the leather ammunition pouches from the saddlebags.

Reaching the lake, I lit the candle, then moved away from the light. I hoped to spot the men the candle drew before they spotted me.

Several minutes passed before I saw two men in a canoe, paddling toward the candle. After beaching its bow in the shore mud, one of the men slipped over the side and waded ashore, a musket in hand. I could see him plainly in the moonlight. He was dressed in peon garb, and he glanced nervously up and down the shoreline. He was clearly not a militiaman.

I put a black scarf over my face.

"Señor," I whispered.

He swung the musket at my voice.

"Stop! I'm your amigo."

"*El Alquimista,*" the peon-rebel whispered.

They had nicknamed me the Alchemist because it appeared to them that I could conjure ordnance and ammunition out of earth and sky.

My apparition-like appearances and the weapons and gunpowder I so mysteriously produced must have seemed like acts of supernatural sorcery.

I threw him the bags. "Adios, amigos."

Something crashed in the brushes. The frightened rebel turned and fired his musket.

It was brown—a deer.

Ayyo! The shot would be heard by all the king's men in the province.

I had to get away. I ran for the mule as the rebel ran for the canoe. His escape would be easier than mine.

I urged Rodrigo through the dense trees and brush. I'd stay off the trail until I hit the main road. Traveling blind over broken tree- and brush-choked terrain, Rodrigo might very well flounder, but I had no choice. I needed cover.

If there was a Spanish patrol in the area, they'd likely stay on the trail. As I rode, I unbuttoned my shirt—in the event I had to reach for the holstered pistol under my arm. Lifting my pant leg, I also had access to the smaller gun strapped to my leg.

I hit a sheer rock wall and had to leave the trees and brush for the trail. As soon as I did, a militia patrol rounded a bend and the point rider spotted me.

He raised a hue and cry, and I quickly slapped Rodrigo's romp: "Andale! Andale!"

Turning in the saddle, I unlimbered my shoulder weapon. I only had one ball in each pistol, and I had to make each shot count. Even with quick reloading, I'd have little chance of firing a third shot before horsemen were on me.

I cocked the pistol. I couldn't aim true, since I was bouncing up and down on Rodrigo's back. Still, it was a maneuver I'd practiced before—pointing and shooting by instinct, not by sighting in the target.

I pulled the trigger, the flint showered sparks over the flashpan, and the chamber powder detonated.

My bullet blew the lead man backward—out of his saddle.

No time to reload. I unlimbered the pistola from my ankle holster.

Another man exploded backward out of his saddle, joining his comrade in royal militia hell.

The rest of the patrol wheeled their mounts and fled.

To the gachupine, the royal militia were little more than peon labor. No one ever accused their patrols of dogged determination or death-defying valor.

Patting Rodrigo's neck, I slowed him to a brisk trot in order to save his strength.

And to reload my weapons.

I'd killed Spaniards before and would no doubt kill them again. The fight would go on until the last gachupine was driven from our land—or had been hanged by his entrails from his palatial home's crystal chandeliers.

Still I took no pride in killing.

It was just part of the job.

Ultimately, I only wanted to survive.

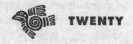

NOT EVERYTHING IN my life was blood and toil. An hour later, returning to the village, I spotted a woman on horseback, someone whom I knew—and adored.

Maria de Rosa.

A pretty young mestiza—*Ayyo!*—I longed to court her. Or more truthfully, *bed* her.

A hot-tempered firebrand with raven-hued waist-length tresses, her black eyes were hard and flat as a diamond-back's. Even as she routinely ripped my ego to pieces with her superior learning, and patronizing insults, her mind-numbing beauty invariably reduced me to stupid stammering.

She was on a painted pony, off to the side of the road, handing a bundle to a man on a bay mare. When she heard my mule coming, she turned. I was visible in the moonlight, but I decided to hail them anyway . . . in case the stranger—not knowing me—reached for a weapon.

"It's me, Maria, Juan Rios."

"What are you doing out here so late? Running errands for your gachupine master?"

The vicious words cut me to the quick. She thought me a humble servant, the "good indio" who humbly bowed his head and served the gachupines without objection.

Maria was an impassioned revolutionary fighting for the shout of freedom the fray had made on the steps of a church at Delores.

And her dedication to the revolution inflamed my desire for her even more.

Like myself, she kept her activities secret to avoid arrest. To ensure that I did not jeopardize the rebels I was
supplying, I kept my own activities secret even from her.
The one time I had courted her, she ranted about "Aztec
piglets" such as myself who "prostituted their talents for
gachupine swine." While I sought to entice her into my
amorous arms, she worked her own agenda, trying to
rally me to the revolution—to help her distribute revolutionary pamphlets in which she railed against the viceroy
and his royal tyranny in tropes of fire and blood.

How she managed to keep from being arrested when
her father had the only printing press in the area was a
miracle. Her father was bedridden, her mother taken by
fever five years earlier, so she had free rein not only to
run the print shop but to issue her politically charged
leaflets.

I had to play the good peon and reject her recruitment
efforts since my role in that revolt, while covert, was far
more critical than hers. Perhaps if I'd told her of my own
deeds and dreams, my wartime work for the Hidalgo revolt and what it cost me, the guns I had run and the men
I had killed, my hairbreadth escape from the viceroy's
slave mine, and how I still fought for the revolution, she
might have viewed me in a more romantic light.

But such confessions were impossible. Besides, Maria
would have me turning out weapons by the hundreds—
right up until I was hanged.

Truth might set some men free, but all it would bestow
on me was a taut noose and the hangman's ghoulish laugh.

She was a true witch. Whatever she did—or how she
belittled me—she bewitched me. Her long dresses—while
exquisitely feminine—were discreetly split in the middle
to allow her to mount and ride a horse spread-legged.

Like a man.

Not that she in any conceivable way looked like a man. The love of my life looked like a man as much as I looked like the Virgin Mother.

After I passed by, I turned in the saddle to bid the lovely señorita vaya con dios.

She glared at me and leaned toward the other horseman, and gave him the bundle.

Then kissed him.

Ay caramba!

I fought the impulse to pull my gun and shoot the bastardo out of the saddle.

Instead I urged Rodrigo onward.

Maria! Why do you torment me? I wanted to yell at her.

I took deep breaths of the night air. The woman could read and write, ride and shoot. She was a firebrand, who did what she wanted—and what she wanted most was to be deemed the equal of any man.

I admired her wild heart, her warrior soul. Aside from her sensuous beauty and voluptuous charm, I admired her . . . *rebelliousness.*

Even though she undeservedly despised me.

But when I saw her kiss another man, my double life tore at my soul—especially when I recognized him: Gomez, a small-time bandido who claimed to be a revolutionary but was more likely a double agent—a royal spy.

I didn't like or trust him—even before he kissed my woman. He hung around the village pulquerías, not drinking peon's pulque, but Spanish wine. Eh, to choose wine over the juice of the maguey plant was good sense, even if pulque was the nectar of indio gods. Peons drank pulque not for its sour milk but because it was potent and cheap— we couldn't afford to get drunk on good wine. This Gomez drank wine while buying pulque for the peons around him.

He also sympathized openly with the insurrectionarios. Dangerous talk. So dangerous it was suspicious.

He had obviously impressed Maria with his rebel talk.

She had no doubt buried him alive in mountains of her virulent pamphlets.

Madre Dios, if Gomez was a royal spy—as I had always secretly surmised—he would not only betray Maria to the militia, but her father, his print shop, and all those to whom she distributed her dangerous diatribes as well would all be in mortal peril.

Ayyo! She could unintentionally lead the viceroy's secret constabulary of police and spies to countless friends and colleagues.

The thought of Maria swinging on a gibbet sickened me to my hell-bound soul.

I pulled Rodrigo into the bushes off the road and waited for her. I resisted the impulse to ride back and confront her and Gomez with my suspicions.

Had I found them conjoined, I would have killed him.

I was still fighting the impulse when she came down the road. I called out her name gently to keep from startling her. The full moon still shone, but she had real courage. In this time of rebellion and outright banditry, most men would not ride at night, certainly not unarmed.

She slowed her horse to a walk. As I came alongside her, I saw the pistol she had ready to use.

"Why are you looking at me like that? You are not my master. I can kiss who I want."

"Gomez can't be trusted."

"I'll trust anyone I want. He's a real man, not a woman in pants who makes weapons to be used against our people."

I took a deep breath and gritted my teeth. To call a man a woman was the worst insult in the colony. If she were a man . . .

"Gomez can't be trusted. He's *too* eager to flaunt false sympathy for rebels," I said.

"Mind your business. Or your master's business. That's what you do best."

"Not all of us have a father who provides us with a business to run. I pay for my own frioles—and I'm under bond."

"I take care of myself," she snapped. "And my father, too. Go your way, Juan Rios." She waved the pistol at me. "I don't need your concern or your protection."

"Gomez may well be a royal spy."

"Arturo is a brave patriot. He's fought with Morelos and Guerrero."

"With Hidalgo, too, I'm sure." I sneered. "No doubt he has stood before the viceroy's firing squad more than once, caught the bullets in his teeth, spit in Death's Eye, and has never known or shown fear. How many notches for dead militia does he have on his—"

She made a very unladylike remark about my manhood—lack thereof—and whipped and roweled her horse away from me, leaving me on my slow-footed mule to eat her dust.

I headed for the nearest pulquería to drown my pain.

Perhaps Gomez would be there. If he was, we could discuss his many services to the insurrection—the parents he had lost, the jail time he had served, the wounds he had suffered, the men he had killed.

He could tell me all that while I pounded his head on the floor.

PART IV

BOOKS AND RECORDS OF THE "SAVAGES" OF NEW SPAIN

The Spanish invaders acted as if they had encountered a tribe of savages rather than nations populated by twenty million people when they arrived in what became New Spain and began to destroy the knowledge and culture of civilizations thousands of years old.

Prince Ixtlilxochitl, the brother of the last king of Texcoco, a Nahuatl empire that competed with the Mexica for dominance in the Valley of Mexico, described the paperwork of an empire in his *Historia Chichimeca:*

"They had scribes for each field of knowledge. Some dealt with historical records, the annals of the people and wars, others recorded the genealogies, the records of the lineage of rulers, lords, and noblemen . . . other scribes kept the law books and matters of rites and ceremonies. Priests recorded all matters concerning the temples, festivals, and calendars. And finally, the philosophers and learned men were charged with painting all the scientific knowledge they had discovered . . ."

The recording, done with pictographs similar to Egyptian hieroglyphics, was done in books now called "codices." A codex was a strip of paper made from fig tree bark, cloth from the maguey plant, or deerskin. Usually about six inches wide, it could run thirty feet or more. The strips were folded and glued to wood covers.

So many pages were needed for record keeping, the Mexica/Aztecs demanded nearly half a million sheets each year from states paying tribute.

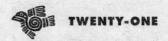 **TWENTY-ONE**

Bᴀᴄᴋ ᴀᴛ ʜᴇʀ print shop, Maria finished the latest pamphlet savaging the viceroy and his royal minions. All her diatribe needed was her nom de guerre—the name under which she signed her furious pronunciamentos, using a male signature to cover her tracks: "*El Revolucionario.*"

Her rabid rhetoric throbbed with blood and thunder and hellfire.

Because it was late in the evening, Maria did not have enough time to typeset her torrid tirade. Hand-setting the movable type would take her at least two hours, and then she would have to print the pamphlets.

Still, she was too energized for sleep.

She turned to another pamphlet. Her conversation with Juan had given Maria a topic that rankled her to the bone: the failure of New Spain's most talented people—including its brutally oppressed peons—to commit themselves and their abilities to the insurrection.

Quill in hand, paper before her, she paused—and pressed her palms against her temples. She needed to get Juan out of her mind . . . particularly the shameful episode where she flagrantly—and maliciously—kissed Gomez in front of him.

She had kissed Gomez because she knew Juan wanted her and she was angry at him—incensed that he refused to back the rebellion even though it needed him badly.

She didn't even like Gomez. He stank of soured sweat, garlic, and chewing tobacco. She kissed him to infuriate Juan.

That she had used Juan's honest and gentlemanly affection for her to torment him shamed her. Maria swore no matter how angry she became with Juan she would not do that again.

Not that she'd gotten away with her ruse scot-free. As if to punish *her* for her charade, Gomez had tried to drag her off her horse as soon as Juan was out of sight. Hammering his temple with her pistol butt, she had ridden off, racing toward Juan.

She'd hit Gomez hard enough to fracture his skull—and hoped that she had.

She would never tell Juan that, however.

Nor would she use Gomez again to deliver her pamphlets.

She'd be lucky now if Gomez didn't break into her home, whip her like a dog, and use her like a puta.

Maria didn't say anything to Juan because she feared he would track Gomez down and kill him. An act of machoism that would bring the viceroy's constables to both their doors. Juan would kill over a woman but not for the cause of freedom.

And she despised him for it.

She returned to her pamphlet, writing:

Every man and woman who has the physical or mental ability to battle oppression in this benighted land must use their God-given gifts to drive the tyrannical viceroy and his greed-crazed gachupine slave drivers out of the colony.

Her head pounded. She could not get Juan out of her head. Juan was so unforgivably selfish. Although Juan refused to discuss his job, a worker at the shop told her that Juan designed and fabricated exquisite firearms and powder that were famous throughout all of New Spain but for which Felix stole both credit and recompense. A gifted, industrious gunsmith/powder-maker, there was

not another hombre who possessed skills more important to the revolution than Juan.

Were he to commit those talents to the revolution, he
would be *the* indispensable hombre.

Damn you, Juan Rios. Why do you waste your talents,
working as little more than a peon for the gachupine slave
masters?

She refused to conform to the strict dictates of the existing social order. Why couldn't Juan be as courageous?

"If you only had courage, Juan," she muttered, fury
flooding her veins, *"you'd be a frontline soldado like myself!"*

Maria had to admit that she'd come out of a home envi-
ronment in which freethinking and the equality of all
people—even that most radical notion of all, the equality
of women—had been openly discussed. And her father—
a respected pillar of the community—had always earned a
good living.

Born of a Spanish father and an indio mother, she was
a twenty-year-old mestizo. Nuns had taught her mother
to read and write, and her mother had taught not only
Maria but many of the local peons as well.

Her father, Francisco, was a bookish man, more suited
to be a professor than a businessman, but having the only
printing press in the community and surrounding area,
he not only did commercial printing but once a week put
out two sheets of current events of community interest.

He had founded the printing shop at Lake Chapala ten
years after the first printing press was established at
Guadalajara. Printing had come to the Guadalajara region
later than other major cities of the colony. Mexico City
started its first printing within a couple of decades of the
Conquest, and Puebla the following century. Printing,
however, was not established in Guadalajara for another
couple hundred years, in 1773. Moreover, the government

rigidly restricted the content of printed materials, limiting printers primarily to Church tracts, the viceroy's pronouncements, and approved businesses.

Nonetheless, Francisco owned the works of Rousseau, John Locke, Voltaire, and Thomas Paine—the thinkers who had done so much to inspire the American and French Revolutions. Maria read them, even though her father forbade her to mention the authors' names when she left the house—or even mention that she had read them. Throughout New Spain men adamantly asserted that reading subverted a woman's sense of self. Reading, many men argued, disoriented women and disrupted their equilibrium, making them anxious, angry, and restless.

While her father held more liberal views, he also had a business to run and a family to support. To express opinions contrary to the viceroy's or Church's dictates could conceivably lead to the royal militia, or even the Inquisition, dragging the dissident out of bed in the middle of the night.

People had been jailed and tortured for far less.

Her father's library contained only thirty-eight books, including seven in French, a language he had taught Maria to read and speak. Even so, the de Rosa library was the largest collection in the area. Though her family was far from rich, what extra money her father could squirrel away had not gone into secret hiding places but into buying books. Furthermore, books were exorbitantly expensive. Most of them had to be imported from Spain, which between duties and transport fees increased their cost exponentially.

"These books are your most valuable inheritance," her father had told her. "They are magic carpets to people you'll never meet, places you'll never see. They will teach you everything—from the printing and fabrication of books themselves to the construction of ships. However, they are not just storehouses of knowledge but the sacred repository of our culture and customs, of our science and mathematics, of our history and religion."

To Maria, the printed word was also a weapon. She wasn't the subtle erudite thinker that her father was but a *doer*. Even her horseback riding reflected a preference for action over passivity. While men wore pants when riding a horse, women were not only denied the same privilege, they were forbidden to ride horses and therefore condemned to trudge the earth like dray beasts—a condition that was irrational, destructive, and unjust.

Most women accepted this prohibition without protest.

But not Maria.

She designed and stitched together a split riding skirt, which allowed her to ride horses like a man. Scorning scurrilous remarks about her "failure to know her place," she was her own person.

She carried her uncomplicated way of thinking about horses and pants into life, love, and politics. To Maria the equality of people and the sexes was logical, reasonable, just, and self-evident. Inequality, on the other hand, was unjust—a social ill that she and her comrades needed to stamp out.

Justice for all was her creed and cause, her heart and soul.

Throughout his career, her father had resolutely refused to print controversial or seditious articles. Two years ago, however, a horse had thrown him, breaking his hip. An intractable infection set in, and the hip had never healed. Leaving him too incapacitated to run the print shop, Maria had run it for him, keeping up all his accounts—including the conservative weekly bulletin, which she printed at the royal government's behest—to ensure that she did not offend the officious officials governing the area.

But at night she wrote, typeset, and printed what she thought and felt.

Her biggest customers were the church and the local government, both of which Maria privately despised. But she took their money, then plowed it back into her own clandestine operation, printing up pamphlets dedicated to their overthrow.

Maria understood the consequences of her actions. The difference between her and her father was that she had something to say to the world—and was willing to risk all to say it.

Moreover, she loved what she did—reveling in the lyricism of language, the satisfaction of finding the right word or forming the felicitous phrase, the potential for powerful language to inflame the passions, plant the seeds of revolt, challenge injustice, repudiate lies, and change the world. To arrange letters of movable metal type into sentences that expressed ideas and inspired dreams of freedom and incited deeds of honor and justice . . . that enterprise seemed to Maria the noblest undertaking any person could aspire to.

Each of us must fight for freedom in our own way, she wrote. *The curate, Fray Hidalgo, raised his voice on the steps of a church. I raise mine with my pen. You must use your own specific skills and personal cunning with which to depose the despots.*

Maria spent nearly an hour venting verbal violence onto paper with quill and ink.

She honestly believed paper, ink, and a professional printing press could give wings to . . . *truth.*

Well, Maria, if you wish to break truth out of prison, she thought, *print the thing tonight.*

Time is a bandit—a fleeing bandit.

Do it now!

Her printing press had a wood frame with an iron

platen. She'd heard that in Europe large printing companies had started using presses made entirely of iron, but such an advance had not reached the colony.

First Maria had to arrange her type letters into words, organizing them into the publication which she had composed. To that end, she placed them piece by piece in a composition stick—a long, narrow tray—into which she occasionally stuck in blanks, when she needed to straighten out or "justify" her right-hand margin. She next slipped in a wood brace which would hold the type tight when she had filled the tray.

She placed the composing sticks faceup on the printing bed, inked the type, placed a sheet of paper on top, and brought the heavy metal platen down to press the paper against the inked type.

When she was done, she had two printed pages of inflammatory fury, which urged the insurrection onward and upward.

Maria printed one page at a time. When she finished, she set the pieces of type back in the type case, one by one.

Printing was slow, tedious work . . . but so was setting fire to a nation. When she had completed her act of sedition, she sat back and shook her head. The more she thought about it, the more ashamed she was that she had kissed Gomez. What Juan must have thought of her . . .

Leaving the shop to return home, she wondered what it would be like to kiss Juan.

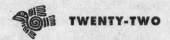 **TWENTY-TWO**

Ａyyo! pulque — the nectar of the gods! I could understand why Quetzalcoatl went loco in the cabeza after a night of this. I had a belly full of pulque and a brain fuming with jealousy and anger. And I didn't have the capacity of a god. I didn't even hold it well for a mortal man. The sour beer was enough to steal my wits even without the magic mushrooms, which Quetzalcoatl had also consumed along with the potent brew. Playing cards—*losing* at playing cards—had not improved my disposition either.

I left the pulquería with two thoughts burning in my head: Find that traitorous bastardo, Gomez—and plant my boots deep into his cojones. No, I should kill him instead. Slowly. Painfully. While he begged and pled for mercy.

Why not? I had killed men before in the service of the revolution—men whom I did not know and whom I did not hate.

I knew Gomez, and to know him was to *loathe* him.

My second thought was to find Maria, rip off her clothes, and have my way with her. Let her learn the way of a man and a woman. Let her learn what it's like for a real hombre to mount and ride her . . . namely *me*. Let her know the screams of ecstasy—*her* screams of ecstasy—when I brought her to the passionate pinnacle she so clearly needed and . . . *craved.*

Sí. I would avenge her affronts to my much-abused dignity.

But when I reached my mule, hauled myself up, and took a few deep breaths of night air, the reality of my life hit me in full. Not Juan the Peon who cleaned up the shit of his Spanish patron. I cared nothing for *that* life.

But Mazatl the Aztec Deer who ran arms and explosives for the rebellion, to me that person meant . . . *everything*. And the Deer could not jeopardize *his* fight for freedom over petty slights and hurt pride.

Maria was half right.

Half my life was a lie—and I did enrich my master making guns, molding bullets, and mixing gunpowder for the gachupine oppressors.

I was on the main road leading out of town when I spotted a cadre of royal constables in front of the de Rosa print shop.

I veered off onto a side street, tied Rodrigo to a post, and approached the shop on foot. Other residents in the town knew what was happening at the shop—like me they skulked in the shadows, watching the constables through dark windows or hid on balconies and roofs.

Off his horse, holding the reins, Gomez stood in front of the building as other officers carried out the printing press, paper, and other supplies in a growing pile that would soon be a bonfire. He was talking to a man standing by a coach.

I knew the name of the man Gomez was conversing with—Colonel Madero. I recognized his silver peg leg. I was right about Gomez. He was a royal spy, and he worked for the most infamous spymaster in the colony. Madero was the head of the viceroy's secret police and spy network. He dressed in an ebony duster with silver-thread embroidery along the lapels, a matching linen shirt, and a broad-brimmed hat with a flat crown and hatband of two-inch silver conchos. Looped around his wrist was a jet-black rawhide quirt with three-inch triple-poppers.

Over six feet tall, Madero had piercing wide-set eyes, an aquiline nose, and a sweeping coal-black mustache that made his teeth gleam white as burnished ivory. I've heard that his wide, glittering smile never reached his eyes and his hard obsidian eyes remained cold and wary no matter how dazzlingly his smile blazed.

I'd never seen him in person before, but I had heard that his soul was "black as the grave."

A bad hombre for sure—with a heart dark as death.

The most dangerous man in the colony, many averred.

He was called El Toro . . . but this bull had a brain, too. His quest for malefactors who rebelled against the king was unrelenting, and once he got their scent he never forsook the hunt—even when the hunt was based upon rumor, gossip, and dubious evidence.

The colonel had spies and informers throughout the colony . . . and was notorious for promiscuous torture, roadside justice, and summary executions—much of it pointless. People whom he merely suspected of plotting against the king and viceroy were routinely surprised with the nocturnal knock, the crack of his quirt, and the business end of his red-hot smoking pistola.

Losing a leg while fighting the French invaders in 1808 during the Dos de Mayo uprising in Madrid had done nothing to improve his chronically grim mood or arrest the dark demons that haunted his pitiless soul.

The loss of his leg had, I am told, made him even meaner.

His peg leg was said to be solid silver, but that much silver would have cost a fortune and weighed a ton. I personally believed the peg to be silver-plated hardwood.

Madero's peg leg was also feared—given his alacrity for driving it into the kidneys and cojones of prisoners and suspects.

And Gomez had led him to Maria.

I was certain they didn't have her yet. I knew she sometimes composed fiery tracts at night, but by this hour she was sure to be home. But they would have her soon.

A constable came out of the shop with a sheaf of papers and showed them to Madero. I could guess what the papers were—fire-breathing pamphlets. Maria had printed a leaflet no doubt advocating revolution . . . in her usual incendiary style.

Those pamphlets would now be her death sentence.

Madero pointed toward the road out of town that led toward Maria's house. Barking orders, he detailed Gomez and a patrol to arrest Maria and her father. Gomez and two constables mounted and headed down the road.

Three armed men dispatched to arrest a woman and a crippled old man. I hoped they brought extra ammunition.

The house was two miles down the road. The rough terrain would not allow me to cut around them. If I followed them and they heard me coming, they would ambush me.

There was no way around it. They would get there before me.

I had no choice but to ambush them *after* they apprehended Maria and her father.

I made a promise to myself to kill Gomez first—just in case I couldn't finish off all three.

PART V
THE SWORD VERSUS
THE PEN

MARIA AND HER father lived in a Spanish-style casa consisting of two stories of whitewashed adobe brick and a courtyard, all of it surrounded by a high whitewashed adobe wall. What would the three men do when they got to the house?

I followed them as closely as I could, pondering that question.

The men would grab her and subdue the sick father. When they were unable to get the old man on a horse, they would have to load him onto the family's small carriage and—

No, there would be none of that. Those bastardos would kick open the front door and charge in. Maria would probably grab her father's rusty old musket and get herself and her father killed.

One thing was for certain—Gomez was a brutal swine. A beautiful but naïve rebel, Maria would be delivered to Colonel Madero—a man who was arguably the most malevolent monster in the colony. Even the most murderous bandidos shuddered at the thought of falling into the hands of the man with the silver peg leg.

Gomez would not be satisfied with simply taking a ripe young woman like Maria back to Madero. Not until he and his compañeros first had their way with her.

And her father? They'd kill him rather than let him testify about the rape. Besides, it would be easier than dragging a cripple around.

I gave Rodrigo my heels and swatted his rump. He barely broke into a trot.

It was the best the lumbering old hombre could do. I had nearly busted its stump-broke heart eluding the Spanish patrol. Cocking my shoulder-holstered gun, I tucked it into my belt for quicker access. I also cocked the gun holstered to my leg and decided to hang on to it. That was two shots.

There were three of them. I hoped and prayed I'd have time to reload.

I was not optimistic.

Gessoed a brilliant alabaster, the house and walls shone in the luminous moonlight.

Then I heard the piercing screams.

Maria came running out the wall gate. A man came out behind her and grabbed her by the hair, jerking her wildly back. She went down as two other men came out the gate. The man who had grabbed her hair jerked her arms behind her and held her as another man—I was sure it was Gomez—grabbed the bottom of her night-shirt and brought it up, baring her legs.

They heard me coming. Poor Rodrigo groaned and blew long rolling snorts that targeted me as much as the blindingly bright full moon.

The man still on his feet reached for his pistola.

I could have picked him off with a shot—even with me on a charging mule—and I almost did. But I held my fire. If I killed him, that left two others—and I would have only one more shot.

I took the reins in my teeth and pulled out the pistola, which I'd shoved under my belt. The ankle gun was still in my left fist.

The next best thing was to drop the man without a shot. Using Rodrigo as a battering ram, I charged the constable, reins in teeth. The man got off one shot with his own handgun. I saw the flash and felt the impact on Rodrigo's chest at almost the same time. I kicked my feet free of the stirrups and slipped sideways off the saddle as my old amigo went down.

I hit the ground, rolling.

But I still hung on to my pistols.

My momentum also carried me into the shooter who made the mistake of trying to holster his pistol before grabbing his knife. Pistols were expensive—not all constables even had one, and he worried about damaging his gun. Holstering the pistola instead of dropping it, however, cost the constable a second or two—time that he did not have.

Using my shoulder as a battering ram, I knocked him off his feet, then rolling off him, I raised both my pistols.

The man holding Maria released her—and charged me with a knife. I shot him in the chest, then dove and rolled again, more out of instinct than logic, but I had sensed a shot was on the way.

It came from Gomez's pistol.

Rising to my knees, I shot him between the eyes. His head snapped backward, and the bullet drove him to the ground.

I rolled again and leaped to my feet. The man I'd slammed into was onto his knees and rising. I laid the butt of my pistola atop his head as hard as I knew how . . . as if I were hammering spikes.

His skull cracked audibly, his eyes rolled back until only the whites showed. Almost instantly he began hemorrhaging from the nose and ears. When I checked his throat, he had no pulse.

Maria was on her feet. She stared at me, her pretty face twisted with terror at the attack.

"My father," she cried, then ran past me.

Reloading my pistols, I made sure Gomez and both constables were dead, then followed her inside.

I found Maria in her father's bedroom, on her knees

beside him, sobbing. The old man was on the floor, not stirring. A piece of rope was around his neck. They had strangled him.

We had no time for grief. I crouched beside her and took hold of her arm. "We have to get out of here. More of them will come."

"Go away." She pulled away and shook her head. "I have to bury my father."

I got up, forcing her to her feet. "Don't be a fool—they'll be coming for *you*. You're already gallows-bait with three dead constables in your front yard. When Colonel Madero arrives, he will order his men to take turns on you, then drag you to the nearest tree and hang you. If I'm here, they'll flog, castrate, and hang me, too."

"I can't leave—"

"Stop it! You know we have to go. We need money, blankets, food—some tortillas. Grab what you can. Throw it all in a sack with some clothes and all the money you have. I'll get the horses ready."

I made sure my mule was dead and then checked the constables' horses, which were tied to a hardwood hitch-rack in the courtyard. I selected the best two for our mounts—a big roan and a chestnut. I found a goatskin water bag, a cross-buck pack, and a horsehair mecate in their tack shed and designated the third horse, a high-spirited gray, as our packhorse. The mecate would be our lead rope, and I affixed it to the gray's headstall. I collected the powder flasks, ammunition, pistols, and saddlebags from the three dead men. They only had one passable musket, which was sheathed to Gomez's horse. Knowing Gomez, his musket and mount were stolen. I could not imagine him paying money for such things.

I loaded their three pistols and put them in saddlebags with the spare ammunition. I tied them to my saddle. The pistolas were in bad shape but might be useful for close-range combat. I had an old grain sack tied to the dead mule, containing a change of clothes, a blanket, and the crumbs of tortillas I'd eaten earlier.

Except for the guns and ammunition, I would lash everything to the pack animal, including the food and water bag.

I went back in the house and found Maria kneeling beside her father, praying. She had dressed. Luckily, she had changed into one of her discreetly split riding dresses. I grabbed a sack sitting nearby, which I had told her to fill with tortillas and any money her father had kept in the house.

When I took her arm again and led her out to the horses, she pulled away. "Wait. I forgot something."

Ayyo . . . When she came back, she had a small sack hanging on her side from a cord over her shoulder. It looked heavy. I assumed she'd brought the family gold hoard or perhaps some expensive jewelry.

I helped her onto a horse and tied the big sack I carried from the bedroom onto the packhorse.

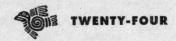

TWENTY-FOUR

We RODE FAR into the night, putting time and distance between ourselves and Madero's constables. The road west led back to town and into the hands of Colonel Madero. It would also connect to the road that went north to Guadalajara. When we reached the lake, we would take the road leading south.

"The capital is south," I told Maria, "but that is not our destination. We're heading for the China Road, which runs from Mexico City to Acapulco. Guerrero still holds much of the region."

Like Veracruz, the main port on the east coast of the colony, the Acapulco region on the west coast was tierra caliente—a hot, wet zone. Beginning on the sandy beaches of the tropical Pacific Coast, the terrain rose inland, finally reaching up to the plateau. Across the plateau in the Valley of Mexico lay the capital, Mexico City, which was said to glitter in that valley like a crown jewel.

General Guerrero was born and raised in the tropical region. A motley mix of races—Spanish, indio, africano, mestizo, mulatto—Guerrero spoke all the languages and dialects. Since the Spanish considered these people inconsequential beasts of burden, Guerrero owned their love and their loyalty.

Having lost everything already, his supporters had little, if anything, to lose, which made them truly dangerous adversaries.

While I had never met Guerrero, as his "Alchemist" I had donated many arms and much explosive to his Cause over the years. He would recognize my code name when I gave it to him and welcome Maria, too. The printed word might not have been mightier than the sword, but it could inform both the sword and the sword's supporters. Printers and pamphleteers were invaluable to the Cause. They were its very vanguard.

Maria knew nothing about my insurrectionist history and dealings. I told her we would head for rebel territory without mentioning my connection. She was silent, but I knew our destination had to please her.

Near dawn I finally said to her, "We need to rest the horses."

We also had to get off the main road. Not only might Madero's constables catch up with us, but the viceroy had couriers who raced the length and breadth of the colony, informing other constables of escaped fugitives who might be headed their way. From the footprints we left in Maria's yard, they would know there were two of us. Constables in the communities up ahead would soon be watching for a male and female on the run.

We found a clearing concealed by trees far from the road. I did not want to risk a fire but thought the site remote enough for a cold camp. We'd have to eat the cold tortillas and cold beef she'd brought even though the early dawn air carried a chill and a fire would have been comforting.

I untied Maria's supply sack from the spare mount. Opening it up to get out the blankets and tortillas, I found books . . . a small painting of Maria's mother and father . . . female things . . . and books . . .

Books.

"Where are the tortillas and blankets?"

She stared at me. "What . . . what?"

"The supplies—never mind. We'll have to make do tonight. We'll buy blankets and food. How much money do you have?"

She shook her head. She was still dazed, but was coming out of it. "I don't know. Nothing. I didn't bring any. There was no room in the bag."

"You should have left this other stuff behind."

"Some things are more valuable than money," she said, glaring at me.

I stared at the sack she had hung over her shoulder. "What's in that?" I asked, pointing at it.

She opened the sack and took out a book.

"Another book?"

"It's my favorite. Sor Juana. I shall read her for comfort."

A volume of poetry by Sor Juana. The poet-goddess of the colony. Dead for over a hundred years.

No tortillas.

No blankets.

No money.

I crossed myself. I was suddenly feeling very much in need of the Christian God.

Santo Maria.

We needed a plan. And a miracle.

PART VI
UN MAL HOMBRE

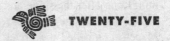

TWENTY-FIVE

GUN-MAKER FELIX BAROJA was in bed when royal officers pounded at his gate.

Colonel Madero sat outside the compound in his light, four-person coach. A soldier sat in the driver's box, the stock of his six-foot buggy whip braced in its cylindrical whip-stand. The coach's woodwork was cedar with silver trim. Its large waterproof mica-glazed storm curtains were rolled up, so Madero could view his surroundings unobstructed and enjoy the cool evening breeze.

The short trip over had been comfortable. The coach rode on firm transverse springs and steel axles, its interior upholstered in plush red velvet with two wide-padded seats. The black-clad Colonel Madero sat in his coach alone, fingering the broad brim of his black flat-crowned hat, his raptor's eyes and mirthless smile ever-present even when he was alone, even when he was rasping the hoarse stentorian orders, which no one dared to ignore or dispute.

As Felix was taken into custody more officers went to the bunkhouse where the single workers lived and to the huts of workers with families.

Madero preferred the coach over horseback for two reasons: Mounting and dismounting a horse with a metal leg was embarrassingly awkward, and in his line of work perception was power. He could never appear vulnerable.

Once when a constable had inadvertently smirked while Madero mounted a horse, he had ordered the constable's wrists lashed to an overhanging tree limb and had commanded his coach driver to take his buggy whip to him. Long after the spine and ribs gleamed white as alabaster beneath the constable's flayed and bloody flesh, Madero compelled the driver to continue the flogging. That Madero had crippled the man for life was of no consequence to him. In truth, when Madero thought about it at all the man's agony combined with his eventual incapacitation only heightened Madero's . . . *arousal*.

He was a perfect officer for a corrupt royal government that was under attack, a man who gauged which way the wind was blowing and went with it.

Coming from a Castilian farming family without wealth or political influence, Madero had risen through the ranks to become an officer. A lieutenant, he had nonetheless shown exemplary courage while leading his company of regulars against a superior French force during the initial uprising in Madrid. Later, when he saw that the royal family, Spain's wealthiest elite, and its aristocratic nobility were supporting the French, he had allied himself with those factions. When desertions to the rebel cause opened up the army's ranks, Madero won promotion after promotion.

As the uprising swept over Spain like a hurricane of fire and the French forces were clearly broken, he had switched allegiances again, working secretly with the guerrillas as a double agent to defeat his French employers.

Madero soon made himself useful to the guerrillas as a spy able to weed out and punish his former friends and allies—now deemed traitors to the Cause.

After Napoleon's defeat, the Spanish king returned to rule the nation he had so unceremoniously abandoned. Instead of rewarding the guerrilla leaders, who had driven out the foreign invaders and whom he had fought alongside for six years, Madero turned on them. Knowing intimately the structure of the guerrilla organization—in particular their hierarchy and principal leadership—he used that knowledge to hunt down and punish the leaders who expected more from their king than capricious arrogance, violent oppression, and self-serving despotism.

New Spain was old Spain's most valuable asset. The largest Spanish colony, it was—in the eyes of the Crown—one vast mountain of silver, whose ore had been created by the Almighty for a single purpose—to be mined and refined by slaves for the aggrandizement of Spanish kings. A mother lode of other raw materials as well, New Spain was also an enormous market for shoddily produced, insultingly overpriced Spanish goods, which their incompetent monopolistic manufacturers could purvey to no one else. Sending Madero to the colony to organize and direct a network of secret police and spies served the Crown not only in its subjugation of the colony but removed Madero from the Iberian Peninsula where his infamous reputation—indeed his very presence—had become an embarrassing liability.

Madero hated everything about New Spain, but most of all, he loathed peons—whom he considered subhuman savages. Criollos too—whom he considered craven, lazy, and untrustworthy—he despised. Of course, he also disdained his fellow gachupines, whom he privately averred lacked "cojones." His loyalty belonged solely to whoever paid his blood bill, and in New Spain that paymaster was the viceroy.

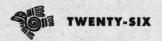

TWENTY-SIX

AFTER HIS OFFICERS reported back on Felix's questioning—as well as on that of the man's workers—Madero stepped down from the coach and summoned Felix.

Still attired in his long white nightshirt, the gunsmith struggled to conceal his fright. Attempting to brazen his way out of his predicament, he stared Madero in the eye and said with a boldness he did not feel:

"I am Spanish, just as you are. The viceroy himself will hear—"

Madero laid his triple-plaited wrist-quirt down across Felix's cheek, cutting it to the bone. Felix collapsed to his knees, sobbing, clutching his face.

"The viceroy will hear what I tell him," Madero said, cracking his bloody quirt's triple-poppers against his metal leg. "Pray he does not hear I had you flogged and castrated as a traitor and that I gladly trimmed the trees on the King's Highway with your gelded remains and gore-covered entrails. You know why we are here, I trust?"

"A mule, one of my mules was found somewhere," Felix said, still on his knees, whimpering.

"The mule was shot . . . and its rider killed three of my men. When I saw the carnage, do you know the first question I asked?"

Felix sobbed unintelligibly, and Madero cut him off.

"Let me ask you my question: What kind of man could charge with a mule three armed constables? What kind of man was so good with pistols he could best three of my men?" Madero shook his head. "Very strange, don't you think?"

"I know nothing of it, señor."

"Of course, you do. Your men were persuaded to talk to my officers. You have a worker named Juan Rios, an indio?"

"Yes," Felix groaned, "and if he's done anything wrong, I promise I will flog the very bones off his back."

"No, señor, you will not punish him." Again, Madero cracked the quirt against his silver leg. "God and the Crown will kill the son of a whore. However, I shall be their surrogate."

"What did Juan do?"

"Didn't you hear me when I said he attacked and killed my men? Don't make me speak twice about this matter or I will have your ears removed from your head and your cojones from between your legs."

"Señor Colonel, I beg of you, as a fellow Spaniard and loyal subject of the Crown, tell me what this worthless Aztec has done. I know nothing—"

"Then know this, señor. One of your mules was found along with my dead men. This Aztec son of a whore used the mule to rescue a female rebel whom I had sent the men to arrest. Moreover, a rebel on a mule had fled a militia patrol earlier. The militia soldiers who gave pursuit said that he was not only an uncanny shot on horseback but that he brandished two pistols."

"Juan took a mule to make a delivery. Perhaps he was waylaid and the mule stolen."

"Your men tell me that Juan is a crack shot with a pistol and musket. And that he carries the two when he leaves the compound. Perhaps he sought to keep those weapons a secret. If so, he failed. His coworkers found out."

"I know nothing about his marksmanship or pistols."

"Sí, sí, you keep saying that, that you know nothing, which puzzles me. You run a gun shop and a powder plant, yet you do not know that this Aztec makes weapons for you as well as for himself?"

"I swear before my Lord and my king—"

Madero backhanded him full across the face with the whip, opening his other cheek to the bone.

"You make a mistake when you appeal to God and Crown to support your lies," Madero said to the now prone, sobbing man. "I know that when you left the compound to collect bills for your annual trip to the capital, you left Rios in charge of your business and that he has also been making guns and powder . . . right under your nose. From what your workers tell me, he is the true master of the craft. Do you know what the viceroy would do if I told him that you taught an indio to make guns and gunpowder? Indios are not permitted to own a weapon—let alone learn how to make them. And gunpowder? To teach an indio how to make guns *and* powder would mean a stay among the Inquisitors' smoldering coals and hot smoking pinchers, its Iron Maid and flame-shrouded stake."

"God in Heaven," Felix sobbed, writhing on the ground.

"Someone has been supplying rebels with munitions. They call him the Alchemist—as if he conjured guns out of air. But what if he obtained the balls and powder from your shop?"

As Felix quaked, Madero wondered how much mordida the man would tally up to avoid the viceroy's wrath and the Inquisitors' tender ministrations. Unlike large hacienda owners whose illimitable wealth was so inextricably enmeshed in land that they were frequently cash-poor, Felix ran a prodigiously profitable, cash business. Madero could bleed him till hell froze over.

Of course, the charges were so serious Madero knew

he would have to cut the viceroy in, but for enough mordida that swine would countenance—no, pardon—a regi-
cide or Judas himself.

Moreover, the trembling sobbing wreck at his feet had
committed not so much a sin of commission as omission.
He failed to effectively oversee a bond slave. True, the
consequences had been grave, but Felix himself had
harmed no one with his own hand or even wished the
Crown ill.

Felix was loyal to the Crown clear through.

But what of Juan Rios and Maria de Rosa? He assumed they would head east on the road that would eventually lead them south. He sent messengers to spread the
word.

And set out to pursue them himself.

TWENTY-SEVEN

THE NEXT NIGHT I made a deal with a ranchero to take the three horses in exchange for a strong mule, a sack of tortillas, a blanket, and eight silver reales. That was the extent of our finances—enough money to feed us for a couple of days.

We rode half a day, and by the time we stopped to eat, Maria had redoubled her disdain for me.

"You are so stupid," Maria said. "The horses were worth many times what he gave you."

By now the only thing about me she respected was the saddle blanket I had given her during the night ride when I saw her shivering—despite her failure to bring one for herself.

Only the fact that she had lost everything—including the last living member of her family—kept me from pointing out that we would be much better off if she had spent her time tracking down the money sack her father had hidden in the house instead of a book of poetry.

"We are lucky he gave us anything," I said. "The man knew we were on the run. Had the horses carried the royal brand, we would have gotten nothing."

Since Madero's constables and spies often worked undercover, they rode unbranded horses to conceal their affiliation with the viceroy.

"Why didn't you at least get two mules? Two would carry us much faster."

"Because a woman riding a mule would attract attention. A woman riding behind her husband would not. If you're going to be a rebel, Maria, perhaps you should start thinking more like a bandido. They both live lives on the run, relying on secrecy and subterfuge to survive."

"Don't tell me about being a rebel. You are nothing but a—"

I turned away from her to pack the mule, and she was quiet for a long moment. She finally came up behind me.

"I'm sorry. You not only saved my life, you faced death with great courage. It's just that . . . that . . ."

"You suffered a great loss—"

"You could be doing so much for the revolution. It eats at me."

"Give me time," I said gently. "I am now an outlaw on the run. Perhaps I will someday be the rebel you want me to be."

"I've ruined everything. I killed my father with my stupidity, I ruined your life. We'll probably both be hanged because of me. I didn't listen to anyone. I thought that God would protect me, because I told only the truth."

She sat down and sobbed. I sat beside her, not knowing what to say. She had told me her father was in great pain and only wanted to die, but his religion had kept him from taking his life. But he didn't deserve to die violently at the hands of Madero's killers.

I hadn't told Maria that I had trafficked arms for the rebels for years because I didn't know what was facing us. I had already killed and risked death to defend her— and would do so again—but if I was killed and she was captured, knowledge of my activities would increase the penalties against her.

Maria's only crime was writing pamphlets—nothing as serious as my own irremediable sins.

I asked myself whether I had lost anything in taking Maria under my feeble wing. The resources and support I had had were now lost to me. Nor was the construction of a permanent facility in a rebel camp—something similar to Felix's compound—feasible. The rebels survived by staying on the move. Sooner or later, the viceroy's forces would learn of the factory and burn it.

Ayyo, at least I would no longer be a bond slave. What life lay ahead of me—and ahead of Maria—was now an open question.

I lay back and stared up at the sky, my hands behind my head. We would need ten to fifteen days—depending on the route we took—to reach the region where Vicente Guerrero was operating. Meanwhile, I had to keep us fed, moving, and . . . above ground.

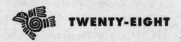

TWENTY-EIGHT

I LED US far into the brush until trees and bushes completely concealed us and we could eat and rest with some degree of safety. Neither of us had gotten any sleep, and I wanted to travel as much as possible at night, knowing we would face fewer travelers and patrols.

Maria was starting to doze off when I leaned over her with my knife. She started to scream, but I smothered it with my hand.

"Shhh. I'm not going to murder you. I'm just going to cut your hair."

"Have you gone mad?"

"I can cut your hair or Madero can cut your throat."

"You want me to look like a boy?"

"They won't be looking for a man and a boy."

"How can you be so sure he'll catch us?"

"Madero will have already sent fast, well-mounted couriers ahead of us. They will distribute our descriptions in every town, village, and crossing—an indio male and a mestizo woman. Even more lethal, they will post rewards on us. Impoverished peons would sell their mothers for a little dinero—let alone for hundreds of reales. Everyone we meet will be an informant, slavering after that reward.

"If that weren't enough, the local constables will set up roadblocks. Everyone will be stopped and questioned. We can't even risk contact with rebels until we reach Guerrero and know it's safe."

I took a handful of her soft hair. I put the blade under it and pulled it through.

She grabbed my wrist with both hands, resisting. She stared at me nose to nose, her eyes blazing with fury.

"You're enjoying this," she hissed.

"You're beautiful when you're angry."

"I hate you, you smug bastardo."

"And I love you even more when you're mad at *me*."

"Then you must be head over heels."

Her eyes were narrowing in rage, her upper lip curling over her front teeth.

"You really do detest me," I said, still grinning.

"Why not? You're scalping me like a savage."

"It hurts me worse than it hurts you."

"If I get my hands on that blade, you're becoming a woman."

"If we get caught, it's hot coals and whips."

I grabbed a handful of her lustrous raven tresses and carefully began to cut.

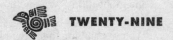

TWENTY-NINE

WE SLEPT SEPARATELY, myself on the bare ground, Maria wrapped up in our horse blankets.

I was in that twilight between dozing and real sleep when she screamed.

"Snake!"

Leaping out of her bedroll, she hopped around, slapping at her body with both hands as if hoping to drive off this fiend from hell.

I got up and rooted through her bedroll.

There it was—a common grass snake.

"It's harmless. It lives on field mice. It wouldn't have hurt you. It crawled into your bedroll for warmth. The poor thing was cold, that's all."

"Kill it!" she hissed.

I pretended to twist its neck and threw it into the woods.

"There, it's dead."

"Others will be back."

"Don't worry, I'll kill them, too. Now let's get back to bed. We have a long day tomorrow."

"Will you stand watch?"

"For what?"

"Snakes."

"You want me to watch over you for garden snakes?"

"Any snakes. They terrify me."

"Not a chance."

Silence.

Then . . . "Please."

A word I didn't expect to hear from Maria. She was a woman who asked for no quarter and gave none.

She was shivering. Her arms were covered with goose-flesh.

I sat down beside her and took her in my arms. "It's all right. Nothing will harm you. I'll protect you."

"Juan, I'm so sorry—"

"Stop it. We have a lot of road to cover. We'll talk about things after we get to Guerrero. Right now we need our rest. And our confidence."

We both lay down on the blanket, fully clothed, and I held her in my arms. She was shaking and I realized that she wasn't just cold, she was scared.

"Oh, Juan, I've been such a fool. I got my father killed. You're on the run because of me. I can't help anyone— least of all myself. I can't even protect myself from harm-less snakes. I can't do anything for anyone. Without a press, I can't even write my pamphlets anymore."

She began to sob again. I held her in my arms more tightly and stroked her soft black hair until she slept.

I don't know when it happened, it was sometime be-fore dawn when the night was the coldest. She snuggled closer against me, pressing for my warmth.

"I love you," I whispered. "From the first time I saw you. From the first time you told me I was stupid and cowardly and—"

To my undying surprise, she kissed my neck . . . and then my cheek.

I kissed her full on the mouth. Her tongue flickered tentatively against my teeth, then probed my own mouth, gingerly at first, exploring the interior until it found my own tongue that it touched lightly at first, then groped and grappled with it deliriously.

I was more than shy. In truth, I'd always been afraid of

her—of her extraordinary beauty, her scathing wit, her searing intellect . . . so often used at my expense. The mere sight of her had intimidated me. More than intimidating—it was terrifying in the extreme . . . like staring into a cocked and loaded gun.

I was the macho man, the secret rebel, the best shot in the colony. But this woman terrified me more than royal constables.

When she placed my hand on her breast, I . . . trembled.

When she slipped her knee in between my legs, my trembling *trebled*.

When she slipped my hand inside her skirt and I touched her and she groaned, I whispered, *"Maria . . ."*

She was shaking again—but this time not from fear or the cold. Placing a finger over my lips, she said softly, *"I know.* But we've both been through so much, and I need you."

With her left hand, she helped me remove my pants.

THIRTY

ANDALE, MANUEL. WE must hurry."

"Manuel" glared at me as she let me pull her up to sit behind me on the mule. Her face was dirty—I had rubbed dirt on it—and I made her take off her earrings and necklace and put on my change of clothes. The pants and shirt were too big, but they would have to do until I could get her some boy's clothes that fit.

Aboard, she put her arms around me.

"Don't hold me so tight." I grinned. "You're my brother, not my lover."

"You did not say that last night, bastardo."

Last night, she had bled and sobbed so much at her loss of innocence I could do little more to console her than swear the eternal love that burned in my heart, in my soul.

Today, however, was different. We were fugitives on the run.

I twisted my neck to glance back at her. "Such language from a lady. Don't forget, God hears these things."

"That was Manuel speaking. The way you cut hair, you should be a butcher, not a barber."

Ayyo. I turn a pretty girl into a boy with ugly hair and I get no gratitude.

From peons laboring in a field of maize, I bought straw hats straight off their heads for the two of us. The hats were sweat-stained, filthy, and well worn—exactly right.

Maria wrinkled her nose at the hat I gave her. "It stinks."

"Good. It's the smell of sweat from hard work—a scent that constables questioning us would recognize."

"It still stinks."

I pulled off the bandanna from around my neck. "Put this under the hat. It'll help cover more of your head."

"It stinks, too."

"Ayyo . . . women!"

We took long detours around the small towns we came upon. Finally, I decided I needed to hear the news and get her "boys" clothes that fit. Entering town a roadblock stopped us, but the constables had little interest in either of us because a ranchero on horseback with his woman sitting behind him was approaching. A constable started to question me, but when he saw the man and woman, he pushed me away and turned toward more promising prey.

Rumors claimed many threats were descending on the colony, ranging from an approaching army led by a long dead priest that would murder all the men and rape the women to something akin to the truth: two rebels were wanted and on the run, a man and a woman. Their crimes varied according to whom you asked—I heard that they were bandidos, murderers, rebels. But the one thing that everyone understood was that a reward was offered.

I bought quill, ink, and paper, and told Maria, "Write. Not well. Scribble. Give us permission to leave Hacienda de la Valle."

"What's that?"

I shrugged. "Who cares? There are haciendas and valleys everywhere."

"Why am I doing this?"

"Because words on a piece of paper will impress a constable if he wants to know what right a couple of peons have to be on the road. He probably won't be able to read it, but he'll know they're words and that will make him fearful, not about what the words say but who wrote them. I don't care what you write—just make it look official and impressive."

She said nothing for a moment. "Juan . . . you are full of surprises. And clever. Too bad you've wasted your talent."

¡Ay caramba! Women! Particularly this one.

Buying the clothes and some food had taken the last of my dinero. I didn't know how we would make it to the China Road, but I didn't worry Maria with it. I had to keep her spirits up. We had a long way to go, and if we were stopped by constables and she showed fear or guilt, we would be finished.

"We have to stay off the main roads. That means our trip to the China Road will take twice as long and be twice as hard. We better get started. We have a lot of territory to cover."

THIRTY-ONE

STAYING OFF THE main road—taking back roads when we could find them, mostly just crossing open territory—was difficult. Traveling was slow, tedious, and dangerous. We slept on the ground, ate cold food when we could steal it, drank water wherever we could find it.

Three days later disaster struck—our mule went lame.

Taking it into the nearest town, I sold it to a butcher for its hide for three reales—knowing the meat alone would be resold for more than that.

But I lacked the leverage to negotiate for more.

Moreover, the money would soon be gone—used on tortillas and beans—and we would be escaping on foot from the king's men. We would be destitute *and* on foot.

Maria asked what we would do. I told her I had a plan but did not give her specifics. My plan was that she stay in a safe place off the road while I went down and robbed a traveler—hopefully a rich merchant or wealthy primate of the Church.

Unable to earn our daily bread by honest sweat, I would do it by the grace of my pistolas.

Ayyo . . . it was now clear to me why the difference between a rebel and a bandido was so minute—both needed a fast horse, a head start, and a good gun.

Having packed a flint and a piece of sparking steel in my traveling bag, I'd had the presence of mind to grab a small cooking pan at Maria's house, and sometimes I'd forage fields for ears of green corn and black beans. Deep in the brush, behind stands of trees, we boiled our contraband corn and beans—when our stomachs growled and burned too painfully.

By the time we reached the town of San Rafael, we were exhausted, filthy, and starved for real food . . . but at least we had circumvented roadblocks and patrols looking for the two fugitives from Lake Chapala.

Interest in the two fugitives seemed to be fading—other news stepping in to fill the void: Near the town of Morena, bandidos had attacked a hacienda and murdered the occupants, a local militia captain had killed the mayor after a dispute over cards, and the richest widow in town had married a man younger than her son.

There was no shortage of horror and scandal.

Juan Rios and Maria de Rosa were old news.

Or so we hoped.

And while I said nothing and tried to put a good face on our predicament, I knew Colonel Madero would never quit the field or give up the hunt.

PART VIII

MONEY, GUNS, AND GAMES OF CHANCE

THIRTY-TWO

WHEN WE WANDERED into the village of Valdero—
a small town on the way to nowhere—a festival was under way. All the things I loved—food, drink, señoritas,
music, dancing, and card games—were in abundance . . .
for people with dinero.

By contrast we were almost broke, saddle-sore, foot-
sore, body-sore, frightened, famished, dispirited, bewil-
dered . . . and without any prospect of better times to
come.

It was just as well.

Since we had not bathed for three days or washed our
filthy threadbare peon garb, we looked like the miserable
tramps we were supposed to be—and in truth were.

The town square was packed with booths selling food
and religious icons.

I was more interested in the card tables.

We stopped at one table to watch one especially color-
ful high-stakes card game. A small crowd had gathered
around it.

A man in black clothes with an extravagant ebony
mustache and goatee—attired in a black frock coat and
matching hat—was smoking a long, thin cigar. He sat at a
makeshift table, playing cards with a portly hacienda owner dressed in a long white jacket and matching pants with
silver stitching. The hacendado had mean deep-set eyes, a
chronic sneer, and a nose like a badly busted knuckle.

But it was the black-clad stranger that fascinated me.

Another man who dressed entirely in black was
Madero, the head of the viceroy's secret police. This man

was not Madero. Still he gave off an aura that warned *Do not trifle with me* . . . and suggested that he was not fit for civilized society, that he traveled a different and far more dangerous road.

The hacendado, on the other hand, was a typical well-to-do landowner, who turned his vast lands and holdings over to an overseer, then spent most of his time in the capital soliciting invitations to the viceroy's garden parties. He thought money bought him everything—including luck with cards, the love of women, and skill with guns.

Watching the game, I observed the hacienda owner rise in his chair, while he stretched and yawned. Ten minutes earlier—taking out a handkerchief, coughing, then blowing his nose—he'd done the same thing.

I knew right away that neither of those two movements were right. They were somehow contrived.

Everyone else however was too focused on the money on the table, the betting, and the cards to notice.

What was he doing?

The realization came to me all at once: He was looking over his opponent's right shoulder at something in the distance.

He was still yawning, stretching—and staring. Since I stood directly behind him, I followed his line of sight.

Something now caught my own eye, and the second revelation hit me like a collapsing bridge: The hacendado had help.

The first hint was a flashing glint of light. Barely visible through the curtain on the second floor of a window across the street, I stared at it, mystified. I could guess the glint's source: Reflecting the bright sunlight was a small, circular lens . . .

A spyglass.

Someone was spying on the hand of the man in

black . . . but how was the person signaling the hacienda owner what his opponent had for a hand?

Then I saw it. Hand signals. Two fingers for a pair. Three of a kind. Two and three for a full house. Other signals were being flashed, but all my attention now was on the black-garbed man.

How could I warn him?

Why did I wish to warn him? Perhaps because I did not like hacienda owners who worked peons to death in their fields and silver mines. Maybe because the man in black was a free spirit, a personality I had not seen since my two uncles deliberately made and kept a date with death.

I moved away from Maria. Positioning myself so that the man in black could see me when he looked up, I deliberately stared at him and then turned my head, glancing and nodding at the glass window behind the hacendado. The spyglass was not conspicuously visible through the curtain, but if he looked closely, he would still discern that something was there . . . something wasn't right.

I was sure he'd take the hint.

Fearing the wrath of the hacienda owner, I moved away from the card game.

I spotted our salvation and headed for it.

Hurrying to keep up with me, Maria whispered, "Where are we going?"

"I'm going to turn our three reales into many more."

"Stop. I'm not going to let you gamble away in a card game the only food we'll see today."

"This is no gamble. It's a sure thing."

And it wasn't cards. I made my way through a group of people watching a shooting demonstration.

The shooting was being done against a half-dozen timbers squeezed together and braced against a stone wall. The distance to the target wasn't great, about forty paces, but the circular wooden targets came in three sizes—small, smaller, and even smaller.

The smallest was a challenge.

The concessionaire was a short man in a brilliant red shirt and black pants, and long greasy slicked hair. He wore a red bandanna around his forehead that only emphasized his thick lips, a thick nose, thick eyebrows, and small devious eyes.

The only pistols he allowed were his own.

The shooter bought one shot at a time with a reale. If the shooter hit the largest of the three targets, the concessionaire gave him back his reale plus one extra; hitting the second target earned him two extra, and hitting the third target earned him three extra.

Almost half of the men were able to hit the largest target. The percentage of hits dwindled as the targets got smaller.

No one could hit the smallest circle.

I sent Maria off to look at things she could not afford to buy or eat, then studied the people shooting. When a shooter was good enough to hit the target, the concessionaire would encourage him, even making side bets with the man. The shooter would keep betting because the more he shot, the more he got used to the pistol and knew exactly how to aim it.

When the stakes were the highest and the shooter could win some real money if he hit, the concessionaire rigged the weapon. He did it when he reloaded the ball and powder for the last shot. Watching him closely, I still didn't pick up on it for a full hour, but finally I caught him.

He gave the pistol barrel a tiny twist.

The man running the concession was cheating.

There is no play in an ordinary pistol barrel. This one was rifled with minute grooves that when the trick barrel was turned would alter the course of the round. Such a small twist wouldn't be detected by someone just holding the gun up and looking at it or aiming it. But the concession owner was changing the bullet's flight by a couple inches. Just as the shooter got his range and perfected his aim, the concessionaire's barrel twist altered the shooter's projected line of fire.

When Maria returned, my courage rose. The other onlookers had wandered away, so I stepped forward. Knowing he might turn away an indio, I held a silver reale in my open palm. I also tried to look naïve.

"May I try, señor?"

Even while grunting a "humph" of contempt, he could not take his eyes off my money. It undoubtedly looked like the easiest money he would make that night.

He gave me the loaded pistol. I carefully aimed and fired, hitting the largest of the targets. Pretending it was pure luck, I asked for my winnings—my reale back and a reale more.

"Pretty good shot, Azteca. Try it again. Go on, try it."

Betting the two reales of mine he was holding, I fired again, hitting the second-largest target.

"Hey, you're one hell of a shot. Let's see . . . now you've got six reales. How much more do you have?"

"Two more, señor."

"I'll make you a deal. You bet all eight and hit that big target again, and you'll walk away with sixteen."

"What if he's able to hit the smallest target?"

The question caught me as much by surprise as it did the man.

The black-clad Spaniard from the card game had been watching. He stepped forward.

"You know this indio," the man asked.

"No, but I saw him shoot, and he's good. I'll make you

a deal. He puts up his eight. I put up ten, too. If he hits the smallest target, you pay him thirty-two. You also pay me another thirty on top of the ten I put up."

"Amigo, you have a bet."

After we put up the bet, the stranger stopped in front of me before he stepped back out of the way. "Don't miss, Azteca."

"Sí, señor."

Out of the corner of my eye I saw the concessionaire give the pistol barrel a little twist as he loaded it. When he handed it back to me, I thought of giving it a twist back but decided not to. With the twist, the round pulled two inches to the left. I aimed two inches to the right and . . . fired.

The smallest target exploded, and the concessionaire detonated in loud curses.

"What are you pulling?" He grabbed the pistol from me and hit me with it. The strike hit me a glancing blow on the head. I restrained myself from pulling out my pistols and putting a bullet in each of his eyes.

The stranger stepped between us. "You owe us money."

The concessionaire stared at the stranger. I could see that he was taking his measure. The cardplayer looked like a man who knew his way around cards and horses, women and *guns*.

Not the sort of man one provoked into a physical confrontation.

The concessionaire made up his mind. He gave the stranger his winnings.

"The indio gets nothing. It's against the law for him to fire a weapon. I'm going to have him arrested."

"Señor," the stranger said, with great courtesy, "you are right. And I'll have you arrested for supplying the weapon."

"The local constable is my amigo, so—"

The stranger's hand moved so fast it was a blur. One moment it appeared empty, the next it was holding the butt of an ivory-handled knife with a twelve-inch blade, three inches at the blade's broad base. The blade tapered to a narrow point, and the stranger had pierced the man's pants crotch with that point.

"You do not wish to offend me, hombre. You've been cheating people with your trick pistol. If I let them know, they'll string you up on the nearest tree—after I separate you from your cojones."

He tickled the man's crotch with a twist of his twelve-inch blade.

The swindler's bladder discharged.

"My dog will feast on your missing cojones, my friend, and I will send you to join your puta-mother and the father you never knew in hell without your manly appendages."

The stranger moved forward till he was nose to nose with the man. He gave him a spectacular grin, and again nicked the man's groin with a twisting, upward nudge of his blade.

The man handed me thirty-two reales. As we left, he was doubled over in front of his concession, vomiting violently.

The stranger said, "You are the best shot I've ever seen."

I shook my head. "It was just luck. I never fired a pistol before."

"Sí, and I've never held a deck of cards in my hands or tickled a woman's flower with my garrancha. Where are you two from?"

"My brother and I work at the Hacienda de la Valle."

Four horsemen entered the square. Constables. They didn't ride in as locals but as men unfamiliar with the town. And looking at people as if they were searching for someone.

Madero would never give up the hunt. That was Madero's reputation. The bull with a brain. He just kept charging.

Maria tensed beside me, and I casually grasped her arm. I didn't want her to run.

"I need coachmen," the stranger in black said.

"Coachmen?" I asked.

"My two coachmen are gone. I caught them stealing and sent them packing. They weren't the kind to watch my back . . . even at a card game. You and your brother want the job?"

"Well, señor, we are heading south, for the China Road—"

"An excellent direction. Point the horses toward the China Road."

THIRTY-THREE

DON'T YOU FIND it strange?" Maria asked.

We had retrieved the team of four from the stable, then harnessed them to the coach. Maria had purchased provisions to eat along the way while I inspected the rims and spokes for damage and greased the axles and hubs.

We sat in the driver's box atop the coach.

Finding coachmen's livery in the baggage boot at the rear of the coach, I fit into my uniform fine. Maria's however needed a tight belt and rolled-up sleeves.

Her new garb did nothing to improve her disposition.

A short-barreled fowling piece—used to ward off bandidos and perhaps to pot birds for dinner—lay on the floorboard under the driver's seat. I knew that kind of gun well, having repaired hundreds of them. It fired wide-pattern buckshot and was murderously effective at close range.

The coachman's assistant was to be a shotgun guard as well.

Unbeknownst to our unsuspecting employer, Maria couldn't even lift the weapon.

Moreover, a quick look at the rusted fittings suggested that it wouldn't fire anyway. I repaired it while we waited for our black-clad boss to tell us to leave. He was currently waiting for a friend, he'd said, and the next thing I knew he was snoring inside the coach.

Earlier when I had watched him kneeling in front of a tree stump, dealing cards to himself, the deck confounded me. It was unlike any card deck I had ever seen. When I told Maria about its bizarre cards—a magician, a female

pope, lovers, justice, royalty, a hanged man, the devil—
Maria said it was a tarot deck.

"For fortune-telling. Rich women love to have their fortunes told, the occult meaning of their lovers' secret sighs,
who they should take for lovers, whether they will have
great wealth. All of it is pure unadulterated idiocy. It will
also bring the Inquisition to your door if the Church finds
out."

Maria was right about our employer—he was an
enigma. A fancy coach with a count's coat of arms on the
doors, he had quickly rattled off his name and title to us:
Count Luis Benito Juarez de Santa Barbara de la Sierra
Madre.

A nobleman no less! A count was just below a marquis
in the hierarchy of nobles. But he was a count with a deck
of fortune-telling cards and no coachmen. And coachmen
for a noble family were not the type hired and fired for
theft. They would be family retainers who spent their entire life in the service of their master. If they stole, they
were given a beating, not dismissed.

"He doesn't look like a count," Maria said.

I don't know what Maria thought a count should look
like, but Luis had the wary eyes and the graceful menace
of a bloodstained, battle-scarred jungle cat who had survived more than one life-and-death brawl.

And emerged the sole surviving victor.

He did not come across as a gentleman of luxurious
leisure.

A coach pulled up, and a middle-aged, expensively attired, strikingly attractive woman with long dark hair, an
enticingly low-cut red silk dress, and a dangling pearl
necklace poked her head out the window. She smiled
pleasantly, almost expectantly. Count Luis climbed into
her coach, his fortune-telling cards in hand.

The woman's coachmen wandered off to drink pulque

and smoke while I reworked the fowling musket's firing mechanism with a file.

Maria dozed.

After about a half an hour the woman's coach began to rock, reverberating with groans of pleasure given and taken. The aching, sobbing groans awoke Maria, and she stared at me.

"Do you think . . . ?" she whispered.

"Servants don't think."

After a while the coach door opened and Luis came out, backing down to the ground, shoving a pearl necklace in his pocket. The matron affectionately touched his cheek. Her facial powders were streaked and her hair mussed.

"The road to Guadalajara," the count snapped up to me.

I froze for an instant. We were supposed to take the road south, not back toward Chapala and Guadalajara. I exchanged looks with Maria and got the coach moving. When we came to the main road that led north and south, the count leaned out the window and said, "To the China Road."

I breathed easier and turned the team south.

"What's he doing?" Maria whispered.

"He didn't want the woman to know which way he was going."

"Why?"

"Maybe she's a lover he wants to part with. Or maybe she'll want back that pearl necklace. Or maybe her husband will want the count's cojones."

"He's . . . *strange*," Maria said again.

No, not strange. He just wasn't what he pretended to be—any more than we were. If he was a count, I was the King of Old Castile. The Spanish had a special word to describe a man who was a gambler and womanizer who took advantage of rich women: *picaro*.

A picaro was a rogue and often a vagabond, but a special kind of villain, a highwayman of the card table and lady's boudoir.

"We have no complaints," I told Maria.

Meeting up with Count Luis was not just good luck, it was miraculous. We could hardly complain about the count's character when we were on the run from the viceroy's hangman and the Inquisition's stake. Anyway, we were finally making good time on the main road. Even if we ran into a posse of constables, they would not dare offend a nobleman by stopping his coach. Even the royal constables backed off when confronted by rich gachupines.

The rich had prerogatives.

Later that night we pulled off the road. The count slept in the coach while Maria and I slept on the ground. But now we were in the lap of luxury, using thick blankets to soften the hard, cold ground.

In the morning, the count stepped down from the coach. He was near Maria but didn't see her. Opening his trousers, he pulled out his manhood and relieved himself.

Maria leaped up and stumbled over a log trying to get away from him.

"Eh, boy, I bet you a reale that I can piss farther than you," the count said.

"He doesn't speak," I said.

"What's that?"

"My brother, he has no voice."

"What happened to it? Doesn't he have a tongue?"

"He's never spoken, not even as a baby. Señor Count, we will get your breakfast now."

I was desperate to change the subject.

THIRTY-FOUR

WE ROCKED ALONG for two days, making good time. Finally we stopped at a roadside inn for the count to relieve his thirst. When he returned, he gave me instructions to a large house. When darkness fell, Count Luis left the coach reeking of perfume that he had no doubt put on to cover the smell of sweat and dust from traveling.

The only other addition to his dark attire was a black mask covering his eyes.

"A costume party," I told Maria as coaches dropped off other guests.

As the hours passed, I wandered over to a group of coachmen smoking and talking to the house's footmen. After I got an earful, I returned and reported to Maria.

"Count Luis is the sensation of the party. Since there's no nobility in the area, the guests were terribly impressed that a count showed up unexpectedly. Still, from what the footmen say, he must be the world's worst gambler. It sounds like Count Luis has lost everything except his boots."

"I hope he doesn't lose his coach."

"And his two loyal servants."

An hour later Luis came out and had me move the coach so that a copse of trees hid it from the view of others. He left and came back with a masked woman. She was middle-aged but like the woman with the pearl necklace, she was still attractive. Expensively attired in red silk, she flaunted her copious cleavage, opulent figure, and a large diamond brooch.

We took a walk in the moonlight to give the count and his newest paramour-of-the-night privacy.

"What if the woman's husband shows up?" Maria asked.

"Hopefully he's dead and buried. If not, you inherit Luis's coach, become a countess, and I'll be your servant."

She stared at me with fixed curiosity. "Who *are* you?" she finally asked.

I stopped and took her in my arms. "What do you mean? Who do you want me to be?"

"I want to know: Who *are* you?"

"A man who has always loved you. Always. Even when you mocked me."

I kissed her cheek.

"I only resent the way you've wasted your talents."

"I have a talent for love, too."

She squirmed out of my arms. "I don't need to get pregnant while I'm on the run."

"And when we're not on the run?"

"We can make love after we're married. When you prove your loyalty to the Cause."

"I see . . . it's my talents you love, not my person."

"Of course. Men are found everywhere. But gun-makers are a rare breed."

I grabbed her and kissed her as my hands worked inside her clothes.

"Get moving."

I jumped away from Maria.

"Get the carriage moving," the count said. He looked at us—his two foot*men*—and shook his head. "You indio brothers have strange customs."

The woman was gone. I didn't know what caused his haste. The prospect of the woman's husband returning . . . or the woman's discovery that her jewelry was missing . . .

"He must be in trouble if he's having us move the

coach at night," I said to Maria. "Pray one of our horses doesn't break a leg."

"Did you notice that he doesn't care what route we take?" Maria asked.

"Yes, he does. He wants us to take him to places where he can gamble and meet rich women."

"What a pathetic way to live. Spending his time playing cards and telling the fortunes of stupid women before bedding them as easily as putas, which is all they seem to be."

"Putas who pay *him*," I pointed out.

"We can't trust him," she said.

"That's all right. He can't trust us, either."

THIRTY-FIVE

"Y OUR EXCELLENCY, PLEASE have another one of these exquisite bonbons." The woman leaned forward to put the chocolate in Luis's mouth.

He let his hand brush against her bountiful bosom as she leaned toward him. Her apple cheeks reddened, and she smiled with pleasure.

"Did your husband suffer much in his last illness?" he asked.

"No, the Lord was merciful and took him right after the evening meal. He was in pain at first, then emitted several massive belches and broke wind like a mule and died . . . with a look of great relief." She popped another bonbon in her own mouth.

Given the ripe rotundity of her bosom, her waist was surprisingly narrow, Luis noted. Moreover, the ample décolletage of her low-cut white evening gown showed her curvaceous cleavage off to maximal advantage. Tonight, Luis decided, he would blend the business of acquiring a new gambling stake in exchange for satisfying the widow's desperate needs while pleasuring himself.

He seldom allowed himself that luxury.

Glancing around the spacious living room, Luis noted that like the hacienda walls outside, these living-room walls were gessoed a dazzling alabaster. The only adornment on the walls were two small crucifixes and a large rectangular mirror in an elaborately carved teak frame. Scattered around the spacious room were four octagonal tables of matching teak, each surrounded by a trio of straight-back armchairs upholstered in soft jet-black leather. A matching leather couch faced a long low narrow table also of teak. Against each of three walls stood an ebony chest featuring a dozen small drawers with brass handles. The fourth wall opened into a vast dining sala at the center of which was a spectacularly long mahogany banquet table and matching straight-back armchairs upholstered with leather seats and backs.

Luis wasn't impressed with the woman's house or her jewels, but the cards had been against him earlier—they usually were—and he had latched on to her at the party because she appeared vulnerable and available.

He desperately needed another stake.

He preferred women who could provide a good brandy and fine Cuban cigars. He didn't see a humidor of cigars, but a filled crystal brandy decanter, surrounded by eight crystal goblets, stood in the middle of a round silver serving tray in the center of the long narrow teak table.

Luis filled two of the goblets to the brim and handed one to the widow. He clinked her glass in toast.

"Salud," she said softly.

"Y dinero," he added.

He took a large mouthful, swirled it around his tongue, then savored the fine brandy as it burned its way down his throat. It was the best brandy he'd had in at least a month. The widow's late husband had enjoyed superlative taste in fine liquors.

"My priest was wondering where Santa Barbara de la Sierra Madre is located. He said he had never heard of your estate."

As if to confirm his doubt, the sleeping priest—passed out on a chair from too much holy wine at the card game— broke the metronomic cadence of his snoring with several short snorts.

Luis waved his hand in the air as if to push away the priest's ignorance. "I have no doubt that a small-town priest is ignorant of many things." He leaned closer, subtly pulling out a deck of tarot cards. "A woman who so recently found herself alone in the world must be interested in knowing what the future holds for her."

With a surprised widening of the eyes she looked on the cards . . . and smiled.

Glancing disdainfully at the besotted, snoring priest, Luis sighed wearily to himself and began to lay out the woman's future. If the priest woke, he would cause trouble, perhaps even putting the local constabulary or, even worse, the regional representative of the Inquisition onto him. A realist, Luis understood that the issue was not that he employed devil cards to summon the occult art of tomorrow-telling. The priest would instead turn Luis in for swindling the widow out of her inheritance—money that the priest had no doubt earmarked for himself.

Luis had learned tarot from his gypsy mother—the woman who had taken him in as a foundling. She had not brought him up out of motherly love—as a professional con artist, she found small children useful as shills in her various confidence games—and as light-fingered thieves. Louisa had taught him well as they worked the towns of Toledo, Madrid, Barcelona—all the countless cities where she and her ward plied their deceptive trade.

During one surprisingly long sojourn in Toledo, a city along the Tagus River in the Castilla la Mancha providence of central Spain, she had taught him the black art of the tarot-reading. She had seduced a wealthy city father and was planning to relieve him of most of his considerable fortune before taking French leave of the old man in the middle of the night. Unfortunately, the old man saw through her scheme and at the last second he denounced her trickery and sent for the police. Luis and his mother had fled in the middle of the night—not with the old man's loot but with the clothes on their backs and the Toledo constables on their tail.

He looked back on that period with some nostalgia. He missed Toledo with its ancient Roman and medieval Moorish architecture and traditions.

That stint in Toledo, however, and Louisa's tarot-card mentoring had served him in good stead over the years, supplying him with a steady stream of revenue when times were hard. As long as he had a reliable retinue of rich widows and a deck of devil cards—with which to charm their fancy and captivate their wits—he would not starve.

Plying that trade was not without its risks. More than once, the devil cards—and the profits they reaped—had brought the law down on him as well. On one such occasion he had employed the devil deck to rob a woman of both her wits and a huge diamond ring that her late husband had lovingly bestowed on her. In that instance so many constables and Inquisitors had descended on him he had actually sought military service as a way out of his mess. Joining the army under an assumed name, he had entered the lists as a cannoneer against Napoleon.

He trained in the army as a cannoneer and because he was intelligent and had a good eye and brain for calculating trajectories, he soon rose to master gunner on a Spanish warship. He had enjoyed the action and excitement, the blood and violence, the thrust of the blades and the thunder of the guns. He was forced to jump ship in Cadiz, however, after knifing an officer over a card game. The officer had claimed Luis had been cheating. Luis counter-claimed that the officer was the cheat. Both accusations were true, but when the officer reached for his blade, Luis proved the superior swordsman as well as the more dexterously deceptive cardsharp.

To avoid the hangman, he crewed on a vessel headed for the colony. By the time he jumped ship in Veracruz, he had cleaned out most of the officers and crew during the all-night shipboard card games. He was ready to set himself up as a New Spain grandee.

Only recently had he managed to pass himself off as a count. His purported coat of arms—adorning his carriage door—announced his nobility everywhere he went.

He had misappropriated the carriage in the silver mining town of Guanajuato after the dice had divested him of everything but his charm. After an all-night orgy of drinking, dicing, debauching, and devil-card-reading, he had borrowed the carriage from the wife—not the widow—of a silver-mine owner with which to return to his inn. Her husband, the count—who'd bought his title—had emblazoned his crest upon the coach doors. Luis learned from a passerby, who had mistaken him for the count, that constables waited at the inn for the gambling, drinking, debauching tarot-reader.

He was not discomfited.

In truth, he had admired the coach and four—and particularly its courtly escutcheon—with such invidious rapacity that he had quickly summoned the coachmen down from their box, ordered them to examine the rear axle, and when they turned toward the rear wheel, he had brained them with his wrist-quirt's leaded butt stock.

Commandeering the coach and four, he had skipped out on the inn and his bill, flagrantly forsaking the concupiscent countess.

He didn't know how long his nobleman's ruse would last before the authorities would be after him in force once more.

But Luis knew no other way to live.

THIRTY-SIX

AT TOLUCA, WE set out south for the China Road.

At the town of Ixtapan de la Sal—famed for its mineral waters—I knew I should reach out to the guerrilla leader Vicente Guerrero. We were in the region where governmental authority was often nonexistent. When the government troops came to town, the local government paid its taxes to the viceroy; when rebel troops arrived, the taxes went to them.

From what I heard, the rebels were currently in the area, which suited me perfectly.

Count Luis had not heard of the town named as a place of "salt." He was pleased when I told him many rich women come to the spas here because the water was known to cure arthritic and rheumatic conditions.

After the count left to look for wealthy widows and games of chance, I told Maria to watch the carriage. It was stabled by the inn where the stable boy watered, fed, and rubbed down our stock.

I then made the rounds of the pulquerías. I had a message system for contacting the China Road rebels: a note left at pulquerías with three words on it: *Alquimista y Guerrero.*

The message would tell them that the Alchemist needed to talk to the rebel chieftain.

I chose only taverns where I felt comfortable with the bartenders.

THIRTY-SEVEN

THE COUNT'S LUCK at cards seemed to be holding up for a change and so was mine. After three days a man strolled up to me in a bar and said "Vicente wants to talk to you. Go to the baño."

The outhouse was in the back twenty paces from the pulquería. I was still five paces from it when men came out of the bar behind me. They were dressed in plain white shirts, trousers, and rope sandals. They had grim faces and brandished machetes.

Rebels, for sure. But which group was the question. Rebel leaders often fought among each other as bitterly as they battled the royals.

"The viceroy sent you to murder the general," said a tall man with hard dark eyes, long hair, and a mean face so sharp and angular it reminded me of the machete he shook at me. "You will die instead."

"No one sent me. I'm the Alchemist, amigo."

"You're a lying killer."

"Take me to General Guerrero."

"Your eyes will never see him and your lying tongue will never speak of him because they will be cut out."

"The general must be told I'm here."

The door to the outhouse opened behind me and a man with a clear commanding presence stepped out. He was of medium height with a broad nose framed by piercing wide-set eyes and a glittering smile filled with white teeth. His dark features contrasted his dazzling smile, accentuating it.

The Spanish were wrong about blood. Mixing blood

created men and women with exceptional powers. General Vicente Guerrero was the proof of that.

I gave him a polite bow. "General. We have never met, but we have communicated many times. I am the Alchemist."

He raised his eyebrows and a pistol. "If you really are the Alchemist, then you can tell me something."

"Sí, señor, what is it you want to know?"

"Tell me the formula for gunpowder."

THIRTY-EIGHT

WHAT ARE YOU telling me?" Maria demanded. "That you personally spoke to General Guerrero and he invited the two of us to join his staff?"

"Have I ever lied to you?"

"You are lying right now. Tell me the truth."

"I spoke to Guerrero—"

"That much I believe. What I don't believe is that you are as innocent as you say. There's something you haven't told me."

There was plenty I had not told her. Guerrero was happy to get Maria as a pamphleteer and printer. And ecstatic to get a man capable of repairing firearms and making gunpowder.

I had to tell Maria the whole truth, but I didn't have time. I told her where she was to meet Guerrero's forces outside of town.

"Why can't you come with me?" she asked.

"I have to tell the count we're leaving so he can replace us."

"Why? He can find coachmen."

"Not if he's on the run from a jealous husband or cardplayers he cheated. He's helped us. I can't go without warning him."

I left Maria and went to where the coach was parked at a stable hoping that the count had left a message about his whereabouts.

The count came rushing into the stable as I looked for the stable man.

"We have to get out of here. Get the horses harnessed."

"I can't, Your Excellency. My brother and I are leaving your employ—"

Galloping horses came into the stable yard.

"Run for your life!" Luis yelled. He drew his sword.

I pulled both of my concealed pistols.

Luis gaped at me.

"You run," I shouted, "I'll cover your back."

But I couldn't. More horsemen had arrived at the back of the stable building. They had us front and back—a dozen armed men at least, wielding swords, knives, pistolas, muskets, whips, and ropes.

Hangman's ropes knotted with nooses.

Mother of God, Luis had incited a mob.

Luis threw down his sword. "Put down your pistols, amigo. You can kill a couple of men, but they will kill us. I'm not ready to die."

Twelve angry men with hell in their eyes and blood in their mouths descended on us with flailing fists and gun butts.

THIRTY-NINE

AYYO . . . LUIS WAS one bad hombre. Bad at cards, at telling fortunes, at sleeping with other men's wives, at taking their jewelry . . . worse, at ransacking the purses and pride of their husbands. The only thing Luis had going for him was his fast escapes.

Inevitably the day would come when Luis ran out of fast escapes.

And I would be standing next to him.

They took my special pistolas and beat me to the ground.

And then beat and stomped me some more.

I expected to be killed outright—or perhaps dragged to the nearest tree and hung.

I was surprised that after an hour Luis and I were both alive. Bound, for certain, hand and foot, though the bleeding had subsided for both of us. The pain was still there.

What we didn't know was exactly who held us prisoner. Luis had offended many people with his usual bad behavior. But there was some controversy about what to do with us. My impression was that some of the men wanted to give us summary justice—dragging us to the nearest tree—while others wanted to profit off of us.

Luis said they hadn't turned us over to constables since all the royal authority had fled because the rebels were operating in the area.

"What are they going to do to us?"

"Shhh."

A man with a broad black mustache and fiery eyes arrived on horseback. He dressed as a caballero and had a brace of pistolas strapped to his waist. More intense discussions took place.

After a moment, I realized something important. "They sound like a bunch of merchants trying to get the best price for cattle."

Luis muttered a prayer under his breath.

For the first time I felt fear.

I could face a firing squad, hangman's rope, perhaps even to be drawn and quartered but not without fear . . . Luis, on the other hand, was not a man to fear anyone or anything—not even the devil. Especially not the devil. When he got frightened, it scared me.

"What's wrong? What are they going to do to us?"

"Take us to Acapulco to the Manila galleon."

"The ship to the Philippines?"

"They're selling us to it."

"We're going to be crew on the ship?"

"No. Slaves. Doomed slaves on a death ship. We'll never make it to Manila. That's why they have to buy forced labor. Mostly criminals sentenced to death or long prison terms are used."

"Why are you so depressed? It's better than hanging."

He shook his head.

"You think you are getting a reprieve from death? All that has happened is you'll be sentenced to torture, starvation, and unbearable thirst, to wither away slowly and miserably as your bones break and disease rots your skin."

"It's still better than dying."

Luis fixed me with a long hard stare. "As you shall see, young friend, there are worse things than death."

PART X

A GHOST SHIP OF
THE DAMNED

CLUBBED INTO UNCONSCIOUSNESS, Luis and I had been taken from the struggle at the inn's stable to a mule train that carried us to Acapulco and a ship moored in the harbor. Dragged aboard, we were hurled unceremoniously into the stinking, dark, and dank hole.

I came to in the ship's slave hold, where the bilge slaves were quartered.

I counted three dozen of us, wretches chained to thick heavy iron eye-bolts—each circular eye six inches across, forged out of inch-thick steel. Bolted into the hold's deck, a half-dozen chains were padlocked to each wide thick "eye". Each coffle chain passed over the leg irons of each of the six prisoners. We were effectively chained to five other slaves as well as to two deck bolts.

Our clothes were little more than filthy bloodstained rags. My head boomed and throbbed like a bass drum, each beat a thunder-crack from hell.

The thunder-cracks were the excruciating beat of my pulse in my ears.

Putting my hands to my temples I felt damp clotted blood covering my cheeks and neck. I glanced at Luis through blurred, bloodshot eyes. He lay groaning and looked even worse. One eye was so lividly swollen I feared it might be blind. Some irate husband or gambler had clearly wreaked violent revenge on my erstwhile employer.

The man lying next to me, on the other hand, felt no pain at all.

He felt *nothing*.

His nose, ears, and mouth were covered with clotted blood, and his glazed eyes glared sightlessly at the overhead bulkhead—into an abyss of nothingness.

He was as dead as he would ever be.

One man was doing a little better. He was young—he looked barely twenty—and dressed in relatively clean rags. At least they were clean relative to the bloodied, befouled, ripped, and frayed garb the rest of us wore. He sported a short dark ratty beard and disheveled hair. Despite his youth, both hair and beard were streaked with gray. Studying us with a sardonic smirk, he said, "Welcome aboard, mates."

"Aboard *what*?" I grunted.

"A ghost ship of the damned."

"Fuck me," Luis rasped, starting to come to.

"Oh, yes, you are truly fucked," the man said.

"How?" I asked. "Where are we?"

"You're on a galleon bound for hell . . . that Infernal Region whose earthly name is Manila. A voyage of the dead, you sail without hope or respite or redemption, amigos. You're headed to wherever it is the dead go. For people like us, that means straight to hell."

"What are we doing here?" Luis asked. "Who are you?"

"I am Arturo, and we are bilge slaves on a decayed derelict that once sailed the seven seas proudly but now leaks like a sieve, topside *and* belowdecks. The bilge fills so fast and furiously it continually threatens to sink us. No pump can empty it quick enough. One day without our bailing and this tub would be sailing on the seafloor itself."

"You seem in relatively good shape, Arturo," I said.

"I was a crew member, and they look after me."

"What did you do to get here?" I asked.

"Someone filched some water and limes from the captain's private store. I was the one blamed."

"What do we do here?" I asked.

"You're part of the bucket brigade. We bucket out the foul stuff, and pass the buckets from hand to hand through a long line of more bucket slaves to a small compartment just belowdecks—just above the waterline—where the strongest, toughest, and meanest of these wretched slaves on the rail hurls the slop through a hole."

"Which slave is that?" I asked.

"My mate, the one who actually filched the water and limes, then tried to pin the pilferage on me."

"How did they catch him?"

"Someone spoke lies about him. But it seems he had a cache of limes hidden in his own seabag he never told the captain about."

"I've died and gone to hell," Luis moaned, clutching his head.

"Make no mistake, you have. No doubt this place smells worse than hell. The bilge is filthy and foul-smelling, the air poisonous and oppressively hot, the lower holds swarm with rats—as big as dogs. By the end of the voyage, the majority of us bilge slaves will either die or the work, foot rot, and scurvy will cripple us for life. We have it worse—far worse—than galley slaves who used to man oars."

"If we make it," I asked, "what's Manila like?"

"Another bilge. You'll die in their cane fields or swamps from black fever or the snakes. Trust me, here or in Manila, we are sentenced to a slow, foul death—without remorse or reprieve."

"Then we might as well fight," I said. "We die either way."

"Resistance is useless. We are chained when we are not working. We are outnumbered and outgunned. We can't even look them in the eye. Meet their gaze, and they will spread and bind you against the mast, then flay the flesh from your bones with a flogging cat. Your bones will grin through your blood and tattered flesh as white as winding shrouds. Resist a second time, and they will feed you to the sharks. Anyway, in a few days resistance will be academic. We will all be too sick and weak to resist."

"You're surviving."

"They look after me to some extent. It won't last long, however. One day I'll catch the contagion which is rife down here. I'll cough and crap my insides out."

"Why were the limes and water stolen?" Luis asked.

"The voyage back is worse than the voyage over, and this last one was hell. We got stuck in the tropics—in doldrums, stock-still, dead-still. In scorching heat, we sat immobile—without a breath of breeze, with sails slack, the sea bewitched. Racked by scurvy and dehydration, we were all dropping in our tracks from bloody bowels, bloody urine, our skin falling from our faces and backs.

"The captain hoards kegs of aqua pura and barrels of limes in his cabin. I was accused of sneaking into his quarters and liberating a water cask and a bag of limes, then passing them out among the crew. Whoever did it saved the crew from certain death. Some of the crew have not forgotten that a thief saved their lives. Whether I did it or not, they are appreciative. I am paying, however, for their salvation. Unfortunately, the person I spoke of leaked my name to the captain as the thief."

"Tough luck," Luis said mordantly.

"I'm saying to you, never forget: They hold all the cards. You have nothing in your hand. Mess with them, you'll lose—and curse your mother for giving you birth."

"Suppose I stack the deck," Luis said.

"Amigo, I can tell you are a fighter," our bilge mate said. "My advice is do not fight them. I've tasted their flogging-cat. Your pointless resistance will not be worth the price. Believe me."

"How do you know we aren't in hell?" Luis asked.

"Hell begins at dawn. For now it's evening. Do as they

say, and you may see Manila. Don't fuck with them, whatever you do. Hear me, amigo. Because you are gachupine, they will assume you are a criminal sentenced to the galleon for despicable crimes against the Crown. Toward you they will be more pitiless, more brutal."

"But I'm a Spanish subject of the Crown," Luis said, indignant.

"You *were* a subject of the Spanish Crown. You are now a worthless wretch. They know you will die. The only question is when and where. They aren't concerned about tales you might tell later."

"I shall survive this voyage," Luis said firmly.

"Even if you survive this voyage and are not sold off to the Manila slave plantations—where you would die within months anyway from the heat, the swamps, the cane fields, and the fever—you would not survive a return voyage. It is far worse—heat, doldrums, typhoons. Even if all of us die on this voyage, it means nothing to the captain. He'll just buy replacement slaves in Manila— for next to nada. There are always criminals and men who have offended the viceroy. Like the viceroy in Mexico City, the one in Manila rules as if he were an Oriental potentate.

"Señor, understand this: Since you are doomed to die anyway, you are inherently expendable. To them, you are less than nada. You are already dead."

FORTY-ONE

Luis, as usual, didn't listen. As soon as we were unchained the next morning he approached the bilge master, Emile.

"My friend, I am a nobleman—a colonial gachupine of august lineage. My presence here is a farcical fiasco of preposterous proportions. As one gentleman to another, could you get me a meeting with the captain so I can get out of this disgusting hole."

The bilge master brought his wrist-quirt's butt stock—weighted with lead shot—down across Luis's already bloodied, battered, and bedraggled head.

He pointed at three bilge slaves. "Haul this lying piece of shit topside."

Our bucket brigade was suspended for a half hour so we could line up before the mast and watch Luis's shirt stripped from his back, his arms and chest spread on the mast, and the flesh of his back flayed all the way down to the spine and ribs.

We were turned in our traces and marched back into the bilge to recommence the bucket brigade.

When I saw Luis again, two sailors were hauling him down to our so-called sleeping quarters, his back packed in rock salt. His teeth were clenched tight against the pain, and his eyes blazed with hate and rage.

I poured a bucket of bilge water on his back. It was dirty, but cool.

FORTY-TWO

AT DAWN THE bilge master unchained us from the deck's eye-bolts. Rations were hardtack, thin gruel, an occasional piece of salt pork, and rank water. The hardtack was broken off in uneven hunks and was often harder than our teeth. The best hope was to bang it on the deck and hope to break off small chunks to soak in your gruel. You had to somehow hammer the foul stuff into the smallest pieces possible.

The hammering also drove out the weevils, which had burrowed their way into the hardtack and honeycombed its interior. On one hand, the weevils were nauseating, but on the other hand, they alone made the hardtack semi-edible. With enough hammering, honeycombed hardtack would eventually shatter. Without those weevil tunnels, the tack would have been impervious to any fragmentation and therefore too big for ingestion.

The weevils we digested no doubt supplied nutrition as well.

The salt pork and salt herring were indispensable to our nutrition. They also had a negative side effect, however. The officers issued miserably minute water rations, and we were continually, agonizingly dehydrated. The salt-encrusted pork and herring aggravated our thirst unbearably.

I saw starving men ingest the pork without sufficient water to wash it down, then go mad with feral suffering.

As with Luis, the captain cured the thirst of men who complained by spreading them against the mast, flogging their backs to the bone, then salting their flayed flesh, as if they were the pork or herring that had so mercilessly un-hinged them.

If starvation and dehydration weren't enough, the back-breaking drudgery of filling and passing the buckets—each one thirty-five pounds—in the sweltering heat of the holds was unbearably brutal.

All the while, the bilge master, Emile, and his henchmen were on our backs, cursing us on in the foulest terms, de-scribing the hideous sexual perversions that they claimed to have inflicted on our mothers, wives, and daughters. When their threats and curses failed to accelerate our floundering labors, they happily applied their ubiquitous wrist-quirts, which they seemed to wear around the clock.

Our laboring lungs ached for oxygen, which deep in the foul bilge was painfully unplentiful and so putrid it sickened you to breathe it in.

Laboring in lightless, airless holds and suffocating gloom, our bodies were starved for water and food, our lungs for air, and our eyes for light. And Lord knows our labors were necessary—if the ship were to stay afloat. Truly a ghost ship of the damned, that old tub was porous as a colander—top and bottom—and storms flooded the bilge so frighteningly that I often thought the ship was sinking.

The captain must have thought so, too. After a storm, the bilge drivers harried us like harpies from hell, work-ing themselves almost as hard as we did—except their exertions went into thundering curses into our ears and laying the lash across our naked bleeding backs.

Everything Arturo told us had come true. We were on a voyage of the dead. Within two days, rebellion was hopeless.

We were too sick, too starved, too exhausted.

That first day Luis had bragged to Arturo that he would survive this ordeal no matter how horrendous it was. More and more his boast sounded like pompous braggadocio. The question I secretly asked was more relevant to the reality of our Death Voyage.

Should we even try to survive?

Increasingly the ocean-wide looked like a wondrously enticing terminus—a pleasant swim, then an end to pain.

At what point would we choose that long swim over this death voyage to hell?

FORTY-THREE

I HAVE TO say this much for Luis—he was nothing if not resourceful.

If you had something he wanted, you underestimated him at your peril. Arturo's treacherous shipmate in particular. The bilge slave with the safest job, he worked dumping the buckets out a hole just above the waterline. He had the kind of job that might mean the difference between life and death on that hell-ship—he *never* should have turned his back on a man as resourceful as Luis.

One night during an especially violent storm—when we were forced to work a night shift on top of our day labors—Luis sneaked up behind him with a stolen belaying pin. Caving in his skull, Luis shoved the man through the hole where the bilge water was dumped.

When Emile asked where he'd disappeared to, Luis explained that the man had been despondent for some time—no doubt racked with guilt at having robbed the captain. In despair, he had apparently opted for the long swim.

Nor was the murder of Arturo's shipmate the only card Luis had to play. For weeks he had worked his wiles on the bilge master. Reading Emile's palms, he convinced him he could foretell his future. He promised him his predictions would bring him wine and women, health, and wealth. Soon Emile was eating out of Luis's hand.

Luis even inveigled extra rations out of the whip-swinging swine.

Luis brought me along as he moved up the food chain—literally. Ayyo—in truth I had helped shove the man through the hole.

Soon the two of us worked the hole together, dumping buckets of bilge into the sea. The work was hard, but at least we inhaled clean sea air and felt the ocean breeze in our faces.

Nor did the indomitable Luis despair.

"We're getting out of here, amigo. This job is better than working in the bilge, but we're still in peril. Just sleeping in that sweltering vermin-ridden disease-infested hold will kill us. Stay there, we will starve, sicken, and die.

"Nor is surviving this run to Manila a solution. Remember what Arturo told us about this voyage and the one back? The return passage from the Philippines to Acapulco is even worse. The world's longest sea voyage without landfall, we have to sail almost halfway around the world, crossing ten thousand miles of water without sight of land. That's if we don't end up as fever victims or crocodile food in the swamp at a jungle plantation.

"We need a way to get topside—and stay there. Think, Juan, think. We must think of something. There must be *something* we can do."

"A special skill," I said, "if we knew something, could do something of irreplaceable value so that we would be indispensable to their survival or their success."

Luis looked at me sadly—but not without kindness. He ruffled my hair with his palm, affectionately. "But then where would an ignorant indio such as yourself get such special indispensable skills."

"Indeed," I said, "where would I have acquired such extraordinary craft and knowledge?" I hadn't told Luis I was an expert gunsmith.

"Nowhere, which means I must conjure some trick from my infinite trick bag. Whom can I deceive? What preposterous tale can I contrive? How can I convince them we are everything they need?"

"Touch their hearts and advance their fortunes?"

"Well said, amigo. I can see, if nothing else, my mentoring has improved your discourse. Now help me invent a plan."

We returned to dumping the bilge in the sea.

FORTY-FOUR

LUIS DIDN'T KNOW it, but I was considering other possibilities. I'd taken a liking to the talkative Arturo and had plied him with questions about the ship—its officers and crew, the positions and functions, their hierarchy and organization.

Some ideas had begun to churn in my brain.

At bottom, I was as desperate as Luis to find topside sleeping quarters—even more so. I had a reason for wanting to return to New Spain.

Maria.

She was there, somewhere with Guerrero's army. I had to find her. She needed me, and, yes, I loved her.

Moreover, Luis and I were favorably placed on the ship.

The powder room was in a ship's hold above the bilge and not far from where we poured out the buckets. Luis and I could actually see into the powder room when the ship's cannon master entered or left his compartment.

Addressing a crew member—heaven forbid a master sailor—was a flogging offense, so speaking to him carried certain risks. I didn't see how I had much choice, however.

Luis and I desperately needed another berth.

One afternoon as he was entering the powder magazine with a waterskin, I approached him.

"Cannon master, I want you to know I am an expert gunsmith and an accomplished powder-maker. Luis here is an unmatched cannoneer."

"Really?" He motioned me into the powder compartment. As with my own powder shop, there was no metal anywhere—nothing that could strike a spark. Otherwise it was a sparse, Spartan facility—powder kegs, a work-bench, and a wood stool.

"So you say you know powder, indio?"

"Sí, señor."

"What kind of powder is this?" he asked, holding a small bag up to my face.

"I need to see the grains, Patrón."

He poured some in his hand so that I could examine it more closely.

"Tell me its purpose—cannon, musket, pistola, demolition. Is it pristine or degraded. Come on, Aztec bastardo. Tell me."

I was afraid to touch it—for an indio to even touch black powder was a crime. Still I believed I could discern that it was the sort of fine grade that was corned for pistolas.

"Look closely at it."

He lifted his palm up so I could see the grains.

"I believe it is—"

He flipped the black powder into my wide eyes. Grabbing me by the back of the head, he ground the granules in his palm into my burning orbs.

As I howled with pain and ripped his grinding, twisting hand away from my eyes, I accidentally knocked him down. In a towering rage, he got up and laid the weighted butt stock of the quirt against my head.

When I came to, he and his assistant were dragging me into a firing hole. Bending me over a cannon, he beat me brutally for—what he called—my "insubordination."

The assistant's parting words when I was dumped back in the bilge slaves' compartment were: "Never speak to us again."

Well, as bad as it was, at least he had not turned me over to the captain who would have lashed me to the mast and stripped my back with a flogging cat.

For two days Luis and I debated the relative benefits of killing the powder master and his assistant. Aside from the pleasure it would give me, I saw none. Luis showed no surprise when I explained I was a master gunsmith.

Ever smarter and more devious than me, Luis saw a benefit where I didn't.

"Killing him would leave the ship without trained powder and cannon handlers. El Capitán would have to use you, no? You could get me assigned as the cannon master."

"Killing him is not a good idea," I said, shaking my head. "We'd be the number-one suspects, and as Arturo said, we are utterly expendable. They would flog and feed us to the sharks as soon as look at us."

"So we just rot here till we die?"

"No, we find another plan—one with at least some dim possibility of success."

PART XI

I will have you keelhauled . . .

Capitán Zapata

AS THE DAYS went by, I secretly watched the cannon master and his assistant prepare the black powder with which to train the cannon crew. They didn't actually make the powder, as I had so often done. Instead, the powder master examined it for dampness, adulteration, the proper proportions of the ingredients, as well as the size and texture of the granules.

Ships were inhospitable places for powder storage, dampness and seawater being everywhere. Then there was the absolute life-and-death necessity for certifying that the powder was properly mixed. If the grains lacked the proper coarseness, the huge quantities of powder—which cannoneers routinely rammed into the muzzles of their big guns—could blast them out of their firing holes and into fiery death and watery graves.

Two things began to bother me about the cannon master. He was our ticket out of the bilge—and its certain death—but he was blocking our escape.

I also had not forgotten his grinding black powder into my eyes and the beating I got from him and his assistant.

My fevered brain had formed a plan, which might bail us out of the bilge, ensconce us permanently above-decks, and punish the cannon master for his unprovoked abusiveness.

When he left the powder magazine for his midday meal, he left behind the batches of cannon, musket, and pistol powder that he was preparing for the test at the end of the week. When he finished his work, I wanted to get my hands on it.

For that, however, I needed help—the ever-resourceful Luis.

When I laid out my plan, he clapped me soundly on the back.

"Amigo, I am pleased that my backbreaking tutelage was not wasted. You have indeed been an apt pupil. With each passing day, you remind me of myself—more and more. You are utterly without conscience, are you not? You cannot say you were born that way. My example has been your teacher, is that not so? To get us out of the bilge you would murder anyone aboard this ship, and you would do so without hesitation."

"If they tried to keep me down there."

"All that counts is your survival and success. You would murder the innocent *and* the guilty, the just *and* the unjust . . . if it got you out of the bilge and off this ship."

"I wouldn't describe it that way, but as God is my witness, I will get off this ship."

"Well spoken, my Aztec bastardo. Spoken like . . . like . . . why, like *me!*"

"But to get the cannon master and his assistant out of the way, I must get into the powder room. Can *you* get me in there while the cannon master is enjoying his midday meal?"

"I am the grandmaster of surreptitious entry. In all sincerity," Luis said with a sly smile, "I can penetrate any lock on this earth like a knife through butter."

"The padlocked door looks formidable."

"Leave it to me."

FORTY-SIX

I NEVER DOUBTED for one second that Luis would get us into the powder magazine.

Which he did with stunning skill, no doubt sharpened by much practice picking locks.

After that it was up to me to heighten the power of the black powder used for cannons.

I found a keg of excellent fine-grain pistol powder—the only keg they had since everything else was degraded. Pouring the cannon powder that had already been prepared by the cannon master into an empty keg, I dumped most of the pistol powder into the cannon-powder container, coating the top with a thin layer of cannon powder.

Being of a finer grain, the pistol powder would burn at a faster, hotter rate. In *small* quantities such an accelerated burn rate is perfect for propelling a pistol ball. In *large* quantities such fine powder would increase the cannon's explosive potential.

I doubted the cannoneer would be in jeopardy. A cannon can absorb an enormous explosion and even split without killing the cannoneer. Or at least not quite killing him.

The blast could disable the cannon though.

Still, I was not going to err on the side of moderation in doctoring the cannon powder. Luis and I had only one chance to get off the bilge gang and out of their sweltering, stifling, disease-choked sleeping quarters. I wasn't going to skimp.

My hope was that if the cannon misfired, the cannon master and his assistant would be blamed and Luis and I would win spots working in the powder magazine and at one of the firing holes. Why wouldn't the captain want us there? We would be the only two men on the ship who knew both cannoneering and powder-making.

Maybe Luis was right. Maybe I was secretly as cynical about life and death as he was. As the hours before the test crawled by, I felt that way: I no longer cared whether those testing the powder lived or died.

All that mattered was *me*.

And my friend, Luis.

FORTY-SEVEN

THE CANNON TEST was scheduled for midafternoon. During the previous three hours I had prayed perhaps for the first time since I was a child and knelt with other parishioners in Fray Diego's village chapel.

I prayed very simply that the scheme would work.

During the last few minutes my prayers became more frantic. I was praying to the most exalted and honored god of my Aztec ancestors—our Aztec Savior, Quetzalcoatl— for divine deliverance from this mortal hell.

I did not even consider beseeching Christ Jesus, the peace-loving Christian savior. I had no doubt that Christ Jesus—who preached turning the other cheek and that peacemakers were divinely blessed—would have despised my deviously violent scheme.

Instead, my Aztec blood rose to the fore, and I beseeched Quetzalcoatl on hands and knees to deliver me from the wrath of the Spanish curs . . . at the very least make the powder strong enough to disable the cannon and disgrace the ship's experts.

At which point Luis interrupted my implorations with a look of fear on his face.

And he was afraid of nothing.

Luis had peeked around the corner and spotted the powder master and the cannon master enter a firing hole.

"I just saw them enter the firing hole. Do you realize which cannon they're testing?"

"No."

He pointed to our forward bulkhead. "It's that big son

of a whore next door. It holds twice the load of the other guns."

I was about to beseech to Quetzalcoatl to cancel my last request when Luis and I heard the cannon master count down the testing of the big gun.

"Three!"

"We have to get out of here," I whispered urgently.

"Never," he whispered his response. "Flight is evidence of guilt. If anyone sees us flee and this thing blows, the captain will spread us out on the mast, strip our backs, feed us our cojones and the sharks the rest."

"Two!"

We both put our hands to our ears and squatted down in the corner, our faces between our legs, empty bilge buckets over our heads.

"One!"

A roar detonated in our eardrums like the crack of doom. That thunder-crack lifted us up and banged us around that tiny compartment like we were rocks in an empty wine bottle shaken by an angry drunk.

Blinded, we were both coughing up stinking, choking, whitish powder smoke. My ears throbbed, my vision spun, my head rang like a mission bell. Every bone in my body felt broken. I choked so convulsively I couldn't get my breath.

Slowly the dense smoke-fog cleared. A huge jagged hole—where the forward bulkhead used to stand—gaped at us. Inside, a massive cannon had peeled like a banana at both ends, most of its breech blown to pieces. Both ends fumed furiously as if it were packed with all the fires of hell instead of our accelerated explosive.

Instead of a firing slit, a huge aperture framed by charred, flaming, broken planks peered out over a blue breaking sea and a cloudless turquoise sky.

Whatever was left of the men manning the cannon was blasted all over the firing hole where we were standing.

The explosion had thrown the cannon master's bloody torso into Luis, knocking him backward into the rear bulkhead. Undismayed, Luis ignored his bleeding right jaw. Instantly on his knees, he bent over the man's remains and rapidly rifled his pockets and belt purse, swiftly purloining several gold coins.

Dropping his pants, he quickly and dexterously inserted them in his rear end.

For safekeeping.

Luis had clearly done this sort of thing before.

He leaned against what was left of our rear bulkhead. I joined him.

"I think the ship's carpenter is going to have his work cut out for him," Luis said amiably. "What do you think?"

"The captain will be short two specialists. It could present an opportunity for two men with experience."

FORTY-EIGHT

We HAD TO get word to the captain that we were skilled powder and cannon experts. He would not need to be convinced that he needed the help of men who worked with munitions. When the ship reached the pirate-infested waters of the Philippines and the Cathay region, it would be an easy kill for marauders if its powder wasn't dry and its cannons ready to fire.

As bilge slaves, that was about as easy as a sewer worker chatting with the king. And more risky, though the beatings passed out had been greatly reduced now that we were weeks at sea and most of the bilge muckers would die under a beating. Arturo told us that bilge master Emile and his assistant would have to take their turn, along with other crew members, when so many of us had died off we could not keep the ship afloat.

We'd have to bribe Emile with gold before he'd convey the message to the captain. We decided against using the money Luis had pilfered from the powder master.

"He'll know we stole it from someone," I pointed out. "We were alone with the powder master and the cannon master. He'll steal the money or turn us in."

Luis had once paid a Toledo barber to pack a large molar on the left side of his mouth with gold after the man had chipped out much of the decayed tooth. "He cut off the leg of a man with a saw before he got to my mouth with his chisel and hammer," Luis said, describing the surgical and dental work barbers performed to supplement their income.

In extreme conditions, he would never be broke—he could rip out his solid-gold tooth.

"Amigo," Luis said to me that night, "things will never get more extreme than they are now."

"Are you sure we have to bribe Emile? He will be doing the ship a favor."

"You know better than I. No one does anything for anyone on this ship—not for free—Emile most of all."

He was right. Also, I knew Emile would not do anything for a slave that would put him at risk. Even conveying information to the captain could result in a good beating.

Still, I saw another possibility.

"We could promise to extract your excruciatingly painful tooth from your lividly swollen jaw for Emile if he carried the message. But only after we meet with the captain. He'll believe us. That side of your face is swollen from this afternoon's explosion. After we see the captain and have been elevated to real crew members, we can tell Emile it wasn't the tooth at all but the explosion. In other words, we lie to him. Who is he anyway? A bad hombre who bloodies our backs."

Luis peered into my eyes searchingly.

"Young friend, my mentoring skills are indeed paying off."

"Luis has a toothache," I explained to the bilge master that night, letting him know that most of the tooth was solid gold. I first told him that Luis and I were experts at powder and cannons. He was inclined to believe me because he already knew that I had gotten a beating from the cannon master for making that claim.

"The explosion proves what a bad state the ship's armaments are in. If you were able to provide the captain with experts on powder and cannon . . ." I grinned and shrugged. He was a stupid man in most ways, but had animal cunning.

"Were you to get me a pair of pliers or a small knife and carry a message to the captain about our skills, I will extract Luis's tooth, which then shall be yours. Just look at his jaw."

Luis clutched his swollen jaw and groaned miserably.

I stared intently into Emile's cruel but craven eyes. I could read fear and indecision on Emile's cowardly face. And greed. No doubt the notion of simply ripping out the tooth and not doing us a favor was tempting. But the resulting infection would not only cost the ship another bilge slave, but word would get out that he did it for a gold tooth.

He could get a severe beating for even approaching the captain with a request from bilge slaves. But rumors about Luis being a nobleman who fell from grace because of a woman scorned—spread by himself, of course—gave him stature as a macho hombre, adding credibility to his claim of being an expert at the implements of warfare.

"Give me the tooth," Emile said.

"We pull this tooth *only* after we see El Capitán." Luis howled like an animal in pain . . . a wolf gone mad with bestial suffering.

Emile insisted that he see Luis's gold tooth.

"An ounce of solid Aztec gold," Luis said, exaggerating the size more than twice. Still groaning and massaging his swollen jaw, he opened his mouth wide and let Emile have a quick peek. "Worth more than you will make in your doomed and desperate life. I swear on the graves of my martyred mother and sainted, belated, and much beloved father that it is gold of the highest purity."

Luis's mother was a puta-swindler and his father . . . nobody knew who his padre was, but Luis was the first to admit that he probably ended his days on a gibbet.

"You two really know guns and powder?" Emile asked.

We gave the poor benighted wretch our widest, brightest, most reassuring smiles.

Luis's grin almost reached his eyes.

The bilge rat insisted on one more look at that treasure trove of Aztec gold in Luis's mouth . . . before he finally agreed.

FORTY-NINE

EMILE'S WORD WAS good as his greed.

When we told Arturo about our plan, he smiled.

"The idiot, Emile, will understand none of this but the captain will from necessity speak to you, even greet you two with open arms if you convince him of your talents," Arturo said. "What Emile does not appreciate—so blinded is he by fear and greed—is that the captain needs you two like he needs air to breathe. We will soon be entering Pirate Alley, where the Southeast Asian pirates hunt merchant ships as if they were rabbits to rip open and gut."

"Through his incompetence, the cannon master has left us defenseless," Luis said. "All the powder in the ship's magazine is now in question. The cannon master has to constantly dry, refine, and remix it just to keep it potent. Cannoneers won't fire it until an expert examines it and determines it's safe."

Emile got the message to Capitán Zapata.

Arturo's prediction was right—the captain sent for us.

We stank so badly he met us upwind on the foredeck. He hardly looked at us once throughout the interrogation. His tone was insultingly insolent.

He knew powder and ordnance, however, and cross-examined us thoroughly on both subjects. He hammered me not only about powder composition but about the texture of the granules, on corning techniques, and on which grades of powder were best for various calibers of cannons.

He seemed even more skeptical of—and more offended

by—Luis than he was of me, the indio. Obviously, he expected indios, whom he thought were little better than savages, to end up as bilge slaves. That a Spaniard with a
reputation for dabbling in black magic and being a cardsharp ended up in this hell of hells meant to the captain
that Luis was intrinsically devious, no doubt dangerous—
and a traitor to his own kind.

Not half-bad assumptions.

Still, he had no other options. The savage and the cardsharp were his only hope.

Capitán Zapata finally said, "If either of you have lied to
me about your skills, I will have you keelhauled until your
flesh has ground off your bones." He sighed. "Tell me what
you need to get started."

We needed help, especially Luis with the cannons. But
he knew better than to personally suggest Arturo. The captain despised Luis with such special vehemence he might
reject him out of contempt for Luis alone. But we had to
say something. Arturo had helped us and he faced certain
death in the bilge.

"The bilge has another man who knows armaments," I
said. "A seaman named Arturo. He was once an artillery
sergeant in the army. We need him to help us with the cannons."

I didn't add that like Luis, Arturo had an unpleasant
mishap with Spain's army that had persuaded him to
change his vocation, geography, and identity.

He actually looked at me. For the first time. Directly. In
the eye. Without blinking. His eyes were red and I could
see his skin was sagging. He looked sick, even feverish. I
suspected he had lost a lot of weight.

He'd been sick.

"We want the seaman Arturo, Capitán Zapata," I said.

"I don't trust him."

I met his arrogant stare. "We need him. You have punished him for wrongdoing. He will work harder for you
now. And with complete loyalty. He won't want to return
to the bilge."

He continued to stare at me, unblinking. "The three of
you will have to be replaced in the bilge."

Giving Luis a withering glance of searing scorn, the
captain turned on his heels and headed for his cabin,
probably praying the wind and stink would not change
direction.

"One more thing, Capitán," I said softly.

He spun around, his face a mask of barely suppressed
fury. For a moment I thought I'd gone too far.

"What?"

"In order to mix powder we need clean skin and clean,
dry clothes. Ideally, of white cloth. We don't want to con-
taminate the powder or get it on our clothing. It could
cause a fire."

He stared at me again, appraisingly—then looked
away. "Very well. The first officer will arrange for it. And
anything else you need to get the cannons ready."

He glanced around to make sure he wasn't being overheard and spoke discreetly low. "I've suspected for some
time that the previous powder and cannon masters were
buying inferior powder and cannonry, billing us for top
grade, and pocketing the difference. As soon as the new
materials arrived they jumped ship and disappeared. The
scum that got blown up were their inept replacements. I'm
especially concerned about our cannonry." He shook his
head with disgust. "I've also been out ill for six weeks and
can still barely get out of bed. I foolishly relied on others."

He stared at us again, no doubt wondering if permit-
ting bilge slaves to take over command of the ship's armaments was a nightmare conjured up in hell during a fit
of fever.

For a moment his eyes grew wild, as if he were staring at demons, and his hand went to the hilt of his sword.

I froze, wondering if he was going to hack us to death. Then he spun around and rushed for his cabin.

PART XII
THE CHIMNEYS OF HELL

THE FIRST MATE, Ortega de Gasset, was a hulking bear of a man with a full beard, a chest like a wine barrel, a nose like a barnacle, and a surprisingly dark complexion for a Spaniard. The galleon's crew was largely self-equipped, favoring for the most part cotton trousers, rope belts, and rope sandals. The mates wore white shirts and trousers with black horizontal stripes, narrow-brimmed straw hats with chin cords, and quirts with lead-weighted rawhide butt stocks looped to their wrists.

Ortega showed us to the quarters of the late cannon master and his departed assistant. Cramped, it had room for two hammocks and two sea chests. We inherited whatever meager possessions they had, including clothes. He had a sailor bring us a large bucket with a long rope knotted to the handle.

"For washing. Tie it off on the rail before you throw it in for seawater," Ortega said. "Lose it, and we'll throw you in after it."

I had no reason to doubt they would.

He gave us a bar of lye soap, a stiff bristle brush with a wood handle, and some clean rags to wash and dry with. Also a large deep pan packed with salt beef, tortillas, cooked beans, a bucket of drinking water, and a lime to share for preventing the dreaded scourge, scurvy.

We ignored the bathing gear. Attacking the food and water, we devoured and drank everything in one sitting. We never even looked up at each other. I'm not sure I took a breath.

We finally got around to filling the roped bucket, after

which we bathed one at a time. The nonbather hauled in more buckets of seawater. We needed six bucketfuls each, half a bar of lye soap, and ample scrubbing to get the bilge stink out of our skin and hair.

Well before we were finished, our raw reddened bodies burned from lye, scrubbing, and the brine.

As powder and cannon masters, we wore the same striped clothes and narrow-brimmed straw hats as the mates—for which I was glad, otherwise some officer on deck would have mistaken me for the bilge slave I used to be and break a belaying pin over my head.

The dead men's clothes fit tolerably, and just as we were dressing, First Mate Gasset came to pick us up for a tour of the cannonry and powder storage facilities. He told us Arturo was being released to join us later.

Luis spent an inordinate amount of time examining the weapons, even climbing on top of the barrels to better peer inside their muzzles.

He said nothing but did not seem pleased.

Nor was I reassured by the condition of the powder kegs, stored in several different sites.

I followed Luis's example and ignored the first mate's questions.

"Please tell the captain," Luis said, "we would like to speak with him in private at his earliest convenience."

"We now need some time to prepare notes," I said.

First Mate Gasset stared at us a long minute, disappointed we were not sharing any information with him.

"Muy bien," he finally said—and left our cramped cabin.

Luis and I stared at each other in silence. For a long time. Finally Luis spoke: "What did you see?"

"El Capitán was unfortunately right—dead right. The only decent batch of powder this ship had was the test batch. After they finished the test, they were finished. The rest of the store is powder for blowing up stumps—if that. A lot of it was spoiled by water on other voyages, then acquired for this ship at a reduced price. The cannonry?"

"Someone replaced whatever cannons they previously had with rusted-out, broken-down junk, probably while the captain was ashore," Luis said. "In fact, a defective cannon might have been more of the reason for the explosion that sent the cannon master to Hades than the tampered powder."

"What's the worst cannon problem?" I asked.

"Cracks. Some of the breeches and barrels have hairline cracks which have been blacked over to make them less visible."

"So we're entering Pirate Alley defenseless?" I asked.

"Even if the cannons worked, you say the powder is only good for demolition work at best."

"What should we do?"

"Tell the captain but otherwise keep it to ourselves," Luis said. "He won't want the word to get out." He rolled his eyes to the heavens. "We will probably end up as shark bait before this voyage is done. Even if we make it, the ship can't return without being refitted with cannon and powder at great cost. When that happens, the Manila viceroy will have the captain's hide.

"But, of course, he will avoid that punishment if the ship is attacked by pirates. Unable to defend ourselves, all of us will be killed."

"We have to assume we'll be attacked," I argued. "Arturo says it's standard procedure for pirates to test the mettle of all ships, backing off only when they see the ship's powder is dry and the cannoneer's aim is good. But we can *hope* they don't attack."

"Hope is for old women and small children. We need a strategy," Luis said.

He stroked the stubble on his chin. "There's no way

you can reconstitute the powder we have so it is munitions quality?"

I had already answered that question twice. "No."

"Perhaps once again we need the hand to be faster than the eye."

"Luis, this isn't about swindling rich widows out of their jewelry, it's about surviving in this hell ship, about fighting murderous pirates with gunpowder so weak, it goes 'poof' and sends cannonballs six feet—the length of our coffins. We are on our way to hell—"

"*Chimneys of Hell*," Luis said.

"Chimneys of hell? What is that? A shortcut to hell?"

"A weapon that would blow the cojones off the toughest pirates."

Just then First Mate Gasset hammered on our door. "Capitán Zapata wants to see you *now*. He's not pleased. When he's not pleased, it does not pay to keep him waiting."

FIFTY-ONE

Luis AND I entered the captain's compartment. First Mate Gasset shut the door and stood behind us. Capitán Zapata was seated at his desk working on the ship's log.

I was sure we'd scrubbed away all our bilge odor and dirt. Still, Capitán Zapata, looking up at us, sniffed, snorted, and glared at us as balefully as if we reeked of burning brimstone.

First Mate Gasset shouted, "Atención!" Snapping to attention, he pulled himself up ramrod-straight. His arms riveted to his sides, he stared fixedly at some invisible object immediately above the captain's head. Luis did the same.

Ayyo . . . Luis and I were no longer bilge slaves. A split second after Gasset and Luis snapped to attention, I aped their example.

Unlike those two, I had no military training, but I also had ample reason to avoid the wrath of the captain. He was far too quick to lash men to the mast, strip off their shirts—then their backs.

He finally looked up from his log. Glaring at us with supreme disdain, his forehead again wrinkled in disgust.

"You examined the powder and cannonry?" he asked, pen still in hand, glancing down at his open leather-bound log.

"Sí, Capitán," Luis said.

"And . . . ?"

"Request permission to speak to the captain alone," I said.

First Mate Gasset bristled, clearly irritated at our

presumption. Capitán Zapata stared at us also irritated . . . but reluctantly curious.

He put down his pen.

"This better be good," he said.

"We understand, sir," Luis said.

At least, however, we had his attention.

"Very well," he said. "First Mate Gasset, you can leave now."

First Mate Gasset saluted, spun angrily on his right heel, and left the cabin.

But he shut the door with care, quietly.

"Well, what is so bad about our defenses that we require utter privacy?"

I glanced at Luis out of the corner of my eye.

"Don't just stand there like statues. Spit it out."

"Señor Capitán," I said, unsure as to how to address him, "how many new crew members did you take on in port?"

"Virtually all the officers. The ship was in dry dock, up on a gridiron for much-needed repairs. I caught something in Manila on the last run and was in my sickbed—down with the contagion." He looked away. "The doctor thought it might kill me."

"I don't know what the cannon master ordered," I said, "but ninety percent of the powder is junk—barely fit for blowing up tree stumps. If you use it to propel cannon shot, you won't get power or accuracy."

"Why did the last cannon explode?"

"Defective ordnance." I was only partially dishonest. As potent as the powder had been, it would not have blown up a well-built cannon.

"The rest of the ordnance?" Capitán Zapata asked Luis.

"Most are as bad as the one that exploded. I could perhaps squeeze three or four worthy of firing light rounds, but we don't have the gunpowder even for those."

"He is saying," I piped in, "that we will enter Pirate Alley unarmed . . . defenseless."

"Dios mío! I am doomed. How could this have happened?"

Luis said, "If the boat was in dry dock and if you were off the vessel—sick and unable to supervise delivery and installation—someone could have replaced your functional cannons with dysfunctional junk. I doubt you took those cracked rusted-out wrecks on your previous voyages."

"I've been too sick to inspect *anything*. The first mate. He was in charge of the ship. I'll have him—"

Luis held up his hand to stop him. "Pardon, Capitán, but you don't want this information to leave this room. If you punish the first mate, we will not only lose a needed fighting man, but his screams will let everyone on board know that there is a serious problem. We have to keep the information from the crew."

"Do not say a word to *anyone*," Capitán Zapata said.

"Sí, Capitán," Luis said. "That's why we asked for privacy."

The captain stood up. "The irony is I'm getting my sea legs back. I'm actually well enough to go out on deck an hour or two a day. If there was anything that could be done to fix the cannons—"

"There isn't," Luis said.

"Without firepower we're doomed. When we reach the Manila coast and straits, the place they call Pirate Alley, marauders will harass us. If we don't drive them back with multiple rounds, they'll swarm us like vultures. We'll never survive that gauntlet."

"Capitán," Luis said, "with your permission I do have one or two ideas. But we would need to take a small detour—to the port of Hong Kong. I know the port well, and know a way to arm this vessel."

The captain stared at Luis, his mouth gaped, as if he had slammed him in the face and called his mother a puta. He appeared even more stunned than when we told him his ship was disarmed.

"Are you loco in the cabeza? Hong Kong is a pirate's haven. It's over six hundred sea miles from Manila. You're suggesting we go there and buy new cannons and gunpowder? That's impossible. Pirates don't sell cannons, they use them to get booty."

"I'm not talking cannonry, not even explosives."

"What then?" Capitán Zapata stared at Luis, incredulous. "What could possibly serve as a substitute for cannon and shot?"

"Something far more lethal," Luis said.

"What is more frightening than cannon shot?"

"The Chimneys of Hell," Luis said.

FIFTY-TWO

WHILE HE STARED at Luis as if my amigo were a madman, the captain looked as if he was getting feverish again.

"Explain yourself," he said. He spoke calmly but his eyes told me he was thinking about having us keelhauled.

"I am sure you know about the weapons called fireships," Luis said.

"Of course. They are Trojan horses filled with fire. Fire has always been the most frightening weapon in any navy's arsenal. A couple of thousand years ago the Greeks invented a combustible we call Greek Fire. They hurtled it in pots, shot it out of tubes, and even rammed flaming boats into enemy ships."

Luis nodded, happy the captain knew about the weapon. "The ancient Chinese commanders crammed ships with combustibles—dry reeds, wood shavings, brush, fatty oil. Locking them to the enemy vessels with hooks and ropes, they set them ablaze, incinerating both ships. The Crusaders employed them, too."

"The English pirate, Francis Drake," the captain said meditatively, "used them against our Armada in 1588. When our ships were anchored off Calais in the Channel, the English sent blazing boats into our Armada's midst, scattering our intrepid navy like a flock of foolish pigeons.

"Let no one forget," the captain said, stroking his chin, deep in thought, "our fireships saved the day at the Battle of Lepanto in 1571. In combination with Venice and the Vatican, we beat the Turks at sea for the first time in history. There were more than two hundred oar-driven galleys on each side, and our fireboats struck terror in their hearts like hellfire itself."

"I myself commanded a fireboat in the Battle of Trafalgar," Luis said.

"Not that you did us much good," Capitán Zapata jeered. "Those British bastardos beat us *and* the French without losing a ship."

"I also commanded a hell-burner against the Bey of Algiers," Luis added.

I wondered how many of Luis's heroic naval exploits were true. I could see from the captain's face he was wondering the same thing.

"The Acapulco authorities advised me of your considerable *criminal* record," the captain said, "forewarning me of your treacherous and deceitful lifestyle. For years both the colony's constabulary and the Inquisition have been after you for your innumerable crimes against Church, Crown, and the stainless honor of Spanish womanhood. If memory serves, the charges against you included the seduction and swindling of wealthy widows, the reading of their fortunes with devil cards—again to divest them of both dinero *and* virtue—and of course for assorted charges of murder-most-foul. After you were so exposed you fled from military service . . ."

"None of that was proven," Luis said, brazening out the embarrassing exposure. "Moreover, none of my alleged misdeeds belies the efficacy of fireships—or their relevance to our plight. Sailors today all ply ships with billowing sails, tar-caulked seams, ropes rubbed down with fat, and holds bursting with black powder . . . pirate vessels included. There's almost *nothing* a ship has these days that isn't burnable, that won't burst into flames if exposed to fire."

Luis leaned closer to the captain. "If fireships can't

get us through Pirate Alley, nothing will. No sight in all of naval warfare strikes more fear in an enemy's heart than a fireship hooked to its side, bursting into flames."

"What alternative do we have?" I said.

"None," Capitán Zapata said, drumming on his desk with his fingertips, impatient with the long-winded Luis. "And most assuredly, the fireship is an awesome sight. Unfortunately, for us, we have no such weapon. Unless, of course, you wish to grapple our own galleon to the enemy, set it aflame, and burn all of us alive."

Capitán Zapata stared at Luis a long hard minute. For a moment I feared he would have both of us spread-eagled on the mast and flogged to the bone. He'd ordered it done to men for less. Instead he shrugged and said, "You're right about one thing: We need a defense against those Manila pirates. What would you use for fireships?"

"Dhows."

Capitán. Zapata studied Luis quizzically. "Have you ever sailed into Hong Kong Bay?" he asked with narrowed eyes.

"On three different voyages, Capitán."

Luis had not told me about that period of his disgracefully depraved life.

"What did you do there?" Capitán Zapata asked.

"Each time our captain made a side trip on his way to Manila, he brought back three chests of opium. It is ten times as valuable as gold in Europe."

"Why?" I asked. I'd never heard of opium.

"It's the greatest pain-slayer in history," the captain said. "When wealthy men and women are in agony—for whatever reason—they will pay a fortune for it. I would have traded my right arm for some during my illness."

"They will pay *anything* the seller asks," Luis said. "If the pain is severe enough, they have no choice."

"I'm sure you benefited as well," the captain said.

"Each time my captain rewarded me with . . . nada. I have hoped and prayed throughout this voyage that I might find cause to visit that fabled city again and acquire for my new and revered captain the same magical powder that he too might grow rich and prosper. I even have prayed that such a captain might be so grateful for my fealty and the mucho dinero which I brought to him that he would bequeath me a minute fraction of his unexpected riches."

"What kind of minute fraction?" the captain asked.

"A paltry forty percent?"

"Or a generous five."

"A pathetic thirty?"

"You get ten percent. Argue any more and you get nothing but pain."

"Muchas gracias. Most generous, Capitán."

Most generous because Luis and I both knew he'd never see any percentage—negotiating with Luis for the captain was a temporary expediency that hanging Luis from the yardarm later would remediate.

The captain pursed his lips. "Most Oriental harbors like Hong Kong are pirate coves, animals to whom our ship will be raw meat."

"Hong Kong has pirates, but the Harbor Lord's revenues rely on repeat business from reliable traders such as myself. He prohibits the plundering of any merchant vessels approaching Hong Kong and forbids attacking any ships leaving Hong Kong which have done business with him. They sail under Hung Pao's protection. Unless you cross him."

"Hung Pao, the Harbor Lord, regards you as a reliable businessman?" The captain's voice conveyed his doubts.

"Sí, Capitán. Hung Pao will give us a red flag with which to deter Chinese pirates all the way to the Manila Straits."

"But will the Manila Marauders honor it?" I asked.

"In a word, no."

"Are you sure you know opium?" the captain asked. "Why wouldn't Hung Pao foist inferior powder on us?"

"As I said, he depends on repeat business, and he only sells opium for silver. Such business is hard to come by. But, sí, for a certainty, I know it."

"I thought the Chinese emperor banned opium sales," Capitán Zapata said.

"Only when it's sold to Chinese for consumption. When Hung Pao sells it to foreign devils for silver, he gives the emperor his cut, and All Under Heaven looks the other way."

Luis paused and grinned at the captain. "I trust you have no scruples in growing rich off a product people cannot do without?"

"I have a ship to save. Besides, as you well know, money speaks the universal tongue, Cannon Master," the captain said. His ice-cold voice and eyes made me shudder. "It is the true lingua franca, not Latin or French."

Suddenly the captain smiled.

His smile—rather than reassuring—was . . . frightening.

I glanced at Luis out of the corner of my eye, and his wolfish leer mirrored Capitán Zapata's . . . *exactly*.

When money was involved, they were brothers in blood.

I felt as if someone had stepped on my *grave*.

FIFTY-THREE

AFTER DINNER THAT night, Capitán Zapata asked us to his cabin, uncorked a bottle of fine Madeira brandy, set out three cups—and opened up his map.

My impression was that he was still trying to convince himself that the mad plan proposed by Luis was his best course.

Locating Hong Kong Island, he sat down and charted the most wind-efficient westerly course.

"We can be there in two weeks. How long do you think it will take you to purchase fireships and teach a skeleton crew to steer and sail this armada of Hong Kong dhows and turn them into Chimneys of Hell?"

"A few days," Luis said. "Dhows are amazingly simple to steer."

"Armament?"

"Juan and I have worked that out. It will be simple—but lethal."

Ayyo . . . we had worked out nothing.

"And you will have no problems acquiring the opium?" Capitán Zapata asked, his eyes skeptical.

"Old Hung and I go way back. He likes me, because I always bring him silver and give no trouble. Hell, I'd like me too if I were him. All that silver? What's not to love?"

Eh . . . I wondered if Luis even knew the man. Could his many trips to Hong Kong be nothing but lies and bravado?

"This is a very complicated way to sail to Manila," Capitán Zapata said with a weary sigh.

"As we stand now, we would never survive Manila's straits and coastlines unarmed—never," Luis pointed out.

The captain shook his head. "I can't seem to trust anyone else on board. Why not an indio savage and a picaro condemned to the bilge gang?"

That night we changed course for the Hong Kong Island.

FIFTY-FOUR

SINCE LUIS AND I were living on deck, I quickly got to know who was on board—crew *and* passengers. I became especially concerned about a mystery man, whose identity was a complete secret. He received special privileges and had no particular duties. Invariably dressed in black, the crew called him "the black ghost."

What concerned me was the way he followed me with his eyes. Like a vulture staring at a dying animal.

His identity was supposed to be a secret, but Luis quickly learned he was a *familiar*, a lay representative of the Inquisition traveling to Manila. Unfortunately for us, our sudden ascent from bilge slaves to crewmen attracted his attention and curiosity.

Even worse, the captain's cabin boy told me that the Inquisitor had ordered the captain to turn me over to him for questioning and that this hound of hell had his "interrogation instruments" with him, and he intended to give me "a thorough examination that may lead to an auto-da-fé."

Ayyo . . . an auto-da-fé was the burning of a sinner at the stake.

He was especially curious how I had learned to work with black powder. And the rumors that Luis told fortunes with devil cards.

The cabin boy warned me that the captain had succeeded in stalling him until we reached Manila because he needed Luis and me until then.

Despite the undeniable logic of the captain's reasoning, the Inquisitor was incensed.

He wanted me on his rack and in his thumbscrews with Luis waiting in the wings for his examination.

When I expressed my concerns to Luis, he seemed unconcerned.

"Amigo, you consider that a problem? You should have been with me on my fireship at Trafalgar, facing down the English Admiral Nelson, or the time I went mano a mano with the Bey of Algiers. Now that was *danger*. This little matter is nothing two men of the world can't make go away like motes of dust in a tempestuous typhoon. Is that not so?"

I could only stare at him, my face a mask of doubt.

He grinned and whispered, "Besides, I have a feeling that long before we reach Manila, the Inquisitor will have to test his ability to swim among sharks." He raised his eyebrows. "An unfortunate accident at sea, no? Man overboard. Hit his head on the side of the boat on the way down so he can't shout for help? Is that not the way of the treacherous ocean we cross?"

Luis had an answer for everything.

I was caught by surprise to be called along with Luis into the captain's quarters that very night.

We were told that the Inquisitor was "lost" at sea.

"What do you two know about this tragedy?"

Of course, I didn't have to lie. I knew nothing. And Luis lied so well . . .

Later, when I asked Luis what he knew about the holy man's mishap, he raised his eyebrows and made the sign of the cross.

"You don't think I would deliberately harm a man of the cloth, do you?"

Of course I did. Besides, a familiar wasn't a priest.

Luis shook his head. "I suppose he fell over the rail

while taking his nocturnal constitutional. All of which only goes to prove my theory that late-night exercise after a full dinner is bad for one's health."

"He *fell* overboard?" I asked skeptically.

"For a certainty. He will be missed and mourned by all."

In truth, no one seemed to care—or know much. If a Holy Brother of the Inquisition could tumble over the side, anyone could.

Increasingly, I viewed Luis as a good man to have in my corner.

Especially since my corner had become such an increasingly violent and precarious place.

PART XIII
HONG KONG

FIFTY-FIVE

HONG KONG.

Near the mouth of South China's Pearl River Delta, the island is thirty square miles of stony earth and raw, barren, infertile rock. Planted directly in the path of the Pacific's most violent storms, Hong Kong is bordered east and west by hazardous reefs. Bounded by the South China mainland, Hong Kong Island itself, and its adjacent islets, its vast volcanic harbor is a highly hospitable refuge from those tempests. Its volcanic hills and scarps of black basalt rise high above the sea—often a half mile high or more.

Hong Kong. Words meaning Fragrant Harbor because of the woods and incense traded at the main bay.

A sanctuary for pirates, slave traders, and opium smugglers, it is home to some of the most cunningly devious and brutally bloody men on earth. Nonetheless; pillaging ships en route to the port or leaving it under its flag of protection is strictly forbidden.

Those who violate these sanctions the Harbor Lord ruthlessly disciplines.

The closer we approached Hong Kong Island, the more reluctant the captain became to enter the pirate domain and acquire his dhow hell-burners and his treasure trove of opium. As we sailed into the big, black, volcanically enclosed cove, Luis continued to press his argument with the captain on why he thought our plan would work.

"As long as we carry ourselves with insufferable arrogance and convince these people we are strong, we will prevail. We appear to be a heavily armed warship with more guns than any pirate vessel afloat. We have no reason to fear anyone. *That* is what our arrogance must convey.

"Furthermore, as long as we are in Hong Kong Harbor, we have nothing to fear. We are safe as if we were in our mother's womb. In the cove and in its surrounding sea lanes the Harbor Lord strictly enforces his prohibitions against violence and plundering of trading vessels. The Chinese never allow a brigand's bloodlust to supersede their greed."

"How civilized," Capitán Zapata muttered under his breath.

"That's inside Hong Kong Bay. If we show fear, Hong Kong's pirates will follow us out of the bay. When we reach the waters of the Philippines, we will be fair game.

"We cannot show weakness or fear in our dealings with these people," Luis said. "All they understand is arrogance and strength."

As we sailed deeper into the harbor, I marveled at the hundreds of double-mast dhows swarming in the sprawling bay. I found the small boats with graceful lines and their distinctive triangular-shaped "lateen sails" things of beauty.

If we wanted to acquire a cheap craft to turn into a fireboat, Hong Kong Bay was the place to shop.

All the colonial powers fiercely forbade the sale of cannonry in the Far East—for fear of inadvertently arming colonial insurgents. And, as Luis had pointed out, the cannons that were available were being put to good use by pirates. With no cannonry available for sale, I told Luis he better be right about being able to acquire a fireboat.

After anchoring in a bay, the captain ordered Luis and me to take a dinghy ashore and conduct the business at hand.

"How will you find your opium trafficker?" he asked Luis.

"Hung Pao's men will be there at the jetty before we set foot on it. His spy dhows have already sped ahead of us and informed him that a large vessel was headed for the bay. If you use your spyglass to examine some of the dhows that seemed to be floating listlessly, I'm sure you'll find they're full of Hung's cutthroats."

"We will need a cover story for the viceroy's customs officers when they examine our cargo in Manila. Otherwise, he'll simply seize the opium for his own account, then jail us."

"Your bill of lading will read tea, spices, and silk cloth. Hung will give you a special price that will be many times cheaper than in Manila. The goods cost him next to nothing. He'll make his profit on the opium. One chest of silver will cover it. They don't see much silver bullion around here. Hung will also plan on us for repeat business.

"If you still can't balance the ship's books, we'll buy some worthless silk and putrid spices for next to nothing and soak them in brine. We'll tell your employers some of the goods got swamped in a storm. That happens all the time."

The captain went over our mission with Luis again, instructing him to only purchase one dhow. "Trying to cross over to the Philippines with more than one of the native crafts would be infinitely difficult. Our sailors aren't familiar with the boats; we won't have a chance to repair them if they prove unseaworthy. We will tow the dhow behind with just a skeleton crew aboard."

I didn't need to be told who the skeleton crew would be. Luis and I would be assigned to the dhow. We would be the ones selected to use it as a fireboat, anyway.

They discussed the type of materials to be stuffed into

the dhow that would prove the quickest and hottest fire when it became necessary. The captain's preference was lamp oils, straw, dried bamboo, and dried palm leaves.

I pointed out that we wouldn't have to pack the dhow full of fire fodder. "We have barrels of gunpowder that won't hurtle a cannon far but I can use to turn a small boat into a big bomb. It'll blow oil and other flammables onto any vessel nearby."

"Combustibles like straw and bamboo which have little value will be a strange cargo that causes talk," Luis said. "We'll have to be discreet about loading it, perhaps bringing the materials aboard in bales and barrels and packing the dhow when we are out to sea. We could use the excuse that we're buying straw for horses we're transporting in the galleon."

Later, when we were alone, I asked Luis if we should go to our meeting with Hung armed.

Luis's smile dazzled like the dawning sun. "Young friend, we *do* think alike, don't we? Of course we will go armed to the teeth. And if we need to draw weapons against a thousand of Hung's Chinese pirates, we will go down in a blaze of bloodied glory, taking a few of them with us, eh, amigo."

Ayyo . . . perhaps a Spanish picaro—or whatever Luis was—thought that dying in battle halfway around the world was glorious, but I intended not to die.

I had to return to Maria's arms.

"I can spare one chest of silver," Capitán Zapata said, "and still have enough to do our business in Manila. If anything should happen to it, if the Chinese pirate leader takes our silver and gives us opium powder as impotent as our gunpowder . . . I will kill myself before the viceroy provides his notion of punishment."

Before we climbed down the rope ratlines to the dinghy, the captain told us in no uncertain terms of what would happen to us if we returned empty-handed. He intended to make sure we suffered severely before he had to suffer.

"How did we become the cause of all the captain's problems?" I asked Luis. "We are more victims than him."

"He needs someone to focus his ire on now that the cannon master is dead. It's the way of the world. Men like the captain kick those beneath him and kiss the feet of those above."

"One more question, Luis. Suppose we face more than one pirate ship?"

"Don't worry, young friend. I have a plan."

He punctuated that statement with an arrogant blast of ear-cracking laughter.

FIFTY-SIX

I HAD NEVER been in an opium den. It was the first place Hung's "honor guard" of vicious-looking cutthroats took us to after we pulled up to the jetty in the ship's dinghy.

Dark and smoke-filled, the room's dimensions were difficult to gauge. Scores of bunk beds stacked three- and four-high blocked my view of the huge hall. Adjacent to each stand of bunks was a brazier, which heated a domed, smoke-filled pot. Multiple hoses were connected to the dome with release valves near the hoses' ends; each pipe serviced a semicomatose opium smoker lying on the bunk.

Walking by one of the bunk stands, I took a close look at their assorted occupants. Dressed in black loose-fitting shirts and trousers, the droopy-eyed smokers stared sightlessly at *nothing,* their mouths twisted in strange, melancholy half smiles.

"Young friend," Luis said. "Hung's men will offer you an opium pipe and invite you to smoke. I will say we are here to buy, not smoke. This is dangerous business. Keep your mouth shut. Open it to talk or smoke, and you will be smoking the red-hot business end of my smoking pistola."

I believed him. But I didn't need the offer of an opium pipe to experience the substance. Ayyo . . . it was enough just walking through the den. The attendants were no doubt immune to the effect after working in the den, but I felt myself getting not just dizzy, but calm and relaxed, with a feeling that life was good . . .

I leaned against a wall and closed my eyes as a

distinguished-looking elderly Chinese man materialized seemingly out of nowhere. Hung Pao, too, was dressed in black, loose-fitting shirt and trousers, and his gray hair was pulled up tight at the top of his head in a pigtail, which Luis referred to as his "topknot."

Luis had warned me not to touch or stare at the topknot. The Chinese were sensitive about their hair.

"Dishonor a man's topknot, you dishonor his whole family. Men have been killed for less," Luis said.

He and Hung Pao gave each other polite, curt bows and Luis did not attempt to shake Hung's hand. He had also warned me that in the Orient and in Arabia hand-shaking was considered disrespectful.

After an exchange of pleasantries—in a language that sounded like squirrel-chattering to my ears—they got down to business.

To my amazement Luis was completely fluent in squirrel-chattering.

Luis had explained earlier that the Chinese consider protracted negotiations an insulting breech of decorum. Both sides are supposed to recognize the proper value of the merchandise and settle on it expeditiously and politely.

So I wasn't entirely surprised when they quickly came to terms.

Almost immediately Hung bowed, and both men were headed for the door. I quickly caught up with Luis. I was light headed after breathing the air in the opium den.

"Hong Kong has a lot of opium smokers," I said.

"It's against the law, but they smoke it anyway. The drug grips them with iron jaws. They can't give it up. It's evil stuff—a true scourge."

"Should we be buying it then?"

"It's only evil if you misuse it. If you are in extreme pain, you'll need opium like you need blood in your veins."

"I hope we never need to smoke or eat it."

"I don't know. The times I smoked it was rather pleasant," Luis said, smiling.

Once more I understood how little I knew about my friend.

After we went through the door, Luis grabbed my arm and stopped me. "Where are you heading?"

"Back to the ship."

"Not yet. Now it's your turn to do some work around here."

I stared at him skeptically.

"What kind of work?"

"You have to honor an ancient Mandarin ritual—actually a sexual ritual. Old Hung demands that you make love to his young, recently widowed daughter."

"What? Is he insane?"

"Not by the terms of his own kind. You see, she lost her husband and bereavement has driven her into suicidal despondency, and old Hung is convinced the only thing which will console her is to have her coals stoked by an innocent youth such as yourself. You see, the old dotard is really quite smitten with you. He mistakes your youth for innocence and your blank-faced stare for inexperience. He thinks you're too pristine to besmirch her. I volunteered my services but unfortunately the old man knows too much about me. He thinks I'm *wicked*. Also I have moral qualms about matters such as these."

"*Moral* qualms?" I asked, incredulous.

"To me, it's a matter of *monetary* morality, young friend. I object strenuously to bedding women down without direct, immediate financial gratification. It's a matter of personal honor—the code of the profession, so to speak."

"She could also be homely as hell."

"A face that would knock a buzzard off a meat wagon? Not likely. I've seen old Hung's wives. They are all *spectacular*. I expect nothing less from his daughters."

"Why am I dubious?"

"A bad attitude indeed."

"This will not end well."

Luis treated me to his widest, brightest, most ingratiating smile. "Young Powder Master, have I ever let you down?"

"I won't do it."

"You will unless you plan to swim back to the colony and your true love."

FIFTY-SEVEN

OLD HUNG'S MAJORDOMO—a middle-aged man in black robes, a long black topknot, a fierce-looking goatee, and narrow suspicious eyes—led me to a room in the back of the Harbor Lord's spacious living quarters.

"My master dotes on his daughter excessively. Fearing she might—in her inconsolable grief—take her life, he has taken her back in under his roof. However, she remains melancholy, staying in her room twenty-four hours a day. Shading the windows, she allows almost no light into the room. She simply lies on her bed and despairs. My master hopes that the charms of a kind and innocent youth might mitigate her misery. Young man, understand you are on a mission of mercy. You may be her last best hope."

I was still incredulous, but as Luis indicated, we lived on old Hung's sufferance. Without his help, we would not leave with our dhow and opium. We would not even survive Hong Kong's harbor.

"How will I communicate?" I finally asked.

"We are a cosmopolitan trading port, young trader. We all speak many tongues, my master's daughters included. Hiring many governesses for his children, our Harbor Lord saw to it that all his children spoke English, French, and Spanish from childhood on."

I studied him intently, still dubious about his and Hung's purposes, but I read nothing in his inscrutable face—and even less in his expressionless eyes. Nonetheless, my misgivings mounted ominously.

"Lotus Blossom," he said, knocking on her door, "I have a young man here."

He pushed the door open and eased me in. Lying on black silk sheets and black cushions was the most impossibly beautiful Eurasian woman I had ever seen in my life . . . also the saddest-looking. With sad sloe almond eyes, exquisite cheekbones, long ebony-black tresses flowing down the small of her back, and an amazingly delicate mouth, she was as astonishingly stunning as she was disconsolate.

And she was naked.

It took me a moment to reconcile that with the fact I was being invited into her room. I supposed despair had distracted her so much she didn't even realize she was disrobed.

The majordomo quickly bowed and departed.

"I'm sorry, young man, that I cannot greet you more hospitably," she said, pulling a black dressing gown of fine silk over her waist and pear-shaped breasts. "Anyway, I seem to be in disarray. But come in. My father has asked me to talk to you. Tell me where you have been, where you have traveled."

My life's story would hardly buoy her spirits. Still, I did not know what else to talk about, and who knew, perhaps my wandering tale of woe might divert a girl who had spent so many years in the seclusion of a single city. My life, so far, had often been frightening, always difficult, but never dull.

I told her how I was captured by Spanish militia and sold into slavery; how, as a slave, I illegally mastered the powder- and gun-making trades; how—fleeing my bondage—I rescued my fair love from certain death; how we traveled New Spain's China Road in search of the rebel leader; and how, with my amigo Luis, I was sold as a slave again, this time to a Spanish galleon.

I even told her how we had blown up the powder and cannon masters and taken their jobs, but how we were now headed toward Manila where who knew what lay in store for us.

"What will happen to you and Maria?" she asked.

"Who knows?" I said. "If I make it back to the colony, I will look for her. But by then she may be old and married with a dozen children and have long forgotten me."

"She will be young and beautiful and waiting for you with open arms."

"What makes you so sure?"

"You. A woman would be a fool not to wait for one such as you. She is not a fool."

"Bereavement has robbed you of your wits."

"Or made me see things as they are."

She cuddled against me and placed my hand over her breast. It seemed natural, as if Maria had done it.

When I kissed her, she kissed me back with unexpected intensity, her lips parting and her tongue pirouetting into mine. Holding me and kissing me tightly, her hand then reached between my legs.

She paused in our lovemaking to smoke deeply from a hookah, after which she extended the tube to me.

"It is only hashish, my friend. It won't hurt or enslave you but will heighten your senses and your pleasure."

If my senses were heightened any higher, I would black out. I'd learned long ago however not to disagree with my masters. I was in her father's house and did what I was told. I smoked deeply, and she was right about one thing: It did heighten my senses. Time lurched, and suddenly everything appeared to me in threes.

Lotus Blossom's two arms were now six, her rapturous lips were not two but six as well, her delicious tongue that so dexterously tickled and tantalized my own were doing so in triplicate. I was not only staring into two dazzlingly sensuous eyes, I was tumbling into six bottomless voids.

When I kissed her breasts, worked my way down her stomach and abdomen, then feasted on the delicate bud between her legs, I savored three of those as well.

When she returned the pleasure, three mouths were kissing and caressing my trembling manhood, my pleasure throbbing three times the intensity.

When she sat astride my hips—taking my manhood into her threefold loins and then bent down to kiss me again—not one woman enveloped me but four.

Four?

Where did the fourth come from?

And why was the fourth perceptibly cooler than Lotus Blossom?

The shades were drawn and the room so dark I could barely see Lotus Blossom. The silk sheets were immaculately and impenetrably black, and absorbed what little light fell on them rather than reflecting it.

Still I could feel a woman coiling herself around my chest and stomach like a . . . like a . . .

Ayyo! I could make the coiling lady out now.

It wasn't a lady at all.

It was a snake!

A macabre monster of a snake!

While I had been bending over Lotus Blossom to address her flower, a twelve-foot python had looped six iron coils around my torso.

"There's a snake wrapped around my stomach and chest," I hissed to Lotus—not unaware that this was the second time a snake had injected itself into my love life.

"He's my friend, Fu," Lotus Blossom explained. "My protector and guardian, he comforts me in my melancholy."

"Tell your friend to let me go. He's starting to crush me."

"If he thinks you don't love me enough and decides you are not good for me, he might very well crush you."

"He's crushing me already," I hissed. "He's cutting off my air."

"That's because he can tell you've stopped loving me and that you're too worried about yourself to truly care about me."

"How can a snake possibly know things like that?"

"He intuits that your pena is softening."

I gave my manhood two energetic pumps, and miraculously, the little beggar leaped enthusiastically back to life.

As my member rose, Fu loosened his stranglehold on my chest.

"When did you first learn of Fu's protective nature?" I gasped, my oxygen-starved brain starting to fill with feverish forebodings.

"Well, Fu did perceive my late husband to be a poor and inattentive lover. At least, I assume that was the reason he crushed the life out of him."

"When did Fu pull off that feat?"

"One night after one of my husband's inept attempts at lovemaking."

"Fu killed your husband in front of you?"

"While I was in my husband's arms."

"That's awful."

"Not really. It wasn't Fu's fault, you know? I explained to my husband that very night that Fu constricted his coils only because my husband failed to heed my amorous needs. I told him he must stop being so erotically erratic, so self-indulgently self-centered, and most of all to stop obsessing so much about Fu's embrace. '*Fu will loosen up when your python perks up!*' I shouted at my esteemed husband during that last evening. I had told him continually throughout our marriage—night after night after night: 'Focus on your lovemaking, my dear! You're losing your concentration! Do you have to be so distracted all the time? Pay attention!' But he was always stubborn. He wouldn't listen. I'd hoped Fu might make him listen, but my husband still wouldn't. He wouldn't attend to my needs. Like myself, Fu finally ran out of patience with him."

"You have to help me," I whimpered. "I can't breathe."

"You can only help yourself, young sir. If you wish to survive Fu's ecstatic embrace, you must not, like my late husband, succumb to insensitive impotence. Do not, like that poor wretch, be a poor and inattentive lover."

"You knew Fu would do this," I hissed between clenched teeth. "*You* have deliberately done this to me!"

"You chose to enter my bedroom . . . You chose to ensnare my heart and to enthrall my loins."

"I didn't think you were this cruel."

"What did you think I was?"

"The most beautiful woman I'd ever seen."

"But then you should have known. You should have understood."

"Understood what?"

"Great beauty is unavoidably, unyieldingly bloodthirsty."

"Why unavoidably? Why unyieldingly?"

"It's the nature of the beast. We have no choice in the matter. If our beauty allowed us to behave otherwise, it would not be '*great* beauty.' It's brutal ruthlessness that makes our radiance so ravishing."

That last statement stunned me to such a degree my lovemaking faltered and my manhood minutely, imperceptibly weakened.

Instinctively, Fu tightened his viselike coils so agonizingly that I almost blacked out from oxygen loss.

Instantly, automatically, without my even realizing it, my stroke accelerated, my manhood stiffened, and his coils loosened.

"Courage, innocent youth," Lotus Blossom said. "No regrets. Never look back. Be of stout heart, and, who knows, you may survive the night. And think of how much ecstasy you will endure . . ."

"How did I get into this?" I groaned, pumping my pelvis with pain-racked effort.

"You're drawn to great beauty like a moth to the flame. Did it surprise you when your wings were singed?"

"I did not seek *this*!"

"You sought *me*."

"Why is this happening?"

"Because of your nature. You're a man. Because you're a man, you could not help but seek me—a paragon of inconceivable beauty."

"I wish I'd never seen you or Fu. I wish I'd never come here."

"It's too late for self-pitying and self-loathing. You must deal with the situation at hand."

"I hate the situation at hand."

"Of course, you do. What man wouldn't? If it makes you feel any better, however, know that you never had a choice."

"What?"

Luis had grabbed my arm and pulled me away from fierce-appearing Mongol warriors on horseback coming down the narrow street.

"Where were you? I found you wandering down the street in a daze. What happened? You breathe too many fumes?"

I shook my head, trying to clear it.

"Luis, did I . . . did you . . ."

"What, amigo? Spit it out."

"Never mind."

I had the strangest sensation—my abdomen hurt like Hades. When I had a chance, I ducked around a building and pulled up my shirt as if I pretended to relieve myself.

I had red welts around my waist.

Ayyo . . .

FIFTY-EIGHT

Luis took me with him in his search for a dhow, and again the negotiations went surprisingly well.

As Luis had explained, Hong Kong Harbor teemed with these vessels—the simplest but most efficient sailing ships on earth. Brought to China by the Arabs centuries before, the dhow quickly came to dominate the East as thoroughly as they dominated Hong Kong Harbor. The most popular sailing ships in all of Asia, we had an ample selection of these amazing boats.

To my amazement, Luis—whom I had dismissed as the most treacherous man alive—was good as his word. Everything he said he would do, he did.

Luis purchased a larger vessel, called a baggala. Sharp-bowed with both a forward and upward thrust, the dhow had disproportionately large sterns, slanted triangular lateen rigging, and an unexpectedly large mainsail—significantly larger than the mizzen.

We acquired the cheapest oceangoing dhow available. We needed it for only one voyage, not for longevity or endurance.

Luis didn't haggle over its condition. He pretended instead not to know the difference between a derelict and a seaworthy ship. He didn't need a solidly built commercial vessel with which to transport cargo thousands of miles through treacherous storm-tossed seas. As long as the boat would survive a single voyage to Manila, he was content.

He bought it so cheap, and his sellers seemed so grateful to part with it, I assumed the boat was stolen.

Ironically, everyone in the harbor trusted this swindler.

Even the crooks selling us the dhow seemed to trust him.

Hung Pao—the most feared, dangerous, and powerful man in Hong Kong—trusted him, and I doubt Hung Pao trusted anyone.

Capitán Zapata—for reasons I could not fathom—trusted him, and El Capitán seemed to trust no one.

Even my resistance was breaking down.

I was starting to understand that being a thief, a killer, and a seducer of wealthy women did not make a man all *bad*.

When the bets were down, Luis was the man I wanted on my side, covering my back.

Like the dhow purchase, the opium transaction proceeded with no problem. Hung Pao turned over the three chests of opium on our galleon's deck, and Luis paid him a chest full of silver seconds later.

Hung handed Luis a red flag with a gold dragon emblem.

"For your safe voyage out of Chinese waters," old Hung then said, suddenly spouting a bit of Spanish. That was not surprising—the Spanish Philippines was a significant trading party for the Chinese.

Luis gave him a terse head nod.

On departing, he and Hung Pao bowed curtly to each other, and the Harbor Lord departed with his silver.

FIFTY-NINE

A DHOW TYPICALLY required more than a dozen sailors to crew it, but despite its size and mass the boat was remarkably simple and easy to handle. Towed behind the galleon with its sails down, Luis believed we could man it with five sailors.

He chose Arturo as the third man aboard. Arturo chose the other two crewmen from men he said we could trust.

In the event we got separated from the galleon, Luis had purchased a "kamal" from Hung Pao. A celestial navigation device used by Arab and Chinese navigators, it was used to determine latitude by finding Polaris's angle above the horizon.

I found the kamal to be a curious-looking device—a small, thin piece of wood about two inches long and one wide, it had a string attached through a hole in the middle. The cord had a series of knots corresponding to different latitudes.

When we were out to sea and would soon have to pack the dhow with explosives and kindling to make it into a floating bomb, we told Arturo the true nature of our mission.

Ayyo . . . our friend was not pleased. Nor were the two sailors he had recruited, though Luis's assurances that he had survived twenty fireboat attacks and was made wealthy by the experiences—as they would be, if they survived this one—helped. That, plus the truth about how unarmed the galleon was, brought them around.

"It's a death run for us," Arturo said. "I'm sorry I ever laid eyes on either of you."

"We will be right beside you, amigo," Luis said.

"Wonderful. We can hold hands as we are blown into hell."

SIXTY

FOR MY PART I set about turning the dhow into a fire-boat.

I started out at first light by laying out five crisscrossed rows of good sail-hauling line, three sets each. On top of those lines I laid out five layers of strong thick canvas sail cloth, ten feet across, on each of the three sets of crisscrossed lines. I had drenched each sail with whale oil the day before, then given it twenty-four hours to thoroughly sink in.

I told the crew of the galleon to pull the dhow alongside in calm waters and lower kegs of what I had referred to as "stump-blasting powder." In addition, I had kegs of metal scrap used to load cannons for short range shots that cleared the decks of opposing warships when they came alongside.

Using a dinghy extended on a painter between the two vessels, I kept a steady stream of supplies coming as I thought of more items I needed.

I asked the captain to round up every bar of strong lye laundry soap in the ship.

When Luis saw my preparations, he thundered at me that I was smoking the opium and that I'd become "muy loco."

We argued when he wanted a "suicide" cannon lowered down to the dhow from the galleon.

"We'll place the cannon below the deck," he said, "right above the waterline. We want it to detonate *through* the bulkhead so that it strikes the enemy at point-blank range right at his waterline."

He was not pleased when I told him that I didn't want the cannon aboard the dhow.

"A ship-killing Chimneys of Hell made of canvas and stump-blasting powder?" he shouted derisively. "I told you what a real Chimneys of Hell was like. We need something like *that*. Build me something like that."

"Yes, you told me what the classic fireboat is like—a ship refitted belowdecks with troughs which lead to portholes projecting 'fire chimneys.' The shafts protrude out from the upper deck. The hole is filled with highly inflammable materials so that when the troughs are lit, the fires set off charges that cause flames to burst out the portholes and up the chimneys.

"Unfortunately, the timing for setting the fires has to be perfect. The ship has to hook on to the enemy's ship exactly on cue—otherwise the ship just bursts into flame. Also the enemy ship will burn from the bottom up—the exact opposite of what we need. We have to torch the masts and rigging *first*, not last—if we want to disable the enemy immediately.

"The fireboats are manned by the best sailors and explosive experts in the fleet because timing and ignition have to be perfect. You have some experience, but Arturo and I are both reluctant fireboat crewmen. You admit that depending on the weather, you may have to add to the crew to sail the dhow to the boat where the pirate leader is aboard. They will not be experienced fireboat sailors, either."

"Amigo, we'll be lucky if others don't jump ship halfway to the enemy dhows," Luis said. "Just fill cannons from the galleon full of blasting powder, cap off the end, and let her blow. All that compression will give you the most powerful bomb in the world. That's all we need."

"Except it will never work. The cannons are cracked, but they're case-hardened, heavy-duty, hand-casted iron," I said wearily. "All you will get is a ruptured cannon, more likely to blow us out of the water rather than the pirate's vessel. We need a material that will blow and spread fire instantly."

I handed him a bar of soap.

"Now if you're going to do something, start shaving parchment-thin slices of soap onto this piece of canvas. We have a lot of soap to shave up. We'll have to mix the shaved soap and the shrapnel in with what I keep calling stump-blasting powder."

Luis's face was a pained mask of skepticism. "Why the soap? Are you going to wash the pirates' mouths out with it?"

"No, those razor-thin soap slices will melt into sticky fiery glue when the powder heats up and blows. Then we're going to *stick* fire to their ships."

"How do you know?"

"I once saw a black-powder grenade blow a bar of soap all over soldiers during the revolt of Hidalgo. They couldn't get the fire off their bodies. Water and dirt wouldn't put it out. I tell you it's *fire glue*."

Luis stared at me, still dubious.

"Okay, how do you get the compression we need?"

I pointed to a barrel full of seawater—also filled with three pieces of canvas sail cloth.

"We wrap the whole package in saltwater-soaked canvas, rope it off tight, then have the ship's sailmaker sew it up even tighter. We set it out on deck for the rest of the day, letting the sun shrink the saltwater-soaked canvas. I assure you, our compression will be tighter than tight."

"If your design fails—"

"We'll meet in hell, amigo."

PART XIV
PIRATE ALLEY

ON THE VOYAGE from Hong Kong to Manila, Luis took time out to give me a detailed lesson on ships, cannonry, and the galleon's disgraceful lack of preparedness.

Luis knew *everything* about cannons, naval and warfare, and fortifications. Moreover, he knew everything about what a well-armed well-appointed vessel should have, which meant he knew what we did *not* have.

"It's not a proper galleon," he explained to me. "The ship is smaller than the galleons that usually make the Acapulco-Manila run. It only has three masts when four would be better, eight sails when ten are best, and worst of all, it's undergunned—twenty-two cannons, twelve of which are twelve-pounders, ten of which are twenty-pounders—about half the firepower the ship should have had.

"It's a mongrel," Luis said, "a leaky old ship that's a constant struggle to keep afloat with tar-and-horsehair caulking as the planks spread wider—and of course endless bilge-bucket brigades.

"The worthless tub had usually been running supplies between New Spain and Peru and was rushed into the Manila run after another ship was sunk by pirates."

He threw his hands up in exasperation. "The ills of the ship illustrate why Spain is no longer the most powerful empire on earth. Our best leaders died in the war against the French and we are ruled by a king and court fools who are not capable of cleaning stables much less the ills of an empire."

I knew, of course, how the Spanish had conquered the

One World, but was curious about how they had won the Philippines, a big foothold in the Pacific. He told me about brave men who set out on an endless ocean to gain not just treasure and empire, but knowledge.

"The Portuguese explorer Ferdinand Magellan—representing both Portugal and Spain—led the first Spanish expedition there, landing at Cebu in the Philippines early in the sixteenth century. The islands were inhospitable even then. The natives murdered Magellan a short time later in a fight on the nearby island of Mactan.

"Thirty years later our king, Philip II, asked Andrés de Urdaneta, a navigator, to lead an expedition from Mexico to the Philippines and to chart an advantageous return route. Five earlier attempts had ended in disaster. In 1565 Urdaneta reached and established a mission—again on the Philippine island of Cebu—then commenced his return to New Spain.

"Sailing in the high latitudes, around 36 degrees north, he exploited their auspicious winds, eluded the southerly typhoons, and reached Panama in 123 days. This became the route of the Manila galleon run and enabled us to colonize the Philippines. Having a foothold there created Eastern markets for the goods of Mexico and Peru and the supply of silk and other goods from the Orient.

"Three further expeditions ended in disaster, but Philip II, who we call the most Catholic of kings, and for whom the islands are named, was undeterred. Dispatching Miguel López de Legazpi to the Philippines, he established the first permanent settlement in Cebu in 1565. The Spanish city of Manila was founded in 1571, and Spain controlled most of the coastal and lowland regions from northern Mindanao to Luzon by the late sixteenth century.

"Inquisitors, friars, and soldiers converted the natives to Catholicism in their usual short order—often using the sword when the Bible didn't convince the natives.

"Legazpi fought off Portuguese ships and Chinese pirates, but he could never subdue the Philippine Muslims of Mindanao and Sulu, whom we call Moros."

Luis shook his head. "We pretty near ruined the Philippines, amigo, just as we did New Spain. We brought in New Spain's encomienda system so that the natives were conscripted into backbreaking labor on Spanish-owned farms to the financial advantage of the plantation owners.

"Manila quickly became one of the Crown's most lucrative colonies. The galleon trade with Acapulco assured Manila of commercial dominance. Exchange of Chinese silks for Mexican silver attracted a large Chinese population.

"The heirs of pre-Spanish nobility were known as the principalia and played an important role in the friar-dominated local government—the same as in New Spain."

"Something tells me I will hate Manila," I told Luis.

"Yes, if we reach Manila in one piece, you will positively *loathe it*."

"We don't have to reach it. I loathe it already. It sounds too much like New Spain, too many of the same injustices."

"Never fear, young gun-maker. We will probably not live long enough to suffer its cruelty."

SIXTY-TWO

THE SHIP SAILED on, pulling us behind it as we transformed the dhow into a fireboat and my education about ships and the sea increased.

"Galleons were originally caravels, young friend, a vessel dating back three hundred years," Luis explained one day as we worked combustibles on the deck. "Their design has changed over the years. I've heard that the caravel was originally broad-beamed, a vessel of 50 or 60 tons burden, with some as large as 160 tons. About seventy-five feet long, those caravels were smaller and lighter than the galleons of a century later.

"The early caravels had forecastles and aftercastles that tended to catch the wind and make the ship unmaneuverable, so we left them off our galleons, making galleons longer, leaner vessels. We also increased the number of heavy guns until they ran the full length of the ship's broadside in one, two, and finally three tiers. The big galleons we called ships of the line because they could serve as powerful warships in a line of battle."

Now that I was a sailor, these ships fascinated me.

"How big were these 'ships of the line'?" I asked.

"A sample ship of the line through the seventeenth century could run two hundred feet in length and displace twelve hundred to two thousand tons with a crew of six to eight hundred men. Their armament was arranged along three decks: the bottom-deck battery consisting perhaps of thirty cannons firing balls of thirty-two to forty-eight pounds. The middle deck would have as many guns firing twenty-four pounds. The upper battery would carry thirty or more twelve-pounders.

"The ships could follow each other's wake into battle. By maintaining the line throughout the battle, the fleet, despite obscuring clouds of smoke, could function as a unit under control of the admiral. The formation maximized the fighting power of the broadside and marked a final break with the tactics of galley warfare in which individual ships sought each other to engage in single combat by means of ramming, boarding, and so on.

"The provisions were little better than the bilge slaves' rations and the daily routine was the same as ours: washing down the decks, caulking, repairing rigging."

"In short, the job was backbreaking even then."

"Young powder-maker," Luis said, "it was ever thus."

SIXTY-THREE

WE'D SAILED UP the Manila coast without mishap, and for a while I thought we might make it without doing battle with pirates. In fact, we were less than a hundred miles from the Manila Straits when we encountered them—three enormous gangha dhows, each one almost two of our baggala dhow.

Each dhow featured two small twelve-pounder cannons, which gave them six more working guns than we had. Moreover, their rails and decks teemed with flamboyantly clad brigands sporting black head scarves, billowing shirts, and loose-fitting trousers of crimson and black. They brandished pistolas and knives, axes and cutlasses, bows and arrows.

These were professional killers, not the gallows-bait and prison-fodder manning our vessel. The only weakness I saw were the pistolas. There was no way, in this damp climate, the pistolas would be capable of repeated firing. They were for show, but the rest of the weapons were deadly.

Midday, the wind was calm, the waters almost flat. We couldn't have outrun them even if we wanted.

We brought the dhow alongside the galleon so we could confer with the captain as to the demands—and battle—we expected.

Bribing them with silver was not an option. They would only take it as a sign of weakness.

The brigands dispatched a dinghy to within shouting distance of the galleon. A Spanish-speaking pirate—a rough-looking, one-eyed, bald-pate rogue in a crimson shirt and black trousers—stood in the bow, and shouted: *"You cannot cross our waters without paying our tax levies. One chest of gold—or two chests of silver—and we'll be on our way . . . pay or die!"*

"In a pig's ass they'll be on their way," Luis said. "The captain knows that they're testing us—to see how effective our cannonry is."

"Tell them we'll bring them a quantity of silver and a gift of jade from New Spain for their leader," the captain told Luis. "Tell them we'll give them some opium so they can have pleasant dreams. They'll correctly interpret our concessions as a sign of weakness but won't attack until they have that much in their hands."

"They'll be slavering for everything else we must have on board," First Mate Gasset said.

"Just tell them," Capitán Zapata said.

Luis shouted: *"We are giving you a dhow loaded with silver and gold and jade. Opium! We have opium for you! Three chests each packed with riches and opium—one for each ship."*

Luis then whispered to me: "If we give them three chests, all three pirate vessels will converge on the dhow. They will not entrust their share to the other ships."

The bald bandido was as surprised as our own crew members who had been kept in ignorance but now heard the proclamation.

"Get out the polished brass coins—that glitter will look like gold at a distance," the captain said. "Also the flour, which from a distance should counterfeit opium."

While the pirate went back to the mother ship, a large dhow much more ornate than the other two, sailors on the galleon lowered chests of "booty" down to us with ropes and nets.

Every so often, Luis smiled and waved at the pirates, then pointed eagerly at their tribute.

Ayyo . . . the pirates must have thought they had died and gone to the Garden of Allah or whatever paradise full of celestial virgins they subscribed to.

Once loaded, we looked at each other. Five of us, on a suicide mission none of us wanted to be a part of.

We pushed off for the pirate leader's dhow, raising a single small sail. The enemy wasn't far and we were not in a great hurry.

SIXTY-FOUR

LUIS POSTED TWO men with muskets, one on the bow, the other on the stern, to discourage any pirates who might try to board us before we reached the flagship.

The pirate captain, easily the most gaudily dressed of the bunch of cutthroats, stood at the railing and stared at us. I knew what was going on in his mind—he couldn't believe his good fortune, which made him wonder whether it was a trick.

Luis brandished the open chest packed with our glittering "gold" coins of polished brass. He even opened the barrel of flour that at this distance would pass as opium. So they would understand what we were giving them, he shouted: "Gold! Opium!"

The other two pirate dhows edged closer to the flagship, their leaders no doubt planning to board when the booty was handed over to the captain.

We were a moment away from coming alongside the pirate vessel when Luis whispered, without breaking his glittering smile, *"Now."*

Using the slanted sail as a cover, I lit the ten-second fuse on my canvas hell-burner—the slanted triangular sail blocking the pirates' line of sight—and ran it up the mast with a block-and-tackle. Swinging the boom around, I dangled the canvas-packed bomb directly over the pirate dhow—until the bomb touched the base of their triangularly slanting mainsail.

The pirate captain went into action, shouting commands.

Arrows flew as the five of us went overboard on the

side of the dhow away from the pirate boat. One of the crewmen Arturo had chosen screamed as an arrow caught him between the shoulder blades.

By the time I came up to the surface, Luis was already twenty feet from his dhow, swimming like a shark, our dhow still providing cover from the fusillade of arrow fire from the pirate ship.

I went back under as the biggest explosion I ever heard sounded behind me. A horrendous hailstorm of wood and rusty scrap iron hammered the seas around me; the underwater concussion from the blast waves pounded, shook, and convulsed underwater.

When the iron hail ceased and my breath ran out, I surfaced. Like Lot's wife, I could not resist looking back. I almost turned into a pillar of wet gasping smoke-choked sea salt. Gathering together had doomed all three pirate boats.

The trio of pirate dhows—composed of tar-caulked planks, greased rigging, and highly flammable canvas—had converged all of those combustible components into three colossal red-orange fireballs.

Around me dropped and drifted a scattering of charred spars and other burnt-out wreckage of the pirates' dhows.

Even at a hundred feet, the heat from monstrous-size fireballs blazed like smoking, scorching forges.

Otherwise *nothing.*

My canvas-shrouded bombs had vaporized the brigands.

The pirates and their dhows had simply ceased to exist.

I could not see one dead floating body.

All I saw was Luis, Arturo, and the third seaman swimming furiously for the galleon, looking forward to a welcome mug of brandy.

And Luis said it was not a Chimneys of Hell, I thought.

PART XV
IMMODERATE WRATH

[I]mmeasurable strength and of immoderate wrath, the wrath that passes exhausted but never appeased—the wrath and fury of the passionate sea.

—Joseph Conrad, *Typhoon*

SIXTY-FIVE

F OR TWO DAYS we plowed a furrow of rapidly fading foam across a tranquil turquoise sea. The captain and Luis both now believed we were safe. We were a half day from the entrance to the Manila Straits and at least two days from landfall. The voyage was going well—fair winds and calm seas.

But nothing lasts.

Slowly, perceptibly, the weather began to change. The air grew damp and dense. The sky turned dull, dreary, leaden, and dead. Suddenly, angry and slate-gray, the sea was riven by rising swells.

Even more ominously, the wind and swells died—for nearly three hours.

That lack of wind, however, was short-lived. The wind began to build again but this time with mounting menacing power.

Within an hour the swells recommenced. First they were random and isolated. Then they struck in multiples and grew in size until our ship was then rocked by violent unending rolls . . . one after another.

The waves burgeoned all around us in height and force, breaking and banging over the deck, hard enough to tear the riggings loose—until the canvas howled and the spars shrieked, the swells knocking us off our feet.

Arturo quickly gave lifelines to Luis and me to wrap around our waists and lash to the mainmast. He shouted something—no doubt profane—at us but the groaning ship and the storm's roar drowned out his words as if he had never uttered them.

The last coherent word I heard any human being speak was when Capitán Zapata roared over the tumultuous blast of the storm: *"TY-Y-Y-Y-P-H-O-O-O-O-O-N!"*

Typhoon—the most terrifying word in any sailor's mind.

No longer turquoise and tranquil, the dark sea over-reached, overpowered, and overmastered. The tall, curling waves sailors called combers rose forty, fifty, sixty feet high and more, towering over the ship, breaking over us like avalanches, flooding us not with molten magma but Himalayan mountains of salt water.

Occasionally one of these climbing waves would lift us up onto its precarious peak—as high as fifty and sixty feet—where we would balance on its foamy summit, and then be dropped like a rock into the depths of the wave's trough . . . either to be lifted up again on the back of another crest for another hair-raising rise-and-fall or wait in the trough for more collapsing waves and their hammer blows of hell. Despite the rope around my waist, I was lifted off my feet and thrown up, hitting my head and crashing my shoulder into the mast.

How long we rode it out, I do not know.

Seconds ticked off like minutes. Minutes, like hours. Hours like days.

Time on loan from hell.

The sun died and darkness reigned—universal, undifferentiated . . .

At some point, the sea turned unusually calm. For the first time in untold hours, I heard a man's voice.

"The typhoon's dead eye," Luis said.

We floated in black nothingness . . . a ship of the dead on an unmoving sea.

When the sea awoke again, we longed for the stillness of the typhoon's eye. Starless and sunless, the sea rose in its unchained dead-of-night wrath, black as India ink.

We couldn't see, but we could hear—the rumbling roar of the rushing wind, of masts and rigging ripping and howling above the sea and the wind, of spars breaking and crashing to the deck, of men screaming with the terror.

I was lifted, slammed back down, whipped around, and banged against the mast as the wave crashed against us and almost vertical waves rolled us.

Every bone in my body felt broken.

The sea was flogging us all to pieces, bloodying our backs with its cruel cat-o'-nine-tails on the flogging rack of its hellish fury.

Just when it couldn't seem to get worse, the waves returned for a second, even more brutal, attack. They crashed down on us from all sides at once—from heights of sixty feet and more.

The ship groaned and screamed, throbbed and sobbed like a dying animal, raging at its fate; and periodically piercing the groaning and roar of the ship and sea—as if in eerie replication of the ship and sea—I would hear the hideous shriek of a dying man.

Not that the sea or the night cared. Into the impenetrable dark of a night sea without end, we were banged and slammed.

When the storm brewed, I had asked Luis why we didn't take cover down below, but he told me the holds were even more treacherous than the sea-slick wave-crashing deck. The cargo had all broken loose. Everything was blasting through the compartments as if fired from cannons—pots, pans, knives, shoes, guns, chairs, cups, buckets, barrels of provisions, silver coins, bloodied, sea-battered and -bloated corpses.

Capitán Zapata needed me and Luis from time to time in the pilothouse. We crawled there, tying our lifelines from support to support. Holding the wheel steady took every muscle in a man's back and shoulders, legs and arms, fists

and wrists. He and Arturo needed relief, and we all took
agonizing turns at that torture instrument struggling in pain
to hold the wheel steady . . . for dear endangered life.

The gale had long ago ceased to be a mere act of an indifferent nature but the blood-crazed revenge of a living,
breathing beast in its death throes, up on its hind legs,
clawing at the world with final violence and brutal rage,
the ship's horrendous howls at times strangely and eerily
emulating the genuinely human howls that occasionally
cut through the ear-cracking sounds of the storm and the
sea.

All the while the breaking waves and cross-waves had
swollen in both force and fury. When we caught a crest,
we rode to breathtaking heights—fifty, sixty, seventy
feet. The crash back down cracked every joist and spar,
plank and beam of the ship.

Still the waves increased in both frequency and size.

We survived two eighty-foot monsters—but the last
drop cracked the main mast a dozen feet above the main
deck.

If the typhoon kept up, it would not only strip the ship
piecemeal, the galleon would break up and sink—vanish
forever into a sea that leaves neither hole nor trace nor
proof of life.

"Eh, amigo," Luis yelled.

I looked up from my own darkness and was shocked
that I could actually see my friend grinning at me on the
other side of the thick but now cracked oak mast. He was
looping his lifeline repeatedly around the mast. Tying it
off, he lashed the loose end of my lifeline to it.

We were now tightly secured to that main spar.

"Amigo," Luis said, "you have to tell me one thing—
you know, before we die. Between amigos. After all, we
have nothing more to conceal. That girl you disguise as a

boy. You go to a lot of effort to keep her alive. She must be much woman in bed, no?"

He treated me to his widest, wickedest grin.

"You'll never know, you picaro bastardo."

He treated me to a long laugh, echoing high above the devastating din of the typhoon.

Another wave swelled under the ship, lifting us with torturous deliberate speed up onto its crest. The wave was like a slowed-down wild bronco, who, in his vertically rocketing leap, jackrabbitlike breaks free of the earth, achieving the highest, hardest buck of his whole hell-bent life—except in my wild wrenching awareness everything was now radically slowed down, as if by supernatural intervention.

Seen through my distorted senses, the great, curling wave raised above the raging sea with godlike languor.

The ship rode the bronco's arching back—riding perhaps the highest wave in earthly history, a tsunami of a curling, breaking swell, first 40, then 50, then 60, 80, 100, then an unbelievable 120 feet in the air.

We hung there in abeyance, poised for all eternity, it seemed, on the froth of that peak.

God, this is beautiful, I said softly to myself.

And then God dropped us.

The drop would have been bad enough. The trough beneath was impossibly deep and improbably distant—no creature on this earth could have survived such a steep plunge—but even worse, high above us was also an entire Pacific Ocean of a wave, collapsing like the Mountains of the Moon into the Valley of the Shadow on mortal men.

I wanted to pray. Christ was out of the question. Jesus would never countenance my warped view of His Peaceable Kingdom—my joy at the bombs I built that vaporized both brigands and dhows or my delight at the Inquisitor's long, lethal, late-night swim.

Quetzalcoatl? I suppose I could have prayed to him, but I didn't.

I had never heard that Quetzalcoatl had a sense of humor.

Which a god would need now—were he to understand me and my life.

Or that of Luis.

Or of my blessed, beautiful, and forever beloved Maria.

So be it.

I prayed to no god, no mortal being, no divine everlasting—nothing, nobody.

I didn't pray at all.

Triple-lashed to the cracked remains of the mainmast, I stared into Luis's mad laughter and mischievous grin— a grin that finally reached his dead-as-the-grave eyes.

Grinning back at my friend, we both waited out our rapidly approaching decline and fall.

Or more accurately, we rode the fall.

To the end of time.

"You know I always liked you," Luis shouted.

"Señor," I said, allowing Luis a sardonically savage smile. "If you liked me less, I would be back in the colony eating tortillas and drinking pulque."

Again, his laughter howled high above the storm.

"I do want to thank you though," I shouted over the howl of the typhoon, "for everything you've done for me—my enslavement into the bilge gang, my murdering of the powder and cannon masters, my massacre of the pirates and their dhows, and now my pointless death in the midst of a howling typhoon. I want you to know—I want you to know—"

"—know what?"

Luckily, with the wind-whipped rain lashing my face,

he could not see the tears flooding my face—tears of joy and love and laughter.

"I would not have missed it . . . for . . . the . . . *w-o-r-l-d*," I roared at the top of my lungs, stretching the last word out.

"Me *n-e-i-t-h-e-r*," Luis bellowed above the storm.

"Then I'll see you in hell," I howled into his laughing, leering face.

"I'll keep it hot for *you*."

Luis's insane laughter cracked and rolled like thunder through the hammering rain and raging wind.

His hysterical laughter was infectious, and I found myself joining him.

Yet even as the last of our laughter rang through the night, I paused to consider Luis's remark and ponder what hell *would* be like.

Would the Nine Hells be my fate?

I found the subject curiously fascinating. My mind was working clear as a bell, and I meditated on its implications.

But it was no matter.

Soon Luis and I would both have more definitive responses.

After all, the ship's terminus in the trough and death wave's crash were now at hand.

Then the answers would come for sure.

The closest I came to an answer was Luis's last reverberating words, roaring at the top of his lungs:

"Remember me when the lights go out!"

I heard no more, and I never felt the ship hit.

Or the biggest wave in the world—possibly in the history of earth, being, and time—that was about to break over me.

The crash knocked me cold.

Everything went black.

Time and the night closed over me—a giant fist dragging a lost soul down, down, down into a nether sea.

Eternity closed, and the night that knew no end finally knew an end.

It knew *nothing*.

My wildly wrenched, violently deranged awareness went black . . . black . . . black . . .

. . . *black as the abyss.*

The abyss grabbed me by the throat and pulled me toward it.

I went along for the ride.

The spinning pit beckoned.

Beckoned.

Beckoned.

And I dived in.

PART XVI

Out of the night that covers me.
Black as the Pit from Pole to Pole . . .

—William Ernest Henley, "Invictus"

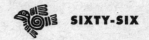

SIXTY-SIX

WHEN I CAME to, I was lashed stomach down onto the shattered spar that had once been the galleon's mainmast. The beam's forward end—two feet above my head—had cracked and broken off at a sharp ninety-degree angle, creating a crudely pointed prow.

I wasn't in a mood to appreciate our good fortune. My temples rang like church bells . . . which all the harpies in hell were currently hammering on.

Luis stared at me.

For once he was not grinning like a skull.

"I thought we'd lost you, amigo," he finally said. "You were bleeding from the nose, ears, *and* mouth when I spread-eagled you atop this spar."

"You should have fed me to the fishes," I groaned. "I hurt all over."

"Enjoy it. The hurt says you survived the storm and the shipwreck. The hurt says you're still alive."

"I never thought we'd survive that last wave. We still haven't made it."

"Really? Look to your starboard."

Through pain-blurred vision, I stared over my right shoulder . . . at white shining sands backed by dense green jungle.

"That's either the Garden of Eden, the Kingdom of God—or I've lost my mind," I said. "Whatever it is, it's a ways off. A half-mile?"

"More, and you never know about these ocean currents. They could sweep us back out to sea. Can you swim?"

"The dead man's float maybe."

"Your head hurts, eh?"

"Like it was run under a drop forge."

"Okay, I'm going to back-kick this log toward the island as best I can. I have to find us a hospitable cove where we can beach—not reefs or rocks which will cut us to pieces. If I feel us being sucked out to sea, however, I'm pulling you off your seafaring throne and you're joining me in the drink. You're going to have to swim. We'll make it. I never thought we'd make it off the bilge gang."

. . . We'll make it.

Luis had lashed me belly down on the spar in the dead of night in a typhoon, somehow kept me on top of it all night and morning, and now was propelling me—still strapped to the spar—toward a sunny sandy beach and lush lavish greenery.

All my life I had judged people not by the strength of their faith, the grace of their bravery, or the size of their soul, but by their appearances.

I had judged Luis by his appearances.

And had sold him short.

He was my friend—the only one I'd ever truly had— and I had sold him short . . .

"Luis, leave me."

"What is it you are hiding from me, amigo?" he said, both hands on the shattered beam, kicking us toward land with his feet. "What is it your amigo does not know about, eh? A fortune in gold bullion? Now you want to cut me out, no? Maybe you have a rich beautiful widow desperate to have her tarot read, her fortune told."

"Luis, I can feel the current pull—away from land, back out to sea."

"Never fear, amigo. My tutelage is serving you well. We *will* get to shore and prosper. We will swim not in salt water but in putas and pistols, brandy and dinero, wine and song. I know about these things.

"TR-U-U-U-S-T M-E-E-E-E-E!!!!" Luis thundered, dragging the words out as he steered us toward the island across a placid pristine sea.

SIXTY-SEVEN

IN THE LAST quarter mile the currents forced us to abandon the spar. I left it oddly ambivalent. I had not forgotten that Capitán Zapata had lashed Luis against that spar and flogged him to the bone.

Yet that same spar had later saved both our lives—an irony I would not forget.

In the end, however, the spar drifted back out to sea—from whence all three of us had come—with a merciless sluggish speed.

"Amigo," Luis said, "I know you hurt, but you must swim like all the hounds of hell were at your back. At dusk, sharks enter these shallow waters and feed on the fat straggling bottom-feeders. We have no time to lose. The sun is fading fast."

We were fatally exposed, but more important, I did not want to let Luis down. We had been through too much, and he had done too much.

With almost superhuman effort, I began to swim—arm over arm, hand over hand, struggling to match him stroke for stroke, kick for kick. My leg and shoulder muscles blazed like balefire. I was not only sick and exhausted, in truth I'd never swum all that well. Luis, on the other hand, was a strong, skilled swimmer, and studying his strokes, I attempted to imitate him.

Luis had told me once that the containment of pain was the highest of all the fighting arts, and I had not understood what he meant.

I understood now.

I hurt.

I hurt all over.

Unfortunately, pain was a luxury I could not afford. Since Luis would not abandon me, our survival meant I had to defeat my pain. Not that I had any confidence that I could accomplish that. I was not brave enough to swim through so much agony and exhaustion.

In the end pain would break me down and wear me out.

Unless I could contain it.

Contain it how?

Contain it where?

Elsewhere.

Well, if so, I had a lot of pain to contain. My head throbbed unbearably. My shoulders and thigh muscles burned, rivaling the agony between my temples.

In fact, my limbs hurt so much I almost forgot the blinding agony in my head.

Contain the pain, I said silently to myself.

You can't control the world, but you can control yourself, Luis had told me another time. *You can control yourself.*

Almost without willing it, I felt my awareness detach from my body—in fact *leave* my body. Even as I swam, my awareness was projecting itself high overhead, where it watched my pain-racked body hack haltingly at the water, forcing itself toward the shore.

Put the pain elsewhere, a voice whispered in my brain, no, . . . to my brain. *Contain it elsewhere and . . . kill it.*

Suddenly the pirate dhow sailed into my awareness. I was back on our own dhow with Arturo and about to blow up the brigand's boat.

Put the pain there. Let the pirate dhow own it.

I stared at the pirate dhow's huge slanting triangular sail. And placed the pain . . . *there.*

Adios, brigands.

Adios, dhows.

Adios, pain.

Again, the fire-burner's blast.

Again, the pirate dhow detonated and disappeared into the . . . sea.

The pain disappeared.

The containment of pain was the highest of the fighting arts.

Renewing my efforts, I strengthened my kick and lengthened my stroke.

SIXTY-EIGHT

WE REACHED SHORE shortly before dusk—and before the sharks came out in force. We were both so drained and dehydrated, we weren't thinking clearly. All we thought about was water, food, and sleep.

We headed into a lush, thick green jungle of reeds and palms, stringy vines and flamboyant fronds. Finding a stream, we dropped to our knees and lowered our faces into it. I would have drunk till I burst, but after a half-dozen slurps, Luis pulled me back.

"Drink too much at one time, and you'll founder like a horse," he said.

Next, Luis scaled a coconut palm. He hurled two nuts down onto some rocks below, splitting them like apples. Afterward we cleaned out the white meat inside.

I never ate anything better in my life.

Sleep overwhelmed both of us almost at once. Falling asleep by an open stream with no protection from predators—animal or human—is never wise, but we seemed to have no choice.

Once we got water and food in us, we collapsed.

Our limbs and eyelids became heavy as lead. Blind exhaustion and black oblivion buried the horrors of the last two days.

We slept.

Luis later told me that at the time our sojourn in Morpheus's arms seemed like a gift from the Greek gods of yore.

"Beware all Greeks bearing gifts," he said.

We might have slept three days for all I know.

There would come a time in which I wished we'd never awakened.

When I came to, it was late morning. The sun was shining, tropical birds that looked curiously like flamingos fluttered around the stream. After all those months at sea, my eyes were starved for color, and that jungle stream had color in abundance.

A dazzling rainbow spectrum of garish hues.

The gaudy jungle, however, was not what held my attention. Instead, it was a man bending over me, smiling— but with the tip of a short scimitar-looking knife pressed firmly against my throat.

"Lovely day," I said pleasantly.

He smiled back with equal pleasantness, and for a while I wondered if we would not get along . . . despite the strange thornlike adornments impaling his nose, lips, and ears. Bones, I thought, he's wearing pieces of bone.

A dozen or so strange, grayish, potato-shaped fetishes were festooned to his belt.

Unfortunately, the longer I stared at that belt and its appendages, the more I was disturbed.

The potato-shaped objects adorning his belt were . . . *shrunken heads!*

"Don't panic," Luis said calmly. "We shall get along famously. I can tell. In fact, I believe they are about to invite us to . . . *dinner.*"

SIXTY-NINE

WE DIDN'T SUFFER an overly long march to their village—though I, for one, was in no burning hurry to get there.

The smell of roasting meat permeated the village. A disproportionate number of the thatched-roof grass huts boasted cook fires just in front of their entranceways—fires framed by big spits with turning handles, on which were turning and roasting choice cuts of meat.

That the village boasted so many meat-roasters wasn't reassuring. In coastal villages, game was rare and the villagers—I had understood—typically supplemented their reduced meat intake with fish, which were available in abundance.

I was even more dismayed when we turned a corner, and I gazed on our new lodgings: *A huge bamboo cage, which already housed six captives.*

The fierce-looking warriors with shrunken heads for decorations gave us each an inhospitable shove into the cage.

The occupants we joined in the cage were similar in color but wore different body decorations and tattoos than the spearmen who took us captive.

Luis immediately struck up a conversation with a man who spoke some Spanish. His name was Raphael. He had been a worker at a Philippines mission run by Spanish priests before he washed ashore on the island after the fishing boat he was on sank in a storm.

"Where are we?" Luis asked him. "What in God's name is going on?"

"Whatever's going on, I assure you," the man said, "it has nothing to do with God—not unless your God advocates the consumption of human flesh."

I chose not to explain that my Aztec gods had demanded precisely that from their subjects.

"They feed us as much as we can hold—and then some," Raphael said. "But not out of their love of humanity. They're fattening us up."

With long hair, dark eyes and skin, a broad nose and mouth, and high, wide cheekbones, the Spanish-speaking native could have passed for one of the island cannibals who had captured us.

"How did the other men end up on this godforsaken island?" Luis asked.

"Their ship needed food and water," he said. "The captain sent them ashore to forage for provisions and a small army of these heathen hellhounds descended on them. When the captain saw how many there were, how ferociously they attacked, and how they were manning their outrigger canoes, he pulled anchor and sailed off, leaving them to face their man-eating fury. What about you two?"

"Shipwrecked survivors," Luis said.

"A typhoon sank our ship," I elaborated, "and we made landfall on a sinking spar."

"You were better off in the typhoon," Raphael offered.

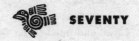

SEVENTY

As THE DAYS passed, our newfound friend regaled us with tales of this most inhospitable of regions. The rivers were so crocodile-infested as to be unswimmable. Consequently, escape from this cannibalistic death trap demanded the negotiation of dense, swampy, largely impassable jungles.

The tribesmen themselves were bronze-complexioned with long black hair, wide noses and cheekbones, and small deep-set eyes. They seemed somewhat shorter than Europeans. The hornbill head feathers, which the males favored, indicated social status and pecking order within the tribe. Each feather represented one head which the wearer had decapitated—just as the heads themselves would festoon the wearer's grass hut.

The upper back, shoulders, and upper legs of the men and women were heavily and elaborately tattooed with blue-black bloated scars.

I learned that the local pirates—who were notorious throughout the region for their ferocity—were not from the island but from a more "civilized" island. Known as Sea Dayaks and Ibans, they hailed from a large island called Borneo. Led by Malays, they marketed the slaves and goods they seized.

The cannibals were a similar group but not seafarers.

Nor had anyone ever accused them of being civilized.

Luis and I quickly realized that the typhoon had swept our ship far away from the Manila Straits.

Once—from the vantage point of our palatial abode—we witnessed one of their cannibalistic rituals.

It was hardly inspiring.

During the ceremony several captives—who had been caged and fattened far longer than ourselves—were led up stone steps.

Several warriors seized and subdued them, then unceremoniously brained them with clubs.

Then butchered and dressed them out like newly killed deer for dinner.

When their various loins, tenderloins, and sweetbreads were spitted and rotated over the cook fires—till their body fat crackled, smoked, and popped—the smoky smell of their roasting flesh was stomach-wrenching.

Luis said, "We are getting the hell out of here, amigo. You and I, we are impaling no cannibal's spit."

And I agreed, saying to myself, *I don't care how many victims my ancestors slew and devoured, I will not be one of them.*

SEVENTY-ONE

CAGED, WE HAD too much time to worry about our fate. Small, harmless snakes occasionally slithered in and Luis worked off some of his boredom by trying to make one into a pet.

Once a day warriors would poke us with spears until we undressed. When we were stripped utterly naked, the village women collected around our cage, where they excitedly ranked our respective male organs.

Raphael explained, "When these cannibals cut off our male parts, the pieces are apportioned solely to the women of the tribe in the deluded belief that devouring a male stalk will help make them pregnant."

"A thousand putas have gnawed on my garrancha," Luis grumbled, "and none of them got pregnant."

"The most monumental member is reserved exclusively for the chief's wife and is to be eaten first. The rest are devoured in descending order, the smallest to be ingested last," Raphael said.

The women seemed unsettled by my member . . . not so much by its immensity—which was not inconsiderable—but by its complexion, which was lighter than their males', who were almost as dark-complected as africanos.

They feared that my manhood's coloring would clash with their duskier hues, bestowing variegated light-and-dark blotches on their babies like the zulzi snake.

The women's fear of my organ had one positive effect. They were determined to kill, cook, and consume me next to last.

Luis was to be last. His member was not only lighter

than mine, it was so shockingly stupendous as to intimidate stud bulls and jack mules.

We stood in line, watching our cell mates barbarically brained, then brutally beheaded. Soon—despite the ferocious fears our male stalks provoked—we were at the line's head.

They were ready to bash, behead, and dissect us.

But Luis was nothing if not resourceful. He had already figured out that these cannibals would not eat anyone who was sick. He prepared a scenario that he was sure would deceive even the most cynical savage.

While we were waiting, he forced me to eat poisonous berries, which not only sent me into convulsions, it made my face blotch in the exact same manner the cannibal women feared my manhood would discolor their babies. While I convulsed in genuine agony, Luis went into action. Bending over me, he began sucking one of our pet snakes out of my ear.

The trick was pretty weak, but my convulsions and discoloration were genuine, which distracted Luis's audience from his sleight-of-hand.

They now believed Luis a genuine sorcerer.

Communicating with body lanuage and grunts, they named Luis head shaman. He promptly appointed me deputy shaman. Instead of feeding them, we would be feted.

My amigo was nothing if not resourceful.

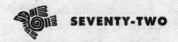

SEVENTY-TWO

LUIS AND I quickly learned these cannibals had strange sex customs and brewed lethal varieties of liquid spirits.

We discovered both these facts that very night during a ritual celebration in which the chief intoxicated us with some of their potent drinks and forced us to perform sex on his wives.

As best as I could tell from the sound, the names of the wives were Bari, Bati, and Badi. The chief now believed that if we inseminated them with our supernatural seed and godlike organs, the offsprings would be divinely endowed.

The wives weren't that bad-looking, but something about copulating cannibals repelled even my sexually liberal amigo. Not even Luis—whose ethical standards in erotic encounters was ludicrously low—could stand the lustful demands of the cannibal life.

Especially when the three cannibalizing wives pondered our private parts, licked their lips, and slavered *hungrily*.

The next night in the wee hours before dawn—after the natives had collapsed from drink and debauchery— we fled into the jungle and the dark.

Unfortunately, the cannibals knew the surrounding rain forest like monkeys know mangrove swamps and sharks know the sea. By dawn, they were almost on our heels, and gaining fast.

Every step of the way was agony: We were eaten by mosquitoes, blood-sucked by leeches, gnawed by ants, spat at by snakes, snapped at by crocodiles.

The sweltering tropical heat melted us right down to our marrow until we resembled tallow-dripping candles.

By late morning the cannibals' wolfish howls were re-verberating up our back trail.

Moreover, Luis—accustomed to horses and carriages—had never raced through swamp-choked thorn-ridden jungles barefoot. His feet—soft and spoiled from a life-time of leather boots and thick socks—were bleeding and blistered.

Once negotiating a high vine-tangled ridge we slowed down and caught a downhill glimpse of our pursuers.

It was hardly an inspiring sight.

Besides long composite bows and quivered arrows, the cannibals brandished eight-foot hardwood blowguns, as lethally and meticulously reamed-out as rifle barrels. Their arrows and darts were both poison-tipped, their fa-vorite toxins distilled from the fermented flesh of rotted corpses.

As we paused for a second look, a crossbow bolt almost hit Luis. A crossbow was a complex weapon, second only to a firearm in its lethal abilities. It wasn't a weapon that the primitive islanders would have.

Someone other than the cannibals were chasing us.

I groaned miserably.

Trained warriors armed with crossbows and prehis-toric savages were *both* dogging our tracks.

And both were trying to capture and kill us.

SEVENTY-THREE

ALMOST AS SOON as Luis ducked the crossbow bolt, an elephant came crashing through the foliage. It came right at us, knocking Luis aside and nearly trampling both of us. A dozen soldiers quickly surrounded us, their lances and nocked arrows pointed at our chests.

"Look on the bright side," Luis said. "They may kill us but at least they won't eat us."

Trussed up by the neck and wrists with heavy hemp ropes, we now marched with the soldiers of the local sultan. Luckily, their sergeant was the offspring of a Spanish sailor who had jumped ship in the sultan's domain and a local woman. His Spanish was rough, but serviceable.

We had a long, hot, tedious walk back to the sultan's palace, and the sergeant-at-arms, Sergeant Marquez, was as miserable as the rest of us. Tall, angularly thin, in a tan baggy uniform with a cylindrical military hat and tight breeches shoved into black knee-high boots—his clothes, like ours, were drenched in sweat.

Luis proceeded to entertain him with dazzling sagas of personal heroic deeds. Having served six months on a Manila slave-labor plantation as an overseer—Marquez had no love for the Spanish overlords, but respected them as a power in the region. As Luis related to him our miserable misadventures at the hands of Spaniards, the sergeant was genuinely sympathetic—Luis having managed to get around the fact that he was also Spanish.

Moreover, Marquez had soft eyes, a ready laugh, and a decent soul. He described our predicament to come and offered some useful advice.

"The sultan," Sergeant Marquez explained, "will be interested in your capture by and escape from the cannibals."

In fact, the sultan hated the cannibals as much as we did.

"The cannibals have raided his villages—for booty and human flesh both—and the sultan continually dispatches hunting parties to rescue the captives. Some cannibals are killed for sport. Some of them, our elephants trample to death."

Those who survived were eventually sold at slave auctions, where the man-eaters brought high prices.

"Slave masters," Sergeant Marquez explained, "dote on cannibals, frequently making them slave drivers. The only thing a lazy slave fears more than an overseer's whip is a cannibal licking his chops and flashing his razor-sharp teeth at him when he's slacking off."

In other words, the sultan's soldiers hunted cannibals for fun *and* profit, and one of these hunting parties had saved us from the dinner pot.

During the long walk Luis amused Sergeant Marquez with obscene tales of the women he seduced, the men he killed, the wars he won, most of which I no longer dismissed as the demented illusions of a fevered brain.

Soon the good sergeant was captivated.

"I will help you prosper in our fair land," the kindly sergeant said. "Due to your country's military presence in the nearby Philippines, the sultan is continually trying to improve his facility with your language. His most favored aides all speak Spanish and wish to improve their command of the tongue as well. I will suggest that were he to keep two enterprising Spanish-speaking men around his court, he and his advisers could increase their fluency in the Spanish tongue."

PART XVII

Are you saying there is no such thing as
dirty money?

—Juan Rios

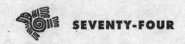

Sᴇʀɢᴇᴀɴᴛ ᴍᴀʀǫᴜᴇᴢ ᴡᴀs good as his word. He got us an appearance before the sultan. Moreover, he was sympathetic to our plight. He loved Luis's tale about buying dhows and opium in Hong Kong, blowing up the pirates, convincing the cannibals of our preternatural powers, our refusal to marry his daughters, and our escape across the swamp.

We stayed in the palace over half a month, eating, sleeping on daiwan cushions and sheets of finest silk. Each day we appeared before the sultan where we—mostly Luis— discussed and answered questions not just about Spanish weapons, warships, and battle tactics, but those of Europeans in general.

It became obvious that the sultan was not just improving his Spanish, but getting information he could use in future wars.

One night, however, after a glorious evening of music, laughter, and storytelling, we were told the soft treatment was over.

Marquez told us that the sultan considered letting us stay in the palace, as he was impressed especially with Luis's abilities and his stories. "He is bored with his tedious courtiers and viziers and you amuse him. But as foreigners, you would not survive palace intrigues."

The kindest thing that could be done for us would be to find us positions where we were safe.

"Slavery," Luis said, after Marquez finished. "We're being sold into slavery."

We were taken to the auction block in chains to await our turn.

"I spoke to a merchant named Anak who trades with foreigners," Marquez said. "I assured him that buying you two would be good for his business. He often deals with weapons of war. There is much need of such instruments in our land. And knowledge of languages."

Both of us spoke Spanish, of course, and knew a bit of Latin because most of our education came from priests, but Luis had traveled widely and knew other tongues, as he demonstrated so well in Hong Kong.

Luis counted off the situation on his fingers as we waited for Anak the merchant to finish his haggling with the slave auctioneer.

"One, the sultan's affection for us didn't prevent him from selling us to the highest bidder. Two, his war with Spain doesn't prevent his people from profiteering off that war. Thirdly, his kingdom is at war with everyone all the time. They live in a constant state of eternal conflict."

"So much for loyalty," I said. "The sultan had gotten all the information he wanted from us and now is going to make a little dinero. No doubt Marquez received a cut, too."

Luis, much more the experienced blackguard than I, shrugged off being sold into slavery by our new friends.

"It's the way of the world," he said.

"I wouldn't sell a man into slavery."

"How about Madero, the viceroy's spy and torturer?"

"I'd kill him but not sell him."

Anak, a trader originally from Bali, resembled a short squat ball of brown fat rather than a wealthy, influential businessman. We soon learned that he was a typical trader who worshipped before the altar of greed.

When Luis and I went to work for him, he made his moral priorities clear.

"You are men from far away. You will interpret for me business negotiations in the many foreign tongues I am told you speak. You will translate not just the terms presented, but by interpreting body language, you will inform me of the tricks the presenters employ.

"If you cost me money—whether through negligence or the subornation of baksheesh—or if you work your wiles on my wives, you will eat your penis, testicles, scrotum, and excrement . . . before you die. And you will die a thousand times."

Anak suddenly backed away from us.

"You stepped on my shadow," he said to me, his face working in rage. He shoved his index finger into my chest hard enough to hurt. "The shadow *is* my bodily spirit. Step on my shadow, you step on *me*. If you step on the sultan's shadow, he will have you cut into a thousand pieces."

Anak told us that the sultan not only provided a safe harbor for the Manila pirate crews who attacked our galleon but he shared in the booty. No one viewed piracy against foreigners as a crime but as a profitable enterprise.

The European brigands were worse than the Asian pirates because their ships were bigger. They paid for trading goods when they had to, but if they could commandeer them at gunpoint, they preferred that rate of exchange. It was more profitable.

We had been kept in the palace compound and now it was interesting to walk through the city with Anak orientating us. The sultan's capital was exotic in the extreme—a place out of the Arabian Nights. Besides native islanders, Chinese, Malay, and Europeans participated in its trade—when not at war with the sultan.

The city was a frenzied hive of activity. A receiving

and distribution point for the Spice Island trade, the city's crowded markets, warehouse districts, and docks reeked with the sweet and pungent smells of nutmeg, mace, clove, and pungent peppers. The world market for these goods was inexhaustible and ludicrously lucrative, and the source of these riches grew literally on bushes and trees.

Money bushes.

The major world powers fought and killed each other continually in their efforts to control the islands, while native rulers collected unimaginable riches.

In the harbor, baksheesh, the Asian version of New Spain's notorious mordida, was a way of life. Pirates swaggered openly up and down the streets, having bribed the sultan and his minions for that right. A Portuguese man-of-war would moor beside a Chinese junk, which dropped anchor next to a Malay sampan, while scattered in the bay were English, German, French, and Dutch vessels. For safe harbor and friendly access to rum and provisions, they all paid the sultan's bitter tariff.

"Don't think because you see European ships dropping anchor in the bay that you can escape to them. If you attempt to escape, you will wish you were back in the hands of cannibals. The sultan decrees death for escapees . . . a slow death."

While the ruling family and governing class were Malays, the merchants were mostly foreigners—Chinese traders predominating but also the Dutch, Indian, Arabic, and Persian. Slaves of all colors—including light-complexioned slaves—abounded.

Greed was the only true motivating force. The Spice Islands' easy wealth pitted every person against every other person.

And then there were Eurasian women—the most exotic-erotic women on earth. As God and Quetzalcoatl are my sacred witnesses, I shall never forget the vast array of bountiful beauties bouncing along those boardwalks in their flamboyantly flower-printed sarongs. Most of the women were bare-breasted, golden brown, eyes dark and cunningly slanted.

Many of these dazzling women were readily available . . . for a price.

Of course, they also shared the streets with glowering melancholic Dutch merchants, inscrutable Chinese traders, grinning, nodding Indians, frenetic French, and arrogant English.

The mud-and-straw buildings were a sun-splashed beige—not unlike the adobe buildings of New Spain—but with an Oriental cast—looming three and four stories above narrow, twisting passageways that were packed with stalls where vendors sold everything from live chickens and tropical fruit to hashish and snake oil—the common cure for every ailment under the sun.

Eerie Eastern and Near Eastern music permeated the stalls—the metallic discords of the Arab refrains, the eerie flute of an Indian shaman hypnotizing a cobra, the jarring jangle of chime and bells.

Local industries produced gold jewelry, cotton and silk fabrics, lamps, engraved copper bowls, and sword blades that merchants hawked with arm-waving shouts and avaricious abandon.

While the weather was endless summer and often balmy, black violent thunderstorms blazing with sheet lightning, slanting layered sheets of rain, and gale-force winds were also common occurrences—just as earthquakes, volcanic eruptions, typhoons, and tsunamis routinely ravaged the sultan's domain.

Like the geography, the commerce too had a frenzied quality. Make your money before things change . . . *catastrophically.*

The religious beliefs were as confused as the music. The region was originally animistic, which held that three superior gods oversaw creation, agriculture, and war. Countless numbers of lesser spirits ran the forests, rivers, rice paddies, earth, and sky—some inherently good, some intrinsically evil. Foremost in their beliefs was the theme that everything has spirit—rivers and forests, even the rocks and earth themselves.

Hinduism arrived with its pantheon of gods, and their worship merged with local beliefs. When Islam arrived, rather than displacing the existing religious elements, it meshed with them.

From what I saw, none of the religions were taken seriously in the islands. Islam took hold—but with none of the righteous fervor that had so enthralled the Middle East. When the Islamic muezzin called the faithful to prayer five times a day from the balcony of a towering minaret, only about half of the faithful bothered to kneel toward Mecca and recite their prayers.

In conversation with servants of Anak who claimed to be Muslims, most of them did not seem to know or care where Mecca actually was.

Hindus, who were supposed to view the bodies of meat-eaters as graveyards for dead animals, devoured meat as quickly and voraciously as any heathen. They were equally enthusiastic about drinking.

Superstitions, however, were obeyed in deadly earnest—even by the most religiously unobservant. Superstition carried with it the true force of faith, I learned.

In fact, superstitions far outnumbered faiths in the islands, especially among the people who lived inland, and superstition frightened any islander far more than the most devout Christian could ever dread hell.

Anak explained countless superstitions for Luis and

me—in hopes that we would not violate and bring eternal rack and ruin down on him.

One of the strangest superstitions was that dreams are living realities in which your soul departs your body, returning only when you awake. Since the events in dreams really happened, the maiden you violate in your dream has lost her maidenhood . . . the man you kill is dead.

Hence, you must never wake your master suddenly because his soul may lack the time to return to his body, and he may well die.

To avoid waking their masters suddenly, slaves approached by shuffling their feet or muttering quietly.

Anak held the veracity of superstitions to be self-evident. None of his impassioned beliefs, of course, prevented him from trading with and profiting from heathens who subscribed to none of his myths and whose lives he might have very well terminated in his dreams or whose daughters' maidenhoods he might likewise have terminated during his slumber.

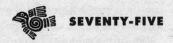

SEVENTY-FIVE

Luis and I settled into a small hut in the back of Anak's residential compound. The warehouse where he counted his goods—and his money—was at the docks.

Our plan was simple: To bide our time until we could escape and ship back to New Spain. We knew the harsh penalties we'd endure if we failed; we had to make it the first time because there wouldn't be a second chance.

"I see incredible amounts of dinero jingling in the pockets of heathen merchants and pirates that should be in the pockets of righteous souls like ourselves," Luis said. "It would be un-Christian of us not to carry back some of this wealth in our own pockets, no?"

Our most immediate problem, however, was sexual: Anak had failed to impregnate any of his several wives. The lack of a male heir created an atmosphere of gloom and discord in the family compound.

His wives had long ago lost all patience with him. They railed endlessly against his failings as a man for their inability to conceive. Anak said he was defenseless against their accusations because none of them had conceived. The only reasonable actions, he said, were to beat them frequently and find a way to make them conceive.

Anak described in detail each and every position of the Kamasutra that he and his wives had unsuccessfully attempted.

Another time Anak took me to a curtained-off stall where he showed me four small gold hollowed-out balls that he'd had stitched up and under the foreskin of his penis. The balls reputedly formed a stiff "ring" around the penis just below the head, which the surgeon had guaranteed would turn his women into his sex slaves.

Moreover, the hollow balls contained a smaller metal sphere that caused them to tinkle like tiny bells.

I never understood the workings of these tiny balls, but sure enough when he shook his member, they . . . tinkled.

Another appliance Anak had employed was a "penis ring" that also promised rock-hard virility. Joyfully intertwined dancing girls—lutes and hip harps slung over their winged shoulders—carved in exquisite bas-relief adorned the jade ring fitted around his member's base. The ring's secondary purpose was the stimulation of the woman's "Jewel Terrace."

"When I engage in sex," Anak said, "I always concentrate on a picture of a person or thing of beauty and grace, an element which the Javanese call 'alus.' It means refined, pure, exquisite, and ethereal. That will assure that a boy with beauty and power will be conceived."

The opposite effect was "kasar," which meant impolite, rough, uncivilized—like the sort of badly played music that habitually brutalized our throbbing eardrums. Negative thoughts result in kasar.

"Kasar," Anak said, "produces ugly, impotent offspring."

In his darker moments Anak feared he was produced through a long, dark night of kasar.

On another occasion, Anak used a Chinese aphrodisiac called the "bald chicken drug" that made a seventy-year-old man so virile that he made so many demands on his young wife, she couldn't sit down anymore.

"But it just makes my member limp," he whined.

In his hunt for remedies, Anak explored the yin-yang tradition of China. Women's yin essence was presumed to be inexhaustible while a man's yang—his essence, his semen—was finite. Ideally, a man would draw the sex act out as long as possible. The longer he remained inside the woman, the more yin—or essence—he would absorb from her.

"When the Chinese methods fail," Anak told us, "I attempt to follow the Hindu Cult of the Phallus. They attempt to incorporate sex into their religious practice."

He showed me a temple, which had numerous phallic representations inscribed on its walls and a giant statue of a stone phallus. Some of the members were so fanatical that they castrated themselves at the temple and threw their severed penis and testicles onto the altar.

One of the phallic symbols was that of the snake. Women who followed the rite adopted a cobra to help them conceive. So the merchant brought a cobra into the house for each of his wives. He gave up the practice after he lost a wife and two servants to lethal bites.

While Anak was desperate to have his wives impregnated, he wasn't willing to have it done by someone else. To ensure their chastity, when he had to be away from home overnight he had their vaginas sewn almost closed.

Anak told us he was seriously considering the Hindu practice of suttee, in which the widow is forced to throw herself on her husband's funeral pyre.

He believed the suttee sacrifice would stop his wives from plotting his death. If he did not impregnate them soon, he feared they would poison him and find a man who would satisfy them.

PART XVIII

ARMS MERCHANTS

Aₙₐₖ HAD A sprawling warehouse packed with assorted merchandise along the wharf. Much of his business
consisted of Chinese imports, including fine Shantung
silks and exquisitely carved jade. Artifacts for Chinese religious occasions and celebratory festivals were especially
popular among the islands' Chinese immigrant population.

We soon learned commercial disputes were resolved
differently than in our own culture.

After we arrived, Anak fell out with another merchant
over the ownership of a slave—each claiming they had
purchased the man. Ownership was to be determined by
"an ordeal of divination." The two parties simultane-
ously lit equal-sized candles. The owner of the candle
that outlasted the other in the burn-down was judged the
true owner of the slave.

Anak described to us another method for settling disputes: a white stone and a black stone were placed in a
bucket of boiling water. The two disputants were required
to reach in and grab a stone. The person who came up with
the white stone was judged the winner.

While inventorying the warehouse, I noted Chinese
firecrackers and festival rockets employed a very low
grade of black powder for combustion.

When I asked Anak why he didn't manufacture cannon
and musket powder, he said that the formula was a closely
guarded secret of the Europeans and that the islanders not
only lacked that formula, they didn't have the ingredients
and manufacturing know-how as well. As for firearms,
they didn't know how to produce iron or steel or how to

fabricate firearms from the materials even if they were available.

I knew the formula was not secret at all but that acquiring and mixing the ingredients—obtaining and incinerating the correct wood for charcoal, gauging the purity of sulfur and saltpeter by color and smell, and "corning" the powder into the appropriately sized granules—did require extensive training, skill, and the proper equipment.

Unless the materials are handled correctly, you end up with low-grade powder for fireworks, the likes of which Anak imported.

Fabricating firearms was different. Anak couldn't simply set up a factory and produce firearms. Even with my knowledge of weapons, such an enterprise would take money and equipment as well as both processed and raw materials. But I knew black powder could power weapons other than iron-forged firearms. During Father Hidalgo's revolution, my compañeros fired reinforced wood cannons when iron weapons weren't available. The wood cannons were best suited to shoot out a batch of nails and pebbles— lethal at close range.

Moreover, the islands were rife with hollow bamboo thick as a man's arm. By stuffing black powder and iron scrap into bamboo I knew I could manufacture crude cannons and bombs. Luis and I both knew that the weapons would pale in killing powder to the ones Europeans used. But . . .

"Patrón," I said to Anak, "I am a master black powder- and firearms-maker by trade. Luis is a skilled firearms expert as well. We could set up a powder- and weapons- making business."

Anak insisted that I demonstrate my skill. I told him I couldn't manufacture and demonstrate effective weapons with his low-grade explosive. With sulfur, high-quality charcoal, and saltpeter I could fabricate my own black powder.

He gave me money for sulfur, and I burned hardwood for charcoal. I was able to separate the saltpeter from urine, which I collected from the cesspit under the pissoirs and the latrines behind the main house.

I mixed the saltpeter, charcoal, and sulfur by weight in ratios of 15:3:2.

We took Anak into the countryside. Luis and I reinforced an eight-inch bamboo shoot with hardwood strips. We mounted the butt end in the ground at an angle and packed it with fragments of seashells. I put fire to the powder in the touch hole and it went boom! The blast shredded a "scarecrow" of clothes propped up ten feet in front of the barrel.

I then placed a bamboo bomb filled with seashells in a small abandoned wood hut. My bomb blew the wood hut to pieces.

Anak stared at the remains of the hut with gapping jaws.

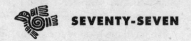

SEVENTY-SEVEN

THE CAPTAIN OF a ship of the line would have howled with laughter at our bamboo weapons. But Anak boasted of our weapons to potential buyers as if they would strike fear in the hearts of Pirate Alley denizens.

Since we had to purchase the ingredients for the powder and other supplies as well, Anak had to trust us not only with his money, he had to allow us to roam the island in search of what we needed. He wasn't happy about it, however. And would only trust us so far.

He assigned us a huge hulking companion with a shaved head and big curving scimitar, which he carried slipped though his waist sash of crimson silk. Favoring white, loose-fitting garments, he habitually wore a red cylindrically shaped hat. Anak told us the man had worn the same clothes when he was a harem guard, which meant to me that he was a eunuch. Ktut was particularly ill-tempered, and I never felt comfortable enough to ask him about his past sexual history.

Luis suggested that we owed ourselves some rest and relaxation. To Luis that meant an erotic odyssey through the local alleyway where prostitutes hawked their wares.

Luis referred to this thoroughfare as "Calle Puta."

The prostitutes plied their trade in gaudily painted sail-cloth stalls—lined up like big bird cages. Each cage had just enough space for a bed and a waiting prostitute. The prostitutes rented the space from the stall's owner, and their trade was openly tolerated. The Hindus believed that a person's dharma—the religious and moral law governing their personal conduct—determined the person's role in life. Thus a prostitute was "born" to be a whore.

As the old adage went, a prostitute is no better than she was meant to be.

Male prostitutes of varying ages and dimensions also rented stalls and practiced their own specialized trade. Occasionally we caught Anak entering their enclosures.

Luis and I quickly discovered that overpopulated Asian countries, such as China and India, routinely sold girl babies into sexual slavery. Purchased and raised by the pimps, they were employed as servants until they were old enough to ply their assigned trade.

In Calle Puta, fortune-tellers also abounded. They belonged to a bizarre tribe from Borneo and were known as basirs. Having both male and female sexual organs, they dressed and acted as women. Deemed intermediaries between heaven and earth, they claimed to unite in their own person the feminine element, earth, with the masculine element, heaven.

One stall housed a retired Portuguese sailor who sold linen penis sheaths, which he claimed prevented both conception and venereal disease. If so, the man should have used his own product. Horrendous syphilis scars scored his face, which it seemed to me undermined his claim that his sheaths prevented "the French Disease."

We passed a woman in a stall who promised to train women to tighten their Jewel Chamber by building up their vaginal muscles. The women who practiced the art claimed they could mount a man and achieve mutual orgasm by merely manipulating certain muscles.

Our guard, Ktut, told us the most expensive women were not in these cages, but inside a building. They had been trained by the woman in the stall.

I chose a woman trained in the muscle art.

Luis was nothing, however, if not self-destructive. While I was experiencing a loving art in Calle Puta, Luis visited Anak's beautiful Balinese wives.

In truth, he had never gotten them out of his mind.

He'd become obsessed. Even though I made him promise to leave them alone, he couldn't control himself. Climbing a vine-covered wall to their balcony one night, he entered a window and entertained them. As he read their tarot—he'd swindled "a Tomorrow-Teller" on Calle Puta out of her devil-card deck—they played a new game he had invented: strip tarot.

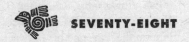

SEVENTY-EIGHT

As LUIS AND I built our gunpowder shop, I was so involved in acquiring supplies and equipment, I didn't have time to worry about Luis's nocturnal activities.

Not until a neighbor told Anak he saw a man climbing up the wall.

Luis, myself, and all the other men in the household denied guilt.

Anak announced that he would conduct a test to see who was lying. He had all of us line up one by one while he applied a heated spoon to our tongues. The theory being the guilty one's tongue would be dry.

It hurt like hell, but all of us passed—including Luis.

Luis later told me the fallacy of the test was that everyone had a guilty conscience for their bad acts. He boasted that he didn't have one.

Next Anak said he would test his pregnant wife—but not with the spoon. That test was for men. The Hindu code of honor required the wife to pass through fire to prove her fidelity to a jealous husband—getting burnt would be regarded as proof of guilt.

Luis and I had to get the wife out of the compound.

Or find a way for her to pass through fire without getting burnt—which couldn't be done.

But I was nothing if not resourceful.

I procured an ingenious Chinese black powder concoction known as "False Fire," which simulated thick flames and generated blinding smoke, but did not actually ignite. His young scantily-clad wife quickly and easily passed through the falsely flickering flames.

Everything went well after that because I was producing profitable black powder. Anak had three children on the way, and his only serious concern was how much money he would take in from our labor.

Luis and I had learned a great deal about the city and the ships in the harbor, including the way the sultan's guards kept an eye on the bay for slaves attempting to escape to a foreign ship. But we still had not figured out how to get the dinero to bribe a ship's captain. Stealing it from Anak was the most obvious route—as soon as we found out where he hid it.

Then word came from the sultan's palace that Luis and I appear before the Bendahara.

"Who's that?" I asked.

Anak didn't respond.

He only shook in terror.

We sat in his courtyard, sipping tea, waiting for him to explain. I finally repeated my question: "Who is the Bendahara?"

"Chief minister to the sultan."

"What's that supposed to mean?"

He finally met my gaze. "It means that you are in serious trouble."

PART XIX

Offend the Bendahara, and you will die one hundred thousand times.

—Anak the Merchant

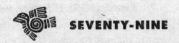

SEVENTY-NINE

JEN MENG-FU, THE Bendahara, kowtowed before Sultan Agung.

The servile deference literally meant "knocking one's head," which was how Jen performed it, prostrating facedown and touching his forehead to the floor.

He was reporting to the sultan about the foreigner "alchemist" who was able to turn the rawest, most inexpensive of materials—including the residue of common piss—into a powerful explosive.

"Great One," the Bendahara said, "the merchant Anak boasts that two slaves he obtained are repairing muskets and cannons and will soon forge their own firearms. The young assistant to the older Spaniard is even said to be a magician with killing powder."

"When you were gone, I had the two men stay in the palace and questioned them. I found out everything they knew about the guns and killing powder that Europeans use."

"I know that, Great One, there was nothing left to discover from these fools after you questioned them." Jen knew better than to infer the sultan had failed in some manner. "Because of your genius in bringing them before you to be questioned, another use of them has arisen."

"Which is?"

"To put them to work making killing powder and weapons."

"That would mean they would know what we have in armaments—and what we *don't* have. You know I don't permit Europeans to become familiar with my arsenal."

"A wise decision. However, we would have nothing to fear from these two. We only need them for the action we are planning against the Dutch. After they finish . . ."

He didn't have to elaborate on the fate of the two Spanish slaves.

The sultan stared at his Bendahara and pursed his lips. "War with the Dutch is coming. We will need these slaves to make weapons for the battle to come."

The Bendahara expected no credit for his scheme. Running the island nation while the sultan hunted animals and dallied with the women of his harem was reward enough.

Excused by a wave of the sultan's hand, Jen backed out of the room. Bent low, he never turned his back to the sultan.

Jen, who was Chinese by birth, was a gift to the sultan from the Chinese emperor twenty years earlier. Jen had ably served the emperor's father for a number of years. The new emperor had told the sultan, on presenting Jen to him, that Jen's administrative skills would surprise him.

At first the sultan had suspected Jen of spying for the emperor. While Jen was coldly calculating, the sultan quickly realized, however, he could not be an effective double agent. Jen was too reflexively brutal and uncontrollably cruel. He lived to inflict pain.

Cruelty was his primary motivational force—his second blood.

When Jen first came to the palace, his proclivities were apparent. Jen's abuse of his servants combined with the sheer viciousness of his political infighting shocked even the sultan . . . who was hardly a paragon of compassion.

In the end, however, the sultan changed his mind about Jen. He concluded that the Chinese emperor, Chia-ch'ing, had sent Jen to him not because he feared the sultan but because Jen scared the emperor.

Jen sometimes even scared the sultan—and *nothing* scared the sultan.

Still, the sultan had to admit, Jen had his uses.

Like many high-ranking Chinese governmental administrators, Jen was a eunuch. As such, he brought to the sultan's East Indies island a three-thousand-year-old Chinese eunuch tradition—political skulduggery.

An educated man, Jen knew that palace eunuchs were not restricted to China or the Islamic Ottoman Empire in Europe. Commonly employed in Rome, Persia, the Byzantine Empire, Italian boys training to become adult soprano singers—otherwise known as "castrati"—were gelded yearly.

Men in some Christian sects had themselves castrated because they believed it would permit them to better serve God.

Eunuchs rose to great power in empires because they guarded their ruler's most prized possessions: power, women, and treasure.

Jen—who had risen to power in China during the long reign of Ch'ien-lung, the father of the current emperor—had guarded the emperor's private *and* public domains with unparalleled effectiveness but also with frightening ferocity.

Tens of thousands of eunuchs served the emperor and the great princes of China. Many, like Jen, had themselves castrated. They simply hired a man who specialized in cutting off the testicles and often even penises. Those who were castrated involuntarily, such as prisoners of war or for punishment of crimes, often had their penis also removed. Chinese doctors had developed a technique whereby they created an opening for the castrated male to urinate after their penis was cut off. Sometimes they simply used a straw.

Jen was a "three treasure" eunuch—his penis and both testicles were cut off. After the slicing, the groin was dressed with a cloth that had been dipped in an oil and pepper mixture. If the new eunuch was able to urinate by the next day, he usually survived.

Not uncommonly, castration led to serious medical problems and even death. Even worse for those who had had it done voluntarily, it did not always create the opportunities expected. Many of the newly created eunuchs ended up homeless and suicidal after they were rejected for government service.

For Jen, self-castration was a road out of poverty. But not all those who chose self-castration had been poor: Many men who were not underprivileged had it done to increase their opportunities to rise to power and privilege. Emperors trusted their eunuchs because usually the eunuch's entire life centered on the master they served.

Following the castration, Jen presented himself at the palace at the age of twenty. After being examined to ensure that his "treasure parts" had been permanently removed, he entered government service in the imperial palace itself.

The Forbidden City, the vast palace compound in the heart of Peking, was staffed by thousands of eunuchs who performed services ranging from domestic servants to palace guards.

Because they were known for their servile flattery to their masters—and utter ruthlessness toward their enemies and even treachery toward their friends—eunuchs were viewed with caution and even apprehension by other palace officials.

Still young and in good physical shape—strong and tall—years from the sedentary lifestyle enjoyed by high-ranking eunuchs, Jen entered the palace guard service.

He rose to officer rank and ultimately organized a system of spies that worked to uncover disloyalty within the palace.

A national organization of secret police known in China as the Tung-ch'ang, the Eastern Depot, had operated for centuries under the control of palace eunuchs. The Eastern Depot sniffed out sedition not only in the palace, but in the entire country. Its torture chambers were called *Zhenfusi,* and it ran its own prisons.

The eunuch at the head of the Eastern Depot reported only to the emperor's chief minister, usually another eunuch, and the emperor himself.

Jen's success in uncovering palace intrigues—real or imagined—brought him to the attention of the Eastern Depot. Five years later, he had the head of the Eastern Depot tortured until he confessed to being a traitor—and Jen took his place as the emperor's spymaster.

As an old Chinese adage went, "Serving an emperor is like serving a tiger." One mistake and you are devoured.

Jen ran the secret police with savage alacrity.

As soon as he had the badge of authority in hand, he carried out a "cleansing" of the imperial staff in the Forbidden City. Hundreds of officials were put to death or driven out of office.

When the old emperor died and his son ascended the throne, Jen's competitor for remaining as head of the Eastern Depot was the eunuch that acted as the tutor and mentor to the new emperor. Jen lost his position. For his years of service, rather than being forced to commit suicide, he was given the opportunity to carry gifts and advice to the sultan . . . with the understanding that should he return to China, he would be executed.

Jen's reputation as head of the notorious Eastern Depot preceded him to the island—and the sultan welcomed him

because Jen had qualifications that warmed the cockles of
the hearts of Oriental despots . . .

Over the years, Jen had grown fatter and slower, and
he found kowtowing more difficult to do gracefully . . .
only his voice grew younger and higher pitched.

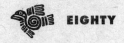

EIGHTY

JEN WENT DOWN the steps of a dark, dank dungeon—
his own Zhenfusi torture chamber—where his resident
torturer practiced the ancient mysterious and esoteric
arts of brute punishment and coercive interrogation.

One cage had originally held four prisoners. It was now
down to three. Jen had suspected the men inside of plotting against his authority and of undermining his relationship with the sultan. However, he had not brutalized them.
He simply left the four men in a cage and withheld food,
only allowing them water—which meant their sole source
of food would be . . . each other.

As an added incentive, Jen had let them know that the
survivor would go free.

The real purpose behind his visit, however, was to discuss the ongoing torture of a Dutch prisoner. The major
power in the East Indies, Dutch influence had waned
during the Napoleonic Wars in Europe. Four years ago,
however, after the 1815 Battle of Waterloo, the Dutch had
begun to reassert their influence. The region's native rulers
had resisted renewed Dutch hegemony, and wars against
the Dutch were breaking out.

The prisoner was a sergeant, commanding guards at a
Dutch fort. Jen was torturing him in hopes of getting more
details on the Dutch military buildup.

At present, however, he had something else on his mind.

"Keep your knives and pinchers red-hot," Jen said to
his black-hooded torturer. "I will have two Spaniards for
you to work on—if they don't do what I ask of them."

EIGHTY-ONE

AS WE WALKED up the street toward the sultan's palace where the Bendahara was also quartered, a shockingly anxious Anak told us: "Do not forget, when you meet the Bendahara in his chambers, you must kowtow to him. Do it respectfully. Your physical safety and well-being depend on it. The Bendahara is the last man on earth you want to antagonize. Offend him, and you will die a hundred thousand times."

Bowing and scraping did not go over well with Luis.

"Get me in a room alone with him for five minutes," Luis snarled. "We'll see how tough he is."

"This is no time for false vanity or your stupid Spanish machismo," Anak said logically, fearfully.

"I still don't see why I have to grovel for anybody," Luis muttered under his breath.

I personally didn't see that we had any other alternative. I also thought Anak was more right than he could ever know. After all Luis and I had gone through, I didn't see that either of us had anything left to be pretentious about. Our ordeal with the cannibals alone should have vanquished the last vestiges of our macho vanity.

We had heard the Bendahara's name spoken during our earlier brief stay at the palace, but had not seen him because he had been gone from the city on a task for the sultan.

Luis was intractable about not kowtowing to "Bastardo Bendahara," one of his gentler epithets for the sultan's much-feared chief minister whom he had yet to meet.

The attitude escalated Anak's stress to the breaking point.

"You two have brought me nothing but misfortune," he whined. "Not only is the sultan expropriating two expensive slaves—and from whose labors I had expected to profit handsomely—those same two slaves have now brought me under the Bendahara's notoriously savage scrutiny. What will be next? The tender ministrations of his Infamous Mage?"

I understood that "a Mage" was a preternaturally powerful wizard, but the word "Infamous" as part of the title threw me off. I asked Anak who or what the Bendahara's "Infamous Mage" was but he was too agitated to respond clearly. He could only grunt frightened incantations to whatever deities he worshipped—and it seemed to me he was willing to worship any and all gods if he thought they would save him from the Mage's "black arts, blacker heart, and foul sorcery."

The only advantage we had was that many palace officials spoke Spanish. Spain's presence in the region had been so widespread for so long, the language had become the international lingua franca—second only to gold.

A huge, ferocious-looking guard led us into the Bendahara's reception room where the court official was seated on an elevated gold chair.

After we kowtowed before Jen—Luis wisely joining the head-to-floor bumping—the minister told us that we no longer belonged to Anak but to the sultan.

Anak bowed and exclaimed eternal gratitude to the Bendahara as he hurried away after he was summarily dismissed.

"Your first new duty," Jen said, "will be to teach our Mage the secret arts of making killing powder and firearms."

The Bendahara stared at us, his eyes half-closed as if he was filtering our images.

"You must obey without question. If you had tried to escape Anak, you would have been severely punished . . . but not killed. For Anak, even after an escape attempt, you would have had a value and he would have stopped short of having you killed. Cutting off your noses would have sufficed.

"If you try to escape the sultan's service, however, or if you were to fail in your assignment, then you are of no worth and you will wish you were dead . . . you will loathe your existence and long for the grave."

Luis and I looked at each other. Neither of us doubted that an Oriental potentate had tortures that would make an Inquisition dungeon master envious.

"You," the Bendahara said to Luis, "will return to your shop with my guards and bring back the goods and equipment. You will no longer work at the shop owned by Anak. You," he said to me, "will instruct the Infamous Mage on the magic of the powder that kills."

An ominous figure—attired head to toe in black—stepped out from the shadows of the chamber.

The Infamous Mage had appeared.

The Mage walked me around a fountain in a lush garden. There, the black silk face mask was removed.

To my eternal surprise the Infamous Mage was a breathtakingly beautiful Chinese woman with large, black-almond eyes and small, delicate features.

EIGHTY-TWO

As WE STROLLED around the fountain, she cast pristine flower petals into its clear depths, hardly taking her eyes off of me as she talked.

"I already know how the killing powder your people call gunpowder works. It was an invention of Chinese alchemists. There was a book written almost nine hundred years after the death of the man Jesus called the *Secret Essentials of the Mysterious Tao of the True Origin of Things*. The manuscript tells us that the killing powder was discovered by Taoist alchemists searching for the elixir of immortality.

"My people delighted in using it for smoke and fire during celebrations but made little use of it in wars. Flying fire was shot out of bamboo tubes and small balls of killing powder were thrown by hand in battles during the age when the most powerful weapon in the West was the bow and arrow."

"But your people never developed it as the power source for cannons and muskets," I said. I knew some of the history myself from Felix's books.

"True, Gunsmith, the killing powder is a Chinese invention, but one we handled foolishly. Had we handled it wisely, we Chinese would rule the world today instead of kowtowing before the cannons of European warships.

"With the killing powder, Genghis Khan would have blown down the castles of Europe and ruled the entire world."

She continued walking around the pond, silently casting petals, but still staring at me.

I found her intense stares disconcerting—and wondered what she needed me for if she knew so much about gunpowder already.

"You know quite a bit about black powder already," I said politely, trying to fill the void.

"I know of the killing powder as a scholar but have never made it. I have no interest in explosives. The weaponry of war and death do not intrigue me because my work is not in taking lives but extending them. However, one does not disobey the Bendahara."

"I will do anything I can to serve you," I said. I spoke the truth, not doubting the chief minister's threat that we would curse life if we didn't meet his needs.

She had said her work was in preserving life. I wondered if she was a doctor.

"What is it," I asked, "that you're working on?"

"I will show you."

She took me to her workplace, a room beneath her living quarters in a corner of the palace compound.

The walls and ceiling were adorned with scenes from the Chinese horoscope and celestial map. I saw paintings of dragons and fish with wings, monkeys and tigers. On a table were oracle bones used in fortune-telling.

A strange chair with the coils of a cobra as the seat and the fanned head serving as the back was against one wall. What made the chair eerie was that the snake seat had real skin and eyes. It wasn't hard to imagine that a large number of snakes had been skinned to cover a frame, but as I stared at the head and the eyes appeared to stare back . . . I wondered *whose* eyes they had been.

Perhaps a hapless slave who didn't prove his worth to the Mage and the sultan's chief minister?

She called the chair a *naga*. "The serpent spirit is a servant of Buddha. When Buddha approaches, the snake coils to make a seat and raises its hood to shade the master's head from the sun."

The room, like the snake chair, had more the atmosphere of magic than practical alchemy.

She showed me her worktable, which was almost covered with bowls and jars with liquids and dry substances.

"The search for what I seek began even earlier than the discovery of the killing powder. Chinese emperors have long dreamed of a fabled elixir called Dancing Water. It is written that a few drops of this magic drink promises eternal life."

"You drink it and live forever? I see why emperors would want that." If I had all their privileges, I'd like to live forever, too.

"It was believed that a fountain of the elixir existed on an island found on no nautical charts. More than two centuries before the birth of the man Christ, the great emperor Ch'in Shih huang-ti sent the most powerful alchemist in all China to the Eastern Sea in search of it. It's said that the alchemist found the isle called Nippon instead, though that is not proven because he never returned to China."

She pointed to a bowl containing a green powder. "This is jade. Because of its beauty and rarity it is believed that if a person ingests it, their life will be extended. The same for gold, cinnabar, and saffron. I use these substances plus many others, including the hearts of elephants and turtles, beasts known for their longevity, in my search for the elixir."

I cleared my throat. "People drink gold and jade?"

She gave a quiet laugh. "Not in molten form, but only after it is turned into a fine powder and dissolved in rice wine. The most distinguished book on secrets of alchemy, the *Tan Chin Yao Ch'ed*, describes the concoction."

She went on to describe how sulfur, an ingredient in gunpowder, mercury, used in silver mining to separate silver from other ore, and the poison called arsenic were substances also used in the search for the elixir.

Ayyo . . .

She read my thoughts and gave me a smile that conveyed her own unspoken amusement.

"Gunsmith, you are correct in wondering whether the powders of immortality can also be deadly. It is written that many Chinese emperors died from drinking elixirs concocted by their alchemists. I am very careful of what I give the sultan to drink because I would be tortured if he should fall ill after ingesting an elixir."

She indicated that her discourse and our walk were over. I returned the polite bow she gave me and she said in parting: "Tomorrow you will begin teaching me about the killing powder. The sultan has some weapons called muskets and pistols gathered over the years but few work. You and your companion will repair the weapons and show me how they are made. At other times, you will give me instructions about the killing powder while your companion works with the weapons."

EIGHTY-THREE

WE ARE IN trouble," I told Luis after I joined him in the small, dark monk's cell-like room we shared in the palace compound. I whispered, knowing that the walls have ears.

"I can teach the Mage to make black powder, but in this climate where it's always so wet you can almost drink the air, keeping the powder dry will be a constant problem. I'll never be able to show her how to make powder as good as what I made in the colony. As for cannons and muskets, they lack not only the makings of a foundry, but even if they had a foundry, they don't have the iron, bronze, or steel to produce weapons.

"The best I can do is give them hand bombs they will never keep dry and bamboo cannons and muskets that will shoot a ball about the same distance they can spit."

"Anything that explodes will impress them."

"True—until they duel with the Dutch or Spanish, pointing their bamboo cannons at ships with real ones. The same with the firearms. The Mage is an alchemist who thinks in terms of mixing a few ingredients together, maybe some iron and copper and poof! A musket pops out. She would need a blacksmith's shop, a foundry, and—"

"Don't worry," Luis said, displaying his eternal confidence that he would have a trick up his sleeve to save us, "we need only to stall them long enough to arrange an escape. With significant gold in our pockets to ensure that we return to New Spain in a grand style."

He locked eyes with me. "Amigo, from this moment on,

we must watch our backs and plan our escape. We must get off this island even if we have to swim."

I didn't point out that the Bastardo Bendahara had probably already guessed that we would make escape plans as soon as we were out of his sight.

The next morning I got up early, met with the Mage, and began instructing her on the curious art of black powder manufacturing.

To my surprise, the shop was against a wall inside the palace compound. Used to skulduggery and machinations, the Bendahara wanted to make sure that he could keep an eye on our activities. The fact that we might accidentally blow up the palace had not occurred to him. I said nothing because I didn't want to begin my task by showing up a man who loved to torture underlings.

Luis worked in an adjacent shop, servicing the sultan's old muskets and pistolas.

Ayyo . . . a stray bullet into my powder room and Luis and I would leave the island like Chinese rockets.

Luis also had five iron cannons to work with, purchased by the sultan from pirates who took them off a European merchant ship.

I had only the opportunity to walk by the cannons and had kept a straight face when meeting Luis's eye. The cannons were worthless. Cracks had been sealed with lead . . . which worked fine if you wanted to keep out water, but did almost nothing to keep in the combustion of gunpowder.

The Mage told me they had six iron cannons until the sultan's chief general had his men load one with black powder bought from the same pirates. The general and his "cannoneers" had not survived the explosion.

Clearly they didn't know how to mix and handle black

powder, nor how to gauge whether a cannon was safe to fire.

The cannons bought from the pirates were not repairable. They could have been melted down and recast in a proper foundry to produce poor quality but usable barrels, but a foundry didn't exist on the island. From the stories I heard, I was certain none existed anywhere in the Far East or Pacific islands.

They had four other cannons, small, inferior Chinese models that a glance at their thin, rusted, iron castings told me would explode the moment they were fired with enough power to send a ball against a fortress or a ship.

Knowing that my lifespan was directly connected to how enthused the sultan and Bendahara were about the munitions project, as the Mage showed me junk firearms and black powder that you could hardly blow a nose with, I did a lot of smiling and nodding and making nonsensical listening responses.

Luis, of course, outperformed me. I could hear his exclamations of wild enthusiasm as he talked to a military officer about the worthiness of the firearms—muskets and pistols we both knew couldn't be repaired because there were no spare parts or a way to make parts. Cannibalizing parts from one weapon to another would result in only a few usable weapons—for which they had little usable gunpowder.

"We'll need bamboo and hardwood in large and small sizes to test the killing powder," I told the Mage. "That way we will be certain we have the correct proportion of ingredients before we test it on the sultan's expensive firearms."

I didn't add that it would permit us to stall disclosure of how worthless the armory would be. By strapping more hardwood or bamboo on the barrels to be fired, I would be able to make cannons that would fire a deadly blast of pebbles, seashells, and whatever other small items we could stuff into it.

After the sultan's army challenged with wood cannons a typical European warship like a "French 74," a two-deck ship of the line armed with 74 guns capable of hurtling a ball over a mile, the punishment Luis and I would receive from the sultan would strike terror even in Aztec priests who had skinned people alive.

Knowing the Chinese love and awe for rockets, and figuring it might also buy us a few days delay, I told the Mage I had ideas for developing and deploying explosively tipped bamboo rockets.

The Mage suddenly bowed deeply and I turned to find the Bendahara had appeared. I gave him a small bow.

"Your Excellency," I said.

"Walk with me and tell me your impressions of our armaments."

I joined him on a path in the compound and talked about the state of the weaponry. He was no fool, so I didn't inflate my evaluations of the weapons. By now, other Europeans would have told him what was wrong with the arsenal. Much of it was obvious. The knowledge he wanted was my ability—and inability—to make the necessary repairs and provide effective gunpowder. And I had no intention of cutting my usefulness short by telling him I couldn't meet his goals.

Ayyo . . . I saw no percentage in explaining to professional torturers the folly of their ways.

EIGHTY-FOUR

THE BENDAHARA TOOK me to a courtyard where two men awaited.

"You will be witness to a duel," he told me, explaining that the two men were nobles who each claimed that the other had offended him. They were going to settle the dispute by a fight to the death.

"The choice of weapons is knives," the chief minister said.

That would have been my choice, too, considering how fast gunpowder turned damp in the tropical climate.

As servants prepared the men for the match, the Bendahara explained to me, "One man is bigger than the other. His longer reach gives him an advantage over the smaller man. To ensure that the fight will be of equals, I have had them bound as you see."

One man had an arm tied behind him, the other man had both arms free but had a length of rope tied to his legs in a manner that let him still move about, but forcing him to take shorter steps.

I realized that the man whose arm he'd tied had the longer reach and the man whose feet he'd hobbled was the faster of the two.

It also struck me that from what I had heard about Jen, he would care little about the justice or correctness of the outcome, but would have ulterior motives for lengthening the bout. Looking about casually, I saw what he was up to: The handicaps not only equaled out the match based upon the relative strength of the two combatants, but would make the match longer and more enjoyable to the Bendahara and the rest of the "audience."

I spotted the onlookers peeking out from bushes and windows.

The minister had no doubt given invitations to what the combatants thought was a private fight to the death.

The weapons Jen provided them were blades of equal length and sharpness.

"What do you think of my fairness?" Jen asked.

"You have the wisdom of Solomon, Your Excellency."

"Solomon?"

"An infinitely wise king, my lord. When two women each claimed they were the mother of a newborn babe, Solomon settled their dispute by offering to sever the baby in half. When one woman protested, and the other said 'Cut away,' Solomon gave the baby to the woman who protested, saying she had proven herself to be the true mother."

Staring at me, he stroked his beard and nodded approvingly. "No," he said, "I am even wiser than Solomon. For troubling me with their petty squabble, I would have had the two women scourged, and then sold them and their child into slavery."

"Very wise, Your Excellency," I croaked.

He flipped his hand at the two combatants who kowtowed to him, then rose and faced each other. They bowed and began the dance of death.

"There is court gossip that the larger man is a friend and that I have created a pretense at equality to give him a better chance at winning because the smaller man is the better fighter."

I nodded. "Faster and shorter can give an advantage."

"The gossip angered me for two reasons. The first is the claim that I arranged the match to help a friend. As long as these foolish courtiers have worked for me, they still do not know me at all."

"In which regard don't they understand you, Excellency?"

"Claiming that I would go out of my way to help a friend. Will they never understand?" He then treated me to a small derisive laugh and a smile of mean merriment. *"I have no friends."*

As the two men circled each other, rather than enlightening me as to the second reason why the court gossip annoyed him, the Bendahara compared the war between nations with the two-man struggle before us.

"In any engagement, there are always questions of who is the bigger opponent, the more mobile, the more reckless, the more aggressive. Who is forced by necessity to take the defensive or adopt the offensive. So it is with nations. The bigger, more aggressive, more powerful, more mobile opponent will usually win the fight.

"But not always. A general can prevail against a larger force if he is clever enough. The greatest military strategist of all time, Sun Tzu, wrote twenty-three hundred years ago that if your opponent is in every way your superior, you might still prevail."

"How?"

"You must, Sun Tzu said, hold hostage what your adversary holds dear."

While Jen talked, the two men in the "ring" slowly circled one another, sparring and feinting with their daggers, each looking for an opening.

"Enemies may spar with each other interminably," Jen said, "but at some point in the contest a moment of truth arrives and a decisive blow must be struck. The sparring can go on endlessly, but the decisive blow—when it is struck—usually takes less than a second.

"The same in war," Jen said. "After all the planning, all the preparation, the clash of arms and armies, all the sparring, victory or defeat can come down to a quick decisive blow that destroys the enemy."

The two knife-fighters closed, the bigger man shouldering the smaller man up against the low wall, which enclosed the fighting area. To block the man's overpowering strength, the smaller man had to drop his blade and grab the other man's knife arm with both hands.

As they struggled, a person in black suddenly appeared from behind a black curtain, draping an adjacent doorway. Sneaking up behind the bigger man, he slipped a knife in the man's back.

The person in black immediately ducked back behind the black curtain and was gone.

"Surprise is the mother of victory," Jen said. "Now you see, Gunsmith, that the most decisive blows against a more powerful enemy are delivered through stealth and cunning. Thus we must defeat our enemies through unexpected stratagems—ploys which they could not anticipate."

In other words, through treachery, I thought.

The Bendahara stared at me without smiling. "The second reason is that I would help one of my favorites. The talk offends me because the fools believe that they can anticipate my moves. The demonstration today will once again let them know that they will never know from which direction I strike."

He waved me away with a flick of his wrist and I walked back to my new workplace.

He had gotten his message across loud and clear: He had surprised the courtiers by having his favorite, the bigger man, killed, to turn the tables on the courtiers who had guessed that he was planning to aid the man.

And the message about never knowing where and when he would strike was a double-edged sword: The other side of the sword was hovering over the necks of his two new gunsmiths.

PART XX

Great Beauty Is Invariably Bloodthirsty.

—An Ancient Adage

WHILE INSTRUCTING THE Mage on gun and powder fabrication the next day, I asked her how the sultan planned to use the firearms and gunpowder.

"The greatest treasure of our region is not gold or silver, we find neither under our ground, but the pungent and fragrant nuts and seeds found in the islands that Europeans call the Spice Islands. For a long time, the Spanish, Portuguese, and Dutch all battled for control of the islands and the trade in their spices. The Dutch won control, but during those many years while European nations were occupied by the wars of the warrior-king Napoleon, the Dutch loosened their grip on the trade.

"For twenty years the sultan has collected tribute from the native leaders on the islands in return for protecting them from predators and pirates. But now the Dutch have returned and the native leaders will no longer pay the sultan. They say that the great warship the Dutch sent to once again dominate the islands is too powerful to resist and offers better protection."

"How does the sultan plan to get back control?"

"He has invited the Dutch governor to come here and negotiate a treaty. The Dutch believe the treaty will acknowledge their dominance in exchange for a small payment to the sultan. But he will have a surprise for them."

"His arsenal of cannons and other European weapons?"

"The Dutch governor won't leave the ship, but instead of welcoming the ship when it enters our harbor—"

"The sultan will open fire on it."

She clapped her hands. "Exactly. You see, you and your

friend have been given a great and glorious task. Imagine the rewards you and your companion will get when your weapons sink the warship."

Ayyo . . . I could easily imagine what our "rewards" will be.

I could also imagine that after blowing away our artillery positions, the Dutch warship would turn its guns on the palace and the rest of the city.

"But more important, Gunsmith," the Mage went on, "the sultan is fighting the Dutch to honor his religion. For centuries the European powers had crusaded against the Muslim states of North Africa and the Middle East. The sultan believes it is his duty to Allah to fight the infidels."

I was taken aback by the Mage's response. I had never considered that the sultan would war on another nation as a matter of religious principle. The powerful men in the history of New Spain had not really been motivated by religious fervor, but military honors, sexual despoiling, and a lust for treasure.

I had never heard of a potentate taking a bloody military stand based primarily on heartfelt religious beliefs.

"What does the sultan plan to do with his control over the Spice Islands once he gains it?"

"Give them back to the Dutch for a much greater payment than they offered before."

Now that was a kind of religious fervor I recognized.

EIGHTY-SIX

THE LONGER LUIS and I stayed in the islands, the more urgent it became that we had to escape. We were not cut out for the claustrophobic confinement of palace life—with a sword hanging over our heads. Nor was I comfortable with Luis's endless need for dangerous sexual conquests—just as he once found his way to the quarters of Anak's lonely wives, he now talked about invading the sultan's harem.

"The girls stick their heads out from behind window curtains in their second floor rooms to watch me work." He grinned as he whispered, "Sometimes they expose more than their faces to me."

Ayyo . . . nothing was sacred to Luis and nothing was more sacred to a potentate than his harem girls . . . except for his treasure, and Luis even talked incessantly about having learned of an underground passage we could use to blow our way into the room that was reputed to be filled with chests of gold and gems.

It was inevitable that we would eventually run afoul of the wrath of the sultan or his vicious chief minister because Luis violated a vestal virgin, I failed to kill enough Dutch, or we violated any one of an endless number of taboos and be subjected to the death of ten thousand cuts—or a hundred thousand, whatever it was. Not that the number mattered—who would be counting?

I had also noticed a change in the way the Mage acted toward me. She had become extremely friendly, finding reasons to touch me or brush against me when we were working together.

I found her attractive, but sensed an aura of dark mystery and even danger emanating from her.

Devising an escape plan—and acting upon it—became more urgent every day.

Luis had much more freedom of movement than I did because he made finding parts and scouting for gunpowder ingredients reasons to leave. His efforts would inevitably bring him to the warehouses along the docks and the taverns where foreign sailors and pirates gathered. Luis was too smart to put out feelers about buying passage for two slaves. "The captain who loses the most at cards and doesn't want to return home broke is the ship we will book passage on . . . the night before it is about to be carried out of the bay by the tide."

I had an idea formulating in my head on how to cover our escape, but needed to work out the details—along with how we could kill ourselves if we failed and were captured.

EIGHTY-SEVEN

THAT NIGHT THE Mage summoned me to her room. She sat in the oversized green cobra chair. Reclining on its coils, the Mage rested her nape on the snake's throat . . . just below its hooded gape-jawed head.

Smoking from a silver hookah, the Mage motioned me over.

I had already discovered the Orient was a land of dream dust. My indio ancestors who used many dream-making drinks and smoke in their rituals, including pey-ote mushrooms that took one on journeys through time, would have appreciated the preoccupation in the East with dream-making.

Handing me her hookah, she bade me sit at her side on the snake's coils. I knew not to decline the offerings of the Mage—any more than I would have disobeyed the commands of the sultan or the Bendahara. Her wrath could be every bit as lethal as theirs.

"Smoke deep," the Mage said. "The smoke will make you see."

"Yes, Mage," I said. "I am yours to command."

I didn't have to ask what was in the pipe. A whiff of opium hit me the moment I walked in the door. And with it remembrances of another place where I had smelled opium and visited a woman of beauty and mystery. And a snake.

I sampled the pipe. I had never smoked opium, and it jolted me with jarring force. My drug-deranged brain quickly and suddenly transformed the Mage into the cobra-hooded naga. As she looped coil after iron coil around me, I writhed in her serpentine embrace. I twisted, however, not so much out of fright as enchantment . . . I was mysteriously enthralled and eerily aroused.

Then I dreamed we were in bed—locked in the throes of passion. I soon realized, however, that part of the experience wasn't a dream. We *were* in her bed . . . amorously entwined. I knew the experience was real, because the sensations were too convulsively carnal, too ecstatically intense.

For sure, I had a woman in my arms, not an opium-induced image.

Yet at the same time her lovemaking was . . . *un*real. Her magical mouth seemed all around me—everywhere at once, preternaturally powerful, capable of consuming me whole. Her lips laved my soul with the grace of angels even as her tongue teased and tantalized, tortured and titillated my tingling flesh. All the while her body undulated around mine—lithe and slender.

In the dark of her bed, surrounded by the erotic mists of our opium dream, our bodies communed and commingled as one . . . in a night without end, void of reprisals, regrets, or recriminations.

Hers was a body and a soul that wanted only me. A transcendent lover, she suffused every ounce and inch of my being with her own—with the beatific soul of an earthly goddess and the bodily desires of an incredibly erotic courtesan.

Compared to my past life, the Mage's boudoir—where I writhed in ecstasy in her arms and charms—seemed perfection incarnate.

Could this be the paradisal peace I was born for—a lifetime with the Mage?

Could this be my true destiny and destination?

I dreamed such dreams for a while and they were sweet. But not for long.

Nothing, in the end, is as it seems—not in the real world and never in a land of dreams.

EIGHTY-EIGHT

I HAD COME back from instructing workers on how to bore pieces of hardwood into cannon barrels when I saw Luis talking to the courtier who supervised the servants that brought us food and drink. Luis seemed to be gawking.

"What did he tell you?" I asked Luis after the man left. "Has the sultan built special racks for us in his dungeon?"

Luis shook his head and stared at me wide-eyed. "A very strange land. He told me that the Mage is also called the Exotic Eunuch."

"The what?"

"Shhh, lower your voice. He said the Mage is a three treasure eunuch that had all her male parts removed but went a step further and had a Jade Chamber—"

I walked away, unable to hear any more. I felt as if I'd been kicked by a mule in the stomach. I went into the workshop to be alone. I had never told Luis about my feelings for the Mage or that I had made love to her, but I think he guessed I had feelings for her. He was too smart an hombre not to read me like he reads others.

The door opened and the Mage came in. She had a big smile but it faded when she saw my face.

"You're . . . a eunuch?" I asked, my voice quivering.

She recoiled as if I had struck me and backed out the door, her eyes tearing, her chin trembling in and out. Pressing her hands to her face, she turned and fled.

Luis came in a moment later. Here was a man who wasn't intimidated by pirate fleets and island-smashing typhoons, yet he had an expression of deep concern.

"Amigo, I think it is time we leave this island."

# EIGHTY-NINE

WE MADE OUR plans as we corned gunpowder a day later. I had already decided we needed a diversion that would stun and occupy not just the palace guards, but the spies and guards the sultan had posted at the wharf. In other words, capture the attention of the entire city.

"We're going to blow up the palace," I told Luis. "Or at least make it appear that way."

We would create a smoke and fire display like we did for Anak's unfaithful wife. But this time on a grand scale, doing what Luis told me the French called a *pyrotechnie* display when they created dazzling fireworks for their kings at Versailles.

"I've kept a good quantity of high-grade powder dry in pouches. It will ignite the lesser grade stuff that I'll mix with other ingredients and put out so much smoke and the appearance of fire, it'll look like the palace fell into the mouth of a volcano."

I would provide the smoke screen for our escape, but we wouldn't get any farther than a rowboat at the docks if Luis didn't get us money and passage.

"I've had my eye on a Portuguese captain who has been losing every night at cards. His ship is sailing with the morning tide and he won't want to go back to Lisbon with his pockets empty."

"What if he wins tonight?"

Luis grinned. "He won't. He's lost so consistently, you'd think the player who's been winning against him has been helped by the gods."

He didn't need to explain.

"We'll need gold."

"I'll gather that the moment you create your diversion. Anak's wives during moments of ecstasy and gratitude confided in me that he keeps a sack of gold at the bottom of the well in their courtyard. He fishes it out with a long hooked pole he has hidden in the bushes. When people rush to see the palace on fire, I'll go over the wall and fish for it."

It was a wall he had become very proficient at scaling.

I busied myself preparing the fuses and series of explosives that would go off one after another turning the palace into chaos. I needed a slow fuse to begin the process because I planned to be outside the palace gate when the volcano erupted.

Both of us had freedom to come and go from the palace because we were constantly hunting down supplies, but we also knew that the wharf area was being closely watched for escape attempts.

I did not see the Mage that day or night and she was not at the workshop when Luis and I arrived that morning to launch our escape. The Portuguese ship was sailing with the tide and the time was right, but we both were hesitant because Luis was unsure about the ship's captain.

"He lost so much at cards, he won't be satisfied with just the gold we offer. He'll want everything we have and a promise to give him our firstborn as bond servants. He'd rip out my teeth if he knew I had a gold filling."

I had not slept well but had terrible nightmares of nagas and other creatures tormenting me.

Ashamed, I had not mentioned my agony of learning the truth about the Mage to Luis . . . and good friend that he was, he ignored the subject and told me funny stories about his life as a picaro on the city streets of his beloved Spain.

We were surprised to find the Bendahara's chief aide waiting for us when we arrived at the workshop.

"The Bendahara commands that you prepare a demonstration for the sultan today to show him how the killing powder will launch balls from cannons and muskets. It will take place in two hours."

The boot-licking bastardo paused and gave us an arrogant smile.

"He commands that you use the metal cannons, not the wood toys you have been playing with."

As soon as he strutted away, Luis and I stared at each other.

There was no possibility of firing the weapons with full charges. And to load a cannon with less than a full charge would show that they were worthless . . . as were the cannon masters.

The avaricious Portuguese merchantman captain had suddenly become our only hope.

"I'll get the explosions going," I said.

"I'll get the gold and meet you at the dock."

After Luis hurried off to get "supplies" for the demonstration to make for the captain, I went into the workroom to set the fuses and make final preparations.

The fuse I selected that would trigger the smoke and fire volcano was a slow one. It was for the powder I'd kept dry but had diluted the explosive power of because I wasn't trying to blow up the building, just start an inferno that spread faster than a contagion of the plague.

I lit the slow fuse and turned away to get my cloak that was hanging from a hook. The cloak would come in handy to keep off rain and to hide my European features from people on the street.

Then I heard something that caused me to turn around.

The sound of the fuse—it wasn't the fizzle of a slow fuse but one that was *racing*.

I froze and gawked at the incredibly fast rate the burning was speeding for the gunpowder container.

The door was closer to me than the end of the fuse. I jerked it open, pulling it toward me and got one step toward getting around it when I felt as if I was hit by a bolt of lightning, a fireball from hell.

Then I heard nothing, saw nothing, felt nothing.

Time passed, I don't know how much, a great deal of time to me, but perhaps only seconds for an observer.

The light faded, darkness came, and my mind shut down. At last light came again.

I couldn't hear anything, but my body was on fire.

I pushed up with my hands and the heavy door slid off me.

The smoke was blinding, and I was choking.

But choking was good. It got my lungs working, my body functioning. As Luis once told me, pain was good—it told me I was alive.

Secondary explosions from batches I'd planted around the area were detonating one by one. I knew these things rather than saw them because the smoke was already black and thick.

I realized the blast blew upward and out, knocking off the roof and flattening the walls in every direction. The door had shielded me from most of the blast.

I crawled and choked, stumbled and staggered to get away from the heaviest concentration of the bellowing smoke. Panic was all around me. People ran and shouted, men and women cried out in fear and panic, trying to escape what they believed was an inferno. At the moment, I had no idea of how much damage had been done or if the entire palace compound was going up in flames.

My lungs were on fire by the time I got out of the palace gate and past the now abandoned guard post.

My feet kept me moving as if they were wise and all-knowing because my mind wasn't able to direct them or anything else about my body. I knew I was hurt, that I had been scorched by the blast, perhaps so much flesh had been ripped off I was a skeleton.

I saw a man on horseback, then literally ran into the horse as the man stared at the flames and smoke erupting from the palace. He shouted in surprise as I pulled him off the horse. He fought back and I pulled my knife from its scabbard and slashed his cheek. He ran and I took his horse.

When I slipped off the horse at the wharf, Luis ran from the dinghy he had tied to the dock to help me.

"Dios mio! What happened?"

"The Mage," I croaked. "She spiked our powder in secret and replaced our fuses."

"Why?"

I stared into his eyes, silent.

Luis stared back, nodded once—and said nothing.

He understood.

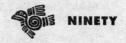

NINETY

L UIS HAD BEEN right about the Portuguese captain. He had not actually held us upside down to shake coins from us, but had gone a step better—after we boarded the ship and Luis gave him half the gold from Anak's well, he took the other half also and then had us stripped naked to make sure we weren't hiding even a copper.

Stripping me down had exposed innumerable wounds and burns. Not even Luis has escaped uninjured—the right side of his face was slightly swollen from a blow he took when he ran into a guard at Anak's.

After I finished howling from being washed down with salt water on the deck by Luis, we retired to the cubbyhole assigned to us—a room just big enough for two canvas bunks.

The room stank of the sea and sailors but I was able to crawl into the narrow bunk and "enjoy" the pain.

"The Bendahara gave you the torture of a hundred thousand cuts," Luis joked.

Ayyo . . . worse than my pain was the knowledge that we would have to become bandidos when we got back to the colony. No, bandidos in Portugal because we have no dinero left to pay for passage from Lisbon to Veracruz.

"Señor Azteca, never fear and never doubt your amigo," Luis said.

He had been practicing dealing cards by the light of a candle and now placed the candle by me. He spit into his hand and the "swelling" of his jaw disappeared.

Bloodred rubies glowed in his hand.

"Madre dios," I whispered. "Anak had a treasure in the well."

"Not Anak. A gift to me from the sultan's harem girls."

I gaped. "You didn't—"

"Amigo, I earned these gems a hundred times over." He grinned. "That's how many of his wives needed to be serviced."

NINETY-ONE

LOTUS BLOSSOM HAD told me that great beauty was unerringly bloodthirsty.

At the time, I didn't understand or appreciate her wisdom, though she was obviously an example of the expression's truthfulness.

Now I had been blinded by great beauty; when I stared into the sinfully sensuous eyes of the Mage, I was mesmerized by her perfect features, unearthly charms, and seeming innocence.

At the time I was making love with her, however, I had become increasingly preoccupied. My distraction had less to do with her than with my revulsion at life under the sultan and the Bendahara, my self-loathing at having to bend to their vile will, and my desperate longing to leave the islands and return to the land of my youth and the woman I truly loved.

I could, of course, explain none of my loathing to the Mage.

The islands were her world. Whether she loved them or loathed them, she was in them and of them. They were her life, and were I frank with her, I would challenge everything around her.

For all I knew, she might have conveyed my feelings to the Bendahara.

I would have found cold comfort there.

Instead I said nothing, but in my obsession to escape the islands, I drifted away from the woman I lusted after.

She didn't replace my love for Maria. I learned that there were different forms of love and that my feelings for the Mage were different from what I felt for Maria. I wanted to make love to the Mage, but Maria was the woman I wanted to spend my entire life with.

She had used the knowledge I gave her of the killing powder to set a trap for me, of course, replacing my slow fuse with one that suddenly raced and enriching the potency of the gunpowder I had prepared.

It was a miracle I had survived. Had I loaded the powder in a cannon and fired it, the flying iron shrapnel would have sent me to the Nine Hells in a hundred pieces, much like I sent the ship's cannon master and his assistant when I altered his brew.

"She tried to kill me," I told Luis.

He shook his head and pulled his mustache. "Perhaps it is even more complicated. Who knows? Maybe the Dutch governor is not a fool and paid that eunuch bastardo Bendahara to kill the sultan's new cannon masters. Perhaps kill the sultan himself. Didn't that scheming bastardo of a chief minister say we were to demonstrate the gunpowder for the sultan himself?"

My amigo, as a master of skulduggery, had great insight into the minds of others with a like mentality.

The next morning as I stood at the railing and let a cool ocean breeze fan my raw skin, I read the note I'd found in the pocket of my cloak.

Gunsmith,
If you read this note, it means you escaped my revenge and that I am no longer on this earth because I will have followed the only path open for me to wipe clean the dishonor that failure to kill you has brought me.
    By now you will have guessed that I prepared the killing powder to take your life.
    You make a mistake when you toy with a heart that

loves you—especially in our remote realm. Our smiles, caresses, and words mean nothing to you. Nothing is ever as it seems. We each live in a box which is in another box within another box.

Never assume you understand our dreams, our lives, or our land. Most of all never believe you know our hearts. Or that you know the last word of any human heart . . .

To break a heart is to break the universe.

Never forget . . .

The One Who Loved You

In retrospect, I should have paid more attention to her fragile feelings, her vulnerable heart.

Great beauty *is* bloodthirsty and I had taught her the bloodiest of arts—the art of war.

NINETY-TWO

Veracruz, 1820

OUR PORTUGUESE PIRATE ship took us from the Spice Islands to Goa on the Indian coast, past the Horn of Africa, around the Cape of Good Hope, and up the west coast of Africa to Lisbon. At the Portuguese capital, we boarded a ship flying the royal Spanish flag that took us to Veracruz.

We sailed on the *Canción de Málaga*—the *Song of Malaga*—a four-hundred-ton merchantman ship with a crew of thirty and a dozen guns.

Luis had considered going back to Spain rather than the colony but eventually decided against it.

"In the colony I am a wearer of spurs," he said with a malicious grin, "flogging and roweling a fortune off the backs of your bastardo Aztec brothers and puta sisters. In Spain I might as well be an *Aztec.*"

For Luis, Veracruz was only supposed to be a stopover on the way to Mexico City and for me a short stop before I passed through the capital for the China Road. From conversation with the Spanish sailors, little had changed in the colony in the two years I had been gone. The viceroy still ruled as a potentate in Mexico City while General Guerrero conducted hit-and-run guerrilla operations in the region extending from Acapulco on the west coast up and over the Sierra Madre del Sur to the Valley of Mexico.

Two years separated me from Maria. I wondered for the thousandth time where she was . . . and who she was with. Did she have a husband? Child? Had the harsh guerrilla's life broken and destroyed her? Had the royal militia captured and killed her? If she was still alive, could I even find her, would she want me, love me?

One thing was certain—politically and socially the colony had not changed. The gachupines still ran everything, the criollos still chafed at their traces, bits, and whips but silently suffered their humiliation for the sakes of their prize horses and fine haciendas. My Aztec brothers and sisters still sweated dirt and blood while their children starved and their masters reveled in luxury and leisure.

"Ten years ago the priest Hidalgo proclaimed independence and a hundred thousands of my kind—myself included—rose up against the Spanish," I told Luis as we sighted the fortress island Castillo de San Juan de Ulua that commanded the approach to Veracruz harbor. "Guerrero has been fighting for ten years, five under the priest Morelos and the last five as generalissimo himself."

"And you Aztec aboriginal savages are still under our Spanish heel." Again, my good amigo gave me his most devious grin. "God must be telling you that you deserve no less."

"Señor Picaro, call me a savage again and I shall rip the heart out of your chest in the manner of my Aztec ancestors."

Luis grinned. "Don't spoil my resurrected aristocratic status. I have to get used to being a wearer of sharp spurs again."

Most of the talk in Lisbon and on the voyage to the colony revolved around events occurring in the Americas at places besides New Spain. Revoluciónarios were breaking Spain's South American empire apart at the seams and liberating colonies from their gachupine masters.

Simón Bolivar, a thirty-six-year-old criollo from a wealthy, aristocratic Venezuelan family, had defeated a Spanish army at the Battle of Boyacá and entered Bogotá in the South American Spanish province of New Granada. Much of the northern region of South America was joining Bolivar's independence movement.

The flames of revolution were spreading from the Isthmus of Panama to the tip of Tierra del Fuego.

Ayyo . . . while much of the Americas was a pandemic of revolutionary fever, in New Spain the revolution had stalled, stuck in the mud and jungles along the China Road on the west side of the colony where Guerrero periodically took control of the road, only to have it wrestled loose again when the viceroy sent an army to escort imports as a ship arrived.

The vital trade route on the east coast, from Veracruz to Jalapa, had briefly been under control of guerrilla leader Guadalupe Victoria, but the Spanish had finally managed to overwhelm the outnumbered guerrilla forces. Victoria had been driven into the jungle and was rumored to be dead.

We heard other rumors about startling events in Spain. In 1819, the king prepared to send large forces from Cadiz to New Spain to put down the rebels. But on January 1, 1820, Rafael Riego, the commander of a battalion at Cadiz, proclaimed a liberal constitution—and the concept had spread like the revolutionary firestorms in South America. "Liberals" had gained the reins of government, commanding the Spanish legislature in Madrid called "the Cortes."

The Cortes had taken actions against the Catholic Church, suppressing the Jesuits and decreeing that the Church fell under civil authority. Issuing pardons to participants in New Spain's ten-year rebellion, it invited the colony to send representatives to it.

"The decrees of the Cortes in Madrid have no effect in New Spain," Luis told me, after he talked to other passengers. "With the king busily battling the liberals, the viceroy knows he must answer to the colony's powerful gachupines and criollos, not political usurpers on the continent."

As we approached the sandy coastline of Veracruz, the talk shifted to a more imminent threat—black vomit, the scourge of Veracruz. Characterized by sky-high fevers and black, bloody vomiting, this plague had threatened— and often killed—anyone who came near the Veracruz coast.

The Spanish called it *La Ciudad de los Muertos,* the City of Death, and passengers and ship crews often went ashore sniffing vinegar pomanders or handkerchiefs soaked with aloe. Both Luis and I sneered at the prevention methods—if the remedies had worked, thousands would not have died each year from the infliction.

"These true believers claim God decides who lives and dies," Luis said. "Still they sniff vinegar in an attempt to fend off God's judgments."

Religious pronouncements from a man who broke God's laws with joyful abandon.

"I've faced pirates and enemy warships and never flinched. I tremble, however, every moment I breathe the toxic air of Veracruz," the ship's captain said. "It's the unhealthiest place in the Spanish world."

The rich gachupines who controlled most of the commerce didn't live in the city year round, but had houses at Jalapa, a coastal mountain town sixty miles inland. Mountainous altitude saved Jalapa from the suffocating heat, brutal winter winds, and vicious mosquitoes of the coast.

"They come down from Jalapa to the tierra caliente only when business forces them," Luis said, repeating what he learned about the region from the captain, "and only in the winter season."

Tierra caliente, the hot region, was also what they called the China Road area where it ran down to Acapulco.

"How come people living in Veracruz can breathe the miasma and only small numbers die?"

"They're intermarried with Aztecs. Indio blood is more lethal than the miasma," Luis said.

I didn't know if he was serious or still practicing being a gachupine.

Luis slammed me on the back. "Don't worry, amigo, it's the dry season and the miasma is not so potent."

He said that for five months, May to October, the rainy season, the risk was much higher.

"But we must still be careful on our way to the capital. They tell me that on the way to Jalapa one passes swamps that stink of the poisonous miasma."

The "dry season" was also the time of el nortes, the savage storms that came in off the sea during the winter months. The captain kept us out to sea for three days to avoid being driven aground by the violent winds that blew landward.

The "port" of Veracruz was the waterway between the fortress island and a pier jutting out from the city. The bay was too shallow for ships to reach the pier, so passengers and freight were taken ashore on rowboats. But before that happened, we had to pass inspection from both customs and the Inquisition.

A port customs official that came aboard told the passengers and crew that a hundred people a week died during the summer.

"We drove a herd of cattle through the streets each afternoon," the port customs official said, "so the cattle could clean the air by breathing in the deadly fumes."

A priest who came with the customs official validated Luis's position about God and the miasma: "When God says it's time to go, you go, and neither vinegar nor cows will save you."

The customs officer didn't contradict the priest. I

didn't blame him—the priest was from the Holy Office of the Inquisition.

Luis muttered something foul under his breath at the sight of the Inquisitor. We were told on board that the liberals in Spain had outlawed the Inquisition.

"The colony has a head of its own but no brain," Luis said.

I kept quiet—trying to look dull and subservient and fade into the background—rather than call attention to myself, something that neither of us needed.

I happily played the role of Luis's servant.

Purchasing false papers in Lisbon, we traveled unchallenged—with no questions asked about the blood taint on my race. My name now was Joaquin Ramirez.

Now, both the government official and church representative went over the names on the passenger list, comparing the names to those on their own records. I wondered if our real names were on the list . . . or had we been reported lost at sea en route to Manila? The latter was most likely.

I watched as the Inquisitor removed a written play from the baggage of a passenger and questioned the man about it. The play was by an Englishman named Shakespeare. The Inquisitor had never heard of the playwright—nor had I—and seized it because it was written by an Englishman.

After passing inspection and giving a "gift" to the customs official and a "donation" to the Church, the notorious mordida, Luis and I and other passengers were rowed ashore and deposited on the pier.

Standing on the pier and staring at the building ahead, the pier appeared more able to handle el norte storms than the town itself. The jetty was made of stone cemented by mortar and was partly paved with flat pieces of iron.

"The iron's from the ballast of a ship," the chief oarsman told us as he threw our baggage up. "The captain left the ballast behind in order to take aboard more silver from the mint at Mexico City. The silver was for the government in Madrid, but it ended up in a pirate's chest."

As we walked toward the main square, we were surprised to find the houses were not entirely constructed of wood. A passenger walking with us said, "The buildings are made of a coral mortar. The same is used for the roofs and pavement. They manufacture it from stony coral reefs called madrepores." The man waved his hand vaguely at the distance. "Few trees grow in the hot zone. Mostly just mosquitoes, miasma, snakes, spiders, rats, sand, and that bastardo el norte."

Despite the unusual building material, the shape of the houses was familiar: Two and three stories with flat roofs, they were enclosed by tall Spanish-style walls. Balcony-like galleries with wrought-iron facades overhung interior courtyards.

The houses framed narrow rows along broad, straight streets. The housefronts looked like long straight rows of tombstones lined up horizontally in a cemetery.

"What is that smell?" Luis growled, holding his nose.

It turned out to be the blue-green, bubbling sludge running through the gutters.

"Wait till it gets really hot and that sewage boils up over the curbs," our fellow passenger said.

"The stink in this godforsaken city," Luis groaned, "would knock a zopilote off a meat wagon!"

"Not really," the man said. He pointed at the big vultures swaddling along the streets—hundreds of them. "The zopilotes and the street dogs thrive on it." A dog was alongside two vultures chewing on the dead carcass of another dog. "The dogs and zopilotes keep the streets clean. Without them, the stink would be even more unbearable."

A vulture flew over my head, leaving a wake of stink as it passed. I knew my Aztec forebears believed vultures sacred, but they must not have smelled the buzzards of Veracruz.

NINETY-THREE

Luis and i checked into an inn and were given small rooms furnished with a benchlike bedstead, a single sheet, and nothing else. The slates of the window shutters kept out rain but not the mosquitoes and street noise.

Ordering a bottle of brandy, Luis joined a card game in the public room below, while I took a walk. I was happy to be back in the colony with my feet on dry land. Though it was already past summer, the day was still warm with the hot-wet sultry feel of the tropics.

The marketplace sold goods out of small stalls, set on the ground on blankets. Most of the people selling fruits, vegetables, meat, fowl, and fish were peons. Few cuts of meat were offered—ratty-looking strips hung from poles, drying without salt. The fruits and vegetables were also stringy. As one would expect, however, fresh fish of all kinds abounded.

A town of sixteen thousand people, the main square reflected the plaza mayors in the colony's other cities: government buildings with the governor's palace on one side and the main cathedral on the other. Most of the walkways around the square were roofed to shelter them from rain and sun. Shade trees lined the plaza's walkways where passersby casually smoked, talked, and strolled.

I walked past the main buildings, including the cathedral. As I approached the governor's palace, I was tempted to ask the guard at the entrance whether Juan Rios and his amigo "Count Luis" were on the viceroy's list of desperados wanted for capital crimes, but I continued on my way instead.

With the heat and mosquitoes pressing in on me, I decided that I should leave Veracruz as quickly as possible—and find Maria.

I would not rest until I found her.

Or found out what happened to her.

If Madero or anyone else had harmed her, I would hunt them down and kill them.

In the most barbaric manner of my ancestors.

I bought a big broad-shouldered roan, two pistolas whose flintlock firing mechanisms I would upgrade, a knife with a thirteen-inch blade and a brass haft that I sheathed on my hip, a machete, water bags, blankets, a sack of tortillas, dried meat and fish—enough to last several days—and a proper change of clothing. I would be crossing a sandy desert and a steaming swamp along those coastal plains. Still I did not want to look like a beggar when I reached the Plaza Mayor in the capital.

I hid the pistols under my clothes since indios were not allowed to possess them and slung the machete just behind me on the horse.

Keeping the gunpowder dry in the humid climate would be a struggle. I knew from my days with Felix that not only was Veracruz's humidity bad for gunpowder, but ships sold their defective gunpowder to the city's unsuspecting merchants. I'd done my best to inspect it, but you never really knew until you test-fired it.

I would not put on new clothes until I left the city. I still needed to dress as humbly as a peon.

During the weeks on the ship, I had created a walking-cane pistol that would fool any attacker with fatal consequences, and I left this for the Marquis de Bargas—otherwise known as Luis—the Swindler and Seducer of Wealthy Widows and the Prince of Devil Cards.

Sí, Luis was no longer a count but had given himself a promotion almost as soon as we hit land. A marquis was just below a duke. I hoped he would not aspire to the latter title. The colony did not contain even a single duke and the sudden appearance of one would cause a stir.

His choice of Bargas for his dukedom was appropriate—he said it was a town in central Spain where he once had been jailed for drunkenness and debauchery.

The next morning before dawn I awoke Luis and the puta sleeping with him to bid him good-bye. He was having a rare run of luck and had found a beautiful woman—not yet a widow—to pay for his tarot readings. He assured me he would meet me in the capital or find me on the China Road when his luck ran out.

I told him we would meet in hell as soon as both our luck ran out.

I was making my way down the hallway when a Spaniard dressed in merchant garb hit me with his traveling bag to make room for himself. He didn't say anything . . . just swatted me as he would a dog that got in his way. His wife, who followed behind him, glared at me and I hurried away.

I had unconsciously gone for the gun under my light coat.

A sultan had treated me as a prince among men, and I had survived cannibals, pirates, and war. I sailed the biggest, broadest sea on earth, and circled the entire planet . . . and a low-class gachupine who couldn't afford a personal servant felt privileged to step on my pride.

I was a man, not a worm. I made myself a promise as I continued on my way to the stable to retrieve my horse. I would never again play the role of peon. And I would kill any man who treated me as such.

NINETY-FOUR

A TWENTY-LEAGUE JOURNEY took one from the coastal dunes and sandy plains of Veracruz to Jalapa in the mountains—typically a three- or four-day trip—and it was not usually made alone. The sand and swamp region had many hazards—snakes, fever, and the black vomito were among the most notorious. On the narrow twisting mountain road, dangers mounted, particularly where the most treacherous of animals of all lurked . . . the two-legged variety—starving rebels and brutal bandidos.

Most travelers didn't make the journey on horseback, either, but sitting in a litter strung with poles between two mules. Since long mule trains left the city every few days, travelers frequently attached themselves to them. Coaches were sometimes used as well, but one could not rely upon the road being cleared of fallen rock or not washed away by one of the sudden torrential cloudbursts for which the area was famous.

I didn't want to be slowed down by a mule train and wasn't in any mood for company.

The rude Spaniard had enraged me—a rage I feared that might reveal itself at the wrong time. I knew I had to keep my temper—I was on a mission to find Maria. And talk in a pulquería had confirmed something I had already suspected: Colonel Madero still headed the viceroy's secret police. And he still bore the reputation of El Toro, a relentless bull who continually tore at the soft underbelly of his prey.

I left the city at first light. On the road I passed a band of travelers from the ship, who had hired muleteers to take them up the mountain on litters, with their servants walking alongside. I hurried ahead of them, eating in the saddle and stopping only to quickly change out of my peon clothes. I was anxious not to beat them to Jalapa, but to traverse this hellish terrain.

The tierra caliente along the east coast was monotonous—sand and swampy lagoons. I rode for an hour across desert sands along the seashore before I even saw scrawny vegetation. The only "life" I saw was dead—the skeletons of horses and mules, baked where they fell.

A little over a league out of the city I crossed a bridge over the Vera Aqua and headed inland through more coastal desert, through suffocating heat and blinding dust whipped up by a hot wind. I put my head down, hiding from the sun under my hat and saved my water for my horse, determined to cross this dead land as soon as possible.

NINETY-FIVE

VEGETATION STARTED IN the foothills leading up the mountains, as did signs of civilization—an occasional small village of a dozen or so huts, indio women with long black hair and half-naked children watching from the doorways.

I camped out rather than staying at an inn—in truth, the "inns" were little more than stables in which people slept on the ground with their animals. I wasn't that desperate to have a roof over my head.

As I rode, I practiced shooting, getting used to the guns and when necessary making small adjustments. My assessment of the gunpowder was correct—misfires were frequent. Amateur powder-makers had failed to properly recorn, remix, and revitalize, and I had neither the ingredients nor the corning equipment to reconstitute it correctly.

A furious rush of water thundered down a deep ravine under the long Puente del Rey—the King's Bridge. The bridge and ravine were bordered on each side by high sheer cliffs. The Crown had mounted cannonry atop that cliff and royal militia sentries shouldering muskets walked along the cliff-top on each side of the cannons.

Before the militia had retaken the bridge, the guerrilla leader, Guadalupe Victoria, had often held the bridge and financed his forces with the "toll" he collected from travelers and mule trains.

I climbed down to bathe in the clean fresh waters.

At this point, the road to Jalapa improved and became wide enough and smooth enough to easily accommodate carriages.

I soon approached a smaller mate to the King's Bridge—Puente del Reina, the Queen's Bridge. The Queen's was not as important as the King's and not protected by the army. As I neared it, I heard the sound of weapons firing in the distance and galloped my horse around a bend to get a better look at the road ahead.

A carriage on the bridge was being attacked by five bandidos—two on my end of the bridge and three on the other. The man closest to me was behind the carriage. His partner stood in front of the carriage mules, pointing his pistol at the driver who sat in the carriage box with his hands in the air. The carriage guard was facedown.

The highwaymen on the far side were rolling a log onto the bridge to keep the carriage from driving off. It was a wasted effort—it hadn't dawned on them that the carriage wasn't going anywhere. One of its mules was bleeding from the leg. From a distance the pastern appeared fractured.

The occupant, an aristocrat by his clothes, jumped out with a pistol and sword—ready to do battle.

Brave hombre. I couldn't let road scum kill a man willing to fight five desperadoes rather than throw them his purse or permit himself to be taken for ransom.

Drawing a pistol, I spurred my horse and let out a war whoop to draw the attention of the robbers away from the man with a sword. With the horse galloping and the reins in my teeth, I drew the second pistol.

I aimed at the closest man, the only one in a position to get off a good shot at me. He threw himself to the side as I pulled the trigger—it misfired. *Ayyo!* The best shot in the world and my gun didn't fire because of the damp gunpowder. I dropped the pistol and pulled my machete. Crouching low in the saddle, I went for the same man because he was the closest. He fired in panic as he rose to his feet. The shot went wild. He turned to run and I rose in the saddle and swung the machete. The blade caught him in the back of the neck.

His head flopped backward even as his body surged forward.

I steered the horse to the right side of the carriage to make myself less of a target for the second man near the carriage. As I came along the mules, I rose in the saddle and fired. The bullet stuck the bandido in the chest.

The driver's musket was still sheathed in the carriage box. He stared at me openmouthed as I pulled my mount up to the carriage and grabbed the musket. Praying the powder was fresh, I spurred the horse again, charging the three men on the bridge. They had stopped in their tracks. From their stares, I saw they were hesitating—perhaps unsure about their next move—since they did not know if I had backup.

I helped them make up their minds—I fired and the musket ball found its mark, sending a bandido to his Maker.

The other two lost their enthusiasm for robbery and murder and fled to their horses.

Wheeling the horse, I came back to the carriage.

The man with a sword saluted me with his blade.

"Señor, I am in the greatest debt any man can be to another—I owe you my life."

Staring at the man, I put my hand to my cheek, feeling the scar. It had been a long time since our last meeting.

Nearly ten years since the day he scarred my face and hanged my uncles.

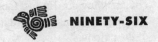

NINETY-SIX

COLONEL AGUSTIN ITURBIDE," he said, introducing himself.

A colonel of the royal militia. Retired, he told me. Another rich, aristocratic criollo who had nothing to do in his old age but count his money and cattle—including his two-legged cattle.

He had done well for himself. He was no longer a young militia captain hunting down and punishing rebels after the great Hidalgo insurrection failed. But he looked too young to be retired, no more than in his late thirties. And he was no overfed hacendado growing as fat and lazy as his corn-fed beef. He appeared in excellent physical condition.

"You are a marvelous shot, amigo."

We were in his carriage. My horse had entered the carriage traces, taking the place of his now dead mule.

I shook my head and lamented the lack of good gunpowder in Veracruz.

"It's so hot and wet in Veracruz," he said, "even people mold and rust. But the two shots you got off, one by pistol, one by musket, found their mark. From a galloping horse. Señor, if I had had a dozen of you in my regiment, the insurrection would have been put down in a year."

"It was luck."

"No, amigo, one hit was luck, two had to be either a miracle or your expert marksmanship . . . and I don't think that God favors me enough to use his precious miracles to save my life."

Iturbide was a tall man, about five-foot-ten, with handsome features—dark hair and gray eyes—and a commanding air. He had the same ruddy complexion of a German passenger aboard the ship that brought me back to the colony.

Furthermore, he was a man who knew he could be gracious and cruel. He said nothing to the driver who had surrendered without a fight—but I saw in his eyes when he looked at the man that when he no longer needed him, the man would be severely punished. The driver's partner had shown courage—and he was strapped to the top of the coach.

There had been no sign he recognized me—but I wouldn't expect there to be. I was no longer the skinny indio boy he'd seen long ago, but in any event, most Spaniards were blind to indios—they thought we all looked alike . . . as did their cattle.

He had finished off the crippled mule with a shot and left it lying on the bridge. "Let the army remove it," Iturbide said. "The bridge should have been guarded. They probably abandoned their posts . . . their pockets full of bandido mordida."

He told me he thought Guadalupe Victoria himself was behind the attack. "The devil is supposed to be dead, but he has more lives than a cat."

I doubted it was the work of the insurrection leader but didn't offer my opinion. Bandidos and rebels frequently ambushed their victims at bridges. Had I thought the attackers rebels I would have hesitated killing them.

At any rate, to Iturbide, "rebel" and "bandido" were synonymous.

I had offered to take the place of the dead guard next to the driver but Iturbide insisted I ride with him. "The rest of the road is safe," he said.

I told him that I had worked as a clerk for a merchant who had perished from the black vomito en route from Veracruz. Iturbide was treating me as an equal, but he was still in the throes of gratitude for my rescue. Tomorrow, if we met on a street, he would probably give me a brief glance and wonder where he had seen me before.

"It's the blood that steadies your aim, señor," Iturbide said. "I assume you are pure-blooded. And that confirms what we all know—that blood makes the man."

The purity of blood was something he wanted to believe. The Spanish were fanatical about judging other Spaniards' blood, believing that while pure blood was superior to mixed blood their pure blood was richer than any other.

I was surprised that he mentioned race. He knew that an indio was not allowed to possess a firearm—unless the indio carried the weapon in the service of a Spaniard.

Mestizos, on the other hand, had no restrictions.

Iturbide asked me to attend a party given in his honor at a hacienda outside Jalapa. "I wish my friends to meet my new amigo."

I begged off, claiming I had urgent business in the capital. My feeling was that the Spaniard wanted me there to show me off—like a prize stallion whose bloodlines went back to the Conquistadors.

I was no doubt now the Grand Criollo's new possession—at least in his eyes.

Iturbide leaned forward and spoke earnestly. "Joaquin, I know what you are thinking—we are of two different worlds. But men like us have a common ground—the battleground. And we have met there not as enemies, but as compadres. I am greatly in your debt. Tell me . . . what can I do for you? Not to repay you, I can do that only by saving your life but to thank you."

I couldn't ask him for his aid in finding Maria. The request required too many explanations about who Maria is . . . and my identity.

"I am set," I said. "But I thank you."

"Are you a rich man?"

"Not at all. But I have some coins in my pocket. I won't accept a reward, if that's what you are offering."

"Certainly I want to reward you, but if you have sufficient dinero, I won't insult you by offering gold. But there is something I can offer you that is longer lasting than the coins jangling in your pocket. A steady income."

"To work for you?" I asked.

"To work for yourself. You're an outstanding marksman. It's a rare talent and one that could earn you a good income. The capital is full of rich men who count their ability with a firearm as one of the proofs of their manhood. You could make a handsome income showing them how to shoot. Unless you own a silver mine, you would do well to take this opportunity. They would especially welcome lessons from an indio."

"Why?"

Iturbide grinned. "A strange sort of pride. They would resent a Spaniard who was far superior to them in shooting."

But not an inferior indio. A twisted sort of pride.

I liked the idea. Not that I cared about rich Spaniards, but I didn't know what I would be up against in the capital or what it would take to find Maria. Iturbide was a very important man and it would be wise for me to keep in contact with him. For all I knew, Maria was wasting away in the viceroy's dungeon. If that was the case, Iturbide and his social circle of powerful friends might be able to help me free her.

The same went for myself. I didn't know if the hangman would be waiting on a causeway, sitting on a chair, dangling a rope between his legs. It would give me a cover story for my presence in the city.

"You understand," Iturbide said, "it's an excuse to keep you for myself. I actually don't want to share you with

my friends, but I will do so only to line your pockets . . .
if you promise to keep some of your methods secret and
only reveal them to me."

Laughing and talking to the charming man as we drank
good brandy and smoked Cuban cigarros, I was reminded
of the casual way he had opened my cheek with his quirt,
hanged my uncles . . . and then sold me into slavery.

In short, I did not trust him—not for a single second.

I wondered what he really wanted from me.

NINETY-SEVEN

Jalapa

ITURBIDE PURCHASED A mule at a ranchero to replace my horse and I parted company with him. He was going off the road to a friend's hacienda and I was proceeding into Jalapa and on to the capital.

When we parted, he gave me a lingering quizzical look and I wondered if finally something about me had ignited the memory of a boy whose face he scarred, but he said nothing. I decided his look was just that of a rich Spaniard appraising a bull he considered buying.

Despite my hostility toward the Spanish who refused to share the colony's political reins and economic opportunities, I found much in Iturbide to admire. He had both personal charm and manliness. And I had to remind myself that despite his charm, the man had not only helped keep peons chained economically to rich merchants and haciendas, but as I knew personally, was infamous for brutality and summary execution of rebels.

Despite the man's courtesy and gratitude, Iturbide saw himself as an aristocrat and saw me as a peon. As a man who supported both the conservative government and the ultra-conservative church, he would not hesitate to have me arrested and punished if he thought I was a threat to his own kind.

The road into Jalapa was in excellent condition and bordered by full green trees and thick shrubs. I paused at the crest of a hill and observed Jalapa in the distance. The city was picturesque, set against grand white-capped volcanic mountains—Perote and Orizaba and other volcanic mountains.

As in Veracruz and most colonial towns, houses were two and three stories, typical Spanish style with enclosed courtyards, but unlike Veracruz, the roofs of these houses were not flat but slanted and tiled.

Cool and refreshing after the heat and mosquitoes of Veracruz, Jalapa was nearly a mile above sea level.

I checked into an inn, another almost empty room, just a rough table and a bench for a bed but I was lucky to get that. Visitors were pouring into Jalapa for the annual trade fair. During that period, the population of thirteen thousand doubled.

I had my clothes washed in an enormous laundry facility; 144 washerwomen, mostly doing clothes sent up from Veracruz. Each washerwoman was supplied with a constant stream of water conveyed by pipes to a stone vessel in which the linen was soaked. Added to this was a flat stone on which they washed. At the end, a piece of lemon was rubbed on the clothes.

The next morning I stopped on my way out of town for a shave and a haircut. I wanted more from the barber than a trim. Barbers were good sources of gossip, and this barber was exceptional.

"Colonel Iturbide is an admired hero," he said. "But there are stories that the militia forced him into early retirement for the misappropriation of funds, some of that money extorted from merchants."

A forced retirement? Money problems?

What does a hero without a command do?

NINETY-EIGHT

AGUSTIN DE ITURBIDE was a man at the crossroads of life. And an attempt to rob and murder him had brought him to a decision in which the indio with amazing marksmanship skills would play a part.

Unlike most wealthy criollos, he had not wasted his time in mindless social events and hunting parties. He had commanded army units against the insurrectionists—even though he had been offered generalships by the rebels.

As a soldier and a hunter, he appreciated Joaquin's ability to handle a weapon. And he knew that Joaquin could not be who he claimed to be—a clerk for a merchant. The story was false, but Iturbide didn't care. He assumed the man calling himself Joaquin had reason to cover his identity—that the sharpshooter was a rebel.

Iturbide knew his own strengths and weaknesses—and his greatest strength and most vulnerable weakness was his extreme ambition. He had a profound belief in his destiny.

Like other criollos, he resented the gachupines. And he had even more reason than some. Despite his family's claim of pureza de sangre, purity of blood, there had always been talk of indio blood in his ancestry, and rumors that his mother was a mestizo. The family angrily denied the rumors but unlike his father, his mother was born in the colony, which fueled the accusation.

He was now thirty-seven years old and he could no longer wait for Accident and Fortune to answer his prayers. He had to do something far-reaching—even desperate—to keep his life from slipping into oblivion.

The standards for all aristocratic Spaniards seeking

glory and fortune were the feats of Hernán Cortés, the conqueror of the Aztec Empire, and Francisco Pizarro, the conqueror of the Inca Empire.

Cortés had burned his own ships so that he and his men would have to conquer indio empires—less than six hundred men against empires that had a population of twenty-five million. His capture of Montezuma, after entering the emperor's city under the guise of peace, was also a brilliant and daring maneuver.

Pizarro emulated Cortés's methods twelve years later when he invaded Peru and set out to entrap the Inca emperor, Atahuallpa. While Atahuallpa was enjoying the hot springs in the small Inca town of Caxamarca in 1532, Francisco Pizarro entered the city with a force of about 180 men. Pizarro invited the emperor to a feast in his honor.

Atahuallpa accepted and arrived at the appointed meeting place with several thousand unarmed retainers, walking into an ambush Pizarro had prepared.

When Atahuallpa rejected demands that he accept the Christian faith and the sovereignty of Charles V of Spain, Pizarro signaled his men to attack. They fired their cannons and muskets against the unarmed indios and charged with their horses. The strange, deadly weapons, noise, and four-legged beasts terrified the indios who panicked and ran.

Pizarro's force captured Atahuallpa and slaughtered thousands of his men.

The Inca king offered to fill a room with gold as a ransom for his release. Pizarro accepted the offer, and the Incas brought gold and silver statues, jewelry, and art objects from across the empire.

Pizarro had the Indians melt it all down into bullion and ingots, accumulating twenty-four tons of gold and silver, the richest ransom ever received.

Once the full amount was acquired, Pizarro ordered

Atahuallpa burned at the stake for being a heathen. When Atahuallpa was tied to the stake, a priest offered to garrote him instead if he converted to Christianity.

Atahuallpa agreed to the conversion and was strangled—a less painful death. The event marked the end of the Inca civilization.

Iturbide knew his own birth year, 1783, was the same as that of Simón Bolivar, the Liberator of the northern region of South America. His own background as an upper-class criollo was similar to Bolivar's.

The Iturbides were minor nobility in the Basque region of Navarre in Spain. Agustin was proud of the fact that his father, José Joaquín de Iturbide, was born in the mountains of Navarre—the legendary pride of the region is the Battle of Roncesvalles where Basques wiped out the rearguard of a French army. The epic legend of the hero Roland immortalized the feat.

His father came to the colony, settled in Valladolid, acquired a hacienda, and was a member of the municipal council. Agustin attended the Valladolid Theological Seminary and learned a little Latin.

In 1797, at age fourteen, he was appointed a second lieutenant in the provincial militia that had eight hundred men in an infantry regiment. He was commissioned at so young an age because he was from a wealthy, aristocratic criollo family.

The regiment hired a few professional soldiers while the criollos were only paid for their yearly month of service.

He married Ana Muñiz Huarte, the nineteen-year-old daughter of a provincial governor. She was not only a beauty, but an heiress—she came with a dowry that included precious jewels. From time to time the wealthy father also gave them loans and gifts of money.

Soon after the marriage he purchased the hacienda of San Jose de Apeo near Maravatio in Valladolid province.

He paid a hundred thousand pesos. His father-in-law and the dowry helped with the purchase.

In 1808–09 in what became called the Valladolid Conspiracy, some young militia officers conspired with others in the community to rebel. The conspirators were arrested after "a criollo with whom they had dealings" informed upon them.

Iturbide reputedly informed on his fellow young officers.

He later claimed he had arrested one of the conspirators himself.

As the son of a prosperous hacienda owner, a hacendado himself, the son-in-law of a wealthy, important gachupine governor, and a product of a Roman Catholic education, his natural instinct was to preserve all those traditions. He was not a political fanatic or libertarian; he was not going to join revolutionaries that wanted to get rid of the society that he was part of.

Iturbide fought the rebels with no quarter asked or given. When he captured a bandido-revolutionary leader named El Manco, named because he had a crippled left hand, Iturbide had him shot, quartered, his head put on a city gate, and his crippled hand exhibited in other cities.

He spread terror among the population through swift condemnation and summary justice. When he captured a rebel position, he often executed the rebels on the spot.

He defeated Morelos in 1813 at the Battle of Valladolid, though Morelos carried on the insurrection two more years.

The criollo officer even showed his ruthlessness with female rebels. Refusing the plea of another officer to spare a woman, he said that in the time of war noble sentiments must always be sacrificed to ugly duty . . . and had shot a beautiful rebel spy, Dona Maria Tomasa Estevasp—among others.

His capture and execution of El Manco brought him prominence and fortified his feelings that he was a man of destiny.

By 1816, a colonel and widely admired, he was appointed commander of the militia "Army of the North" in the silver-rich province of Guanajuato. But a scandal erupted when he was accused by the head of a Guanajuato cathedral, a man who hated him from school days, of financial crimes, burning haciendas, seizing and selling livestock, using troops to convey his own goods, being brutal to prisoners, including female prisoners. The viceroy "cleared" him of the charges but "retired" him.

After falling from grace with the viceroy, he squandered much of his fortune on high living and gambling.

It was 1820 and much of the New World burned with revolutionary fever. Revolutions brewed on half the continent and were progressing on the other half. A time of opportunity, this tempestuous age had launched the careers of Napoleon Bonaparte and Simón Bolivar.

Now opportunity hammered on his door.

Ten years of continuous insurrection had taken its toll on the Spanish commanders who dominated the upper echelons of the officer class. Their reluctance to fight mounted even as rebels dominated the tierra caliente zones in both the Veracruz and Acapulco regions.

Fighting an enemy that one moment held a gun and the next minute was plowing a field, who disappeared into the jungles at will, had dispirited the military commanders.

To say nothing of living with the heat, mosquitoes, and fever in those regions.

Ordinarily, the gachupines hoarded the best military commands for themselves. Gachupines in Guanajuato resented a criollo in command and had engineered his fall.

Now Count Venadito, the viceroy, however, had offered him the Army of the South. But he knew he would find no glory in his new position. The stalemate would continue: Fighting an animal that could not win but who would not be defeated either was not a recipe for glory or career advancement.

The command stretched from the silver mining town of Taxco, about a three-day journey from the capital, to the port of Acapulco, which took over a week to reach. The terrain was difficult, ranging from mountains to jungle. It came with guerrilla raids, dysentery, raging fevers, terrible heat, torrential downpours, bad food . . . but the lack of glory was the main drawback.

Gachupine officers had begged off, pleading illness, family demands, even poverty. No one wanted a command that offered nothing except a holding action.

After the last of his reputation and assets were squandered in a hopeless military action . . . then what? Retire to a hacienda and fight off creditors until he drank himself to death?

No. He would not treat the viceroy's offer as glory's end but as an opportunity.

He had an idea for turning his stalled career around, and the sudden appearance of the Aztec sharpshooter had pushed him into a decision.

His passions were ignited.

Like Cortés, he would burn his ships.

NINETY-NINE

I HAD HEARD countless stories of the capital and its wonders, not just when I was a provincial at Lake Chapala but from the crews and passengers on ships that carried me back to the colony and on the wharfs of Lisbon. With more than a hundred fifty thousand people and ten times that in the surrounding district, it was the beating heart and sacred soul of the colony. From the far reaches of the northern deserts to the jungles of Guatemala, little occurred in matters of politics and the law that was not mandated in the capital.

Nearly a mile and a half higher than coastal cities like Veracruz, the city was in the southern part of the Valley of Mexico. Mountains cradled the valley in all directions. Two volcanoes, Ixtacihuatl and Popocatépetl—both over seventeen thousand feet high—stood sentry duty in the distance.

Nowhere in the colony were the distinctions between the races more pronounced, either. The stronghold of the royal government, the city was the seat of the viceroy and the archbishop, populated by more pure Spanish than any other city in the colony, with more of the Spanish being gachupines than anywhere else.

I needed to find an inn that would accommodate a poor peon like myself, one that I could melt into with others and not attract attention.

Iturbide asked me to tell his servants of my location in the city so he could arrange a shooting demonstration of my marksmanship for wealthy men in the city. I resisted staying within reach of Madero and his spies however.

As much as I would be taken for just another peon, I also had an identifying facial scar.

Still I accommodated him in the hope I could make contacts that might help me locate Maria.

Mexico City stood on the ruins of Tenochtitlán, the island capital of the Mexica Aztecs. But the lakes in the region were now more than half-gone. The water around the city was mostly marshes choked with vegetation and garbage. A few canals still remained and these were the roadways that hundreds of indios traversed each morning. To bring their goods to the markets, they stood in their canoes and pushed them through the shallow channels with long poles.

In the midst of an army of commerce, I crossed on the causeway, shouldering my way past mules stacked high with goods, flocks of sheep, cattle, and the two-legged beasts of burden, indios with loaded packs on their backs, tump-lines of tightly woven maguey stretched taut against their foreheads.

Soldiers had erected and manned barriers, but they appeared bored and uninterested in the long lines of people and goods entering. To keep from standing out, I attached myself to the rear of a herd of milk cows as if I were driving them into the city. I struck up a conversation with a mestizo on horseback who was actually herding the cows. He told me that the animals would be distributed to various squares and the milk sold fresh from the udder.

The heart of the city, the Plaza Mayor, dwarfed any that I'd seen in other towns. I estimated the square to be over two hundred paces in each direction. The viceroy's palace, government buildings, and great cathedral lining the enormous square were bigger and infinitely more impressive than others I'd seen. In the center was an equestrian statue of Charles IV of Spain—a magnificent tribute to the dull-witted king who had turned Spain over to Napoleon in return for a rich pension that never got paid.

The arrangement of buildings in the square and homes down the broad, straight streets was similar to other flat cities I'd seen, but the streets were much wider, the buildings larger and grander.

The two- and three-story houses were often twice the height of houses in other towns because each level was as much as fifteen or twenty feet high. The ground-floor area was typically entered through thirty-foot-high gates. Without looking inside, I knew the courtyards would have magnificent shrubs, flowers, and fountains. Although some cities at this altitude harbored winter snows, the Valley of Mexico was temperate year round—a land of perpetual spring except for rainy periods when the air was sultry.

As in Veracruz, there was so little snow, the houses had flat roofs. Many roofs had flowers draped down the sides of the house.

The fronts of the houses were of various hues—white, crimson, brown, or light green. They were gessoed through a process known as distemper, though in Chapala we had always said such buildings were whitewashed regardless of the color the painters spread on.

Scriptural verses about Jesus or the Holy Virgin Mother adorned many front gates.

A grand and bustling metropolis, the streets teemed with africanos, mulattos, mestizos, and indios, many of whom worked as servants in the grand houses, their own sleeping quarters above the stable. Gentlemen on horseback, their massive black saddles trimmed with silver and turquoise, in black thigh-length riding boots heeled with five-inch silver rowels, and women of luxury in gilt carriages moved along the streets among half-naked peons with just serapes pulled over their shoulders, their wives wearing the long woolen scarves called rebozos.

And everywhere the city's underclass—its hordes of beggars, its notorious lepéros—bundles of rags whose cries and whines would drown out an artillery barrage.

I found a room at an inn that catered to peons. The place reminded me more of a stable than a sleeping place for people.

From the bar talk that evening at a pulquería, I learned that the city was a vast den of gambling iniquity. The fever gripped men and women, rich and poor, priests and beggars alike. Besides the countless illegal gaming houses, the viceroy licensed many legal ones, with the Crown taking a portion of all proceeds.

Luis will be pleased, I thought.

I began my hunt for Maria in the city, not because I expected to find her there, but because the city was the crossroads of all news, rumors, and innuendo—not just commerce and politics.

I sought information the only way I knew how—asking questions and listening to talk in pulquerías, striking up conversations with peons who had gathered to drink and talk on street corners. I couldn't ask for Maria by name, but asked about female rebels and learned the names only of those that had been hunted down and killed by the viceroy's police and spies. I knew I had to move on—to the China Road—but I delayed for several days, hoping that Luis would reach the city. We had agreed that each day we would go to the Plaza Mayor at noon to find each other, but he hadn't shown up.

Pamphlets that supported or opposed the government could be found and I sought them out, particularly looking for one written by *El Revolucionario*. I didn't find it, but I found something interesting in another pamphlet—one which noted that the insurrectionists, who still held an island on Lake Chapala, were supplied by the legendary munitions-maker, the Alchemist.

I read the pamphlet several times. The article blazed with the sort of searing pronunciamentos that Maria penned. This writer, however, had moderated their style . . . perhaps in order to avoid the viceroy's gibbet or the Inquisition's dungeon.

None of this meant that Maria had written the piece. Maria might have merely influenced the writer. Still the piece rang with overtones of her old style. It struck me that the pamphleteer might have studied her old pamphlets and copied her style, modifying them for his own purposes.

The pamphleteer called himself *El Pensador Mexicano,* The Mexican Thinker. The reference to Mexico was to the city, and that gave me hope I'd find him on the streets.

Pamphleteers didn't advertise their movements or whereabouts because they would most certainly be arrested at one time or another. I wandered in the business districts two full nights before I found this self-proclaimed thinker, a seedy character selling pamphlets on a street corner—and not very successfully.

"May I buy a pamphlet, señor?" I asked politely.

The weasel-looking creature stared at me as if I had insulted his mother's chastity.

"My works are not for illiterate peons to wipe their asses with," he said.

He turned and hurried away.

I followed him from a distance across the street and down another, waiting for my opportunity. I was sure he genuinely thought I couldn't read and did plan to use his pamphlet to wipe myself, and I was quietly furious at his insult. He sought not universal rights but the empowerment only of criollos such as himself.

Could he be working undercover for the rebellion? No . . . treating me as dirt had come too naturally to him.

He could hardly be supporting a movement that demanded equal rights for peons.

I followed him down a dark and deserted street lined with closed shops. He mounted a stairway on the side of a store that sold feed and seed that led to a room above.

Not a criollo with dinero in his pockets, I thought. His living quarters were a step up from living above a stable . . . but barely.

After I saw the loft's window light up from an oil lamp, I went quietly up the stairs. It would be unusual for most people to lock a door at night, but I didn't care. I didn't want to knock or enter quietly. I decided I would start out my relationship with this pamphleteering wretch on a basis that would guarantee his sincere and heartfelt cooperation.

I kicked open the door.

The man was standing next to a table cutting cheese. He gaped at me and threw the knife down. "Don't murder me!"

I sighed. "Señor, I have some questions to ask you. If you answer them correctly, I will not cut off your head. If you don't . . ." I pulled my knife out.

"I have no money." He reached into his pocket. "Here, this is all I have, some coppers and a reale."

"I don't want your money." I moved forward, and he backed up until I cornered him. "I want answers."

"Answers to what?"

I took the pamphlet I'd examined and shook it in his face. "This piece on the Lake Chapala insurrection. Who wrote it?"

"I wrote it."

I kicked him in the knee with my boot heel. He yelped and started falling. I jerked him back up and stuck the point of the knife under his chin.

"Listen to me carefully. I'm not going to repeat myself. Tell me where you got the Lake Chapala story."

"A pamphlet I found."

"The name of the pamphlet?"

"*El Revolucionario*."

"How long ago was it written?"

"A month, two months, I don't remember."

I sucked in a breath. Pulling him over to the table, I forced him into a chair. Leaning against the table, I dangled the knife in front of him.

"Now, señor, tell me where I can find this pamphleteer Revolucionario."

"I don't know, honestly, I don't know. You're from the viceroy, aren't you? One of Madero's men. To tell you the truth, I didn't believe any of that nonsense about Lake Chapala, I just quoted it to show how stupid the—"

"Shut up. Tell me about El Revolucionario."

He shrugged and threw his hands up. "I don't know anything. It's another pamphleteer, like me, but I'm loyal to the viceroy—" He stared at me. "You are from Madero?"

"I ask you for the last time, tell me about El Revolucionario."

"I know nothing, but the name and that its political thoughts are radical. I've heard the pamphlet is published by Guerrero's movement. In fact, that—no, it's too ridiculous."

"What's too ridiculous?"

"I've heard rumors that a woman writes and prints the pamphlets, but that's ridiculous. No woman could write such—of course, you understand, señor, the entire pamphlet is trash. I spit on it."

I raised my eyebrows. "So now I am a señor? Perhaps even a patron? What was I when you insulted me on the street?"

"You didn't have a knife then."

I leaned down close to him. "I don't need a knife to kill an insect like you. I could squash you under my boot heel." I looked around the room. Pamphlets were stacked everywhere. "Do you have any more *El Revolucionario* pamphlets?"

I could tell from the way he looked at me that he was changing his mind about my political alliance. He shook his head. "I had a couple, but I sold them."

"You sold someone else's pamphlets?"

"I was hungry. My writing brings much praise but little dinero."

I suspected his praise also suffered malnutrition.

"What's your name?" I asked.

"Señor José Joaquin Fernández de Lizardi." He spoke the name proudly, as if he was introducing a person of distinction. His eyes narrowed. "You're not one of Madero's spies. They all know who I am."

I grinned. "Selling them information?"

He sniffed. "I've been arrested many times. I even spent time in the viceroy's jail."

"For what? Stealing the words of real revolutionaries?"

"Peon, I don't have to—"

I jumped at him and buried the point of my blade between his legs in the wood of the chair. "You know what a eunuch is? A man-steer. Call me a peon again, you worthless worm, and I'll cut off your cojones and shove them down your throat."

When I stepped back, he stared at me and made the sign of the cross on his chest.

"Why did you do that?" I demanded.

"You remind me of someone I once knew. A mal hombre. A loco devil. He had an impulse to cut off a man's cojones, too."

I grinned again. "Good. Remember that when you answer my questions. Tell me about *El Revolucionario*. How long has it been since you saw one of the pamphlets?"

"Weeks. But that's how long it takes to get copies here from the China Road area. Why are you so interested in this pamphlet?"

"It's libeled me. I want to find where it's printed to pay the writer a visit. I'll be disappointed if it's not a man I can turn into a steer."

"Ha! I knew it. The filthy rag has attacked many of our finest citizens, even liberals like me. But I plan on bringing the writer to bay."

"How are you going to do that?"

Lizardi tapped his head. "The pamphleteer stays on the move, moving the press from one location to another, buying paper from different sources, dropping off the pamphlets at different locations to be distributed. But there is one thing that every printer in the colony needs and there's only one source for it."

"Which is?"

"Ink. Printer's ink. It's imported from Spain and there's a royal monopoly on it, not just for the money its sale brings, but to keep track of who's using it. The only way to get the ink is to purchase from the royal warehouse here in the city. I told my cousin who works for the viceroy's administrator of police affairs that they should track shipments of ink that go to the insurgency area." He jumped up from the chair and limped excitedly around the room. "You see, there aren't more than a dozen presses in all of the insurgent area and one of those is not an established printing business because it keeps being moved."

I shrugged. "So you find out the name of the rebel press. How does that help?"

"The ink order, they buy the ink from the royal warehouse and it's shipped to a store in the China Road region licensed to handle shipments." He wagged his index finger. "When the rebel printer comes to pick the ink up at the store—"

"Constables will be waiting."

"Yes, exactly. A brilliant ploy, no?"

I smiled and nodded my head, but I felt like gutting the bastardo.

"Where is this ambush to take place?"

"Taxco, the silver mining town."

Taxco was not far from where Luis and I were captured and I saw Maria last. Invaluable to the viceroy for its silver, it was under royal control although guerrilla forces roamed the surrounding rural areas.

"When did you give this inspired idea to your cousin?"

"Just last week. They are expecting a shipment of ink from Veracruz any day now, so the next shipment of ink for Taxco should leave the capital in three or four days. In another week, the viceroy's men will have the rebel's most important pamphleteer in their hands and I will get my reward."

I was tempted to give him a different kind of reward but held my temper and left.

If I thought it would have done any good, I would have retrieved my horse from the stable that moment and rode toward Taxco to find Guerrero's forces and hopefully Maria. But it would have been futile. The rebels could be anywhere in the China Road area.

On the way back to my room, I made up my mind to leave in two days and reach Taxco a day ahead of the shipment. That would give me time to look for Maria if she was in the town. And I would still have a chance to connect with Luis. Two pairs of eyes on the lookout in Taxco would be better than just my own.

I shook my head. *Maria, Maria, you provocateur.*

That she was important enough for the viceroy to set a trap to catch her showed she had done well for the revolt.

That made her important enough to be tortured in a royal dungeon before being turned over to the Inquisition.

Was she married? In love with another? What would she say when she saw me? Spit in my face and call me a coward who had deserted the revolution? I laughed out loud. That was my Maria, for a certainty. She would wave aside the two years of danger and struggle, slavery and war, pirates and cannibals, and berate me for not having done what she wanted me to do.

WHEN I REACHED the inn, a short-bearded man in a black frock coat and hat was waiting for me.

"Señor Colonel Iturbide commands your presence," the man said.

"It's foolish for you to stay in that filthy inn when there's room in the stable," the colonel told me. He sat behind his desk in a leather chair fit for a king.

I stood before the desk in his study, my hat in hand. A bottle of fine Jerez brandy was on a tray next to silver goblets. I could smell the aroma of Havana cigarros in an open box within reach of my hand.

No offer of a smoke, a drink, and the sharing of tales of women, horses, and the hunt came. I just stood and humbly nodded my gratitude at the chance of sleeping with horses and carriage mules after saving his life.

He didn't know any better. He was not raised to give thanks to the lower classes when they lay in the mud to be stepped on so he didn't have to dirty his boots. He had been an officer in the militia since boyhood. Criollos didn't expect to die in battle—they expected their underlings to take the musket shots.

"Tomorrow we're going outside the city with a group of hunters. You'll demonstrate your marksmanship to them, give several of them pointers. That will start your introduction. I guarantee that by evening, I will have requests from half of them for your services."

Had I been inducted into the colonel's regiment? Was he going to rent me out to his friends?

I felt as if I should have saluted before I left his study.

He gave me a final command before I stepped out of the room.

"There are fine weapons in my gun room that you can use tomorrow. As you know, an indio isn't allowed to own personal firearms."

The stable turned out to be an improvement over the inn. The rooms above the stable were occupied by servants, and I was given a room next to the colonel's gun room. The small room had a lamp and cot, but more important it had an excellent supply of weapons, gun tools, and spare parts for pistols and muskets. And a supply of fine powder made by Felix Baroja, no less. I recognized the spare firing mechanisms, too. The best ones had been made by my own hand.

I went to work immediately improving the pistols I'd purchased in Veracruz. The unrifled barrels would never have the accuracy of the fine pistolas I once possessed, but they would be serviceable.

Iturbide's selection of weapons was good, but I suspected his finest pieces were kept in the house. The ones in the gun room were all unrifled, but the criollos would be more impressed with hitting a target with an unrifled barrel than a rifled one.

I selected a pistol and a musket for the shooting demonstration and improved their performance.

The next morning before it was time to leave for the hunt with the colonel, I sought out the stableman, Raymundo, who had brought the message for me to come to the house last night. I wanted to define the time period so the ink wouldn't be shipped to Taxco before I left for the city.

"I have an amigo who is in the printing business. He's

waiting for a shipment of ink to arrive at the royal ware-house. He needs to find out if the shipment is in from Veracruz."

I gave him a silver coin.

AS ITURBIDE WENT to the side door that led to the stable where Juan and the mounts were waiting, his majordomo, a gray-haired servant brought from Spain by Iturbide forty years ago, told him of "Joaquin's" request to Raymundo.

"Raymundo thought it was strange that a peon would be asking about printer's ink. And have a friend who's a printer."

Iturbide nodded and stroked his chin. "Very strange. You go personally to the warehouse. Tell the manager I want to know if he has word of anything unusual in the works concerning printer's ink."

 **HUNDRED TWO**

THE GROUP OF hunters gathered in a clearing an hour's ride from the city. Iturbide told me on the way over that deer and fowl were brought in to sweeten the hunt. We had stopped to give me an opportunity to get used to firing the weapons I'd selected from his gun room.

I paid no attention to the carriage arriving behind me because I was busy checking muskets thrust at me by hunters who wanted to be told either that their weapon was the finest money could buy—and every weapon was certainly expensive—or that the reason they were a poor shot was because the sights were off, the barrel was off, the powder was bad . . . anything but that their aim was bad.

When I became cognizant of the carriage, the occupant had already stepped down. He now limped toward me. I had a hard time keeping my composure.

Iturbide stepped forward to greet the new arrival.

"Colonel Madero, this is the sharpshooter I told you about."

Still clad in black, still cracking his silver peg leg with his riding crop, the head of the viceroy's secret police gave me a searing look. Not a glance, but a look that took in everything from my head to foot and chilled me to my soul.

"As I told you, Joaquin brought down two rebels with two shots while charging in a full gallop."

I gave the secret police chief a small bow, "Señor, Colonel," and knelt down and buried myself in examining a fowl musket that was misfiring. I wished I could crawl down the barrel and hide. Scar, gunsmith, sharpshooter. Only the name was different. And the geography—I was a long ways from Lake Chapala.

Madero limped around me on the infamous silver peg leg he'd used to stomp prisoners to death.

"Are you indio or mestizo?" he asked.

"I don't know, señor. I was an orphan. My parents were not known."

"Where are you from?"

"Guanajuato," I said. I was familiar with the city because of the many trips I made there to deliver powder to the mines.

"Ha, a beautiful city. And so rich, with its beautiful churches. My favorite is La Valenciana with its sacred image of the Virgin."

I froze. The famous image of the Virgin was in the Basilica of Our Lady of Guanajuato. The wooden image of the city's patron was a gift from the king of Spain. La Valenciana, built by a silver baron, instead was famous for its opulent use of silver. But I was in a difficult spot. Madero was testing me to see if I knew the city—and I had to correct him. But I had to do it carefully. Were I to simply rebut the colonel's knowledge, he might very well lash me to a tree and flog the flesh off my back.

"La Valenciana was not my church, señor, so I am not familiar with the sacred image though I've heard that the church has much silver inside. I attended the Basilica of Our Lady of Guanajuato. We also had a very old image of the Virgin there—said to have been given to our church by the king himself."

To my eternal gratitude, Iturbide terminated the discussion.

"Amigos," Iturbide said, "gather around. Joaquin will give a shooting demonstration."

I was relieved to avoid the police commander's gaze.

I didn't like the way the man looked at me. His manner was superficially polite, but he'd spent a lifetime in intelligence-gathering. His eyes saw through appearances and lies.

Moreover, Madero was notoriously meticulous, and if his reputation for thoroughness was as accurate as I had heard, he would know a lot about Juan Rios, including his marksmanship. I wasn't in a position to deny that I was a good shot, but as I prepared my weapons, I pondered how to present myself. Do I miss an occasional shot, making me a better-than-most marksman? Or do I really impress them as the expert sharpshooter Iturbide has told them I will be?

My instinct was to dazzle them. Anyone could be a good shot—including the fugitive Juan Rios. To be an expert sharpshooter was rare—had that bastardo Rios been one, the whole world would have known about it— and it was a secret I kept to myself.

That was my intention, and Iturbide corroborated that feeling, when he took me aside and forced my hand to shoot to win: "Don Carlos considers himself the best shot in the city. His guns are rifled and were made in Eibar by the best craftsmen. I bet him a hundred reales that you would beat him." He grinned. "If you lose, the money will come out of your hide."

Ayyo . . .

Colonel Madero limped over and took the pistol I had in my hand from me. He turned it to see the name engraved. "I see you're using Don Agustin's guns. Do you have a weapon of your own?"

"Sí, señor." I padded my hip. "My knife."

"What kind of work did you say you did in Guanajuato?"

"Worked for Miguel Balistra, a ranchero. He taught me to shoot the coyotes that came after his cattle."

I didn't claim that I belonged to a hacienda because Madero might know many of the major hacienda owners in the area—but there were hundreds of rancheros in the region.

"What were you doing on the Veracruz road?"

"Returning." I gave him the same story I gave Iturbide—that I had accompanied a merchant who died of the vomito. And added that my ranchero employer had hired out both myself and a span of mules to the late merchant.

I was sure I was sweating. I had decided on the story already, but my mouth was full of cotton as I spoke the words.

"Ever been to Lake Chapala?"

I shook my head. "No, señor."

Walking to the firing point, I thought about how complicated my life had become. I had literally been roped into service by a wealthy criollo . . . and the most ruthless gachupine in the colony had me in his gun sights.

Bastardos, all of them. It was time to show them what an "Aztec" could do when competing with them at one of their favorite pastimes.

"I am ready, señor, when you are," I told Don Carlos.

COULD THERE BE two Aztec marksmen? Colonel Madero mulled over the question and more as his carriage carried him back into the city.

Possibly, he thought. He had never shared his own fellow Spaniards' contempt for the indio. More than the average gachupine, he was a student of history. He knew that the Aztecs, Mayans, and other indio nations had a high culture and brave warriors.

And for both to have facial scars? Highly unlikely. Other words like improbable, impossible, unbelievable also came to mind.

He had been a policeman too long to believe in extraordinary coincidences. He had no doubt that the indio sharpshooter calling himself Joaquin Ramirez was Juan Rios, the rebel gun-maker from Lake Chapala.

One and the same.

Under ordinary circumstances, he would have had the man arrested on the spot . . . waiting for the hunters to enjoy their sport first, of course. He hadn't done it because he was unsure of his actions—it didn't take much evidence to arrest an indio or even hang one. He didn't arrest the man because of Iturbide.

Madero was a cynic and realist about the virtues of his fellow Spanish notables—criollo and gachupine. Men of wealth and power were not generous, especially when it came to the two things closest to a Spaniard's heart— guns and his horses—with women a distant third. Iturbide would be unlikely to advertise the indio's merits and expose his newfound gem to other grandees who would bribe him away.

No, he hadn't arranged the shooting demonstration to simply show off the indio's skills. There had been an ulterior motive.

Something was in the air with the criollo.

Nor had his invitation to Madero to attend the shooting exhibition been an accident.

They were not friends nor did they socialize. They moved in entirely different circles. A bachelor, Madero preferred the elite company of gachupine military and police officials rather than the capital's flamboyant social life, which revolved around effete costume balls and degenerate gambling.

Iturbide had a reason for inviting him to the hunt—for flaunting the indio's skills before him. Something beyond socializing.

Iturbide must know the identity of the indio. The criollo was a high-ranking militia officer. While the viceroy had kept the escape of the pamphleteer and indio gun-maker a secret, it was a "secret" well known to ranking members of the militia, the police, and the viceroy's staff. Madero had no doubt Colonel Iturbide, the leading criollo military officer in the colony, had been privy to it.

So what was the criollo up to?

What game was he playing?

Iturbide had had a setback when accusations of corruption had ended his military governorship of Guanajuato. But he had returned to the service and had been offered the most important military command in the colony, the Army of the South.

He knew most gachupines had begged off command of the army confronting the insurrectionist Guerrero. And Madero wondered about the viceroy's wisdom in offering it to an ambitious criollo.

True, Iturbide had been a loyal defender of the Crown and the Faith. Steadfastly loyal to the royal cause, he had declined offers of command from the rebel priest Hidalgo and other insurrectionists. Instead, he had continually proved his loyalty not only on the battlefield but by the number of rebels—often only *suspected* rebels—he had summarily executed. But he was still a criollo with blood and roots in the colony, not in Spain.

José de San Martin and Simón Bolivar, the traitors leading the revolutions against Spain in South America, had been loyal criollos before they took up arms when the winds of politics shifted. And the news coming from Spain was more depressing every day. The liberals in Madrid had usurped power, putting into jeopardy the power and privileges that men like Madero—and Iturbide—relied upon.

Madero would not have been surprised to learn Iturbide was flirting with the rebels. The viceroy had a list of younger, ambitious criollos who he wanted kept a diligent eye on—and Iturbide had headed the list.

But why had he involved me? Madero asked himself for the tenth time.

Madero had had to restrain himself from striking the indio with his whip as the man lied about his background; then restrain himself as the indio made a fool out of Don Carlos by shooting circles around him.

The escape of the indio gun-maker and the female pamphleteer two years ago were blots on his record. Ones he wanted to remove.

He decided to send a messenger to Lake Chapala to have the gunsmith Felix Baroja brought to the capital.

Madero wasn't a gambler, but a man who counted cards.

The criollo had played a card.

He needed a trump card to play.

I WAS SLEEPING in the stable's gun room when the servant Raymundo awoke me.

"The señor wants you."

Earlier the man had told me he had been unable to obtain any information about ink shipments. He was not a good liar. I realized I had been foolish to even attempt to get information that way.

"Get out, I need to splash water on my face," I told him.

After he left, I put on my shoulder pistol and strapped on my leg gun. It was the middle of the night, at least to me. A request at this hour put me on guard. I heard Iturbide's carriage arrive back from a party and his voice and that of his wife a while ago, so perhaps it was not that late to these people of leisure.

Conversation on the way home from the shooting demonstration had been minimal. Iturbide had given me ten reales as a reward for winning him a hundred. Don Carlos had been a good marksman, but I had been angry and had imagined Spanish faces with each shot. They all went true. Besides, I could tell that rifling marks in Don Carlos's barrel needed to be bored. They were filled with residue of gunpowder and lead balls.

Back in the city, I put down a good quantity of the criollo's supply of wine I found in another part of the stable. The wine was not in a cellar because there were no basements in the capital. Digging down more than a foot or two brought a flow of water—the city was built on reclaimed territory that had been lakes. I heard the only basements in the city were secret dungeons of the viceroy and Inquisition.

I had planned to head out for Taxco at first light. Now I regretted not having left sooner—as soon as I heard Raymundo lie to me. Besides, leaving the city at night was not a good idea. Few people left after the sunset and their departure would attract attention of the guards and bandidos.

Nothing was going to stop me from leaving however. I had to get to Taxco before the printing ink shipment.

Iturbide was seated in his library drinking brandy before a roaring fire. I picked up a slight movement behind tall curtains. I had an idea who might be hiding there. And why.

A large book was open facedown on the table beside him. He poured a goblet of brandy and gestured at it.

"Take a seat, Juan. This is good brandy, I have it brought from the best vineyard in Jerez."

"Thank you, señor."

"My friends were suitably impressed with your marksmanship. You even aroused Colonel Madero's interest."

The remark was a threat.

"What did you think of the men on the hunt?" he asked.

I shrugged. "Typical wealthy criollos. Too much food, too much brandy, too full of themselves. They wear the finest boots, with the sharpest spurs, while their workers go barefoot."

He chuckled. "You don't like us Spanish, do you?"

There was no use to keep up the pretense. "That's not true. It's not the Spanish I dislike, I have met many Spaniards I admire. The common people of Spain are little different than the common people in the colony. What I don't like are gachupines who come to the colony to get rich off the sweat and blood of peons or criollos born to riches and laziness who won't share the power or wealth of the colony. I am told my father was Spanish. He was a great man, full of compassion for all. Before you hanged him."

Ayyo . . . it had not gotten past me that he had called me "Juan."

He tensed and stared at me. A slight movement of his right hand told me that he had a pistol under the small table in front of him.

He nodded. "Yes, I see it now. From the first moment I saw you, I had a sense that there was something familiar about you. Not the scar, I cut your face but never saw it healed into a scar. I knew that a gunsmith and marksman named Juan Rios, a man with a scar, had evaded the viceroy's police a couple years ago.

"I didn't put the boy I'd struck and shipped off to the mines together with the notorious gunsmith. It's been what, six, eight years?"

"Nearly ten."

"Yes, soon after the fall of Hidalgo. It was Tula, wasn't it? The boy with the priest and the Aztec. You bear the mark I gave you. You know, of course, I did it to save your life. I don't know why, I suppose God was directing my hand that day. He apparently had plans for both of us. Of course, had I not given you some punishment, my men would not have respected me. How did you go from a boy being shipped off to the mines to a gunsmith's profession at Chapala?"

"God isn't always on the side of you Spanish. I knew how to make black powder and work with guns."

"Since we met along the Veracruz road, I assume you had been in contact with Guadalupe Victoria."

"No. I was returning from a trip abroad. I haven't been in the colony for two years."

"But you're still involved with the rebellion."

He was referring to my attempt to get information about the ink. "I'm trying to find an old friend."

He nodded. "Yes, of course. The pamphleteer you rescued from Madero, an attractive woman, I'm told. You escaped together, now you want to find her. And she's with Guerrero. Waiting for printer's ink?"

"I don't know where she is. I inquired about the ink on the chance she might buy it herself."

"It's a woman writing and printing pamphlets for Guerrero—probably your amiga. Colonel Madero knows more about her than I do."

He stared at me over the rim of his goblet as he sipped brandy.

"Do you know why I asked you here tonight?"

"You have a proposition. If I refuse, you'll signal your man behind the curtain—is it your majordomo?—and the one listening at the keyhole . . . Raymundo? They will start shooting. Since they are probably poor shots and you are a good one, if it comes down to a fight, I will kill you first . . . before you are able to pull your pistol from under the table."

I had to give Iturbide credit—he didn't blink. But a small smile told me that I had discovered his plan.

He shook his head. "It would be a pity to wake up my wife and children with gunfire. And all that blood to clean up. Why don't we instead come to a mutually satisfying agreement." He turned in his chair. "Benito, please step out from behind the curtain."

His majordomo appeared, musket in hand.

"You can go to bed. And send Raymundo to his bed, too. I want complete privacy."

After the servant left, Iturbide asked, "Do you know what I want?"

"I can think of three possibilities. I've heard you are taking charge of the army fighting Guerrero. You believe I can give you information about his location or strategies. I cannot."

"Your second guess?"

"To enlist me as a spy for you in Guerrero's camp."

"The third?"

"You want me to kill him?"

"Will you?"

"No. I would kill you before I'd kill him."

"Of course. But all three guesses—while excellent—are wrong. I have a much simpler task in mind, one that I believe you won't find offensive. I want you to carry a message to Guerrero."

That caught me by surprise. "Write it out. If I run into Guerrero, I'll hand it to him. But there's no guarantee I will ever seen him."

"This message must go from your lips to Guerrero's ear only."

"What is it?"

"I want to meet with him. Personally, no intermediaries."

"He will think it's a trap."

"Of course. But you must assure him of my honorable intentions. I will also agree to conditions which will guarantee his safety and which will confirm I am not deceiving him."

"He will want to know more than just the fact you want to meet with him."

"Tell him I want to discuss the future of the colony. It's that simple. I cannot tell you more."

I stood by the fire, my back to him, while I digested the message.

To suggest that there could be a "future" for the colony other than Spanish domination was inherently treasonous.

Was Iturbide, perhaps the most influential criollo in the colony, suggesting a future without king and viceroy?

I turned to face him and he said, "Don't mistake my intentions, Juan. My blood is Spanish, my home is New Spain, my loyalties are to both. I want only the best for the colony. Things are spiraling out of control in the Old and New Worlds. Undesirables have grabbed power from the king in Madrid and rebellion is exploding everywhere in Spain's American colonies that will help neither criollos nor peons. We need to manage these changes."

I knew peons like me were not included in the "we" Iturbide suggested must manage the changes. And I knew better than to ask him to elaborate on his message. If my interpretation was right, he was already risking everything—his reputation, fortune, his very life.

"Why me?" I asked. "Why not someone you know and can trust?"

"Who can you trust in this benighted world? Moreover, I already know you have courage, honor, and resolve. You don't like criollos, but you are a man who rises above politics to do the honorable thing."

"How do you know that?"

"A few days ago on the Queen's Bridge you rode into a battle against your own kind to save the life of a criollo. You never thought about what you were doing. You saw me outnumbered and you reacted. Besides, you are a man of conviction and intelligence. You worked secretly for the insurrection for years, playing the loyal peon while cleverly supplying badly needed munitions. Your true loyalty is to the cause of your people. It's a dangerous mission to carry a message to a rebel leader. Dangerous to the sender and the messenger. I need a man who can accomplish the mission."

I gave him a little bow. "I hope, señor, for both of our sakes, that your estimation of my abilities proves true."

"The task may be more difficult than you think. You have not been in contact with the rebels for two years. You must also watch your back and your mouth. Half the people you meet in a pulquería claiming to be revolutionaries will be Madero's agents." He stopped and grinned. "I'm sure you have some experience in these matters. Leave my house before the first light. I will be on the China Road in a week to assume my new command. My whereabouts will be well known to all because I move with an army. Find Guerrero for me. Then return to me with his reply."

"How will I contact you? I can't ride up to your sentries and ask for you."

"Through my servants. I'm taking Benito and Raymundo with me."

I had a final question. "Why did you expose me to Madero?"

"Leave Madero to me. The viceroy's spy is a very complicated man, who requires complicated handling. For the time being, let me handle him."

"That tells me nothing."

He threw me a pouch. "Go with God, Juan Rios, and bring me back news that the rebel general wishes to meet."

He had one final comment for me as I turned to leave. "We are now even, Juan. I saved your life, you saved mine."

Back in the stable, I opened the pouch. The additional ninety reales that Don Carlos had lost betting against me was in it. A reward for finding Guerrero. But it didn't fail to occur to me that if I was caught by Madero, Iturbide would claim that I had stolen the money and fled.

An interesting hombre, this criollo. And the way he thought was also intriguing. He said we were "even." Had he forgotten that he hanged my uncles? That some criollo—perhaps he himself—had executed my mother and sister?

We were not even. We simply had a stalemate until the next cards were dealt.

On my way out of the city I stopped at the best inn in the city, a hostel with a reputation for having high stakes card tables. I left a simple message for Luis: *Taxco*.

Rich or poor, he would inevitably end up at a card game at the inn after he got to the city.

PART XXII

WAR TO THE KNIFE

THE MINING TOWN of Taxco was a three-day journey from the capital. I made it to the outskirts of town in less than two.

The city was not under rebel control. A rich town, with much silver, the viceroy fought hard to make sure it remained in royal hands. But the town marked the rural region where the rebels held sway in villages and towns all the way to the Pacific Coast, so the army was better prepared to check strangers than in most towns.

I needed to circumvent the soldiers' checkpoints on the main thoroughfares leading into town. Like the ones at Mexico City, they occasionally pulled someone out of the line for close interrogation—either to look busy or because the person piqued their interest. As at the capital, I decided companionship was the best disguise.

I rode up beside a muleteer bringing in a line of pack animals, and asked him about the safety of roads in the area. Muleteers loved to relate the hardships and hazards of their trade. This one delivered mining supplies to a store on the road that led to the main mines on the other side of town. I asked him if he ever delivered black powder for the mines.

"No, the store sells it, but to transport it is very dangerous. All the rebels want it, so you can only transport it with a company of soldados, and often a full company is not enough."

We entered the town, ambling by the soldiers, jabbering like coworkers.

I was on my own in the town but unsure as to how to

proceed. I couldn't risk roaming the pulquerías, asking for Guerrero and dropping off my old nom de guerre— flaunting my former fame as the "Alchemist" would be suicide.

Instead of finding Guerrero I'd more likely find a cadre of constables kicking in my door at the inn, after which I'd find the dank, dark confines of an interrogation cell staring me in the face.

My first priority was finding and protecting Maria. After I was certain Maria was safe, I would focus on delivering Iturbide's message to Guerrero. As the rebels' voice in print, she would know how to find the general.

Rumors concerning the guerrilla leader's whereabouts changed day to day, but I was confident that he would never be very far from the main road that ran from Acapulco to the capital. Running through jungle and over mountains, that rugged road transported endless shipments of expensive goods flowing in from Manila and mule trains ladened with silver shipments out of Taxco.

Taxco was in high country, built on the side of a mountain and surrounded by sheer cliffs and mountainsides. Like Guanajuato, it was a tight town, with narrow, cobblestoned streets that mostly dipped up and down, rather than running horizontally. The central plaza was small, and their cathedral had two soaring bell towers and a dome.

The muleteer turned out to be a lover of poetry and plays. He told me that a famous writer, Juan Ruiz de Alarcón, was born in the city. A skinny hunchback who lived two hundred years ago. I feigned curiosity, but in truth had no interest in long-dead writers.

Muleteers considered themselves knights of the roads and knew quite a bit about each other, not only because they traveled the same roads but often competed for the cargoes. I asked my muleteer friend when the next mule team from the royal warehouse in the capital was scheduled to arrive in Taxco. He said he thought it was scheduled to leave three days after he did, but he wasn't sure.

His uncertainty wasn't good enough, so I had to visit the store that the printer's ink was being shipped to. Asking questions in it would be risky. An Aztec asking questions about the printer's supplies would raise suspicions, not to mention that spies looking for the rebel pamphleteer no doubt abounded. Still, I did not see that I had any other option.

I located the store and was about to enter when I spotted a ghost—*Gomez, the bastardo who betrayed Maria at Chapala.*

Ayyo . . . I'd killed Gomez at Chapala.

Apparently, however, I didn't kill him thoroughly enough.

Madero's spy was back—no doubt after Maria.

And her ink.

I leaned against a wall, a three-day beard and my hat pulled down to block the sun and my face . . . a cigarillo dangling, hoping to melt into the other slackers hanging out in front of the store.

I got a look at his face as he strolled by with a puta. Jesús Cristo! He had a third eye—the round scar where I'd shot him between the eyes.

Too intent on impressing the puta, he didn't see me, but he waved to two men sitting on the curb in front of a barbershop across the street. They yelled greetings back.

Good. Now I knew what three of Madero's spies looked like . . . and that the ink had not arrived.

I also knew that Maria would be in for extremely rough treatment when they grabbed her. Gomez would not waste time in taking his revenge. His dirty shirt and trousers were unkempt, his straw hat filthy and frayed, his face lined and drawn, his eyes hollow and haggard. He was clearly wasting away from drink, debauchery, and no doubt the dreaded diseases picked up from putas.

Nor was I engaging in idle speculation. He'd just come out of a pulquería where peons drink cheap Aztec beer instead of Spanish beers and wine. And he had acquired a cheap whore.

He didn't look like a man Madero would be able to trust with an important assignment. Madero had probably sent him on the assignment because he could identify Maria. No doubt after scraping Gomez out of the gutter for the job.

The humiliation—and punishment from Madero—for failing to arrest Maria and me would have been severe. The stares, which his middle eye inevitably provoked, would be a continual reminder that he was a traitor to his own people and of his failed career as a double agent.

He would remember Maria and me as the two nemeses who brought him down.

Moreover, Madero might have sent other men—not just three. He might also have enlisted soldiers and constables as backup.

I had to keep an eye on the store to identify more of them. Going into the store and asking about ink shipments was impossible, however. With few printing presses in the area, there could not be more than a few shipments of the special ink, so my question would result in shouts for the constables.

If the muleteer was correct about the shipment not being due for several days, at least I'd have some time to prepare.

Killing Gomez rated high on my agenda. He could identify me as I hung around the streets. And he might harm Maria the moment he saw her.

It was almost six o'clock. The store would stay open

another hour. Watching the two men at the barbershop, I realized their lax attitudes were not faked. Therefore, the ink had not arrived. Gomez wouldn't be bedding a whore if there was a chance the ink purchaser was showing up at the store.

Ayyo . . . once again in my life, I needed a plan. A couple of them. Killing Gomez would get rid of one snake—but I would face a whole nest of them after him. Standing out in the middle of the town square with a pistola in each hand was going to bring nothing but a quick death for Maria and me. I needed something that would give me the fighting power of a dozen men. Something I knew better than I knew women.

The muleteer had told me of a store on the road to the mines that sold just what I needed.

BEFORE I LEFT town, I bought sugar, metal pots, and buckets at a store. No, I wasn't planning to bake a cake but I would be mixing up batches. Then I went to the mining store and bought mercury canisters, black powder, saltpeter, and fuses. On the way back to town, I started looking for a place to house my workshop. I spotted it off the road that led back into town—a poorly kept house with an outlying building that was little more than a three-sided lean-to. The open side of the outer building faced away from the road. A donkey cart stood next to a corral that held a melancholy burro. I needed some of the animal's hay, too.

I wasn't a lover of burros. A mule was the offspring of a jack donkey and a female horse, but the similarities ended there. Mules lived up to their reputation of being stubborn, but they were smart, lived off the land, and were the workhorses of the colony. But burros were erratic. The bastardos would lick the hand that fed them one moment . . . and kick their benefactor in the cojones the next.

Nonetheless, the beast would play a small role in my plan—so long as I did not have to wrestle a burro along with a gang of Madero's killers.

The woman of the house was a mestiza widow—barely twenty years old. With long black hair braided down her back, the straight nose of a Spaniard and wide flaring cheekbones of an Aztec, she was unusually attractive.

"Yes, señor, I have no man. I have not had a man for two years. He died in the mines, leaving me only this small abode. I am alone in this humble home. Of course, if you are sure you need privacy, I can stay with my sister and her family."

When I assured her I did need privacy, she stared at me with disappointed doe-sad eyes, her manner subtly seductive.

Still, she was happy to accept my money and to rent me the lean-to, the cart, and the burro. I paid her for a week but intended to be gone much sooner.

I prepared two types of bombs, starting with a smoke one. Black powder smoked, but not enough. Adding sugar and a little sawdust I found at the wood pile, I made saltpeter burn slower and dirtier, creating a much heavier whitish haze. I had to play with the mixture before it erupted into thick clouds of dense, billowing impenetrable smoke.

I also needed something with a bigger bang and sharper bite than a smoke bomb. Adding saltpeter to the blasting powder, I made it burn faster and hotter. When the powder was tightly confined, it would detonate on ignition . . . which is where the mercury canisters came in. They made excellent bomb casings.

The king had a monopoly on mercury—a substance that was critical to the separation of silver from those baser elements in the ore and that came packed in metal canisters. Consequently, mercury canisters were available in abundance.

It would not be the first time the canister bombs were used in a colonial battle: In 1810, Father Hidalgo's army of "Aztecs" attacked the fortresslike granary in the silver mining town of Guanajuato. During the siege, the Spanish defenders threw mercury canisters filled with gunpowder and triggered by short fuses down on the indio attackers.

I planned on putting them to even more effective use.

I SPENT TWO days making compounds and occasionally checking out Gomez, his companions, and the store.
I was consequently near the store when a carriage carrying a wealthy Spanish general famous for his military
exploits arrived in town.

General Luis Benito Juarez de Santa Barbara de la
Sierra Madre gave me a sweeping greeting with his wide-
brimmed hat. "You—Aztec guttersnipe!" he thundered at
me, his face split in two by a wickedly scintillating smile.
"I'm in need of an ignorant indio carriage driver."

His driver had fled into a pulquería as soon as the
carriage pulled up. The man looked like gallows-bait
the "general" had commandeered off a prison ship.

"Where did you get the carriage?"

The question was, of course, rhetorical. I knew where
Luis had gotten the carriage—the same place he had acquired the general's rank . . . the same place he got all of
his other titles.

"I won the carriage in a game of chance."

"You actually won for once?"

"I meant a different kind of gambling. My opponent
thought he could defeat me on the field of honor—
pistola to pistola . . . after he had accused me of cheating
at cards. A ridiculous charge. I had only marked half the
deck."

"You have a dead man's carriage?"

"I have *my* carriage. And I made the trip from the capital to here in haste after receiving your message. I bought
fresh mules on the way."

"I take it the carriage owner—late owner—had a stash of dinero on board?"

Luis grinned. "Enough to keep me in mules and cards and women, but now I am broke. So, tell me, what are we doing in Taxco? Is there a mint here we are going to rob? A rich widow who desires a reading of the tarot?"

"Maria."

"I was afraid you would say that. Is she with the rebel army or in prison?"

We sat in his coach, smoked, and drank as I brought him up-to-date with Iturbide and Maria. And Madero's agents.

"Ahhh, a man who cheated death," he said, about Gomez.

"Not for long. I've been watching him and the two men I've been able to identify as Madero's agents. They stay away from him. He's a pariah, probably because Maria and I got away. He spends his time eating and drinking and fucking."

"The best time to attack a man is when his pants are down, eh, amigo? But it would be sacrilegious to kill a man when he's with a puta. The rule is that you wait until he's finished and has paid the girl—before you kill him."

"I agree that going after him with his pants down is best. But I don't want him to go to hell with a smile on his face. I have another plan."

I WAITED OUTSIDE the pulquería while Gomez gorged himself on frijoles, tortillas, and hot peppers, washing it down with pulque. Hour after hour he gluttonized. A call of nature should have been required at some point. I couldn't believe that this bastardo took so damn long to come to the outhouse behind the pulquería. Slovenly gutter-trash that he was, he didn't bother closing the door. He dropped his pants, flopped his naked ass over the hole, and gave a disgusting belch as he let loose frijoles from his other end.

He frowned at me, trying to bring me into focus as I paused next to him and leaned down and touched something by him with my cigaro.

As I walked away, he yelled, "What the hell you doing?"

I mumbled something.

"What?"

I waited until I was at the corner of the building before I turned and yelled back: "Kiss your ass good-bye, you son of a whore. I lit a bomb fuse under your rear end."

I got one step around the corner before the outhouse blew.

A BAD PLAN," Luis said. "It is only right that we rescue your love. Where is the justice when I am hanged for something noble instead of my splendid life of sin?"

"Perhaps God will deem it payment due," I suggested.

"I have hid from God most of my life. Attracting His attention would be a strategic blunder."

He walked beside me as I positioned the donkey cart next to the cathedral. Night was falling, most of the town had closed down to attend a special cathedral service commemorating the death of a mine owner. The mule train with supplies for the store had arrived earlier, and the general store was still open—no doubt at the insistence of Madero's men.

They would be waiting for whoever picked up or inquired about the printer's ink.

Now I knew there were six of them . . . two in front, two inside the store, two in back of the store.

General Luis's fancy carriage was also waiting by the general store, parked across the street. Two of us. Six of them . . . and Maria caught in the cross fire.

Ayyo . . . not a happy picture. I thought of eliminating a couple more men—Gomez was not the only one who had a call of nature—but that might arouse suspicion. Rumors had it that sewer gases had exploded and killed Gomez. An easy explanation for Madero's men, who no doubt found the three-eyed derelict an embarrassment anyway.

I was up the street near the cathedral when I saw the rider. A slender youth on a mule appeared on the street, heading for the store. A nice disguise. If I hadn't traveled with Maria and turned her into a boy myself, I wouldn't have recognized her.

I gave the signal to Luis and headed for the carriage.

The youth rode up to the store and tied the mule's reins to the post ring in front.

As she went into the store, I heard a whistle—Madero's men in front signaling that the suspect had arrived.

I set the fuse at the carriage and hurried to the back of the store.

The explosion in front seemed to shake the whole world. Ayyo . . . perhaps I had put too much gunpowder in the carriage. The explosion of the donkey cart Luis set off near the church was lost in the bigger explosion.

Luis had wanted to let the animals go up with the explosion but I had insisted that they be released before our grand display.

Both explosions were more smoke bomb than blasts. The idea was to drive hundreds of people from the cathedral into a street full of smoke. Luis was to throw two hand bombs . . . carefully, so they didn't hurt anyone. In other words, he was to create mass panic, diverting the two in front.

The first man who approached me got off a shot but it went straight into the dirt—after which I killed him. Then I shot the other man. His pistol went off when he dropped it as he hit the ground.

Luis was to take out the two in front, which left two inside the store.

With Maria.

And I didn't have time to reload.

I heard her scream—even as I was charging in with my machete.

Maria was already battling Madero's two men.

Ayyo . . . this is why God gave indios knives. As one of

the men swung around to face me, I gutted him, twisting the long blade. He stared at me in surprise and agony.

He hadn't bothered to draw his pistola to fight Maria. I pulled it now and using him as a shield, put a bullet in the middle of the other man's chest.

I had aimed for his heart, but the weapon was not accurate.

Maria had kind words for me as I rushed her out the back.

"Bastardo, it's about time you came back."

Luis was waiting with the horses when we came out.

We mounted, Luis tossing a canister bomb into the back of the store.

"Just to keep them busy," he said.

The amount of smoke left people with the impression that the whole town was going up in flames. No doubt their fears were kindled by the fact that so many of the buildings were made of dry-rotted wood.

We rode out of town, leaving frantic townsmen behind us fighting the "fire" they thought was raging as militia poured into the city to assist.

No one noticed that three dangerous revolutionary "criminals" were escaping.

WE SEPARATED FROM Luis outside of town. He'd planned to return to the capital on horseback. He had wealthy widows and games of chance yet to conquer. Not to mention another carriage and title to acquire.

Meanwhile I had other business.

First with Maria.

We didn't speak until we were two miles out of town. We stopped and dismounted to let the horses rest.

She stared at me, examining me as if she were staring at the face of a stranger. I saw questions, anger—at last relief on her face.

"Maria," I said, "I love you."

"Really?" she asked, her mouth curling with disdain. "Then why were you gone for so long?"

"Maria, I traveled around the world—the whole *world*—to return to you. I never stopped thinking of you."

"Did you think I was going to wait for you? To spurn other men because you were lost somewhere in the world and might someday come back?"

"Well . . . no, I didn't . . . I—"

"Of course I waited for you because I love you more than life itself."

She stepped to me and on tiptoes, kissed me.

We came together as lovers long apart, bonded by love and our passions.

PART XXIII

BLACK INDIO

GENERAL VICENTE GUERRERO crouched behind a rocky escarpment on the high stony hilltop.

As usual, his guerrilla forces were outmanned, outnumbered, and outgunned. His only hope was to *outthink* his opposition—Lieutenant Colonel Moya and his infantry regiment, a full four hundred strong, which would be coming down the narrow valley slope before him.

Moya's regiment was on its way to join up with the Army of the South and its new commander, Colonel Iturbide.

Guerrero had to outwit them. He had nothing else in his hand. For that, he needed a better view of his prospective battlefield.

He had survived nearly ten years of warfare, half of that time as commander of the last major force to carry on the revolution, by understanding the terrain better than the enemy did.

He already understood his opponent—Lieutenant Colonel Moya. A tenacious adversary, Guerrero had fought him before—and he had not defeated his regiment in the field, which did not particularly bother him. Guerrillas did not prevail through victory in the field. In their way of war, citizen "irregulars" prevailed against regular troops not in set-piece battles but an inch at a time—through the employment of hit-and-run, through the pillaging of supplies, the disruption of communications through the interdiction of couriers, and the targeted assassination of officers.

The word "guerrilla" had been born when old Spain's

courageous common people changed the Art of War for all time, when they fought and eventually defeated an infinitely superior, unspeakably ruthless foe—Napoleon and his vast horde.

During that mano a mano combat, the guerrilla tactic of firing a single musket shot . . . then cutting, running . . . was born. The tactic originated out of necessity. The guerrillas had only a single lead ball or two to give to each fighter, so the guerrilla had no other choice: He had no extra musket balls.

Necessity proved to be more than the Mother of Invention and a viable strategy. It proved the path to ultimate victory: Even if one had many more musket balls, to stand and fight a hugely superior force was suicidally stupid, and in the case of the guerrillas, they were almost always outnumbered.

Well, at least, the Spanish army he waited for would not catch him by surprise—surprise was his key weapon.

The Spanish force was composed of 40 cavalry and 360 infantry. Guerrero arranged his ambush so scouts leading the way would not stumble onto his men. Moreover, most of his men were coming up behind the long line of Spanish troops. A smaller unit secreted in rocky terrain was to spring up and fire at the front column, then quickly retreat. When the mounted troops surged forward to chase, the guerrillas to the rear would attack.

Staring out over his prospective battlefield, Guerrero remembered Xavier Mina, his hero and mentor. The Spanish guerrilla leader who—more than anyone—created the strategy that eventually drove out the French and for a time led the insurrection that promised to drive the Spaniards out of New Spain.

To Guerrero's eternal, inconsolable sorrow, Mina had died fighting for the rebel cause in the colony.

Barely nineteen years old in 1808—when Napoleon

grabbed Spain and the Spanish guerrilla movement rose to drive the French back over the Pyrenees—Mina had left the study of law and become a guerrilla leader under his uncle.

Captured by the French in 1810, he spent four years in a prison. Released from prison, he joined the liberal movement confronting King Ferdinand who had reassumed the throne.

Mina went to England, then to the United States where he organized a force of three hundred to invade New Spain in defense of the independence movement.

After winning several battles—in one case against a Spanish force six times larger than his own unit—he was captured and summarily shot.

Though he died at twenty-eight years old, he had experienced more of life than most people who lived three times longer.

Vicente Guerrero understood that he, too, had been through the needle's eye during his own thirty-eight years. A "black indio"—his mother was indio and his father had African and Spanish heritage—he had become a rebel leader despite the fact he had been a mule driver.

Unlike the educated, worldly priests Hidalgo and Morelos who had led the rebellion before him, Guerrero was illiterate. But he made up his deficiency in book learning by having an instinct for military tactics. He had been fighting now for over ten years and had lost battles but not the war.

He was aware of his weaknesses and understood part of his success was his knowledge of the terrain and knowledge of the inhabitants who could relate to both his black and indio heritage. He kept much of the rugged, rural region from Taxco to the beaches at Acapulco under his authority but was smart enough not to venture into open field combat or attempt to hold large cities.

Iturbide, the new commander of the Army of the South, had a force of twenty-five hundred men, including four hundred very loyal troops from his old regiment of Celaya. Guerrero's force was half that size and more than a match. But that only created a stalemate because if Guerrero attempted an outright victory, the viceroy could pour thousands of troops into the battle.

Guerrero had proved many things about the strength of the peons of the colony, including the fact that the men and women of color and mixed blood were as strong and brave and intelligent as any Spaniard, that the test of purity of blood that determined one's place in life was a lie and a perversion.

He fought for the right of all people to have political, economic, and social rights regardless of their bloodlines.

When the independence movement erupted and Father Hidalgo called for patriots to rise and fight the gachupines, Vicente's father, Pedro, supported the Spanish side, believing that racial progress could come without revolt.

When Vicente announced he was going to join the insurrection, father and son had a heated political argument in the family mule corral as Vicente packed a mule for the trip to the Bajio where Hidalgo was raising an army.

Pedro first pleaded with Vicente and then disowned him, his only son, declaring that no family member should ever again talk with Vicente.

Vicente, meanwhile, made his way up the Pacific Coast from Acapulco to join the revolt, gathering a force along the way with which to join the rebellion.

Another rebel with a mixed racial background was the dark-skinned priest, Father José Morelos. Although Morelos and Hidalgo were both priests, they had very different backgrounds. Like Vicente, Morelos had earlier been a mixed-blood mule driver in the Acapulco region. His father was a carpenter. Although Morelos was registered at birth as pure-blooded Spanish to avoid the harsh laws discriminating against people of mixed blood, his mother's racial roots included indio and africano.

He had worked for years before attending seminary school and had nearly starved to death while getting schooling. In contrast, Hidalgo's parents were pure-blooded criollos and hacienda owners.

While Hidalgo raised a ragtag army that in spirit and goals resembled the Children's Crusade as much as a military unit, Morelos learned how to fight from the way it was being done on the Iberian Peninsula—guerrilla warfare.

Made a general by Hidalgo, Morelos went back to the rugged Acapulco region and launched a grassroots revolution while Hidalgo's army met and were ultimately vanquished by the Spanish.

Morelos assigned the twenty-seven-year-old Guerrero to serve under officer Hermenegildo Galeana, descendant of a sailor who left a British pirate ship and settled at San Jeronimo, a day's walk up the coast from Acapulco.

Father Hidalgo faced a firing squad in 1811. Morelos, entrenched in the Acapulco region, carried on the battle until he was captured and executed in 1815.

For the past five years after Morelos's death, Guerrero had kept the torch burning . . .

AT LAST, LIEUTENANT Colonel Moya's force was entering the trap Guerrero set.

When the front line of the Spanish cavalry and infantry were in musket shot, Guerrero gave the signal to open fire.

After firing a round, he ordered a retreat. Seeing the backs of rebels, the lead cavalry unit took up pursuit.

When the quick moving cavalry separated from the militia infantry and gave chase, Guerrero raised his hand and whispered, "Now, amigos."

His trumpeter blew a signal and his second unit attacked the rear of the militia column, inflicting casualties and grabbing pack animals. As the mounted troops wheeled to go to the rear, ten men rose from another outcrop, fired, and retreated to delay the rescue.

Their purpose was not to obliterate the regiment. For Guerrero one rebel wounded—as opposed to four royal troops killed and more wounded, compounded by the loss of the eight mules packing supplies in the course of a terrifying rout of Moya's regiment—was a significant victory.

One of the mules carried a cask of fine Spanish brandy intended for the new commander of the Army of the South. That night over a campfire dinner, Guerrero gave a mock salute to General Iturbide, who of course wasn't present but who had supplied them with so much bounty and who had suffered another bitter loss at the hands of another one of Guerrero's guerrilla units.

"Muchas gracias, El General."

XXIV

CHANGING OF THE GUARD

AY . . . SEÑOR ALCHEMIST, modesty is for widows and maidens."

Maria said that after I refused a commission as a colonel in the revolutionary army. I accepted the task of being the armaments master of the guerrilla force but refused the commission because I didn't want to wear a uniform or learn even the minor military decorum practiced by the rebels.

She accused me of not accepting a commission as an officer because it would be easier for me to escape royal forces if I was not wearing a uniform . . . and what could I say? The woman was a mind reader.

Having experienced a world of knaves ranging from man-eating savages to avaricious sultans to pirate kings, I was cynical about just about everything except for my love for Maria and my desire to drive stakes through the hearts of the gachupines—I had not fought and thought my way around the entire world to come back and be the humble indio to gachupines who wiped their muddy boots on peons.

Prior to setting up a munitions compound to repair weapons and work gunpowder, I did accept an assignment from General Guerrero to carry a message back to Iturbide, with Maria accompanying me.

At dawn, Maria and I headed toward Chilpancingo, "Place of the Wasps."

Over two hundred years old, the town lay in the Sierra Madre del Sur along the Huacapa River. To the rebels, it had a greater distinction than age: It was the site of the first revolutionary congress—called by Father Morelos—and the site of battles with the royals.

Maria told me Iturbide kept that area under constant surveillance, not only because it was an important town on the China Road but because it sometimes was occupied by the rebels.

She and I also discussed our respective lives quite a bit. Even though she knew about my prior work for the revolution, she still seemed skeptical of my commitment to the cause. In fact, my gun- and powder-running to the rebels only infuriated her because she felt I'd betrayed her by concealing it from her—even though I was protecting her in the process—and protecting the cause.

I already knew I could not win with this woman.

In turn, I directed some of my feelings about her activities to her. I felt she was endangering herself writing pamphlets and by letting her emotions run away with her good sense.

She should have known her trip to Taxco for printer's ink would be monitored.

At one point on our journey, however, I crossed the line.

"War is a man's job," I definitively proclaimed.

Again, I felt I was under the 120-foot tsunami of a wave. She detailed for me all the heroines of the revolution, including a woman whom Iturbide had ordered shot. She thundered:

"Manuela Medina, Maria Fernanda Creek, María Louisa Martínez, Gertrudis Bocanegra, all died fighting. Antonia Nava was a general who won many battles. And there was La Corregidora, Doña Josefa, who sparked the revolution by sending a message to Hidalgo and Allende that they were to be arrested.

"Maria Tomasa Estévez—she and other women and men faced firing squads ordered by Iturbide without a trial.

"Not the least to face a firing squad was Gertrudis Bocanegra Mendoza, who created an underground network of women freedom fighters. She was taken prisoner, tortured to give the names of conspirators, which she never did, and was executed. She was fifty-two years old and had four adult children, all of whom rallied to the revolution. Before she died, her husband, son, and son-in-law had fallen in battle.

"Is my life any more important than these brave women?" Maria asked.

"It is to me," I said.

She requited my love with a look that was hard enough to cut diamonds.

I wilted under her stern gaze.

I had come to realize that a woman's scorn was often more lethal than a man's pistola.

MY INSTRUCTIONS FROM General Guerrero were to meet with Iturbide and evaluate the man's proposal.

If I was satisfied that Iturbide had a reasonable plan for independence, I was to tell Iturbide that Vicente will meet him near the town of Acatempan to make an agreement.

The exact location of the Acatempan meeting would not be established until the guerrillas had made sure the royals were not setting a trap.

We reached Chilpancingo, where I had to talk to Iturbide. I told Maria to be prepared to fade into the surrounding wilds if I did not return.

I also told her I believed Iturbide—who was not a gachupine but a criollo who resented being lorded over by men born in Spain—genuinely wanted to join forces with Guerrero.

"What Iturbide wants is true independence from Spain," I told Maria.

"It's a trick to trap and kill us," she said.

"No, it's a miracle. The revolution has gone on for eleven years. Hundreds of thousands are dead, and no one has won."

"I'm surprised Vicente would agree to meet with Iturbide," Maria said. "He's too smart to fall for that trick."

"He agreed because he sees an opportunity to end the stalemate."

Iturbide greeted me as an old comrade . . . but only because I had something he wanted, of course.

He got down to business immediately.

He walked with me away from the hearing of others and told me his proposal—a unification of the forces under the joint command of him and Guerrero and a march on Mexico City to drive out the gachupines.

"Madrid is too weak right now to support the viceroy. He has to draw his support from the criollo leaders in the colony. That support will fall away from him when my fellow criollos see that between General Guerrero and myself, we are bringing peace and prosperity to the colony."

He stopped and locked eyes with me.

"I have a plan to take effect after the gachupines leave," he said. "One that will make the colony an independent nation."

Acatempan, February 1821

GUERRERO WAS GOOD as his word. When I arranged for an evening meeting with Iturbide in a wooded enclosure outside of Acatempan one cool night in February, the rebel general arrived on time on his favorite warhorse—a big broad-shouldered roan. He was dressed in black casual clothes, wearing a matching wide-brimmed low-crowned hat of well-worn felt—its dark leather hatband was embellished with silver conchos—and ebony-hued leather riding boots, heeled with rowels.

General Iturbide, on the other hand, was decked out in a tan dress uniform of his own design and a short cylindrically shaped general's hat. The front of his uniform was weighted down with medals.

Their honor guard's garb reflected their superiors— that of Guerrero's the casual catch-as-catch-can attire of irregulars, Iturbide's men decked out in formal Spanish uniforms.

The two men dismounted and studied each other in awkward silence, standing only a few feet apart. For over a decade they fought as sworn mortal enemies, trying by any means possible to kill each other. Had they met, blood would have flowed. Even now, each wore a brace of pistols strapped to his waist. For a moment I wondered whether they might use the weapons.

Iturbide spoke first—his tone friendly but pompous: "I am honored to finally meet you—a patriot who like myself has cherished the dream of independence and freedom. We have both survived much bloodshed and disaster to maintain the sacred flame of liberty and to keep the dream of freedom alive . . . a dream whose realization I sincerely believe is within our grasp."

Guerrero replied, "And I, señor, congratulate my country upon recovering a son whose valor and knowledge have all but destroyed it."

To my utter astonishment Iturbide's eyes teared over.

Then Guerrero gave him the abrazo—an embrace.

With shocking celerity they came to terms. Iturbide and Guerrero would jointly publish a plan that would make the colony independent from Spain, referring to the colony as Independent Mexico. The plan had three major provisions: creation of a monarchy with limited powers (the throne would be offered to a Spanish prince); Catholicism as the official state religion; and racial equality.

Iturbide's and Guerrero's forces would join to form the Army of the Three Guarantees.

The Plan was cleverly designed, I thought—it created a monarchy to satisfy church and conservatives and independence to satisfy the rebels. But I knew too well that words on paper are not always reflected in the acts of their authors.

I knew that the events that were taking place at a clearing in the colony had more to do with events in faraway Spain than they did with events in New Spain.

Spain was in the throes of political and armed chaos. Because Ferdinand VII had betrayed the guerrillas who saved Spain from the French, Spanish liberals were forcing the unpopular king to make political concessions.

Those concessions frightened the criollos of New Spain. While they despised gachupine rule by the mother country, at least they were left alone to enjoy their vast wealth. They also kept their hands off the Church. Most of the wealth in the country was owned by the conserva-

tive, land-owning criollos and the Church—and these
two rich, powerful factions realized that the revolutionary movement would come to power in the colony once
the liberals in the mother country had their way.

Facing the inevitable, the rich criollos and the Church
had made strange bedfellows in a secret plot to free the
colony from Spanish rule: They had decided to make
peace with the revolutionaries and make the colony independent of Spain, but in a way that would keep the status
quo.

Iturbide had fought Hidalgo, Morelos, Guerrero, and
most of the major rebel leaders over a decade; now, after
nearly eleven years of bloody warfare, the heads of two
opposing armies would join forces and fight for Mexico's independence from Spain.

Their coalition army would have the first chance of
succeeding since Cortés had wrested an empire from the
Aztecs.

To ensure that his soldiers and important criollos
would support the plan, Iturbide said he wanted a hundred copies printed to be distributed.

Guerrero changed the wording that Iturbide presented:
Guerrero said the third clause, providing for racial equality, was too vague. He had it reworded to specify that all
people, including black, indios, and mixed bloods, had
civil rights.

The two longtime enemies embraced again as if they
were old friends . . .

"People will remember this night for all time," Maria
whispered.

"What?"

"This abrazo de Acatempan." The embrace at Acatempan. "The day all Mexicans became free and equal. It's
too bad that so many patriots didn't live to see this day."

As we walked away from the two leaders, Maria said, "He achieved high rank and wealth by killing."

"Who?"

"Iturbide. He killed thousands."

I shrugged. "So did Guerrero."

"There's no comparison. Vicente Guerrero fought for freedom for all. He fought back against despots and tyranny. Iturbide served those who wish to enslave and exploit us."

I knew she was right—I knew it from being around Iturbide that the man did not have a democratic bone in his body. But it was a time for hope, not nay-saying.

She was quiet for a moment and then asked me, "Can a man who fought brutally against freedom for all suddenly change his skin and claim to desire liberty and equality?"

"We'll soon find out."

Maria's secret printing press was hidden at the nearby town of Iguala and she printed the declaration, which included freedom and equality for all peons—blacks, indios, mestizos, mulattoes.

Maria cried with joy as she read her proclamation—but told me again of her misgivings about the preening, strutting Iturbide.

"I keep wondering, Juan," she asked, "whether we will get rid of one devil of a tyrant for . . . another."

As I took the printed materials to Iturbide, an old acquaintance stepped out of the general's tent laughing: Madero, the viceroy's secret police chief.

"I will serve you well, General. My flogging post will work overtime to keep you informed."

I ducked back around the tent's corner, so they couldn't see me.

But I couldn't believe my ears.

The infamous torturing bastard was now Iturbide's chief of police.

"Grab your things. We're heading out," I told Maria.

"To where?"

"You're right. Regardless of Iturbide's intentions, he's allied himself with that torturing killer Madero. Guerrero can't trust Iturbide now. He will need a strong ally."

"Who?"

"Guadalupe Victoria."

PART XXV

The Art of War is the Art of Deception.

—Sun Tzu

Jungle, Veracruz Region

THE BAREFOOTED, HALF-NAKED man stared at the bunch of tortillas hanging from a tree branch.

It reminded him of the live chicken he had seen hunters hang from a branch to attract jaguar, the king of the jungle.

Had he not been hungry—emaciated from over two years in hiding and running, living off whatever he could find or catch with his bare hands—he would not even have stopped and stared at the tortillas.

He had been so long without human companionship, prepared food, music, and conversation, that a bunch of stale tortillas brought sensations of happier days, gayer moments.

He had not always been a naked, white-skinned savage, hiding in tangled sweltering jungle with nothing but a ragged blanket draped over his shoulders. He had once ridden tall in the saddle at the head of an army.

His name was Guadalupe Victoria, though that was not his birth name.

Once he was the most hunted man in the colony. That troops no longer beat the bushes for him in no way indicated disinterest. It only indicated that they thought he was dead.

To those who stood in the way of making the colony a republic with freedom and equality for all, he was the most dangerous man in the colony . . .

. . . *Born in 1786, the miserable escapado was Don José Fernández y Félix—a criollo of good family.*

He adopted the nom de guerre Guadalupe Victoria—

the Victory of Guadalupe—as a tribute to the revolution and the patron saint of New Spain.

Like Mina, he had left the study of law to fight in the revolution, joining Morelos's army in 1812 after the downfall and death of Hidalgo.

During the siege of Cuautla—when Morelos and his insurgents escaped from the town after a long, bloody siege, and the angry Spanish general, Calleja, (who beat Hidalgo in the final battle) savagely slaughtered the inhabitants—he had been badly wounded in the thigh.

He rose quickly in Morelos's army. In 1814 Morelos made him a colonel and sent him to assist the rebel general in charge of the Veracruz area.

Spain's two lifelines were Veracruz on the Atlantic and Acapulco on the Pacific, with Veracruz the most important many times over. If they could control the Veracruz–Jalapa road, the rebels could economically strangle Spanish interests.

Victoria was small-built, curly-haired, and had a pleasant, courteous disposition. The commander of the Veracruz region immediately assumed Victoria was too weak and incompetent to lead. He was wrong. Victoria was bright, and an excellent tactician, courageous, and intelligent. He raced on horseback from one defense to another. He was invariably the first to attack the enemy and the last to withdraw.

The locals as a whole were friendly toward the rebellion, but distrustful of rebels because many of them were little more than bandidos and murderers. Victoria, on the other hand, treated prisoners with respect, never tortured or killed them cruelly as some generals did.

The people repaid him with a loyalty they did not give the other rebel leaders. His men called him "Don Guadalupe" while some of the other leaders ridiculed his name change.

Some critics disparaged his name change as romantic vanity.

After the death of Morelos in 1815, the Spanish government offered indultos (pardons) to those willing to give up the fight. Many leaders and common soldiers took them, leaving two leaders fighting in the two main economic pipelines of the colony—Guerrero in the Acapulco region and Victoria in Veracruz.

As resistance evaporated in other areas, the Spanish focused their main effort to get Victoria. He was not only important because of Veracruz, but he, along with Guerrero, were symbols of the continued vitality of the independence movement—and he was a criollo.

Twenty times, the official organ of the viceroy, the Mexican Gazette, announced that Victoria had been killed; then he would suddenly reappear, at the head of a guerrilla unit, make an attack, and melt away . . .

The Spanish instituted another tactic in the Veracruz area—any village suspected of giving any aid to the rebels was burned, its lands confiscated, its inhabitants arrested and often enslaved.

Using overwhelming force and brutal tactics, Victoria's forces were defeated. Victoria, however, was also keenly aware of the despair and fear not only of his men but of the people whose support was necessary; but rather than personally surrender and take a pardon, he went into hiding in the jungles to wait for the tide to turn back to revolution.

He disappeared into the jungles in late 1818, avoiding massive searches for him and intimidation of anyone who could help. He ended up living as a hermit, eating off the land, keeping on the move with long, shaggy hair, ragged clothes. Skinny and barefooted, his skin and feet torn by thorns, often ravaged by fever, cuts and bruises festering into sores and burrowing insects.

Finally, a decomposed body was identified as Victoria's and the hunt wound down.

Two and a half years later, in February 1821, the independence movement erupted again with Iturbide and the Plan of Iguala.

When word reached Veracruz about the Plan of Iguala, two followers set out in hopes of finding Victoria alive. They found a footprint they recognized as that of a white man because of the shape created by having once worn shoes.

One of the indios tied a bundle of tortillas from a branch where it would be in open sight. Several days later, Victoria found the tortillas and spotted the men, who ran at the sight of the aberration and stopped as Victoria kept shouting his name.

Emaciated, his hair and beard were long, his nails had turned into claws; he was naked except for a tattered blanket.

He was led to the messengers from Guerrero who had launched the search for him.

"Don Guadalupe," Juan said, "your people need you."

$\mathbf{A}$FTER MARIA AND I brought Guadalupe Victoria back from the dead, we returned to General Guerrero, who had another mission for us. He told us that the two armies would slowly move toward Mexico City but that Iturbide needed to gather his criollo support from the Bajío before they attempted to take the capital.

"A couple of small deeds need to be performed for the revolution in the capital before we attack the city," Guerrero said.

One "small deed" was for us to distribute a proclamation about the plan of government the leaders have agreed upon.

"It's not a perfect plan," Guerrero told us, "but there is something for all classes of society, even the Church. We need to let the people know so they don't continue to support the viceroy out of fear they will lose their possessions. Only the gachupines have to fear a loss."

He wanted us to print and pass out thousands of pamphlets in the capital—hopefully without getting caught.

"Can we print them here and carry them into the city?" I asked Maria.

"No. The city guards might very well find them during a search. Already word is racing to the capital that the revolt has grown and the entire colony is at stake. Goods that passed unnoticed before will now be checked."

"There are three presses in the capital," Guerrero said. "You must get discreet access to one of them long enough to print the pamphlet."

"Printers prepare pamphlets for some writers," Maria

said, "and rent their equipment to others who can do their own typesetting and printing. But they're careful not to let their presses be used for seditious purposes."

"On the other hand, maybe I do know someone who has access to a printing press," I said, thinking of the worm Lizardi. "I think I can persuade him to support the cause."

The second "small deed" was to evaluate the viceroy's preparations to defend the city.

"Take four good men," Guerrero said. "And strong mules for them to ride. Use them to carry your observations to me. Their lips to my ears. Put nothing in writing."

I set out for the capital with Maria and the four guerrillas. I had packed the mules with religious relics manufactured in the area in the hopes that if we were stopped and searched by royal forces, they would not harass those of us who work for God.

I also packed pistolas, muskets, and extra ammunition.

This time I packed our money and food.

I'd learned not to entrust Maria with anything practical.

Mexico City

AFTER WE RENTED a small house with a stable to work out of from a rebellion sympathizer, Maria and I paid a visit to Lizardi. The Bookworm was again full of revolutionary zeal—as long as he didn't have to do any of the fighting and shed the blood. But oddly enough, Lizardi was not unreceptive to helping us—he admired Iturbide, so much so he asked: "Why would a prince of criollos like Iturbide ally himself with indios and bandidos such as you and that blackguard Guerrero?"

I quickly lost patience with the man. With my knife to his throat, I said, "I have not forgotten what you did, Lizardi." I slammed him against a wall, cutting off his windpipe with one forearm, and with my other fist tickling his throat with a knife blade.

"May God forgive me for failing you, amigo," he asked, whining, gasping for air.

"You set the viceroy's constables onto Maria by telling them to follow the ink. Not very nice of you considering you had also been stealing Maria's words."

I tickled his throat hard enough to draw some blood before I released the pressure and let him breathe.

"I do sometimes set my own type at night at a printer's," he said. "Perhaps I could run off the copies you need. Better yet, you two could run them off while I'm at the opera and in plain sight of dozens of witnesses."

"You're scared," I said, grinning maliciously. "I like that. It means you'll be careful. Just remember I'm the adversary you have to fear. If I come back for you a second time, I won't be so nice. I'll feed you your own cojones washed down with a fine Jerez brandy."

I told Maria after we made arrangements with the worm and left, "Not everyone will want to follow General Guerrero and Iturbide. Half the people trust Guerrero and hate Iturbide. The other half are the opposite. But almost every criollo curls into fetal positions, clutches his gold, and fears that the revolucionarios will divest him of it."

Still the little snake came through. Maria and I printed the pamphlets, and had our guerrilla friends distribute them surreptitiously.

Meanwhile, I set out to gather intelligence on the viceroy's plans for the defense of the city. I'd always found that the best places to get information were the pulquerías and inns where soldiers drank, gambled—and talked.

Making the rounds, I ran into my old friend who had unceremoniously lost his widow-swindling savings to his Unholy Trinity—Women, Wine, and Cards. Back to hustling, his fellow cardplayers had just caught him stacking the deck *and* dealing them seconds.

I spotted him just as his hotheaded cohorts were about to gut him throat to balls with a hooked skinning knife. Nearby was an open bag of rock salt. They were going to flay him whole and salt and dress his carcass like a deer.

Dios mio, this was getting ugly fast.

Flinging a chair against the wall—just to get their attention—I pulled both my pistolas.

"No one gets to kill or maim that man except *me!*" I said emphatically.

We were horribly outnumbered but my outburst did allow Luis to twist out of their grip and join me back to back in the cantina. I did kill one man when he stuck a gun in my face, and another for bringing a knife to this gunfight.

Most of the time I used my pistola as a club.

We fought our way out, however, eventually making it to the small house that Maria and I had rented.

"Ah, amigo," Luis enthused, "I am so glad you found me. You have again saved me from a fate worse than death, worse than getting caught shaving a deck. I was so desperate for dinero, I'd actually considered seeking a *job.*"

"You're not even capable of hauling bilge buckets."

"Eh, I considered something worse than that."

"What could be worse?"

"I was so broke I considered taking a job working for the viceroy at the black-powder cave."

"Chapultepec?" I asked.

"The same."

Chapultepec—which my Aztec ancestors called the Hill of Grasshoppers—was a mound near the city. About two hundred feet high, it contained the viceroy's "summer palace"—which was actually a fort built to retreat to in case of trouble. The viceroy also had a cave in the side of the hill enlarged and turned it into his gunpowder storeroom.

When Iturbide's forces reached the city, I assumed the viceroy would distribute the gunpowder to the defending forces, more of whom were arriving daily.

"An officer of the guard offered me a job," Luis said, "after he found out I could work with gunpowder, a job I would have taken only out of sheer desperation. It's not only dangerous as hell, I assume Guerrero had targeted all that powder for usurpation or detonation."

In that moment I realized we might pull this revolt off after all . . .

LUIS AND I clandestinely observed the movement of
gunpowder in and out of the cave. We also saw that cannons and balls were being stored in the open courtyard.
Mule carts pulled cannons on two-wheeled carriages.
Sometimes the carts were loaded with cannonballs.

The opening to the cave had been finished in mortar
with heavy wooden doors that were two feet thick. An
adobe wall as thick and five feet tall surrounded the compound.

Wagons carrying gunpowder arrived at the guard sta-
tion, the only way in, and were thoroughly searched. Loads
of cannonballs were also checked, but the cannons themselves were barely looked at.

I was familiar with the transportation of gunpowder because I had done it myself. I knew that finished powder
should only be stored in copper kegs and transported covered with sealed leather pouches. The wagon bed should
be lined with leather and if possible wagons without metal
anywhere, even axles, were used to keep sparks from occurring.

The gunpowder was being transported to the compound
in wooden kegs similar to small wine barrels. That made
them easier to blow up . . . but blowing up a cart wasn't
the objective.

I wanted to blow up the entire cave.

To do that, I considered sending a keg into the cave
with a false bottom that had a burning fuse inside.

"That can't be done," Luis pointed out. "If the fuse is
concealed, it will burn out from a lack of air. If there are air

holes, it will be seen, heard, smelled . . . or more likely, ignite the keg, the wagon load of gunpowder, and blow us all to hell long before it reaches the cave or the compound."

Luis's negativity was fueled by his boredom with the cause. He preferred the action of the gaming table; and he was feeling increasingly lucky.

I let him know that I had devised a surefire plan.

"We'll blow up the cave by hitting it with a cannonball."

Luis stared at me, dumbstruck. I had never seen him fail for words, not even in a typhoon, but now he stared at me with disbelief.

He finally muttered, "You are loco in the cabeza."

MARIA WASN'T IMPRESSED with my plan.

"It's suicidal," she said.

Perhaps.

"Even if it succeeded, you'll be blown into little pieces."

Probably.

My plan depended on the fact that the one thing that wasn't closely examined by the guards at the compound gate were the cannons . . . there was no reason to examine a cannon because the purpose of checking incoming wagons was to ensure that no insurrectionists were hiding in the wagon.

"A cannon is a cannon," I told them. "The guards won't search one if we pulled it behind a wagon as if it's for the arsenal."

"And what do we do with this cannon—assuming we can find one at the nearest pulquería."

"We load a cannon with ball and powder. You can't tell a cannon's loaded by looking at it, not unless you light a match and look in the barrel and have it blow up in your face."

My plan was to load the cannon and have it all ready to fire, then bring it to the compound. Once it was inside, while maneuvering it into position to be stored, we would point it at the door to the powder cave, light the cannon, and send a ball into the cave.

"Even when powder isn't being moved in or out, the cave door is usually left open during daylight to help keep it dry."

When it blew, it would be a miracle if anyone in the compound survived.

"We can give ourselves a small chance by reinforcing the bed of the cart," I said, "that the cannon is pulled behind. We light the fuse, jump into the cart, and pray that we're not blown to hell."

"Will that work?" Maria asked.

"Probably not," I said.

Maria said she was coming.

I told her she wasn't.

I told Luis on the other hand he wasn't getting out of it.

"Never fear, amigo, I'm starting to get into the spirit of dying for a good cause instead of for my sins. By the way, I don't suppose you have a touch of brandy around here, and a few of your rebel friends who would like to engage in a game of chance besides the dice they throw with the viceroy's hangman?"

NOW ALL I had to do was to come up with a cannon. Clearly, I had to steal one, which unfortunately would not be easy. A better plan was to buy one that someone else had stolen. Fortunately, the government in the colony had become even more corrupt as taxes went to support the wars and other problems of the king in Europe. That left public officials even more reliant on squeezing out bribes so they could support their families.

"A supply sergeant," Luis said, letting me know who had access to cannons. "An ordnance sergeant who works with cannons is less likely to sell a cannon because he won't be able to account for it being missing. But supply sergeants spend their entire military careers buying, selling, trading, and bartering for supplies . . . naturally keeping aside a bit of each transaction for their retirement."

The only vulnerable artillery pieces I could see were defective—cannons waiting to be reconditioned. The last thing I needed was for our cannon to blow us up rather than fire properly.

The defective cannons were being shipped back to Spain for repair because the colony lacked skilled workers and the equipment to rehabilitate them. I had the skill to repair a cannon but not the equipment or the time.

Still, I was nothing if not resourceful.

Luis and I finally procured a cannon from a willing supply officer he met at a card game, the man becoming more willing to sell his soul after he lost regimental dinero that he brought with him to the capital to pay for boots. He

could easily divert a cannon that was waiting to be sent out
for repairs.

Our story to him was that we needed the metal to forge
plows . . . and then, of course, the application of mordida
to him personally closed the deal.

The age-old bite was incorrigibly convincing.

At the shop of a blacksmith—one friendly to the
revolt—I made quick repairs. The work wasn't that oner-
ous. I didn't need a battle-ready piece that could hurtle a
ball a mile or more, just one that could fire a quick shot
at very close range.

At that range, it didn't even have to be that accurate.

Also, since I had been pondering the arcane art of
powder detonation, I forged a few other things.

I PARTED WITH Maria on the morning that the plan was
to be implemented, warning her again to stay away from
the compound. Her tears surprised me. They were the result of love and passion—for me and the revolt. She not
only feared for my life, she wanted to help strike a blow
against the viceroy.

Luis and I drove the mule-drawn cart with the cannon
carriage hitched behind it. When we reached the compound gate, we were subjected to only a brief inspection, though a careful one, of the wagon to make sure no
rebels or explosives were hidden anywhere in or under
the wagon.

At first, the guard seemed hesitant, so I told him the cannon came not from the field but from the viceroy's palace.
The moment he heard the word "viceroy" he snapped to attention and waved us through to the compound.

Inside the compound, however, a crisis erupted. We
were directed to a spot where the cave's opening was not
within our line of fire.

We disobeyed the command and instead turned the
cannon so its muzzle was pointed toward the open cave
door.

An officer stepped forward, shouting: "Put the cannon
where you're told."

I smiled and nodded and pretended to be unable to handle the mules. The officer pulled his pistol and pointed it
at my head. "Put the cannon where I told you or I'll put a
bullet in your head."

"That's not friendly," Luis said, grinning at him.

"Change of plan," I informed the martinet.

Luis pulled a pistol from under his coat and shot the officer in the head.

Now I had to fire the cannon . . . which was easier said than done. Not only was the cannon unreliable, and possibly defective, I had loaded it with an exploding, incendiary cannonball filled with gunpowder and pitch-soaked flammable packing.

Igniting the powder close-up could be fatal if the breech flew apart, so I'd forged a couple of iron bullets at the blacksmith's shop. When this hit the cannon's flint-firing mechanism, sparks would fly.

I drew the pistola from my shoulder holster and fired an iron bullet into the cannon's powder hole.

The bullet's sparks and searing heat detonated the cannon, sending the ball toward the cave.

We both dove for the ground as the cave blew. The concussion battered me, knocking the breath out of me as the world turned more black, violent, and chaotic than when we were being tossed into the sea by a typhoon.

The entire cart went flying as well as the kicking and braying mules; the cannon flipped over and smashed to the ground next to my head.

I was half under the cart, scared out of my wits, my senses stunned, when I heard hooves by my head and a familiar voice in my ears.

Charging into the compound was a two-wheeled carriage pulled by a single horse with Maria at the reins. Maria jumped off and helped both Luis and me aboard.

She hustled us out of the compound, leaving behind the cries of the wounded, the silence of the dead, and numbed soldiers staggering around trying to figure out why their world suddenly exploded.

We were both so battered and smoke-begrimed that no one tried to stop or detain us.

We looked like everyone else, stunned and numbed, covered with dust and bleeding from a thousand small cuts.

MARIA TOOK US to the house, where she patched our wounds.

Later, when she told me she was going to the print shop to compose a pamphlet about the rebel triumph at the munitions site, I begged her not to go.

"The viceroy will be in a killer mood," I told her. "A major blow has been struck, and he will have every soldier and constable in the city looking for rebels to hang."

Giving Maria orders was like telling the wind which way to blow. She had a mind of her own, and it obeyed only her passions.

She was gone two hours when one of Guerrero's men came to the house and told us that the print shop had been seized by constables. Maria was taken, along with the printing press.

It didn't take me long to figure out how Madero knew where to find her—Lizardi had sold her out.

With the sudden appearance of inflammatory pamphlets in the capital, Madero had no doubt rounded up all the pamphleteers that had been troublesome in the past, my friend Lizardi among them.

It would not have taken much to squeeze information from the whining little rat.

Luis offered good advice when I told him I would hunt down the pamphleteer and slice him into little pieces.

"If he has any sense, he will already be gone from the city, if he's not being held in the viceroy's jail for aiding rebels. And we have something more important to do. We must find and rescue her."

He was right on all accounts.

"I'll find out what happened to her," he said. "You stay off the streets. Now that they have her, they will be expecting you to come to her aid. They'll stake her out like you did those tortillas to lure Victoria."

Luis was able to check around the city and use silver to palm to find out what happened to her.

She'd been taken to the Inquisition dungeon.

In Mexico City, the Inquisition's headquarters was both infamous and familiar—Luis was able to quickly find out where it was headquartered.

"It's common knowledge on the streets that the Inquisition's headquarters is in a palatial building across from the Dominican compound people refer to simply as 'the convent.' The hounds of the church have been led by Dominicans since that devil Bishop Torquemada first started burning the unfaithful at the stake."

"Convent" did not refer to a place just of nuns, but was used to indicate a compound where either monks or nuns lived.

"There's also a church on the grounds," Luis said. "Along with the secret prison."

The holy office, I'd been told by my padre-uncle, was not only concerned with heresy and other capital crimes, but punished minor offenses such as witchcraft, the casting of spells, bigamy, polygamy, sodomy, and the possession of pornographic and other prohibited books.

After Luis left to get a good look at the Inquisition's premises, the landlord of the house we had rented, a supporter of the rebellion, told me what he knew about the place where the Inquisition conducted its secret interrogations and torture.

"The paved court in front of the church has a large flat stone with a square hole in its center. That's where the stake victims were tied to when they were either whipped or burned in an auto-da-fé," he said.

"Auto-da-fé" meant act of faith.

An act by the Church to horribly burn at the stake men and women who dared deny its authority or its claimed monopoly on the bounties of God.

The Holy Office of the Inquisition was situated across from the church square.

"It's said there are underground cells that prisoners drown in when the water rises. Rather than using some common sense that any deep hole dug in the city will eventually fill with water, these demon priests call the drowning an act of God."

I cut him off when he started to tell me about the Inquisition's interrogation methods, but I already had heard about them. The tortures were notorious throughout the colony but rudimentary. One consisted of attaching the victim to a rack and shoving a funnel down his throat into which were poured jugs full of water. I'd heard survivors say that the water torture was so painful almost no one could endure it.

My uncles believed that a most profitable venture of the Inquisition was the persecution of wealthy Jewish widows who claimed to have converted to Christianity. The widows were vulnerable and more likely than their late husbands to fail to keep up a pretense that they had really converted. The women were tortured into confessing to imaginary satanic crimes, which in turn gave the Inquisition the right to confiscate their estates. Typically the Crown received a third of the plunder, the Church a third, the Inquisition a third.

I knew that the Inquisition had always been hard on women. My padre-uncle had been clear on that score. Claiming they exposed sexual acts that deviated from simple procreation, they tortured women cruelly, justifying their torture on the grounds that they were elevating marital moral standards. All the while the Inquisitors would attempt to force confessions of oral, anal, and satanic sex, lesbian encounters, promiscuity, bestiality, and bigamy out of the tortured women.

Such confessions were predictably unreliable.

From the woman's point of view an Inquisitorial experience was little more than sexual sadism, pornographic voyeurism, and financial freebooting hiding behind churchly black hoods and religious regalia.

The words "sadistic pornography" seemed to my padre-uncle especially appropriate to a scene in which men, masked in the attire of institutional respectability, stared closely at the naked female body bent and twisted, listening to and recording in writing the moans, cries, and pleas for mercy. Meanwhile the cords stretching their body on the rack were gradually tightened and pitchers of water slowly poured down the throat.

The accused might also be tilted with her head toward the ground and her feet in the air while the torturer poured water into her mouth to simulate drowning with the water torture technique.

Because of my padre-uncle I understood what Maria was going through at that very moment.

The priests were torturing her about the whereabouts of her comrades-in-arms.

Even though she was under the viceroy's sentence of death, I knew she would refuse to tell them anything.

That was Maria.

By the time Luis returned, I had already decided how the two of us would attack the Inquisition jail and make the rescue. And I was desperate to get started.

"We can use the same kind of smoke screen that I used in—"

He shook his head emphatically. "I rode by the place

in the carriage of a widow with an eagerness for me to divine her future love life from the tarot. You can forget about a direct assault to rescue Maria."

"I can't let them—"

"They already have done with her what they want to do. Now you can only get her killed in an escape attempt that will fail."

PART XXVI

Tenochtitlán, 1520

They came on in battle array, the conquerors, with dust rising in whirlpools from their feet. Their iron spears shone in the sun; their pennons fluttered in the wind like bats. Their armor and swords clashed and clanged as they marched; they came on with a loud clamor, and some of them were dressed entirely in iron . . .

Their great hounds came with them, running with them; they raised their massive muzzles into the wind. The dogs raced onward, before the column; they dripped saliva from their jaws.

—Aztec description of Cortés's army, recorded by Bernardino de Sahagún in *Historia General de las Cosas de la Nueva España*

Several thousand Aztecs were killed by Alvarado who had been left in charge of the city while Cortés was away. When we returned, Alvarado told Cortés that he had attacked the people while they were holding a festival in order to take them while they were unprepared because he feared they plotted an attack on the Spanish forces.

Montezuma had helped calm the people after a great rage erupted, but his own people had turned on him and hit him with stones.

I have already told about the sorrow that we felt when we saw that Montezuma was dead.

When the Aztecs beheld him thus dead, we saw that they were in floods of tears and we clearly heard the shrieks and cries of distress that they gave for him, but for all this, the fierce assault they made on us never ceased, and then they came on us again with greater force and fury, and said to us, "Now you will pay for the death of our King and Lord and the dishonor to our Idols."

When Cortés heard this he said we should sally out from the city over the causeway and that the horsemen should break through the Aztec squadrons and spear them with their lances or drive them into the water.

Cortés ordered his steward to bring out all the gold and jewels and silver. More than eighty friendly Tlaxcalans and eight horses were loaded with gold and much gold still remained piled in heaps in the Hall.

When we were spotted racing for the causeway, Aztec

priests beat drums from atop the great pyramid. Thousands of their warriors came at us from the plazas and canoes as we fought to the causeway.

On the causeway we met many Aztecs armed with long lances. Cortés and the captains and soldiers who passed first on horseback, so as to save themselves and reach dry land, spurred on along the causeway and they did not fail to attain their object, and the horses and Tlaxcalans laden with gold also got out safely.

So ended la Noche Triste, the Night of Sorrows.

             —Journal of Bernal Díaz del Castillo, Conquistador

Mexico City, 1821

I PUSHED MY way along crowded streets toward the central plaza, dressed in the traditional uniform of an Aztec warrior, a Jaguar Knight.

I'd been thinking for some time about the name given to the Spanish retreat from the city after a surprise attack and massacre of indios—the Sad Night. Cortés managed to get away with most of his men and most of his hoard of stolen gold and to live another day to defeat our indios with his superior weapons and knowledge of war.

The celebration on the streets was part of an annual festival reenacting the night three hundred years earlier when Cortés and his band of men fled Tenochtitlán—today's Mexico City—largely because his lieutenant Alvarado had indiscriminately massacred indios en masse.

After the massacre, the Mexica Aztecs drove the Spanish and their allies out of the city and had pursued them on a dark, rainy night, the famous Noche Triste, Night of Sorrows, June 30, 1520.

The only reason why it was called a "sad night" for the Spanish is because the victors write history.

Three hundred years later my indio compatriots were still roweled and raked bloody by the sharp spurs of the gachupines.

But on this one day Aztec warriors, such as myself, could dress in full regalia, while brilliantly attired militia troops marched, the wealthy and their ladies watched from balconies, and the streets were thronged with excited crowds, food vendors, and begging-thieving leperos.

Meanwhile other "Aztec warriors" glided across the lake and landed on the shore in boats . . .

The heart of power and privilege in the city resided in the Plaza Mayor. Flanked by the great cathedral and the palace that first housed the conqueror Cortés, for centuries it had housed the viceroys of New Spain. On the north side of the great plaza was its colossal cathedral, and on the east side the viceroy's palace. Dominating the middle was the equestrian statue of Charles IV, the incompetent King of Spain who died two years before.

I moved anonymously through the crowd, just another indio dressed up in warrior garb. Standing on the steps and leaning against the wall of a building, I could see over the crowd. I could even see the viceroy approaching a pavilion that had been set up so he could view the festivities.

Fearful I might be recognized—even though my features were concealed—I tensed. I was on a dangerous mission. If I were spotted by the viceroy's secret agents, I'd be killed on the spot.

Still, I was moved. Caught up in the spirit of the times and the celebration, the teeming mob of Aztecs reminded me how far our people had come—and how close we were to Padre Hidalgo's dream of freedom that he shouted eleven years before.

We were planning to turn the world upside down. The Christian God and Quetzalcoatl only knew how many will die before it was over . . . and all hell was about to break loose.

I saw a familiar face in the crowd—an old enemy.

Madero of all people was coming down the street right toward me.

He didn't recognize me because of my indio outfit . . .

and passed me by like I wasn't even there. Gachupines pride themselves at seeing through indios.

I had to stop myself from killing Madero where he stood. It was too soon to kill him.

I had something more important to do.

TODAY WAS MORE than a religious festival. It was an execution as well—the viceroy was going to hang four rebels. Three of them weren't really rebels. They were murderous bandidos who well deserved to hang.

The fourth one, however, was my beautiful, blessed, and beloved Maria.

The prisoners were held in iron-barred cages on carts lined up at the gibbets. Maria's was the first in line.

I couldn't see her from where I was, but I knew she was there, trapped like an animal, frightened, terrified.

The viceroy wanted to make an example out of her. After all, there were precedents: Iturbide and other commanders notoriously did not shrink from executing women.

Word had already reached the capital that Iturbide had turned renegade and united with the rebels. He was marching on the city. As he did, support for the viceroy was evaporating. The wealthy criollos who constituted the foundation of royal power were slipping out from under the gachupines as they came to realize that radicals in Madrid could take away their privileges in the colony.

The viceroy was putting on a spectacular show for the people of the city—not out of love for the people, I was certain, but to flaunt them with the might, majesty, and power of their gachupine masters and intimidate them into slavish subservience.

His heavily armed, uniformed military had already marched en masse into the Plaza Mayor to guard and patrol the celebration, to let us know we were still under the gachupines' spurs and heels.

The viceroy and his high-ranking entourage sat in a canopied pavilion erected for them near the center of the Plaza Mayor so that they would have a 360-degree view of the celebration and parade. The parade was already in full swing with long lines of women trooping by, dropping large bundles of flowers—hundreds of which had been strewn at the base of the pavilion in honor of the viceroy.

Other batches of flowers had been deposited under the statue of Charles IV.

It was part of the insanity of how we dealt with our leaders that statues of even the most careless, uncaring, and stupid could be immortalized by monuments.

I went up a side stairway of a building that I had left my horse tied behind. I took two muskets with me and a length of rope concealed in a rolled rug, and got myself into position.

Disguised as an officer of the guard, Luis was suddenly in front of the viceroy's pavilion on horseback. I could not repress a terse smile when he honored the viceroy's august assemblage with a flamboyant sweep of his captain's cap.

I could not hear his words from that distance, but I knew what he was saying: He was telling the viceroy that if he did not obey his every command, Luis would have him and the cream of gachupine and criollo society in the pavilion blown to holy hell . . . Your Excellency . . .

I saw the shock on the viceroy's face as he was told he was sitting on a powder keg. The officers around him were already going for their weapons.

I had to give the viceroy credit—he was a man who thought fast. Shooting Luis would not solve the problem of sitting on a powder keg. And Luis was too well dressed and mounted, the rebel army advancing too close, for him to assume that it was an idle threat.

The viceroy shot up from his seat and gave a command for the soldiers to stand down.

Luis had told the viceroy he would give him a demonstration of how earnest he was about the threat.

I had already braced my musket on a small wood gable by the time Luis waved his hat a second time. Pulling the trigger, my bullet hit the "bunch of flowers" under the statue of that imbecile, Charles IV. The big bouquet actually concealed a tightly packed pouch soaked in pitch and filled with gunpowder. When the pouch and inflammable pitch-soaked packing ignited, the bouquet blew, blasting Charles IV and his horse into pieces.

I switched the empty musket for the loaded one.

As people milled about in fright, Luis remained rocksteady in front of the viceroy—utterly fearless as he pointed at the garlands of flowers that completely surrounded the pavilion.

I smiled sardonically knowing that Luis's next communication to the viceroy was to point out that the pavilion was a small island in a sea of gunpowder.

The viceroy must have also suddenly realized that the pavilion was surrounded by hundreds of fierce-looking Aztec jaguar-warriors in full battle regalia—warriors who had lost their initial sense of panic and understood that something was happening they had never seen before: The main gachupine in the colony, a man with the power of a king, and all the lackeys and bastardos that courted him were in terror of a single rebel.

Once again I saw the viceroy shouting orders. From the actions I saw officers take, the soldiers were still being ordered to stand down.

Luis spoke again and I knew he was telling the viceroy he only wanted Maria, that the viceroy could hang the others *twice* if he so chose. They were murderous criminals who deserved nothing more than a dropping trap, a taut noose, and a farewell of "May God Have Mercy on Your Soul."

Nodding his agreement, the viceroy stared at Luis in stunned silence as Luis trotted his mount over to Maria and ordered a constable to open the cage.

A priest wearing the sign of the Inquisition on his robe stepped between Luis's horse and the cage. I couldn't hear what the priest said, but apparently Luis didn't like the comment because he lashed out from the saddle and caught the priest under the chin with the toe of his boot.

My heart beat wildly as I saw Luis reach down and help Maria swing onto the mount with him.

I forced myself not to look at Maria, not to wonder what they had done to her, but to turn back to watch the viceroy.

From his facial expressions and the frantic words I knew were being thrown at him by those around him, I knew the viceroy was on the verge of ordering the troops to open fire, calling what others were telling him was a bluff.

Already soldiers had started removing bunches of flowers away from the pavilion.

Luis raised his hat again . . .

Squeezing the trigger, I fired at a bunch of powder-packed flowers sitting atop the base holding royal, noble, and church flags.

Sympathetic detonations blew up the other rigged bouquets. The base exploded and the forest of flagpoles toppled.

The viceroy's facial expression told the story: He shouted and the guards stood down again.

As soon as Luis and Maria were out of musket range, I shot into the bunch of flowers at the pavilion. The powder blew, setting off a chain reaction of blasts. They didn't kill anyone on the pavilion but the smoke and fire created panic.

More people were hurt stampeding off the pavilion than by the explosion.

I would have killed the viceroy, but a messenger from Guerrero had warned us that harming the viceroy would make the rebels appear to be heartless killers and turn the leading citizens against us.

But it was a spectacular climax to Noche Triste—the Night of Sorrows.

Abandoning my muskets, I raced to the back side of the building and tied the rope off so I could climb down. I figured that by now constables would be coming up the side stairway I had taken to the roof.

I hit bottom and turned around to find my horse was gone.

Someone stole my horse? was my first thought. But a man stepped out of a doorway.

Colonel Madero pointed his pistola at my chest. He seemed to change sides so often, I wondered if he had trouble remembering what side he was on.

"It's just you and me, Azteca. You are the only mark on my years of enforcing the king's law."

"You're supposed to be on the same side as me."

He shrugged. "I am on all sides until the last card is turned over. But this is personal with you and me. I'd kill you no matter whose orders I obey tomorrow. Put your hands behind your head."

"How did you find me?"

"Informants are everywhere," he said with a grin.

"Not around here," I said, glancing around. "I don't see a soul—least of all yours."

"I never claimed to have one." Again, he grinned—the ghastly grin that never reached his dead eyes.

"No one else is here?" I asked once more, looking around.

"I'm selfish. I wanted your death all to myself."

"Shooting an unarmed man with no chance at all is hardly a compliment on your manhood. But then, perhaps you have none."

Again, the ghoulish grin. "How's this?" Backing up five feet, he lifted his pistola toward the sky. "You have a pistola under your belt. Go for it."

My hands were still at the back of my head. There was no way I could lower them to my belt gun, unlimber it, cock the trigger, and kill him before his gun hand returned to my chest . . . and blew a hole in it big enough for Cortés to march his army through.

I didn't have a prayer in hell of going for that gun. And he knew it. But what he didn't know was that my hand was not clutching the back of my head but the thirteen-inch steel dagger in my back sheath.

I fell backward at the same time I flung the dagger.

Madero's pistola fired.

On my rear end, I clutched at my own pistola, but stopped.

He stood upright, his whole body suddenly convulsing as the pistola dropped from his hand.

Blood poured down from the blade of my knife wedged in his throat.

"Madre dios!" he choked.

"Y el Diablo," I added.

He dropped to his knees, clutching at the knife, but unable to control his convulsions.

I shot him between the eyes. Not to put him out of his misery, but to make sure that he kept his appointment with the devil.

I found my mount tied to a tree around the corner. Appropriating Madero's sheathed belt saber, I strapped it onto my mount. Swinging on, I unlimbered my pistola as well. I might need them.

As I rode toward the causeway, soldiers were fleeing for their lives, panic-stricken, in full rout, while mobs hurtled insults and rocks at them.

The combined forces of Iturbide and Guerrero were entering the city.

This time the fight for independence from the spur-wearers would succeed.

Maria and my amigo were waiting for me on the other side of the causeway, tears in her eyes as she watched the waving rebels' banners and flags of the vanguard approaching the city. Even Luis's eyes were misted, though I would never dare to have pointed that out.

"Next time," she said, "when I am being tortured, rescue me quicker, Señor Alchemist."

As we hugged, I wondered what she meant by "next time."

The revolution had succeeded.

New Spain would now be independent.

We Aztecs would be free and equal with the criollos, no?

Ayyo . . . I knew it was not time to put away my pistolas yet.